L.A. Love Lessons
The Complete Trilogy

PG Forte

Copyright © 2014 PG Forte

Chapultepec Press

ISBN: 978-1-880370-21-6

Cover artist: PG Forte

Editor: Devin Govaere

First paperback edition

Praise for LA Love Lessons

Dedication

For John.
My very own Scorpio Soul Mate.

Table of Contents

Waiting for the Big One

Gabby Brown refuses to consider her best friend Derek for the role of soul mate because she fears sex will ruin their friendship.

When she meets Zach, she's convinced that he could be The One. But, Derek has ideas of his own, and they don't include sharing Gabby with anybody.

Chapter One

It was one of those perfect mornings, the kind that only ever seems to happen on a Sunday. You know the ones I mean, don't you? Just before noon, all lazy and warm.

The city of Los Angeles was steeped in sunshine, snuggled about as deep into the weekend as it could get. It seemed like everyone was laid back and happy, except for me and the dozens of other drivers who were trying to move west along Hollywood Blvd, headed toward Fairfax, going nowhere fast.

They'll tell you Pisces is a patient sign, but you can't really label the fish. We're complex people. We combine the best and worst of all the other signs. And the truth is, I hate to wait.

So, there I was, stuck at yet another red light, when it hit me. It wasn't just me who was waiting and it wasn't just now. All of Los Angeles was in the same boat, all of us, all the time, waiting for the big one.

For most of us, that means our big break, our shot at seeing our name in a star on the Walk of Fame. It's the role that'll lift us out of obscurity. It's the hit that'll soar to the top of the charts. We're all hopeful romantics—like Kathleen Turner, in *Romancing the Stone*. We're always certain it'll happen with the next deal we make, the next audition we go out on, the next person we meet.

Take me, for instance. Any day now, with just a little bit of luck, I could go from being plain old Gabby Browne, aspiring actress and dog walker, to Academy Award Winner, Gabriella Giacomo.

And if fame doesn't get us, no doubt the earthquake will. That's the other thing everybody's waiting for, the big eight point, nine point, ten point shaker that scientists say is bound to occur.

The one that'll rock this town to its knees. Even hopeful romantics have to admit it seems inevitable. How could any place with this much surface glamour not be doomed?

But this morning, I was waiting for something a little more personal. I was waiting for The Big O: the elusive, G-spot, ultra orgasm, the kind I'd heard about, read about, yearned for, but had not yet experienced.

Don't get me wrong, it's not as if I'd never had an orgasm or anything. But, to date, they'd all been the standard issue, plain vanilla kind. Nice, but nothing I couldn't give myself any day of the week if I wanted. What I was hoping for was something more life-altering, soul-searing, rock-my-world passion. I knew it was out there, waiting for me. All I needed was the right guy to help me find it.

I knew he was out there, too. He was my Twin Flame, my Split Apart, my Tantric Soul mate; the man who would love me madly, passionately, loudly. All night long. They say good things come to those who wait, and I was certainly counting on that being true, but he was taking a long time to get here, and I was growing impatient.

Finally, the light turned green and I made it to where *I* was trying to get—The Body Electric—for my first workout of the week, and definitely my favorite.

Power Yoga with Derek Novello was never an easy class, but with Derek calling the shots, getting whipped into shape was almost a pleasure. I hurried up the walkway toward the two-story Hollywood Deco building, smiling in anticipation, enjoying the trickle of the fountain in the courtyard, the tinkle of the wind chimes in the topiary, the sweet scent of sandalwood.

"You're late," a voice growled the minute I set foot inside the deserted anteroom.

I froze for an instant, heart pounding in my chest, as I recognized Derek's dark-chocolate voice. Then I turned, making one of those slow, graceful pivots I'd been practicing.

Derek has the kind of chiseled features the camera loves. Even now, with his thick, black brows drawn into a frown that had them almost meeting over the bridge of his classically perfect nose, his face was sensual, expressive, intense.

He was looking yummier than ever today, with his two-hundred-push-ups-every-morning-before-breakfast arms folded across a tight black tank, putting all those lovely muscles on an in-your-face display. The black workout pants he wore, on the other hand, were disappointingly loose, at least in front. But experience had taught me that when he turned around...ooh, baby. They'd likely mold to his glutes in a way that would make my own pants grow damp.

Was I in a rush for him to turn around? Uh-uh. 'Cause he's also got the fiercest brown eyes, the most delicious looking lips and, oh, I thought with a tinge of sadness, if only we weren't friends.

"Traffic," I explained, trying to rein in my runaway lust, trying to resist the urge to run my fingers through the dark waves of his short hair. I'd always made it a policy never to mix sex and friendship. It was something Derek knew full well, though he continued to tempt me. "You wouldn't believe all the cars on the road today."

"So? There's always traffic, that's no excuse. Besides, you only live twelve blocks away. You jog, you hike, you exercise—give me a break, Gabe. Are you really going to tell me you couldn't walk that far? You could get here on time if you wanted to."

I sighed, feeling even more regretful. The truth is he looks even sexier when he gets worked up, and since he's a Scorpio, that happens a lot. "Don't be silly, Derek. This is LA—no one walks here."

Derek rolled his eyes. "Go get dressed."

Sexy or not, I hate it when anyone's annoyed with me. It's a Pisces thing. We want everyone to be happy. Luckily, I knew just how to make Derek's day.

"I'm sorry, Sensei," I murmured in my breathiest, most contrite sounding voice. I dropped my chin, laced my fingers together, and peeked up at him adoringly, like the blondest damned geisha you've ever seen. "Won't you please forgive me? I promise it'll never happen again."

A muscle twitched at the corner of Derek's mouth, showing me how hard he was trying not to smile. "It better not. You know the rules. Don't expect me to make exceptions for you just because we're friends."

Well, that was ridiculous. Scorpios *always* make exceptions for their friends. That's still the best way to tell when they've written you off. But as I bit my lip and took a step closer, I knew that wasn't the case with us—yet. There was a hot, hungry look in Derek's eyes, though he was still pretending to be indifferent to my act. 'Course that all went to hell in an eye-popping, jaw-dropping hurry when I flashed him the twins.

"Damn," he muttered, blinking appreciatively as I tugged my top back into place. I gave him a wink, then turned on my heel, and marched off toward the lockers.

"You still have a few minutes before class starts, Der," I called over my shoulder. "You might want to use the time to rearrange that package of yours. It's bulging."

Chapter Two

I'd known Derek for just over a year. He used to be friends with my ex-boyfriend, Bobby. Bobby's a Libra. Sweet tempered. Fun loving. Good-looking. A liar. So, okay, maybe that last one is not necessarily a Libra trait, but it was definitely a Bobby trait., which is why we're no longer together.

When I first met him, Derek was involved with Claire, owner of The Body Electric and, technically, his boss. Claire's a Leo. She's older, flamboyant, charismatic, nice when you get to know her; but, like all Leos, she has to be the one who calls the shots. For a while, I guess Derek was content to play Ashton to her Demi, but I knew it couldn't last. They broke up shortly after I ditched Bobby, which is when Derek and I really began to hang out.

I know what you're thinking. I should have ditched Bobby sooner, and gone after Derek even before he left Claire, right?

Wrong. That was never an option. Derek and I share some unfortunate character traits. We're both faithful, loyal, committed, and even if I never had a guy for a best friend before, I do know a thing or two about friendship.

Friends don't break up each other's relationships. That's rule number one. They stick up for each other like the Train song says, even when you know they're wrong.

Being a Scorpio, this all comes naturally to Derek. Scorpio's a fixed sign. Once they get an idea in their heads, no matter how stupid, they stick to it until hell freezes over or they come to their senses, whichever comes last.

It's been harder for me. When it comes to matters of the heart, we Pisces are not really known for our constancy which, believe me, is putting it nicely.

If either of us had been unattached when we met, things might have been different. As it was, our relationship started out platonic, and I was sure that was how it was going to stay.

That isn't to say that I never thought about how things might have been. I thought about Derek the whole time I was changing and all through class as well. To tell you the truth, I was a little annoyed with us both. I suppose it wasn't Derek's fault I could always get him with the submissive routine; there are lots of guys who dig demure. But it was one more reason added to the list of why we could never be anything but friends.

I'm too independent to play that kind of role for more than a couple of minutes at a time. Any longer and I'd be bored out of my mind. Pisces are mutable water—flowing, changeable, unrestrained. That's what makes us such good actors. Give us a role to play and we're happy. But try and make us play that role for life. No way.

It would take someone like Grace Kelly to pull off a stunt like that. You know what she was, don't you? Yeah, that's right. A Scorpio.

By the time class started, Derek had recovered his composure. His little soldier was no longer standing stiffly at attention and, trust me, I looked to see.

As I said, I was annoyed with myself, too. It's a bad idea to tease a Scorpio. They're ruthless. You can always count on them to find a way to turn the tables, to give back more than you'd bargained for, and that had certainly been the case this time around. Derek and I had both gotten an eyeful and now his cock was just about all I could think of. Wrapping my hand around the thick shaft. Wrapping my lips around its swollen head. Wrapping my legs...well, you get the picture.

He, of course, didn't even seem to notice I was in class. I was having an off day, too. I could feel it, you know? I wasn't holding the Asanas long enough, I wasn't pushing myself hard enough. Hell, I wasn't even trying on most of those stretches. It was the kind of thing that I could always count on to draw Derek's attention for some hands-on coaching. But not this day. From the way Derek was behaving, you would have thought I didn't even need an instructor. By the time class ended, I was in a really bad mood and there was only one way I could think of to make myself feel better.

* * * *

I have a confession to make.

Derek and I might not have had a physical relationship in real life, but in my fantasy life things were very different.

Take the showers, for instance. I know you've seen the films where there's a hole cut into the wall of the girls' shower room. There's always some guy on the other side of the wall who gets off on watching naked chicks soap themselves up. I knew there was no such hole at The Body Electric, but that didn't stop me from pretending there was or from pretending Derek was watching me as I touched myself.

I wouldn't say it was a regular part of my routine, but some days, especially days like this, when I didn't have to rush off to an audition, I'd take my time getting undressed. I'd stall and dawdle until I had the room to myself. Then I'd hit the showers for a little one-on-one.

I wouldn't call myself an exhibitionist, but I *am* an actress. And, if I were certain I was alone, I'd push the curtain open and watch myself in the mirror. Never miss a chance to hone your craft, that's my motto. Or, it should be, anyway.

I'd rub soap over my breasts, admiring the rosy flush the hot water had given them, and pretend that Derek was watching. I'd roll my nipples between my fingers and pinch them until they'd harden. Then I'd slip one hand between my legs.

"Faster." I'd imagine him growling, his eyes blazing as he stepped out of the steam to stand before me. "Don't stop."

I'd imagine my breath catching at the sight of him, my heart speeding up. "Derek, what are you doing in here?" I'd ask, glancing nervously around.

"Watching you," he'd say, and then he'd pull his cock free of his pants and stroke himself. "Getting hot for you. Getting hard."

Now, given the tent-pole he'd raised when I flashed him, I realized I'd been shortchanging him in the size department. As I adjusted my imagination to accommodate my new knowledge, I found myself getting hot as well—faster than ever before.

It made my pussy drip just thinking about it. I slid two fingers between my labia and gasped in surprise at the heat and slickness there. God, I was so ready. There was only one thing missing—

"I want you," I murmured to my imaginary Derek. "I want to put you inside me."

That wasn't possible, so I made him shake his head. "Not yet. I like the way you touch yourself. I want to watch you get off. I want to come while I'm watching you."

"But, Derek, I..."

"Do it."

Unfortunately, watching myself wasn't doing it for me today. I closed my eyes and rubbed harder, imagining Derek's hand keeping pace, sliding up and down his shaft, faster and faster. My clit swelled beneath my fingers, and I imagined Derek's cock growing harder for me. Pearly drops appeared at the opening as he pumped himself. I licked my lips.

"Please," my fantasy self begged. "Let me have a taste."

"Not yet," he repeated. "Make yourself wet for me."

"I am wet. I..."

"Wetter."

Groaning, I leaned my back against the wall. Water pounded against my chest. I tried to imagine it was Derek's fingers, but that was a bit of a stretch, even for me.

"Spread your legs," he ordered as he joined me in the shower. "Let me see you—now! I want you to come in my mouth."

Ever obedient to his commands, I slid my legs apart and held my lips wide. Water played over my pussy, wet, warm, and delicious. Like Derek's mouth.

"Yes. Like that," I imagined him murmuring as the first spasm hit. I bit my lip hard to stifle my moans as I came and, damn, it felt good.

Water beat against my face as I slumped lower along the wall, feeling boneless and relaxed. My toes curled against the wet tile of the floor. I shuddered for breath as I rode out the aftershocks.

Pisces is a dual sign—like Gemini or Libra. We're quite capable of holding two opposing viewpoints at one time. I didn't think it at all strange I should feel both completely satisfied and totally unsatisfied. I was sated and aching, happy and sad.

But while it wasn't unusual for me to feel this way, that didn't mean I had to like it very much, either.

Chapter Three

"Well, that took long enough," Derek said as I exited the locker room after dressing. I turned, surprised to find him leaning against the wall beside the door, one leg bent up behind him, arms crossed. He came off the wall in one fluid motion and fell into step beside me. "You all done?"

There was a faint, ironic tilt to his smile. *What does he know?* I wondered, as I felt my cheeks grow warm. My eyes narrowed. "What are you doing hanging around out here?"

Derek's eyebrows rose. "Waiting for you. We have a date, remember?"

"A date?"

"To talk about the screenplay?"

"The screenplay. Right. I forgot."

Like everyone in LA, Derek wants a piece of the business. He'd approached me about a month ago to collaborate with him on this movie he said he wanted to write. I thought he had a pretty good idea. A modern-day retelling of a fairy tale, one that rarely gets retold. I, of course, will be cast in the lead role, if it ever gets optioned. But, even though we'd been meeting a couple of times every week, things were still in the concept stage.

"You forgot?" Derek frowned as he studied my face. "Gabe, are you feeling all right today?"

"I'm fine. Why do you ask?"

"I dunno. Your cheeks are all red. You kept messing up in class..."

"You noticed that?" I asked, touched that he had.

"Of course I noticed. It's my job to notice. But I figured something was up, so I..."

He broke off abruptly when I leaned in and kissed his cheek.

"Hey! What's that for?"

"Nothing," I said, smiling happily as I slipped my arm through his. "Just 'cause you're you."

The twitch in the corner of his mouth grew more noticeable. "Well, okay, then. As long as you have a good reason."

* * * *

We walked down to the corner. There's a sidewalk cafe there that's always being mentioned in the Trades, but it's almost never crowded on Sundays. I ordered a veggie wrap and iced tapioca tea. Derek had a soy burger, a side of yam sticks and some insanely healthy organic juice drink, Kombucha and carrot juice, I think. We started out talking about our movie then the conversation wandered off-track, like it always seemed to do. Next thing I knew, we were back to discussing friendship and sex.

"Come on, Derek, everybody knows it," I found myself saying once more. Frankly, it was a position I was getting tired of having to defend. "As soon as you add sex, friendship goes right out the window."

Derek shook his head. "Everybody? Who's that?"

"It's like in *When Harry Met Sally*," I told him, but of course he disagreed.

"Gabe, I keep telling you. You're missing the whole point of that film. Billy Crystal was wrong. She was right, he was wrong. You're a feminist, you should love that."

I pushed aside my plate and picked up my tea. "What about you? How many women friends do you have that you haven't slept with?"

"Besides you? None."

Which was just what I thought he'd say. "There you go. And if you and I had sex we would no longer be friends, either." It sucked, but that's the way it was.

Derek sighed. "There's something wrong with that logic. One of these days I'm going to figure out a way to prove it to you."

"Go right ahead," I told him, feeling somewhat pouty. There was only one way for either of us to *prove* our position, and that was to try it and see. That was so not gonna happen. Scorpios make great friends and horrible enemies. They hold everyone they know to the same impossible standards they hold for themselves. Derek and Bobby used to be real close, but as soon as Derek found out he'd been cheating on me, he cut Bobby loose.

I did *not* want to be cut loose too.

They'll tell you Pisces are chameleons, wishy-washy, overly amenable. But you have to have a pretty sturdy backbone to live your whole life like...well, like a fish out of water. I can be as determined as a Taurus when I have to be.

"What now?" I snapped, suddenly aware of the way Derek was watching me. It was...weird.

He shook his head. "That drink of yours. I'm surprised they haven't had to shut this place down yet."

I popped the straw out of my mouth. "What are you talking

about? What's wrong with my drink?"

That sexy half-smile was back as he said, "Wrong? Not a thing. It's the way you're toying with it. It's obscene."

Toying? "Oh."

Now, for a Scorpio, obscene is always a good thing. Of course, for a Scorpio, butterflies can be obscene. They taste with their feet, you know. Butterflies, that is. But don't let me get started on feet.

A good actress never passes up a chance to practice, especially not when she's got a captive and appreciative audience. It took all of a second for me to find my motivation.

"Hmm," I murmured, as I fitted my lips around the thick straw. If Derek really wanted to see obscene, I was happy to oblige. My fingers lovingly caressed the length of the straw as I slowly sucked first one, then another of the tapioca balls into my mouth. "Mmm." I licked my lips, put my head back, and swallowed, smiling in sheer bliss. "Mm, mm, mm."

"Oh, Jesus."

I know I said it was a bad idea to tease a Scorpio, but there are times when a girl's gotta do what a girl's gotta do. Derek's espresso-colored eyes were looking distinctly glazed as I sighed dreamily and parted my lips to take the straw in my mouth again. "Did you say something, Der?"

"Can we get back to discussing the movie now?" he croaked.

I paused, mouth open, and ran my tongue across my bottom lip. My eyelashes fanned my cheeks. "Of course, we can. We can do whatever you want."

That wasn't really a joke. Like all the best performances, it held a kernel of truth. With Scorpios, you can either do what they want, or you can hide 'til they're gone.

"Right." Derek rolled his eyes. "Nice one, Gabe."

Derek's the only one who's ever called me Gabe. It started shortly after we met. He said that since we were going to be friends, he was going to call me Gabe. Gabby, he said, was a girl's name. And he already had a girl*friend.*

"You're wasting your time with the dog walking job," Derek told me now. "You could be making tons more money charging people to watch you eat."

I smiled, feeling smug. "I'll keep it in mind. Now, I thought you wanted to talk about the screenplay?"

Like I said, it was an intriguing idea he'd come up with. A

modern-day Rapunzel, trapped by her pre-conceived ideas about love, and the man who was trying to reach her. There was just one problem—

"She's a modern woman, Derek. She wouldn't just wait for love to come to her. She'd go out and find it."

"Like you're doing, you mean? You say you want love, too, but I don't see you going for it."

"That's different. I'm a Pisces. A fish. I go with the flow. It's not that I'm waiting, it's more like...like I'm trying to swim *with* the tide, instead of against it."

"That's bullshit. And if you think that's true, you're lying to yourself."

Fish don't like to be forced to defend ourselves. We really hate to be pinned down. We'd rather turn and swim away. Or, at least, change the subject. "Well, if I am, it's your fault. I've asked you to teach me some of those Tantric Yoga techniques but you refused to help. So, what am I supposed to do?"

Derek leaned back in his chair and crossed his arms. "I didn't refuse. I said I'd be happy to teach you."

"You said you could only teach me *hands-on*." And we both knew what *that* meant.

Derek shrugged. "That's the only way to learn some things." He looked at me for a moment and then said, "You know, you're never gonna find what you're looking for unless you're willing to risk something to get it. It's like that Matchbox 20 song. You gotta give it up to get off sometimes. You can't let your fear about what *might* happen hold you back. Love isn't gonna just drop into your lap without any effort on your part."

"Maybe it is, and maybe it's not," I told him as I got to my feet. "It wouldn't be the first time something like that happened, you know. Fate works in mysterious ways."

"I thought that was God?" he asked, looking faintly surprised. "Are you leaving?"

"Fate. God. Same difference." I planted a kiss on his cheek. "And, yes. I am. I have to go. Thank you for lunch."

Derek sighed. "You're running away."

What I was *not* doing was arguing. "As you wish," I replied, knowing he'd get the reference to *The Princess Bride*, hoping it would soften the blow.

I left the restaurant and headed toward my car. I could feel him staring at my ass the whole way and I put a little more sway in my hips because of it, which was no more than he deserved.

* * * *

I stopped on my way home and picked up some stuff for dinner—pre-packaged sashimi and a split of Chardonnay. By the time I got back to my building, my annoyance with Derek had morphed into serious frustration. I was tempted to call and ask if he wanted to continue our discussion over dinner. I knew that would likely send him the wrong signals, but I almost didn't care.

I shouldn't be the only one stuck with the task of keeping our friendship from doing a crash and burn. If he wanted to quote song lyrics at me, then fine. Two could play that game. I could tell him that "just one move would put him by himself" but the truth was I was afraid the shoe would be on the other foot. That he'd be the one to leave and I'd be the one feeling left out.

He'd never actually told me why he'd dumped Claire, and since friends don't kick friends when they're down, I never asked. It could have been anything. And I could be next.

I parked in the garage and was headed for the elevator, so deep in thought I wasn't watching where I was going. That all came to a halt when I collided with something big, hard, and definitely male.

"Oh, no," I gasped as I felt the bag rip. The wine bottle slipped from my grasp.

"Gotcha," my collision exclaimed as he lunged. He caught the bottle scant inches above the cement floor then laughed triumphantly as he tossed it into the air and caught it again. "D'you see that catch? Damn, I'm good."

I certainly couldn't argue with that. He was damn good-looking, too. Kind of like a scruffy, blond, Japanese anime version of Brad Pitt, long, lanky with big eyes and a sweet mouth. He was dressed in a faded black T-shirt that hugged him in all the right places and a pair of worn jeans that did an even better job of it; carrying a box full of clothes and...well, stuff.

"Your split almost split apart," he said as he handed it back to me.

I felt myself blink. *Oh, no, he did* not *just say that?* Chills ran up my spine. I nodded toward the shoe that had fallen from his box. "Better pick that up. You wouldn't want your *sole* to lose its *mate.*"

"Nope. Can't have that, can we?" he murmured as he bent to grab it. He smiled up at me, sea green eyes twinkling, and when our eyes connected, I felt dizzy from the rush.

"Do you live here?" we both blurted at the same time. We

paused and tried again. "Yeah, I do. I…"

"You first," he offered chivalrously.

"A couple of years. I'm in 405. Gabby Browne."

"Zach Harris." He slipped his shoe back into the box and extended his hand. "I just moved in today. I'm in 404. Does that mean you're right next door?"

I shook my head and his hand. "Other side of the building, directly across the courtyard. Our apartments actually face one another."

"Really?" Zach's eyes glowed brighter. His hand tightened on mine. I was sure he was picturing the sliding glass doors that opened from each of our living rooms and bedrooms out onto our balconies, even before he murmured, "I hope you're in the habit of leaving your blinds open."

Funny, that's just what I was hoping, too. I laughed as I answered, "Maybe I am."

"I'll look forward to it."

"Mmm. Me, too."

We talked for a few minutes more, sharing all the pertinent info. He was a guitarist and a Pisces. And I knew. I just *knew* we were fated.

It's Destiny, I thought, as the elevator doors finally slid shut. *It's Kismet. It's a miracle. It's about freakin' time…*

As soon as I reached my apartment, I grabbed my phone.

"What's wrong?" Derek asked, when he heard my voice.

Wrong? I shook my head. Nothing was wrong. It was all very right. "Derek…the soul mate thing? I think I just figured it out."

"Gabby?"

"I need you. Can you come over?"

Chapter Four

I hadn't even popped the cork on my wine before Derek was knocking at my door. One look at his face and I knew he'd run the whole way.

It was late February, and not that hot. And, as Derek had pointed out earlier, it wasn't even that far, still his cheeks were flushed, he was breathing too fast. "Omigod. Derek, are you all right? Come in. Sit down."

He came in, but shook his head at the rest. "I'm fine. Tell me."

"No! At least...here, let me get you some water."

I retreated to the kitchen for a glass. I was as shaken by his appearance as I was touched by the gleam in his eyes. It takes a real friend to be that happy for someone else's success.

Derek was pacing back and forth in my living room when I re-joined him. As he took the glass from my hand, I noticed that his chest was still heaving a little too hard. He was acting so strangely and looking so odd that if it weren't for the smile that kept curving his lips, I'd have thought he was angry.

"You sure you're okay?"

He nodded, drank the water down fast, and handed the glass back. "Yes. I told you, I'm fine." He smiled expectantly. "So?"

"Well, his name is Zach," I said, feeling suddenly shy. Derek's smile and the way he was looking at me were doing funny things to my insides. "He uh, plays guitar. And he just moved into the building today."

Derek frowned. "Wait. Who are we talking about?"

"Zach. The guy I just met. My soul mate."

"The guy you just—? What? Met *when?*"

"Now. When I got home. In the garage."

Derek's eyebrows had risen about as far as they could go. He looked at me for a moment without saying a word, and then shook his head. "I need to sit for a minute," he said as he crossed to my couch.

Well, I could have told him that was a good idea, I thought, as I followed after him. In fact, I had told him, hadn't I? "Derek, you're really starting to scare me. Do you want some more water?"

"Water's not gonna do it. What else you got?"

I had wine, but there was no way I was going to offer him

that. Not when he already looked like a cardiac candidate. "Iced tea?"

"*Tea?* Yeah, that'd be perfect," Derek mumbled. "No, damn it, I do not want iced *tea*. Forget it." He covered his face with his hands and groaned. I watched him, worried.

Finally, he lifted his head and looked at me. There was a different gleam in his eyes now, a look I didn't understand at all. "Tell me," he repeated. "Start at the beginning. And don't leave anything out."

* * * *

"I don't get this. Why am *I* here?" Derek asked, a few minutes later, after I'd told him the whole story.

I couldn't understand why he was being so thickheaded. He knew about my quest for The Big O. We'd discussed it at length. Maybe he thought these things just happened naturally, but personally, I suspected they took planning and work. "You're here to help me, of course. To give me some pointers, help me get this guy's attention. There has to be some kind of sign I can give him, you know, so he'll know I'm interested?"

Even soul mates have to start somewhere and we were both Pisces. Someone had to make the first move. If we both decided to go with the flow, it could take months before anything happened. Most of the time I'd be good with that. But I was really sick of waiting.

"You're a guy. You must have some ideas?"

Derek's eyes narrowed. "You want to give him a sign? Oh, that's easy. Why don't you put on a show for him, like you did for me this morning?"

I must have looked puzzled, because after a minute he added, "Show him your tits, Gabe. That'll get his attention. I promise you. It'll make him think all sorts of crazy things."

"Derek!" I stared at him, shocked—both by his crudeness and the idea. "I can't do that. We just met. I-I hardly know him!"

He sighed. "Gabe, right now I'm wondering if you know anyone. Including yourself."

* * * *

I had a lot to think about the next day at work. Luckily, that's one thing my day job gave me plenty of—time to think. I was a dog walker for Pooch Camp, one of LA's most exclusive pet services. Pooch Camp catered to the darlings of Hollywood's elite, some of the most pampered pets on the planet. My specialty was providing off-leash excursions for up to six dogs at a time, in several of the area's parks.

It's a fun job. Although there were some pets I could have done without, I had no real complaints. Besides being a steady gig, dog walking kept my feet in Pradas and Vasque Calderas, it paid for my classes, and it allowed me to keep food on the table and a roof over my head. Or, as Bobby once put it, to pursue my two favorite hobbies: eating food and living indoors.

I had taken the dogs to Runyon Canyon Park—one of LA's best-kept secrets. One hundred fifty acres, nestled amid the Hollywood Hills, extending from Franklin north to Mulholland, Runyon is secluded, close to home, and gorgeous. The ground is baked hard most of the year, the air carries the rich herbal scents of chaparral mixed with laurel and sage, and the views are exquisite. Hiking through the relative wilderness of undeveloped parkland, with a pack of unleashed dogs romping around you, is guaranteed to leave you feeling like Diana, goddess of the hunt. But that's on a good day.

On a bad day, when the dogs won't behave or the weather is rough, you feel more like Mowgli from *The Jungle Book*—after the pack has turned against you.

Today, the weather was mild, cloudier, and a little bit cooler than yesterday, but no rain yet. The dogs were mostly cooperative. A good day, all in all. And a good thing, too, because, as I said, I had a lot on my mind. I couldn't wait to see Zach again, but I still didn't know how to approach him. Derek had been no help at all.

He'd looked at me, almost pityingly. "Another musician? You're kidding. Don't you ever learn?"

"He's not like Bobby," I said, bristling as I came to Zach's defense.

"Oh, they're all like Bobby. If you're smart, you'll forget this guy. You don't want a musician for a soul mate anyway."

What was he talking about? "You make it sound like I have a choice." Besides, musicians weren't that bad. Sure, they had groupies, and that was always going to be a problem. But, actors were worse. Good actors believed so hard in the roles they were playing they almost had no choice but to fall for their co-stars. Worst of all were dancers and athletes. They were so focused on their bodies, so focused on bodies in general—

"Of course you have a choice. Haven't you ever heard of free will?"

"Sure I have. I just don't see how it applies to soul mates."

It was a ridiculous thing for him to suggest. In fact, every word out of his mouth last night had been ridiculous.

"Show him my tits," I muttered, feeling grumpy all over again. "Yeah, there's a great idea." It was such a Scorpio thing to suggest. Or maybe it was a guy thing—who knew?

As for his other suggestion, that I didn't know myself? Well that was just laughable. Problem was I knew myself too well. I knew I was getting bored with acting, bored with the pace of my life, as restless as a salmon in springtime.

At this point, my thoughts were derailed by Harry. A two-year-old Rhodesian Ridgeback, Harry's a beautiful dog but hopelessly undisciplined. If you knew who he belonged to, you wouldn't be surprised. Like owner, like dog.

Ridgebacks were bred to hunt lions. There are no lions here in LA County, but there are ground squirrels aplenty. I wouldn't think you could mistake the two, but Harry's been known to anyway.

Harry's been known to hare off into the bushes after squirrels or pretty much anything, actually, wasting my time, ruining the walk for the rest of the dogs. Today it was a Gnatcatcher. Two Gnatcatchers, to be exact.

They're on the endangered list, and they aren't supposed to be disturbed. Particularly not in the middle of their nesting season—which, of course it was. Count on Harry to find a pair and flush them out of the brush.

By the time I finished rounding the dogs up, I was covered in dust and sweat, and in desperate need of a shower. I'm pretty sure that's what gave me the idea. I thought about yesterday, thought about everything Derek had said, everything Zach had said, and suddenly, I knew just what I needed to do to attract Zach's attention.

I was left with only one question to answer. Did I have the guts to go through with it?

Chapter Five

I had to wait until dark to put my plan into motion. This was both good and bad. Good, because it gave me time to prepare, bad because...well, did I really want that much time to think?

Luckily, as I've mentioned, it was still February. Dark came early. So early, in fact, that I had barely enough time to get ready. There was so much to do! I had to shower and shave and touch up the highlights of my honey-blonde hair. I had to give myself a pedicure. I had to pick out my wardrobe, put fresh sheets on my bed, fresh towels in the bathroom, and then set the stage, block my moves, choose a soundtrack...

Liz Phair took an early lead in that department. "Extraordinary" and "Why Can't I?" were perfect for the occasion. But "Little Digger" is somewhat iffy as a love song, Bobby always laughed himself silly over "Favorite" and "HWC"... well, it seemed a bit extreme for a first date.

Eventually, I settled on my favorite Maroon 5 acoustic album instead. It was hot, sweet, totally sexy, a little too short, but, hey, that's what the replay setting is all about, right?

I waited until the lights went on in Zach's apartment and I knew he was home. Then I fired up the music, opened the blinds, turned on my own lights, and went into action.

I can honestly say it was the scariest thing I'd ever done.

They say some people never outgrow their stage fright. I was already worried that it might be the case for me. Just thinking about performing naked had the butterflies in my stomach spawning and multiplying.

Luckily, I knew how to deal with nerves. It was simply a matter of finding a character to play and submerging myself in the role. Tonight I had decided to play Claire.

Claire is glamorous, sexy, very self-assured. I'm certain she's never known a moment of self-doubt. That's one woman who lives for the spotlight. I could totally see her doing something like this for Derek, vamping it up until she had him on his knees.

I strutted and twirled to the hot strains of "This Love", tossing in a shimmy or two as I removed my clothes. I'd taken six months worth of belly dancing lessons when I was with Bobby—for all the good it had done me up until now. While I was learning to shimmy, he'd been shaking it up with some waitress in a Venice Beach dive.

By the time "Sunday Morning" started, I was so into the act, I'd forgotten I even had an audience. I thrust my hands into my newly-blonde hair and was dancing naked for myself, eyes closed, swaying to the music.

Thinking of nothing but how good it felt I glided my hands down my body. I reveled in the silky smoothness of my skin and pretended it was my lover's hands touching me. I imagined how much better it would feel when it was his hands on my breasts caressing my nipples into hard peaks; when it was his hands slipping between my legs to massage my clit. I was imagining it all so clearly—his hands tight on my hips as we rocked to the music, his cock nudging me from behind, his voice urging me onto all fours in the center of the bed. The ringing of the doorbell came as a shock. It broke the mood, startling me out of my reverie right in the middle of "She Will Be Loved".

"Damn." I grabbed my robe. I'd forgotten to keep an eye on the window. Was that Zach at my door? Or had I attracted some unwanted attention?

I breathed a sigh of relief when I peeked through the spy hole. "Zach, hi," I said as I opened the door. That was as far as I got. He was through the door in an instant, pinning me against the wall and framing my face in his hands. Kissing me for all he was worth.

And, damn, could he kiss.

His lips covered mine, his tongue filling my mouth with pleasure and reducing me to a mass of jellied bones and molten heat. Blindly, I reached out a hand to push the door shut. Then he was pulling away, leaving me groaning, wanting more but, oh, so not in the mood to stop him as he nibbled his way down my neck.

"That was the hottest thing I've ever seen," he murmured, pushing my robe aside. "Please, tell me that was for me?" He curved his hands around my breasts, pushing them together, staring at them with an expression of awe, wonder, and greed.

I sucked in a quick breath. "Of course it was."

"Thank you," he said as he dove in, face first. The pull of his lips on a nipple had me arching against him. Electric currents of need were flowing in a perfect circuit from his mouth to my sex and back again.

He ran his tongue around the peaks of both breasts, and then tugged again at the tips. He gazed up at me, his eyes wide and hopeful, his smile hinting at wickedness yet to come. "I want to fuck you so bad. Can I?"

I nodded.

"Right now?"

I nodded again.

"Yes!" I heard him whisper as he sank to his knees. "There is a God."

Gently, he pried my legs apart, using his thumbs to spread my lips. His tongue darted out, stroking my clit again and again until my legs started to shake and I clutched at his head to keep myself from falling. Or perhaps to insure that he never, ever stopped. Maybe both. I'm not really sure. I was beyond thinking at that point.

By the time the sweet strains of "If I Fell" were replaced by the hard, driving rhythm of "Highway to Hell", I was ready for that highway myself—I wanted to burn.

Luckily, so did Zach. "You taste amazing," he murmured reaching for my hand and tugging me to my knees. As he kissed me again, I found myself agreeing with him. I thought we tasted pretty good together, too.

He shifted one of his hands to cup the back of my head. Deepening the kiss, he slowly lowered us both to the floor. Then he straightened again. Kneeling between my legs, he unzipped, dug a condom from his pocket, and quickly fitted it over himself. He had a nice cock—long and lanky, just like the rest of him. I licked my lips as I thought of all the places I'd like to put it. Of all the places I was sure I would put it, eventually.

Zach caught the motion and grinned. "I gotta tell you, this is the greatest birthday present anyone's ever given me."

"Today's your birthday?" I asked somewhat startled. He lowered himself on top of me again. I was vaguely aware that the album had started over.

"That's right," Zach murmured, pressing another quick kiss on my breast before moving up to nuzzle my neck. "All day." He rubbed his cock along my slit, coating himself in my juices. "Spread your legs a little wider, baby. Help me get nice and wet for you."

I shifted slightly to comply with his request, feeling suddenly awkward.

"Happy birthday."

I know it sounds stupid. I mean, I knew he was a Pisces, so the fact that it was his birthday shouldn't have been that much of a surprise. All the same, it kind of drove home the point that, really, what did I know about him? Then he flexed his hips and drove another point home and I went back to being mindless once again.

Say what you will about musicians, but what they don't know about rhythm probably isn't worth knowing. As Zach began to thrust inside me, rocking right along to the music, I felt the air grow thick. I was hot, so hot, so—

He reared up suddenly, and grabbed hold of my knees, pressing my legs apart, his movements slowing almost to a stop as he stared at me. I gazed up at him in surprise.

He nodded at my pussy. "Touch yourself. Like you were doing earlier."

I slid one hand over my mound and began to finger my clit as he watched, stroking and circling the swollen nub, growing hotter, growing wetter. I arched my back as I felt all my muscles clench tighter, tighter...then it all came undone.

I spasmed around him and Zach groaned. "Oh, yeah..." He began to move faster again, thrusting harder. Then he threw back his head and let loose with a long, low growl of release.

A moment later, he'd collapsed alongside me. We both lay there, breathing in tandem, gulping air in companionable silence like a pair of beached dolphins.

He stirred first, turning his head to look at me. "We're not done yet, are we?"

Done? Hell, no. Not even. I shook my head.

He smiled. "Good. That's what I was hoping." He got to his feet, reached for my hand, and hauled me up as well. Next thing I knew, he'd hefted me over his shoulder and was running for the bedroom. I was choking with laughter as he tossed me on the bed. I gazed up at him expectantly while he ripped off his clothes, waiting for him to join me. Instead, he did something even better. He lifted one of my feet to his mouth and began to nibble on my toes.

Now, you've probably heard that Pisces rules the feet. I'm not so sure it's not the other way around. I've heard of women who can come just from having their toes sucked, and I'm thinking every one of them is a fish.

Rippling waves of pleasure were coursing up my leg. I was halfway to heaven when Zach muttered "Damn, you're cute" and sank to his knees. His mouth rode the waves toward my throbbing pussy.

I opened my eyes, ready to order him to stop, to go back and do my other foot—but the Mistress routine is not my best role. Besides, right about then his lips found my clit and I gave up the fight. Pisces aren't that big on confrontation anyway.

* * * *

It was just before midnight when Zach left my apartment. It was still technically his birthday, so he was going to meet some friends for drinks. Musicians don't do anything early and they rarely do anything alone. He invited me to join them, but I had dogs to walk in the morning, so I turned him down. He kissed me good-bye, thanked me once more, and turned off the lights on his way to the door, so I wouldn't have to get up again. Pisces are thoughtful like that.

I wrapped my quilt around me but, tired as I was, I couldn't fall asleep. Lazy thoughts kept circling in my brain, like leaves in a fountain, bobbing and spinning 'til I sat up again and reached for my phone.

"What's wrong?" Derek asked.

I felt myself frown. "Why do you always ask that? You make it sound like I only call you when there's a crisis."

"Well, don't you?"

Tears pricked at my eyes as I slid open the drawer of my night table and dug out some emergency chocolate. I've told you how Pisces tends to mimic all the other signs. Well, at the moment, I was feeling as moody as a crab. "No. Stop being mean."

"Has something happened that I don't know about?" Derek asked cautiously.

I chomped on my chocolate macadamia bar for a moment. "Mmm. I took your advice."

"What advice?"

"The strip tease. Did you get that idea from Claire, by the way?"

"Did I—? *What?*"

"It seemed like such a... such a Claire thing when I was doing it."

"Oh, Jesus. Are you fucking kidding me?"

I could hear Derek moving around in his apartment and I closed my eyes to better imagine what the noises filtering through the phone might mean. *Kitchen*, I thought. Glass. Bottle. Pouring. I could imagine him standing at his counter, with the light from his faux Tiffany fixture spilling down on his dark hair, gilding it with a faint green-gold tinge. I could imagine him lifting one of his square glass tumblers to his lips, tossing his head back with a quick motion that would leave his hair in disarray.

"What are you drinking?" I asked, feeling thirsty, feeling like I was right there in his apartment with him, running my hand through his hair to comb it back into place, trailing my fingers down his cheek. He had a nice place, right above the studio. When the windows were open, you could hear the water and the wind chimes in the courtyard below. It was dark and mysterious—just like Derek. It was cozy, crammed with things he'd picked up on his travels. It was warm...

"Never mind what I'm drinking," Derek snapped, sounding *not* warm. "What happened?"

I sighed, breaking off another square of chocolate and popping it in my mouth. "Pretty much what you'd expect to happen, I guess. It worked. He got the message. He came over."

"You *slept* with him? Already?"

Well, I certainly wouldn't put it like *that*. Sleep? No. Not even. Silence hummed over the line. I listened as Derek poured himself another drink.

"How was it?"

"It was great," I replied, sliding back down between the sheets. "But, you know, probably even soul mates don't start out at the peak. Right?"

This time the silence stretched even longer. "I think you're rushing this," Derek said at last. "What do you even know about this guy? Nothing."

"That's not true."

"Prove it. You said he's a musician, right? So, tell me what his favorite groups are. What kind of music does he like? What's the name of the band he plays in? Give me three local artists he'd be likely to follow."

I sighed. "We did talk, you know." Not much, but enough. Music was definitely one of the topics we'd covered. I had no problem reeling off the names of a half dozen bands I felt confident would be at the top of Zach's list.

"But I don't see what good knowing all that is supposed to do for me," I said. "How is that gonna get me what I want?"

"You need to slow things down with this guy," Derek replied, ignoring my questions. "Stop pushing so hard. You haven't made any plans to see him again, have you?"

"Well, sure. He's coming over for dinner tonight," I said, feeling exhausted as I thought about it. Maybe Derek was right.

Maybe I was pushing too hard for this. Maybe it was one of those Zen things where the only way to find what I was looking for was to stop looking.

"Dinner?" The way Derek said the word; you'd have thought it was a foreign concept. "Where—your place? Tonight?"

I snuggled even further beneath the covers. "Mm-hmm. You've heard of it, right? Dinner...it comes after lunch...before bedtime...and speaking of which..."

"Funny," Derek muttered, although I thought the only thing funny was how *un*-amused he sounded.

"Nite, Der," I murmured sleepily. "Sweet dreams."

"Yeah." His voice was quiet. Almost too quiet. "Yeah, you, too."

Chapter Six

The next day was overcast. The canyon was wreathed in fog and prettier than ever. I didn't have Harry with me and everyone else behaved themselves, so I was able to get my whole menu planned for dinner: lemon sole, fresh asparagus, a gratin of braised winter vegetables and a kick-ass white chocolate fondue for dessert.

Of course, within minutes of Zach's arrival, I was having real doubts about whether we'd make it to dessert. He'd followed me into the kitchen when I went for the wine.

"Ever do it on a counter?" he asked as he nipped at my neck.

I smiled at him over my shoulder. "Not with you."

"Hmm. In that case..." He spun me around and then backed me against the refrigerator. I shivered as he caged me there. "How about here? Ever do it here?"

I shook my head.

Zach smiled. "Wanna?"

I smiled back. The possibility was not without interest. Still... "I thought you wanted to eat dinner?"

Zach's eyes were twinkling. "Maybe I'd rather eat you. Can I?"

There was only one answer to a question like that. Just thinking about what his tongue had done to me last night made my pussy clench and my breathing hitch. Before I could get a word out, the doorbell rang.

"Ignore it," Zach said—a suggestion I heartily endorsed. But, obviously, whoever was out there, had no intention of being ignored. The bell rang again.

"Hold that thought," I begged. I slipped beneath his arm and ran to answer the door.

"Whoever you are, you have really lousy timing," I muttered.

I peeked through the spy hole in the door. My eyes widened when I saw who it was. I pulled open the door.

"Derek? What's wrong?"

"Not a thing." Giving me a quick peck on the cheek, he breezed past me. "Wow. Something smells good. Did you cook, Gabe?"

I stared at him. "What are you doing here?"

"Screenplay." He held up a familiar looking spiral notebook. "Don't you remember? We had a date to meet and work on it some more."

"We did not."

"You forgot? Again? That's twice in one week."

"I didn't forget. I..."

"Ah, so you do remember?"

"What?" I shook my head, hoping to clear the confusion. It didn't help. "No!"

"Everything okay?" Zach poked his head into the hallway to ask.

Derek's eyes flashed. The look he gave Zach could have melted steel. Then his face cleared. "You must be Zach."

"Uh, yeah." Zach glanced at me. He had that swim-away-fast look in his eyes. I knew that look and I knew what it meant. Fish society runs on fairly simple rules. There are two ways to survive. Either you're big, or you're fast. Or you're lunch.

"This is my friend, Derek," I explained, hoping to sound reassuring by emphasizing the friend part. *Ignore the teeth*, I wanted to add. *He's harmless. Any resemblance to a great white or a killer whale is purely coincidental.* Problem was, I wasn't altogether certain that was the case.

"Oh, I'm more than a friend," Derek asserted calmly.

We both looked at him.

He smiled at Zach. "We're writing a movie together. Didn't Gabe tell you? She'd play the lead, of course. It's a great role for her. I think this could be her big break."

Zach's face cleared. "Cool." He smiled at me sweetly. "Do you two need to work? I can come back later if you're busy."

"No," I answered, just as Derek inquired, "Were you in the middle of something?"

"Yes," I said, aware that they were both staring at me.

Derek's lips curved up in his usual half-grin. "Well, which is it, Gabe? Yes or no?"

"I'm having dinner with Zach," I reminded him. *And great sex afterwards.*

"Maybe I can join you?"

I knew Derek was talking to me, but his gaze strayed to Zach, who naturally felt compelled to answer. "Yeah. I'm cool with that. Unless there's not enough to go around?"

Once again, they both turned toward me as if I was the one with all the answers. I gritted my teeth and smiled. "There's plenty."

* * * *

What's Derek up to? That was the question that plagued me throughout dinner. He and Zach seemed to be hitting it off. I didn't know why that surprised me so much, but it did. And I really didn't understand why I felt left out. I should have been happy about this. But I was back to feeling moody again. I guess it's just hard to get too happy when you know you're being lied to.

That was the bottom line. I knew Derek hadn't forgotten about my dinner with Zach. And I'd bet anything that it hadn't slipped his mind I was hoping to have the most incredible sex of my life right *after* dinner, either.

Sex never slips a Scorpio's mind.

I'd gotten him alone for a minute in the kitchen just before we all sat down.

"Are you here to play chaperone?" I demanded.

Last night on the phone, he'd cautioned me to stop rushing, to take things slow. Now, I expected to get the full lecture. Instead he gave me one of his enigmatic, pitying looks.

"Hardly. More like the reverse."

"What's that supposed to mean?"

"Think about it," he advised. Then he'd picked up the extra dishes I'd just taken from the cabinet for him, and headed for the table.

I'd been thinking about it all through dinner and was still at a loss. Was he here to watch? Did he want to join us?

My fork slipped from my fingers to clatter on my plate as the thought hit. Did he?

I glanced up. The guys had stopped talking. They were both staring at me. I was pretty sure I must be wearing that swim-for-the-shallows look in my eyes now, too.

"Everything okay?" Zach's smile was gentle, inquisitive. His gaze took in the drops of lemon sauce that spattered the table before returning to lock with mine.

"What's the matter, Gabe?" Derek asked. "You finally figured some things out?"

My gaze shifted to his face. "What do you mean?"

His dark eyes gave nothing away. "Well, you looked like you were thinking pretty hard. I thought maybe you'd had a revelation. Like you'd suddenly discovered what *forty-two* means."

"No," I replied. "Nothing like that."

"You sure? Maybe you've figured out what you really want then? Is that it?"

I picked up my fork and resumed eating. "It's nothing. I was just being clumsy."

"As you wish," Derek said softly.

I nodded, but kept my eyes on my food. *Yeah, I love you, too—but not like that!*

I know fish usually go with the flow, but I really wasn't sure about *this* flow. I mean, sure I've had fantasies about being shared by two men, who hasn't? That didn't mean I wanted to try it in real life or with real people.

Which didn't mean I wasn't going to think about it...

Zach would start it. He'd channel his inner Leo and do something suitably dramatic, like sweep all the food from the table with a single swipe of his hand.

"Ever do it here?" he'd ask, standing at the end of the table, daring me to play along.

I don't take dares—unless I want to. And, oh, did I want to.

I climbed on top of the table, having already mysteriously lost most of my clothes. Purring like a big cat, I crawled toward him. Derek's eyes widened. I could feel the heat of his gaze as I passed him. I could feel his hot breath on my skin and my nipples grew harder.

Then I reached the end of the table and slid between Zach's legs. They both watched me as I lay back on the table, stretched my arms above my head, and arched my back. "Where do you want me?" I murmured mischievously.

"Right here, baby," Zach replied, running a finger along the thin strip of wet satin that covered my pussy. "Right now." He hooked a finger under the lace strap at my hip and tugged, but nothing happened.

"Try this," Derek suggested, handing him one of my steak knives.

"Trust me, baby?" Zach asked as he slid the knife under the lace.

I nodded, and then held my breath as he cut the panties from me with sure strokes.

"I can't sit here and watch," Derek muttered, getting up.

I didn't see where Derek went. Zach was running the point of the blade lightly up my stomach and doing a good job of distracting me from anything else. Carefully, he slipped it beneath the front clasp of my bra. One slice and the bra fell open.

Suddenly, "These are mine," Derek growled possessively, leaning over my shoulders to palm my breasts. "I saw them first."

He was standing so close that I could smell the musky scent of his cock. It made my mouth water. I tipped my head back and looked at him. "You remembered?"

His eyes warmed as he returned my smile. "Natch."

"Snatch?" Zach sounded faintly annoyed as he looked up at Derek from between my legs. "Dude, wait your turn. Learn to share."

Derek's eyes glinted. "I've got plenty to share." The tip of his cock nudged at my cheek. "Open up."

I shivered as Zach dipped his head to take my clit in his mouth.

I shivered again as Derek framed my face in his hands and guided his cock between my lips. Then his hands slid back down to my breasts. I writhed in ecstasy for a moment before another thought hit me. There was still one thing missing.

Luckily, I had all that yoga training to fall back on. I braced my hands against the table and slowly went into a modified Plough posture, bringing my legs over my head, and my feet into perfect position—right in front of Derek's face.

I released his cock from my mouth long enough to beg, "Please?"

His eyes smoldered. "As you wish," he murmured just before his lips closed on my big toe...

The sound of Zach's chair scraping against the floor brought me back to reality.

"What's going on?" I asked, feeling my stomach flip as Zach got to his feet. I eyed them both nervously. *Fantasy, guys. It was just a fantasy.*

Zach rounded the corner of the table and gave me a kiss. "I gotta go. You don't mind, do you, babe?"

"Mind what?" It took a minute for my brain to kick into gear. *What the hell?* He hadn't said *babe*, he'd said...*Gabe.* "Where are you going?"

"To the concert," he said, naming one of the groups that I'd mentioned to Derek last night. I felt my eyebrows crawl right up my forehead when he added, "I know it's last minute, but Derek just gave me a ticket for it."

"He did?" Dumbstruck, I turned and looked at Derek. "You did?"

Derek shrugged. "A gift from a client. I wasn't going to use it. Seemed a shame to let it go to waste."

"Gabe?" Zach asked again. "You don't mind, right?"

See what I mean about Pisces and the flow? Of course Zach would take Derek up on his offer. Of course he'd go along with whatever suggestion he was given. He didn't know how important this dinner was to me. But Derek did.

Of course, I was a go-with-the-flow Pisces, too. I smiled brightly at Zach. "Go ahead. Enjoy yourself."

"I'll walk you out," Derek said. I was still smiling brightly as they left the room together.

* * * *

"What the hell are you doing?" I demanded when Derek came back alone.

He looked at me for a moment before answering. "Come on, Gabe, you're not stupid. You know the answer to that, don't you?"

"You're supposed to be my friend," I reminded him.

"Being friends was your idea."

I felt my eyes narrow. *Liar!* I remembered quite distinctly which of us had first used the F word. It was definitely him. Way back in the beginning, in typical Scorpio fashion, he'd given me a choice: we could be friends, or we could stay the hell away from each other. "You're deliberately trying to mess things up between me and Zach. Why?"

"Because you don't belong with him. You belong with me."

"I don't sleep with my friends."

"Fine. Let's not be friends then."

Pain stabbed at my heart. That was exactly what I'd been trying to avoid. Losing Derek's friendship was more than I could bear. Luckily, Pisces are good at ignoring unpleasantries, so I did. "I can't believe you're trying to get me to cheat on Zach with you." I really couldn't. Derek hadn't even tried that when I was with Bobby—who would have deserved it. Of course, back then he was still with Claire. Not for the first time, I wondered why they'd broken up.

"Cheating?" Derek looked surprised. "What are you talking about? I don't want you to cheat on anybody."

"You don't?"

He shook his head. "Hell, no. I want you to stop sleeping with him altogether." I must have looked as surprised as I felt, because after a moment he shrugged a little and added. "Okay, look, he seems like a nice guy. You can still be friends with him, if you want."

Unfortunately, this was not the right thing to say. "I can?

39

Why, thank you—Master."

Nine out of ten times Pisces will do everything we can to avoid confrontation. We're peaceful. Compassionate. Willing to see everyone's point of view, to take everyone's side, to give everyone the benefit of the doubt. We're nice people. Really. But if you happen to catch us on that tenth time—watch out.

Scorpios, on the other hand, are secretive, manipulative, deceitful, jealous, obsessive, and obstinate—and that's all the fucking time! Which is exactly what I told Derek, in no uncertain terms. Then, just for good measure, I listed a whole bunch of reasons why I—or pretty much any woman I could think of—would prefer someone like Zach to someone like him.

"Okay, fine," he snarled quietly when I was finished. "I get the point. But, there's just one thing."

"What's that?" I snarled back, a little less quietly. I was seething with anger, hurt, resentment, frustration, pretty much anything you could seethe with, in fact.

"Next time you have a problem, don't call me for help."

Never let it be said that Pisces can't give back as good as it gets. "I won't. I'll call a *friend*."

I crawled into bed right after Derek stormed out. I opened my night table drawer, pushed aside the chocolate and pulled out my vibrator, intending to fuck myself into a better mood and a good night's sleep.

After no more than a few minutes, I gave up the attempt. I was *not* in the mood to fantasize about Derek tonight. Unfortunately, I was also not in the mood to fantasize about anyone else either.

Chapter Seven

I've told you that dog walking has good days and bad days, right? Well, Wednesday was bad. It was raining—one of those slow, dismal drizzles that never lets up. It was gray, it was muddy, it was disgusting. It was perfect really because it completely matched my mood. The trail was slick, treacherous, annoying...a lot like a certain Scorpio I could've mentioned. And the dogs, not just Harry, but the rest of them as well, were as wired as an ADD playgroup on a sugar high.

That was for starters. As everyone knows, days that start off bad generally get worse before they get better. Or else they just get worse and stay that way. Today was no exception.

The next thing that happened was that Harry got lost. I blamed that on Derek, too. If I hadn't been obsessing about the previous evening, I might have been paying attention. I called. I whistled. I offered treats. I did everything I'd been trained, or could think of, to do. Then, while I was pondering my next move, the earthquake struck.

Oh, not the big one, of course. This was a mere four point eight. Strong enough to knock me off my feet, but that was about it. And shortly after the ground stopped shaking, I found Harry. So, you might've thought my day was improving, right?

Wrong.

Harry was at the bottom of the ravine. It was muddier than usual, and he couldn't get back up the way he'd gotten down. That wasn't the problem. The earthquake had dislodged a dead tree that had been lying along the slope. Somehow, when it shifted, Harry's collar had gotten snagged on an exposed root. He wasn't hurt, but boy was he stuck.

For all our dreamy otherworldliness, Pisces are very practical at heart. There was no way I wanted to go down there after him. I tried calling Pooch Camp for backup, but the earthquake had knocked out their phone lines. So, I did what any sane person with an emergency would do. I called 911.

Here's a piece of advice. If you happen to be a sensitive, compassionate Pisces, one who cares about animals and expects other people to do the same, and if you happen to be having a really crappy day in the first place, don't call 911 when your dog gets trapped in a muddy ravine. Not unless one of you happens to be dying. I got yelled at for a good two minutes. As busy as they claimed to be, what with the earthquake and all, I'm surprised they had even that much time to waste.

I'm not going to say that what I did next was smart, but I still think it would have worked...if it weren't for the rain and the mud, the tree, the aftershocks. And the fact that it was Harry I was dealing with.

I went down to get him. You probably already saw that coming, huh?

I could tell from the way he whined and wriggled that he was grateful to see me. It took less than a minute, and only a moderate amount of pressure to get him un-snagged. He was so happy to be free that he jumped up and tried to lick my face.

Of course, he knocked me down. Of course, his jumping caused the tree to shift again. Of course, I ended up with my foot trapped beneath the trunk.

Bet you saw that coming, too.

So there I was, lying in the mud with the rain beating down, being trampled on by dogs. Yet I knew there was still worse to come, because I needed help, and there was only one person I could think of to call.

Now, Aries will rage 'til they're blue in the face. Geminis will cut you with words. Leos will bluster and put on airs. But *no one* holds grudges like a Scorpio.

"What is it?" Derek snapped when I reached him. And didn't that just figure? The one time when 'what's wrong?' would've worked.

"I need you," I said, and I bit my lip because clearly *that* was the wrong thing to say.

He snorted. "Oh, you need something all right, I'm just not sure it's me."

"Derek, please. I'm really stuck."

"Sorry to hear that. Why don't you call Zach?"

"Because I don't have his number!" This time I cringed. It *really* was the wrong thing to say.

"Try information. I doubt he's unlisted."

"Don't hang up," I begged. "I don't know what to do. The dogs are going crazy, I'm at the bottom of the ravine, there's this tree on my ankle that I can't lift and—

"You're *what?*" Derek's voice cut across my explanation. "Where are you?"

"Runyon Canyon. The Western trail."

"I'll be right there."

I'll say this for Scorpios, they move damn fast when they want to. But even a few minutes can seem like an eternity when you're trapped under a tree. You can do a lot of thinking in that time. A lot of thinking.

By the time Derek slithered down the slope to land in a wet, muddy heap beside me, the only thing I could say in favor of his appearance was this: I looked worse.

"Are you okay?" he asked, as he looked me over.

I nodded, although that wasn't altogether true. "I've been better."

Improbably, a smile curved his lips. "I have to admit, I like the look."

Considering that 'the look' consisted of a soaking wet T-shirt, coated in mud, and plastered to my chest, I wasn't surprised. "You would," I muttered, sniffling a little as I blinked back tears.

His smile disappeared. "You're crying? Are you hurt?"

I shook my head. The concern in his voice only made the tears fall faster.

"Gabby? Sweetie? What's wrong?"

"Just get me out of here," I begged.

* * * *

It seemed like no time at all before Derek was unlocking the door to my apartment.

I sighed in relief. "I'll be fine now."

He nodded, and followed me inside. "I know."

"You don't have to stay."

"I know." He glanced at the table, where the remnants of last night's meal still lay. "You didn't eat much last night, did you?"

"No," I sighed and averted my eyes. It was too painful to look at or think about.

"Any breakfast this morning?"

I shook my head. I hadn't been in the mood to eat. I still wasn't.

"How about you go inside and get cleaned up and I'll fix you something?"

"Derek, you don't have to do this," I told him.

Gently, he pushed me toward my bedroom. "Yes. I do."

* * * *

There's something about a gratin of just about anything that really hits the spot on a cold, rainy day when you're feeling like shit. Especially if you eat it while tucked into a warm bed. It might have been a little early for the wine, however.

"Are you trying to get me drunk?"

Derek shook his head. "Not much point in that, is there?"

I was going to suggest, again, that he could leave if he wanted, but I didn't want to insult him. Scorpios can be very sensitive...in their own fashion.

Derek borrowed my bathroom for a quick shower while I was eating. Then he put my plate and glass away, and came and sat on the bed. He hadn't put his muddy shirt back on. His chest was all smooth muscle and tanned skin, sheened with moisture, totally delectable. I was having a hard time not staring at his tight abs or the narrow line of dark hair that disappeared into his waistband. I was having an even harder time ignoring the liquid heat pooling between my thighs.

"You know, it's a misconception that Tantric Yoga is all about sex," he said quietly. "It's not. It's about accelerating spiritual growth. It's about raising Kundalini. It's not really about orgasm at all."

"I know that."

"It can take years of practice before a Yogi is ready to join with a partner, someone who complements him, who makes him whole. And then it could be years more before those partners are ready to join with one another in Maithuna."

I nodded.

"Even then, the primary goal is to avoid orgasm. To channel all that sexual energy and use it to reach enlightenment."

"It sounds lonely," I whispered, raising my eyes to his face for the first time since he'd sat down.

He looked a little wistful. "Maybe it is." He shrugged. Then he looked at me. "So, is that what you're interested in learning about?"

I shook my head. "There's more, isn't there?" I'd heard stories. My cheeks flamed. "What about...Amrita?"

"Ahh." A faint smile curled Derek's lips. "The nectar of the Goddess. I see." For a moment, his eyes glowed with heat. Then the fires were banked, but the smile still remained. "That's what you want to know about? Prolonged orgasmic bliss? Female ejaculation? Coming so hard that you faint? They say it's...quite a cosmic experience."

I'd heard that opening oneself that fully, being touched that deeply and intimately by another person could cause you to cry uncontrollably, or to laugh; could lead to an emotional release unlike any other. As I've said, I did a lot of thinking out there under that tree. I knew there was only one person I wanted to touch me like that.

"Show me."

Chapter Eight

Derek lifted one of my hands to his lips and kissed my palm, my wrist, my fingertips. "Are you sure that's what you want?"

A flush climbed up my chest to my face, and I swear I nearly came right on the spot. Speaking was too difficult. I nodded.

Unfortunately, nodding does no good if no one's watching. Derek looked at me questioningly. "Well?"

"Yes."

He released my hand and slowly slid the bedcovers down my legs, his gaze following right along. I had to take a deep breath. My toes curled in anticipation of what was coming.

"Relax," he ordered, but since he was sliding his palm back up my leg as he said it, there was no hope of that happening.

He took hold of my nightshirt next. "Have I mentioned that you have *the* most beautiful breasts I've ever seen?" he asked, pulling the garment over my head and tossing it on the floor.

My nipples grew tighter. My breasts ached for his touch. I'd been waiting so long...

But he only looked. "So gorgeous," he murmured. Then he stood and hooked his forefingers beneath the strip of lace at either side of my hips. "Lift up," he instructed as he tugged my panties down my legs.

"What about you?" I croaked when I found myself naked in front of him.

Resting his hands on my ankles, he paused and glanced at my face. "What about me?"

"Aren't you going to undress?"

His hold on my ankles tightened and he spread my legs wide. "Don't worry about what I'm doing."

"Not possible," I gasped as he slid between my thighs.

He peeked up at me, brown eyes glinting. "You're an actress. Think of it as taking direction."

I would have argued, but his lips closed around my clit, and for a time, I stopped thinking at all. After a few minutes, he replaced his mouth with his hand, slid two fingers inside me, and began to stroke with steadily increasing pressure. Heat spread low and fast, like a huge, warm wave, swelling to a crest—*Oh, God*, I thought suddenly, *I have to pee.*

"You don't have to pee," Derek murmured.

I looked at him, amazed. I'd heard Scorpios were intuitive.

Was he reading my mind?

He smiled. "That's how it feels, right?"

I nodded.

"It's supposed to. Ignore it."

"Easy for you to say," I muttered squirming a little, as I imagined myself wetting the bed.

He stopped and regarded me sternly. "If you want me to teach you this stuff, you have to be willing to do what I say."

I knew he enjoyed calling the shots but, truly, the submission gig had never been a big turn-on for me...until that moment. I fluttered my lashes. "Yes, Sensei," I murmured demurely.

Derek chuckled. "Don't make me laugh," he said...or ordered...hell, maybe it was a threat... I don't know because he began to stroke inside me again and the heat rose even faster than before.

"Close your mouth," he said a minute later.

"What?"

"Haven't I taught you anything about proper breathing techniques?"

Yoga is really big on nose breathing. So, I clamped my lips together obligingly, took a long, deep breath and immediately felt a rush of heat all through my body. My legs started to shake.

"Open your eyes," Derek murmured. "Look at me."

I did, and I swear time stopped. The heat was everywhere now, and when I felt his fingers pull out of me, I wanted to cry. "Don't stop now," I begged him.

"Shh. Do you have any condoms?"

I had to think for a second. "No."

Derek nodded. "Right. Me, neither. Do you trust me?"

Reluctantly, I nodded.

"Then, listen. I'm going to fuck you now, but I'm not going to come. So it'll be okay. Believe me?"

Now, I know what you've heard. Pisces are gullible, naive and far too trusting, right? Well, you know what? Sue us. Nobody's perfect. I nodded again.

A smile warmed his eyes as he stripped out of his pants. I barely had time to register the fact that he was tanned all over and that the erection jutting out at me was even heavier than I'd been imagining, before he'd slipped between my legs again and bent his mouth to mine. I blinked in surprise. It was our first real kiss. All sex and sensuality—not something friends would share, not even in their fantasies. Yet, nothing had ever felt more right. I wrapped my arms and legs around him, wanting to melt right into him. My skin was so sensitized that just the feel of his body, so solid, so warm, all mine to enjoy, nearly sent me over the edge.

He lifted his head and our eyes locked as he slowly thrust into me. My eyes slid shut again. I started to shiver.

"No," he murmured as he pulled back out. "Not like that. Focus."

Groaning, I forced my eyes open once more. Successive waves of hot and cold chills chased themselves over my body as he thrust into me again and again. I think I stopped breathing and I know my nails were digging into his shoulders hard enough to break the skin, but I didn't care. A feeling was welling up inside me that could only be love. A huge, bright bubble that pushed itself to the surface and erupted from my throat in a sob. Tears streamed from my eyes and I clutched Derek tighter as my body convulsed. Joyful. Ecstatic. Inconsolable.

* * * *

I don't know that I passed out, but my mind definitely went blank. Next thing I knew, he was kissing my neck, my shoulder, my breast; whispering words I couldn't hear.

"Oh, my God," I murmured, fighting for breath.

Derek lifted his head and smiled. "So, what d'you think?"

I'm not usually at a loss for words, but this left me speechless. "The earth moved."

His lips quirked. "I'm pretty sure those were aftershocks from the earthquake, but I'll take it as a compliment just the same."

He kissed me again, and then pulled carefully away and got out of bed. I blinked in surprise as he reached for his clothes and started to dress.

Considering how amazing it had been, *that's it* seemed a little inappropriate. But still..."That's it? You're leaving?"

He smiled faintly. "Work."

"But...you didn't come?"

He shook his head. "No."

"Why?"

"Because. Today was about you. Besides, we don't have time for the full session right now."

I think I gaped. "The *full* session?"

His eyes turned smoky. "Yeah. The big one. That's where you come a couple more times, and then we both come together and pass out in each other's arms."

"Oh."

His smile widened. "That sounds worth waiting for, doesn't it?"

I nodded yes, but what I was really thinking was: *more waiting?*

"There's something I've been wondering about," I said as I watched him finish dressing.

He looked at me. "Go on."

"Why'd you leave Claire? What changed? Was it something she did?"

His eyes widened, as though the question surprised him. "It had nothing to do with her. Claire is...Claire. I don't think she'll ever be anything different. I wouldn't want her to be. What changed was I'd fallen for you. Staying with her would have been dishonest."

I sighed. It was as I'd hoped. And what I'd feared. But it was never what I'd intended.

"I'm sorry."

Derek shrugged. "It happens. Look, I've got a class to teach now, so..."

"Why didn't you tell me any of this sooner?"

His jaw clenched. "I tried to. You wanted to be friends."

There was that word again. "What happens now? Can we still be friends?"

He shook his head. His voice was as cool as marble and his answer was pretty much what I'd expected.

"I don't think so."

Chapter Nine

"I'm sorry," I told Zach the next day.

He shrugged. "It's okay. I kind of figured it was coming. I saw how things were the other night." He looked at me for a moment, and then smiled. "Besides, we'll always have the refrigerator."

I stretched up on my toes to kiss him good-bye. "Thank you."

He pulled me in for a hug and kissed me back. Then he kissed me again. I think I've mentioned that he's really good at that. "Mm. Thank *you*. Still the best birthday present I ever had."

"I'm glad," I said as he let me go.

I turned to leave.

"So, um...I guess this means you'll be keeping your blinds closed from now on?"

I glanced at him over my shoulder and smiled. "You never know. I might forget sometimes."

He smiled back. "I'll look forward to it."

* * * *

I know I've said that a modern woman wouldn't sit at home and wait for love to find her. But there are some things that only come in the proper time, like when the tides turn, or when the seasons change. And, sometimes, after you've done everything you can think of to make things happen, there's nothing else you *can* do, except sit back and let what you want come to you.

I really do hate waiting, though.

I waited until I knew Derek was teaching a class, then I left a message on his answering machine; one I knew he'd only respond to if he'd been lying the night before. It might sound odd, but I was hoping that was the case. I had to believe we were still friends, that we weren't really giving anything up, that we'd only added a new dimension to what we already had.

The message was short. Three little words. "I need you."

* * * *

He must have checked his answering machine right after class, because it was only a few minutes later that he was ringing my doorbell.

"What's with the message?" he asked as I let him into my apartment. "What do you need?"

"A friend?"

Derek's eyes flashed—not in a good way. His brows drew together. "I thought we covered this? I told you. I don't want to be friends."

"I know. But..."

"You don't sleep with your friends. I don't know how many times you've told me that, but I got the message, okay?"

I took a deep breath, and asked, "What if I made an exception?"

Derek looked at me for a long moment. "Exceptions are good," he murmured and pulled me close.

I nestled against him, feeling happy, relieved, loved. "I'm so glad you came."

"But, I didn't come—yet." He raised his head and smiled wickedly. "Are you ready for the big one?"

Chapter Ten

Well, that was the question, wasn't it?

Call it stage fright, call it performance anxiety, call it opening night jitters. Call it whatever you want. Suddenly, I was nervous as hell. I'd been building this whole thing up in my head for so long, waiting, hoping. What if I was disappointed? Worse, what if Derek was disappointed? Worst of all, what if I had been right and we ended up wrecking our friendship?

Derek stopped in his tracks just a few steps into the bedroom. Glancing around, he eyed the preparations I'd made: the champagne colored satin sheets, the vanilla musk scented candles, the gardenia blossoms floating in bowls of water.

"Verrry nice," he murmured as he wrapped his arms around me from behind and trailed kisses down my neck. "You've been thinking about this, haven't you?"

I nodded. "All day." In fact, it had been hard to think of anything else. And now... I could feel his cock pressing into the small of my back. I closed my eyes and pressed back. I wanted to cant my hips and grind against him. I wanted his hands on my breasts. I wanted to stay wrapped in his arms forever.

But he was already releasing me, moving toward the bed. He ran his hand over my new sheets and nodded approvingly "I like." Next, he lifted the lid of the fondue pot I'd set up on my dresser, and peered inside. "What's this?"

"White chocolate fondue. I made it for the dinner you messed up the other night."

"Good thing, too." He dipped a finger into the melted chocolate for a quick taste. Then he looked at me and his smile disappeared. "Oh, come on. Don't tell me you're still holding that against me?"

I shook my head. That wasn't the problem. The nervousness was back.

Derek's eyes were troubled as he walked back to where I stood. "What did you expect me to do? Nothing? I'd tried that. It was killing me. I couldn't stand by and watch you waste time with another loser."

"Zach is *not* a loser," I blurted in the instant before I realized that the smarter thing would be to say nothing. Zach was sweet and fun, but did we really want to discuss him now?

Derek nodded. "Okay, well, maybe not. But that would have

been even worse, wouldn't it? You might have stayed with him for months, if that was the case. For years. Forever." His voice was matter of fact, but his face was grim and his words tore at my heart. "I wanted you with me and you just weren't getting that."

Pisces are nothing if not compassionate. Abandoned puppies, orphaned children, wounded men; we want to save them all. Derek was looking very wounded, and it made me forget all about being nervous.

"I'm with you now, aren't I?" I asked. I closed the distance between us and framed his face with my hands, intending to reassure him with a simple kiss. But he pre-empted my kiss with one of his own, sweeping me into a tight embrace, molding me to him, slanting his mouth over mine. I opened my mouth on a sigh and his tongue swept in. There it was again. A rush of heat. A feeling of home. The been-here-done-this, déjà vu feeling that only being with a soul mate can give you.

A man's kiss is his signature. Mae West said that. Pretty insightful for a Leo. I felt like my soul had known Derek's kisses in a dozen different lifetimes. If we'd done this months ago, it might have saved us both a lot of waiting.

I could have gone on kissing him all night, but too soon, he was pulling away. We took turns taking off each other's clothes; slowly, deliberately, breaking eye contact only when the need to see or to taste what we were uncovering became too overwhelming to ignore. I was right about the tan. I was right about a lot of things.

By the time we were both naked, I was shivering, but not from cold. My nipples were hard, my pussy was throbbing, and my chest heaved with every ragged breath I took. Derek's breathing, on the other hand, was steady and even. Calm. Only the clenching and unclenching of his hands betrayed his excitement. Well, that and his cock. Thick, swollen, corded with veins, I didn't know where I wanted it first, but I knew exactly when. Now. No more waiting.

I lay down on the bed and reached for him, aching to feel his arms around me. I had a box of condoms ready on the nightstand, but we could deal with that in a minute. First, I wanted to feel Derek's weight on top of me. I wanted his lips on mine again. Instead, he skipped my arms, sank to his knees, and took me with his mouth.

I groaned, only partly in disappointment. The way his lips teased my clit was certainly nothing to complain about. In fact, it was nothing short of amazing. Better than any fantasy. Then he reached for my breasts and his arms pressed against my thighs, pushing them open. I felt myself spread wide and held immobile—exposed—his for the taking.

I had braced myself on my elbows to watch but now my heart thudded in my chest. As his hands traced over my midsection I arched into them, moaning as they closed on my flesh. He paused and raised his head. His gaze, heavy lidded and dark, lingered on my breasts where his thumbs circled and rubbed the already swollen peaks.

His glance moved higher, and when his eyes connected with mine, I fell into his gaze. Satisfaction and desire laced his smile. I shuddered as my sex flooded with liquid warmth. Heat blazed in my cheeks. Derek's eyes grew even darker. His nostrils flared, as though he scented my arousal.

He dipped his head once more. The first touch of his tongue on my clit had me crying out. I came almost too quickly; sharp, hard, explosive, and I was still shaking as Derek's hands slid away from my breasts to cup my ass. His fingers curved into the crease and he lifted my hips toward his mouth. He lapped noisily at my pussy, and the sound alone was almost enough to make me come again. My toes curled, my fingers twisted in the sheets. When he thumbed my labia wide and licked inside me, it wrenched another strangled cry from my lips.

He glanced at my face again and grinned. Then he flicked his tongue once more across my clit and slid up to lie alongside me. "How's everything up here?" he asked, eyes sparkling.

I had no words, so I kissed him, loving the feel of his arms as they finally tightened around me, of his fingers as they splayed across my back, drawing me closer. I'd wanted to be held like this for so long—ever since I'd first seen his muscles, I think. I slipped my own arms around him and reveled in how good he felt.

Our legs tangled, our tongues touched, and when Derek's hand drifted down to my ass, his fingers feathering soft touches along the crease, I rocked my hips back to give him more. He inhaled on a shuddery little sigh, hands clenching as he pulled me tight against him. His erection nestled against my thigh, rock-hard, just starting to weep. My sudden desire to take him in my mouth and learn his taste as it exploded on my tongue left me breathless.

I prodded his chest until he pulled back to look at me questioningly.

"Your turn now," I murmured, resting my head against his

arm. Smiling up at him I grazed my fingers down his chest and stomach, loving the way his muscles trembled at my touch. "I want to taste you."

"I want that, too," he said. He took hold of my hand and stopped me before I reached his cock. He laced his fingers through mine and stretched my arm above my head. "But not just yet."

He slid his arm out from under my head and clasped my wrist while he kissed me even more deeply. His legs hooked around mine, pinning me to the bed with his thigh. Chills raced across my skin as his free hand slid down my arm to gently trace the curve of one breast.

When he lifted his head to watch what his hand was doing, I nearly whimpered with frustration. What it was doing was causing my sex to ache, and throb and cream. My legs were pressed tight together, and yet I could still feel trickles of wetness seeping from between my labia and sliding down the crease of my butt. At this rate, I'd soon be lying in a pool of my own juices.

"Derek, please," I begged, bucking my hips against his restraining leg.

The corner of his mouth was twitching again as he dipped his head and curled his tongue around one nipple. "Hmm? Please...what?"

Please fuck me! Well, okay, that's what I wanted to say. But Pisces aren't known for being that direct and, although I was quickly getting there, I wasn't that depraved...yet. "I want you."

"I'm glad," he murmured, taking my nipple between his lips and suckling it. I was keening with need by the time he pulled back and laved the tip with his tongue. His gaze was tender as he smiled at me. "Relax, okay? Just enjoy"

"I am. But..."

"Shh." He stopped my protest with a finger across my lips. "Please. Let me love you like this. I've been waiting too, you know."

Yes, and you're still waiting, I thought, biting down on my lip to hold back the words. Obviously, one of us had a rather large, unexpected, masochistic streak. And it wasn't me. I blame it on Pluto. There's something dark and twisted about Scorpio's ruling planet.

Still, if that's really what he wanted, who was I to argue? "Okay."

"Want more?"

I nodded.

"Good," he said, scissoring his legs suddenly, to push my legs wide, and then skimming his hand down over my stomach. His fingers flitted lightly across my clit and then buried themselves in my pussy.

He'd been lying about the aftershocks. It wasn't the earth that had been moving at all the other day. Once again, my own private, internal temblor started as soon as his fingers curved inside me. Three fingers inside, his thumb nudging my clit, his pinky trailing over my slick perineum, each slow stroke released a fresh flow of fluid spilling into his hand.

"Omigod," I gasped as the pleasure intensified.

"Mmm." Derek nuzzled my neck. "So sweet. Can you feel how wet you are?" His voice was rough, faintly trembling.

Eyes closed, I nodded. I felt dazed with heat. I felt molten.

Derek's hand continued to move, stirring up delicious, hot waves that rippled outward from my melted core to every extremity. "You're a goddess," he murmured. "*My* goddess."

I opened my eyes and stared at him, questioningly.

His lips twitched. "What? You didn't know that?"

I shook my head. I don't know what answer I would have made, but before I could say anything, his pinky dipped into my ass, and just that tiny bit of added pressure pushed me over the edge. The waves rolled and crested, engulfing me as I came and kept on coming—so hard it should have hurt.

Next thing I knew, Derek's arms were around me, holding me close, and tears I couldn't recall crying, tracked my cheeks.

"So beautiful," he whispered against my ear. "I could watch you come like that all night."

All night? "Hold that thought," I said, pushing away from him and sliding off the bed. For all I knew, he meant to do just that. Which was great, except for one thing: I wanted to give a little something back, too.

Derek rolled on his back to watch me. "Where are you going?"

I took the pot of fondue off the heater and stirred the white chocolate goo with one finger, testing the temperature. It was perfect. Hot, but not too hot. "It's your turn."

"I told you. That..." he said, breaking off to stare as I let a single white drop fall on the tip of one rosy nipple. His penis jerked. "That's not part of the plan," he rasped, still staring.

I smiled. "I'm an actress, remember? Think of this as

improv."

His eyelids were at half-mast when I returned to the bed and straddled his legs. He drew in a startled breath as I tipped the pot and let a tiny stream dribble onto his cock. I sat back to admire my artistry. It looked so much like cum, I found myself licking my lips. "Mm. Looks yummy."

"What are you trying to do to me?" he groaned.

"Just giving you ideas," I said, giving him a second helping too, while I was at it.

His cock jerked again, and some of the warm chocolate missed its mark, forming a puddle that spread from the base of his cock almost to his navel.

I clucked my tongue in mock dismay as I lowered my head to his belly and licked up the mess, swirling my tongue an extra couple of times in his belly button, but taking care to leave his cock strictly alone. If he wanted to wait...well, then, I guess he could wait.

Derek's breathing was harsh, his eyes mere slits by the time I was done. Now we were getting somewhere. Smiling, I dipped my finger in the pot again, and then smeared chocolate around each of his nipples. *The shiny brown buttons already looked like mini M&Ms,* I thought as I leaned forward to take one in my mouth; now they'd taste like them, too.

I licked them both clean then licked my lips. "Good?"

He nodded, his eyes still trained on my lips.

"Want more?"

Something hot and primal flashed in his eyes as he growled, "Yes. Now."

"What's your hurry?" I asked, as I painted over my own nipples, loving the feel of the chocolate on my skin, so warm and silky. Loving the way his eyes darkened and his cheeks flushed with heat. "Mm, sweet," I murmured, dunking my whole thumb in the pot this time, and sucking greedily.

"C'mere," he rasped, reaching for me, but I eluded him long enough to plunge my finger into the fondue one last time, before putting the pot aside. I leaned forward again and traced over his lips with the chocolate, then leaned closer still. He clasped my head in both hands, sinking back onto the pillows, pulling me down with him. Chocolate smeared over both our faces and our chests as we collided, leaving us with no choice but to kiss, lick, and nibble at each other until it was gone.

Finally, I pushed away from him and sat up. I was breathless and flushed, and gloating over the fact that so was he. "Well, that was fun."

He eyed me quizzically. "I don't think we're quite done yet," he said, glancing down his torso.

"Mm." I followed his gaze, smiling smugly at the sight of his cock, still making no move toward it. "Looks nice, doesn't it?"

Derek all but gaped in disbelief. "You're going to make me ask for it, aren't you?"

I smiled innocently. "Ask for what?" I was pretty sure what was coming next, and he didn't disappoint me.

"Gabby?"

"Yes, Derek?"

"Would you suck my dick, already? Please?"

My smile grew wider. "I thought you'd never ask."

Chapter Eleven

"Oh, Jesus," Derek moaned as I swirled my tongue around the head of his cock. I smiled. I loved the contrasting tastes and textures. I loved the husky timbre of his voice. I opened my mouth wide and swallowed what I could of his shaft. I loved the way he filled my mouth. I loved the thought of his cock gliding deep into my wet pussy. But mostly, I just loved him.

I couldn't believe how close we'd come to missing this. I couldn't believe how stupid I'd been all these months. I cradled his balls in my hand as I swiped away the last of the chocolate, and then ran my tongue down the length of him, just barely nipping at the delicate skin in the juncture where his cock met his sack.

"Stop," he groaned, twisting away abruptly and reaching toward the nightstand. "That's enough."

I glanced up, surprised and disappointed. "Was that too rough?"

He shook his head. "No. It was perfect. Here." His fingers were trembling as he handed me a condom.

I took it reluctantly. I didn't really want to stop. I licked his swollen head again, with its velvet skin and dripping slit. He was teasing me with that tiny taste. I wanted more. "We don't need this yet, do we? I could take you in my mouth."

"Please," he gritted, his teeth clenched. "I *need* to be inside you. Now." His voice sounded tight but determined.

"As you wish," I sighed, feeling almost jealous of the latex sheath as I unrolled it over him. He could have at least let me finish what I'd begun because, this way, hot as he was, he was liable to come too quickly and disappoint us both.

I guess I should have known better.

Derek surged upward, coming to his knees so abruptly that I fell backwards. He grabbed hold of my ankles and pulled me toward him. My butt slid along the slick satin of the sheets until I was pinned beneath him. I could feel his whole body trembling with tension as he carefully aligned himself with my opening, and then paused. I looped my arms around his neck and waited, barely breathing.

He looked at me, his face stark. "You know what this means, don't you? You. Me. What we're doing. You know this is how things should have been all along?"

What, with you on top? But I stopped myself before I could say it. I've told you how unexpectedly sensitive Scorpios can be, and something told me this was no time to make jokes. Besides, I knew what he was really asking. I nodded, reaching out to feather the hair at his temple. "I know."

He held my gaze as he thrust into me. We both sighed in amazement. Then Derek's eyes shuttered closed and he began to move slowly, deeply, deliberately.

Considering that I had already come twice, I really hadn't expected to be ready again so soon, but incredibly, I felt my muscles tightening almost at once. "Yes," I whispered, only partly from pleasure. Mostly, it was in answer to his question. I knew what we were doing, what this night meant—to both of us.

His eyes gleamed as he opened them and smiled at me. "Good." And I knew he wasn't talking just about how he felt.

He picked up the pace until we were both rocking in frantic tandem, racing for the peak and reaching it together. We jerked hard against each other as the tremors slammed us again and again.

Gradually, our movements slowed, our breath returned. Peace, contentment, and exhaustion settled over us like a heavy cloud. Derek collapsed next to me. I half turned to snuggle into his embrace.

"I love you," I thought I heard him say.

I think I nodded. I think I smiled. I think I answered, "You'd better."

But, then again, I may have already been asleep and dreaming of the big one.

* * * *

Well, that was several months ago. Derek and I are still together, of course, and ecstatically happy to be so. I have it all now. Love, friendship, and really hot sex. All with the same great guy. I'm not waiting for anything anymore. Oh, except for one little thing.

Our baby.

He or she—we want to be surprised—is due in March. I'm really hoping for another Pisces.

Love, from A to Z

Total amnesia is not what Richie Valenzuela had planned on when he drugged his cousin. A few missing hours, which could easily be blamed on April's having had too much to drink, was all he was aiming for. And he certainly never expected the reclusive heiress to slip out the club's back door with the sexy guitarist she'd been making eyes at all night.

Zach Harris is sure the girl he'd picked up the night before had told him her name was Angel. Too bad she didn't tell him anything more about herself, because, this morning, it's not just him she can't remember, she doesn't even know her own name!

What April views as a problem, however, Zach sees as a once-in-a-lifetime opportunity; a chance for her to discover who she really is. Not her name or her address, but the important stuff. Her personality. Her likes and dislikes. Her preferences—in and out of bed.

Prologue

Friday Night
Venice Beach, CA

April Valenzuela wasn't going anywhere. No matter how pissy and bad tempered her cousin Richie got, she was staying right where she was—seated at the ridiculously well-lighted, stage-side table in the otherwise dimly lit club. It was Richie who had suggested the table. In fact, it had been Richie who'd suggested this entire night of bar hopping in the first place. He'd dragged her all over the LA Basin, hitting one sleazy nightspot after another, finally landing them here, at this mostly forgettable Venice Beach dive where April had at last discovered something—make that *someone*—yummy enough to make the whole sorry evening worthwhile.

The lead guitarist of the band currently reigning over the bar's small stage was easily the best thing she'd seen in at least the last year and a half. Even scruffily dressed in a faded black T shirt that accentuated broad shoulders and a nice pair of pecs; and torn jeans that molded enticingly around the impressive bulge at his crotch, he was breathtaking. With his tall, sinewy build, devilish smile and angelic, golden curls, he took hot to a whole 'nother level.

And the way he played! Well, that was taking April to another level, as well.

She wasn't sure how he did it. Maybe it was the way he held the neck of his guitar. Maybe it was some complicated picking technique. Whatever it was, it was fan-fucking-tastic. She sat mesmerized, watching his fingers coax music from the strings, feeling every one of those delicious notes as they vibrated deep inside her, making her clit throb and her nipples bead tight. She'd bet anything it was intentional.

"C'mon, let's go," Richie whined again.

"Not a chance."

You couldn't really climax simply from listening to someone play guitar, could you? The longer the god of grunge rock played, the less certain April became. For the sake of research alone, she owed it to herself to stay and find out. She gestured at the empty glasses on the table in front of them. "Look, Richie, if you're that restless, why don't you go get us some fresh drinks? It'll do you good to stretch your legs."

"I don't want another drink," Richie protested stubbornly. "And you should have had enough by now too."

But he really ought to have known her better than that. April would decide for herself what constituted enough. And never in a million years would she admit to the faint wooziness that made her legs feel like rubber. Yet another reason not to try and navigate her way to the door right now. "Richie. Go."

Scowling furiously, Richie pushed away from the table. "Bitch," he muttered under his breath as he headed for the bar.

April shrugged. "Wow, how original." She *was* a bitch, damn it, and even though she wouldn't be caught dead wearing one of those flashy gold necklaces that proclaimed it to the world, she was proud of it. It was a quality she'd developed young, it was what helped her survive the cut-throat family politics she'd had to endure following the death of her parents. It was precisely the reason her grandfather had chosen her to inherit the bulk of his estate when he died six months ago, much to her remaining relatives' continued dismay.

So, if Richie didn't like it, he could kiss her ass. She had no illusions about why he'd invited her out tonight. No doubt he was hoping to hit her up for money. It was the same ploy his father had used only last week, inviting her to lunch with him at his club, and then asking for a loan.

"It's not really a loan, though, is it?" she'd pointed out. "I mean, that would imply you were planning on paying me back."

"I suppose that's true," George had replied dryly. "However, I didn't think you'd be as amenable if I'd called it a gift. Still, I can't imagine that my favorite niece would really want to see me lose the business I've poured my heart's blood into, simply because her grandfather didn't understand the ramifications of what he was doing when he drafted his will."

George's favorite and only niece smiled sweetly. "I guess we'll never know what Papi had in mind, will we?"

In all likelihood, April knew that her uncle was right. Her grandfather probably *would* have bailed him out of trouble. But then, April was also pretty certain that George would never have dreamed of subjecting his father to the continual humiliation to which he'd treated April during the last few years. Her love affairs scrutinized. Her most casual dinner dates subjected to background checks. Not to mention the embarrassment of having her lovers confronted—usually *in flagrante delicto*—with the evidence of their perfidy.

"I know you don't like me to rush into anything, Uncle George. Not without investigating it first. So, I'll get back to you after I've had a chance to check things out."

A little turnaround. That's only fair play, isn't it?

Fair or not, George hadn't taken being turned down well, and most likely Richie wouldn't like it much either. But that was just too bad and, come to think of it, if that's how it was going to be, they could both kiss her ass. She'd allowed them to maintain their comfortable quarters in the family mansion because they were family, because she knew that's what Papi would have wanted, and because, frankly, it suited her to do so.

The thought of living all alone in that big house, with no one but the servants for company, was almost enough to give April hives. As far as family went, George and Richie weren't much, but they were all she had. Still, enough was enough! She was at least as smart as either of them and she was through being played for a fool.

Just then, the guitarist launched into another of those wicked little riffs that practically had her coming in her seat. She squirmed restlessly as heat pulsed inside her, then gasped in surprise when her pussy clenched. *Damn. Almost.* When she raised her gaze to his face, the sultry smile that lit up his eyes only reinforced what her own intuition had already told her. He knew just what he was doing to her, and loving every second.

Not that she wasn't enjoying it even more herself, of course. Her eyes narrowed down to tiny little slits as she felt her labia soften and swell. Heaving a sigh, she reclined in her seat, the better to feel the sensations as they washed through her.

Since this was all the enjoyment she was going to get from him, April decided to make the most of it. "Ooh, yeah, bring it, baby," she murmured as she stretched, arching her back, raking her fingers through her hair. The movement caused her breasts to strain against the sheer burgundy fabric of her blouse, riveting his gaze.

That's better, she thought, smiling slyly, watching as his eyes grew dark. *You like that, do you? Good. Let's see what you think of this.* As her fingers traced the neckline of her blouse, skimming lightly over the curves of her breasts, she longed for the courage to slip her fingers beneath the filmy silk, to massage their aching tips. Or, better yet, to slide a hand between her legs, and help things along. But she wasn't that brave.

She would have liked to take her new playmate home with her, too; to strip him out of those clothes and find out how much of that bulge was for real, to dig her nails into those broad shoulders, to test her teeth against those taut pecs. But all of that was out of the question. She knew only too well what would happen if she tried it. She supposed she really ought to thank her uncle for that insight.

It didn't really matter how hot this guy was, or how good they might be together. One look at the manse, and he'd find himself falling madly in love all right—but with April's money, not her. She'd been there before, too many times, and she'd learned her lesson well. Now, she restricted herself to dating only the equally wealthy. It was safe, if boring, and it led to her spending far too many nights alone, which was the main reason she'd accepted Richie's invitation.

"Here." Two glasses slammed down on the table in front of

her. Her cousin directed a venomous scowl toward the stage as he regained his seat. The guitarist turned away, engaging the bass guitarist in a musical duel. Disappointed, April sat up straight, letting her hair fall forward, hoping to disguise the flush in her cheeks.

"Thanks a lot," she muttered as she reached for her glass. The suspicious gleam in Richie's eyes as he studied her face surprised her. What was that about? Could he sense her arousal? She sipped her drink and nearly gagged at the caustic taste. "Omigod, what is this swill? It's awful!"

"Tequila Sunrise," Richie replied waspishly. "Given the hillbilly ambience of this place, I figured you'd appreciate the irony."

"Well, they need to open a fresh bottle of orange juice, or something, because this stuff has turned."

Richie raised an eyebrow. "Really? Mine tastes fine. Why don't you try it again, maybe it's you."

April gazed at her cousin doubtfully. Since Richie was even more of a food and wine snob than she was, the sight of him guzzling yet another mixed drink, with apparent pleasure, seemed just a little surreal. If there was anything even slightly off about the taste of his drink, everyone in the bar would know it by now. She pursed her lips around the straw once more, and tried again. The drink still tasted strange, but perhaps it wasn't the orange juice, after all. "Can grenadine go bad?" she asked her cousin.

Richie shrugged. "How would I know? Just drink it, okay? And then let's get out of here."

"Mmm. Not just yet," she murmured. She had finally succeeded in making eye contact with the guitarist once again. She ignored the faintly unpleasant taste of her drink and the tingling numbness in her mouth. It felt like her tongue had been coated with plastic, but she sucked greedily, pausing now and again to lick her lips—just to give him ideas.

He smiled appreciatively, but with a faint shake of his head he let her know that playtime was over. By the time April's glass was empty, she was pouting.

"*Now* can we go?" Richie asked as she put her empty glass down with a frustrated sigh. Before she could answer, her cousin's cell phone rang. He took it from his pocket and glanced at it. "Shit," he muttered as he got to his feet. "I gotta take this. I'll be back in a minute."

Frowning, April turned to watch her cousin as he headed for the door. Something was up. She'd recognized the number. Richie was a little old for a curfew, so why was he getting calls from his father at this time of night?

Scattered applause from the surrounding tables alerted her to the fact that the band had finished playing. *So soon?* She glanced toward the front just in time to see the guitarist hop from the stage and head straight for her table. Her heart started to pound and, all at once, an odd, dizzy feeling came over her. Her vision blurred. *What's going on*, she wondered, as she swayed in her seat. *I can't be that drunk, can I?*

"So," he said as he pulled out the chair opposite hers and sat down. "What's it gonna be? Are we gonna play by the rules? Are you going to make me ask for your phone number, wait a few days, call you up and invite you out on a date? Or do you want to save some time and cut through all that crap? Leave with me now and let's go someplace where we can carry through on some of those promises we've been making each other all night."

The room seemed suddenly airless and what seemed like several minutes passed before his words filtered into April's brain. She felt herself frown. "Promises?"

He flashed a dazzling smile. "That's how I see it. Between what your eyes have been saying to me and my fingers have been doing to you, I figure either we owe each other a real good time, or we're just a couple of teases. And, baby, I don't know about you, but if there's one thing I'm not, it's a tease."

April smiled back, faintly, trying to remember what she'd planned to say if he approached her, but her thoughts slipped lazily away. Did it really matter? He was here, he was hot, and leaving with him... was there a problem with that? None that she could see. "Okay, sure. Let's go."

His eyes widened first, then his smile followed suit. "Well, all right. You, uh...think you might need to say something to your date first? Like, Sayonara, or..."

April frowned. "My date?"

"Yeah. Guy you're here with? Sour looking dude?"

"Oh!" She couldn't help giggling at his description; maybe that's why Richie hadn't noticed anything wrong with his drink. "You mean my cousin? No, he's gone away somewhere. Besides, we're not really that close."

"Your *cousin?* Well, all right, then." Still smiling, the stranger got to his feet. "Shall we?" He held out his hand. April stared at it for a moment, waiting for understanding to dawn. Then she took it, and let him haul her to her feet.

He glanced at her in surprise when she stumbled and almost fell against him. "Hey, are you okay?"

"Mm-hm," she murmured, blinking up at him.

"Yeah? You sure? You gonna be all right to ride on the back of my motorcycle?"

What nice eyes he has, April thought. His eyes were the purest sea green she'd ever seen. But they gazed at her questioningly, as though he were waiting for her to say something. "All right," she repeated, smiling encouragingly. "Let's go."

"Okay," he said as he helped her into her jacket. "If you say so. My name's Zach, by the way."

"April," she replied, reveling in the touch when he placed a warm hand against the small of her back and propelled her toward the bar's back door.

He shook his head. "Hold on, I can't hear you. Wait 'til we get outside."

Cool, night air, fresh and slightly misty, wafted over April as they stepped through the door. She sighed blissfully as she breathed it in. Looking around, she was vaguely surprised to find herself in the alley where Richie had parked his Porsche. *Where'd he go*, she wondered, but without much interest. *Is he still on the phone?* Then Zach pulled her into his arms and kissed her, and she stopped thinking altogether.

His lips were warm, firm, oh-so-right. It had been too long since she'd been kissed, too long since a man had held her like this. *How long*, she wondered, but her thoughts felt muddled and hazy, and she couldn't recall.

Zach was breathing hard when he broke off the kiss. "I still don't know your name?"

The glow of the streetlight gilded his hair 'til it blazed like a halo as it framed his face, and the heat in his eyes when he smiled at her left her dizzy. He looked like an… "Angel," she murmured as she snuggled against his chest, hoping for another kiss.

Suddenly, an engine roared to life. Headlights blazed, all but blinding her. Her hands clenched in the fabric of Zach's shirt. "Watch out!" she screamed as a car rushed toward them.

He pushed her hard, shoving them both from the car's path. April felt the hot wind as it passed them, and then she was falling. Arms flailing, she reached for Zach but missed. The back of her head connected with the metal dumpster. Stars exploded inside her skull, entire galaxies spinning out of control.

"Ow," she muttered as the pavement rose to meet her. And then the stars winked out, slowly, one by one, and she was left in darkness.

Chapter One

The next morning
April

It's funny how you can always tell when you're not alone. Even before I opened my eyes, I *knew*. It's not like I could hear the sound of someone's breathing—early morning birdsong and the persistent buzz of a lawn mower drifting in through the open windows took care of that. The bed didn't so much as jiggle and certainly there was no one touching me. But, all the same, I knew. I wasn't alone. There was someone in the bed with me. But who?

Cautiously, I opened my eyes. As an unfamiliar wall flickered into focus I stifled a gasp. *Omigod, where in the hell am I?* Heart pounding, I tried not to panic. Maybe I was dreaming? I closed my eyes, counted to three, and then tried opening them again. The view remained the same: a row of paperbacks, cheap shelving, a stack of CDs, part of a sliding glass door. A random and unremarkable collection of furnishings met my gaze, nothing I could recall having seen before. Even the bed felt unfamiliar, now that I stopped to consider it. And my memories of the previous night? Completely non-existent.

I took a moment to assess the situation. I was naked in a strange bed, under a navy blue sheet whose depressingly low thread count begged the question, *what was I thinking?*

A fabulous question that, by the way. One I wished I'd had the sense to ask myself the night before.

I mean, it was obvious I'd picked someone up. Or, considering my location, I'd been picked up. What wasn't so obvious was why. Because, despite the subtle pulsing in my sex, the slick, swollen softness that let me know that, wherever this was, I'd clearly had a real good time getting here, instinct told me this was *not* my usual milieu.

I lay still a little while longer as I contemplated what my next move should be. Could I slide out of bed without alerting Mr. Right Now to the fact that I was leaving? Much as my body would have liked an encore, my mind recoiled at the awkwardness that was sure to ensue. If I could find my clothes, if I could dress quickly and quietly enough, I could be gone before he even knew I was awake, saving us both from certain embarrassment.

It was a plan, and a good one, but before I could put it into action, the mattress creaked and a heavy, warm weight settled against my back. "M-m-m-morning." An indecently sexy voice rumbled in my ear. An indisputably male arm ensnared my waist. An unmistakably hard cock prodded my ass.

Well, shit. So much for graceful exits.

Biting my lip, I turned to face my unknown bedmate. I'd be lying if I said I didn't fear the worst. But one look at his face and, suddenly, things were making a lot more sense. I mean, if you're gonna screw up and go home with a total stranger, you could do worse than to pick one who looks like a Greek god.

Or who would if Greek gods were blond. I'm guessing they're not, no matter how many times they cast Brad Pitt in the role.

"Uh...hi," I murmured, feeling breathless as I stared into an absolutely gorgeous set of smoldering, sea green eyes. How in the world could I ask his name, or any of the other dozen questions which were begging for answers, without betraying the fact that I couldn't remember the first thing about him, about the night we'd just spent together, about... a lot of things, actually.

"C'mere," he murmured as he drew me close. The throbbing heat deep in my belly did a good job of distracting me from the vague uneasiness nagging at me from the back of my mind.

There was too much here that I didn't understand, too much I couldn't remember, but it was easy to forget about that with his fingers splayed across my bare back. As his hands slid lower, fingers teasing the seam of my ass, I couldn't help but shiver at the touch. Even so, when he lowered his lips to mine, I shoved at his chest, pushing him away.

"Wait," I gasped, unable to shake the feeling that we were moving too fast. Sure he looked good and felt good, but come on, if you'd found yourself naked with a man you'd just that instant laid eyes on, for what felt like the very first time, what would you do?

He cocked his head to the side and regarded me curiously. "You're kidding. What do I gotta wait for *now*?"

Good question. "I uh...well, what were you waiting for before?" I bluffed, hoping to sound less clueless than I felt.

That's when he hit me with his smile. One of those too-good-to-be-true, sinfully sweet charmers, it left me stupefied. "You." He planted a soft kiss on the tip of my nose. "I tried waking you hours ago but you sleep like the dead."

"Sorry about that," I mumbled, feeling even more breathless than before.

He chuckled. "Well, you should be sorry. 'Cause you fell out last night just as we were getting to the good stuff."

"The good stuff, huh?" As far as my body was concerned, I'd already *had* the good stuff. "But didn't we already, uh...?"

His smile turned wicked. "Well, sure. But that was just the warm-up."

"Oh."

This time, when he leaned in for a kiss, I was too distracted to stop him. And, like everything else this morning, that, too, was a surprise. A soft, sweet, open-mouthed kiss. Not wet. Not sloppy. Just perfect. A kiss that, for all its gentleness, breathed passion. The kind of kiss that makes you hot, that makes you never want to stop, that makes you long to give him everything you've got. I'd heard the term soul kiss before, but up until now, it was only words. This kiss gave it meaning.

I was trembling as I clutched at his shoulders. My breasts tingled, my clit ached, I felt reckless, wild with desire. He pulled back, just far enough so that his tongue could trace over my lips and the teasing touches drove me over the edge.

I pushed at his shoulders until I'd rolled him onto his back, then I straddled his waist. He gazed at me, questioningly. I could feel the long, hard length of his cock as it pressed against my pussy. I wanted it inside me.

"Condom?" I gasped, hoping it wasn't the first time either of us had thought of it.

He nodded toward the nightstand. "Drawer."

As I leaned across him, he propped himself up on his elbows and caught one nipple in his mouth. A shudder ran through me. It took several attempts before I could open the drawer, several seconds of fumbling before my hand closed on the foil packet.

My mission accomplished, I started to pull back. But, I couldn't bring myself to break away so soon from his mouth's sweet suction, so I curled into his heat. He fell back into the bedding, groaning as I lavished kisses across his shoulder. I could barely repress the urge to leave love-bites all along his neck.

His hands roved over my back, causing me to groan, "That feels so good."

"You feel good," he corrected as his hands tightened on my waist. He slid me lower, taking my mouth again in another mind-melting kiss. Heat spread thick and fast, leaving me breathless once again.

He tried to roll with me in his arms, but I had other ideas.

"No." Breaking away from his embrace, I slid down to straddle his legs. When my fingers had trouble with the condom, I used my teeth to tear open the package.

His eyes widened. "Tell me you're gonna put that on me with your mouth and I'll be your slave forever."

My slave? "I, uh, umm, maybe later," I stammered in surprise, then silently cursed myself for my stupidity. Later? How likely was that? Embarrassed, I dropped my gaze from his face.

He had a fabulous body, I realized—really noticing it for the first time—with broad shoulders, narrow hips and lean, toned muscles; the kind of body swimmers have. Shit. I just knew he was a surfer. He had to be, didn't he? It would explain so much, from his tan and his sun-streaked curls to this unimpressive room. And how the fuck had I hooked up with one of those? Never mind *why*... although I was beginning to have a pretty good idea about that part.

I would have liked to confirm my suspicions, but asking was out of the question. For all I knew, we'd discussed the subject at length, the night before.

"Something wrong?" he asked, when the silence became a little too lengthy.

I shook my head. "No," I lied, smiling brightly. "Not at all." At some point, I really would have to piece together last night's events and figure out how in the hell I ended up here. But, in the meantime...I was in this deep, there was no way I could back out now. So, why not make the best of things?

I finished unwrapping the condom, hurrying now because the feeling that my being here was an accident, a mistake, all wrong, was stronger than ever. A pearly drop of pre-cum glistened on the head of his cock. I leaned in and swiped it with my tongue, reveling in his velvet skin and musky taste. On an impulse, I swirled my tongue around the plump head as well, smiling as he growled his approval.

I knew he wouldn't object if I continued, and in another time and place, I definitely would have lingered; gliding my mouth over his thick shaft, testing to see how much I could take; and then teasing his sac with my lips and teeth. But I was on a mission now. The nagging voice in the back of my head was getting louder and harder to ignore. All I wanted to do was to get off and get out—as quickly as possible.

Pulling back, I made quick work of the condom and then

climbed on board. I'd taken hold of his cock, to ease him inside, when he stopped me.

"C'mere a minute," he murmured.

"Hmm?" I glanced up at his face, surprised to realize he was frowning.

He crooked his finger at me. "I said, come here."

Sighing impatiently, I released his cock and slid forward, lowering my mouth to within inches of his. "What is it?"

He palmed my breasts as I leaned in close, strong fingers kneading aching flesh, making me shudder. "Relax," he breathed against my lips. "You're too tense. This isn't a race, you know."

"I'm not tense," I insisted, even though I was. I was tense and uncertain, desperate for distraction, anxious and impatient—until he kissed me. Then I melted against him, my worries forgotten, at least for the moment. I kissed him back feverishly, wanting to devour him whole, my mouth and pussy both hungering to be filled.

His arms slid around me, pulling me close, holding me tight. I could feel the tip of his cock as it nudged against my anus, and I shivered uncontrollably. *No. Not there. Not like that.*

Breaking away, I reached between my legs and grabbed his cock again. A tortured groan rumbled from his throat as I rubbed the head along my slit, lubricating it with my juices, and then slowly, slowly lowering myself on top of him.

He groaned louder. "Damn. That feels...so...good."

"Unnh," I moaned in answer, unable to form the words to show that I agreed, hoping he'd understand all the same.

Up and down along his shaft I moved, loving the hot slide of his cock inside me; unable to stop. His hands clutched convulsively at my hips. I could feel his cock swelling and I knew it wouldn't be long before he came. I was getting close myself, but not that close. And still, I couldn't stop. So desperate was my need, I couldn't even force myself to slow down. Anticipating my disappointment, I moaned again in frustration.

Suddenly, he slipped his hand between us, his fingers searching out my clit. "Oh, yes," I sighed as he stroked and tugged. "There. Right there. Right—Ah!" I gasped in surprise, losing my rhythm when his fingers began to thrum my sensitive flesh with quick, light taps that were not quite stinging, not quite painful; harder than before.

"Keep going," he ordered. "Don't stop."

73

My pussy clenched and I gulped for breath, my entire body flushing with heat, because even though he ground the words out through gritted teeth, there was no mistaking the tone. It *was* an order, one that made my heart race and my pussy drip.

Not that I needed any urging. I was already moving again, faster, harder, writhing against his hand, seeking release from the pressure building up inside.

"Now," I groaned as the first spasm shook me and all my muscles seized. "Omigod!"

"Yes." His hands were on my hips again, his fingers tightening on my flesh as he took over the ride, thrusting hard, fast, deep. Hitting all the right spots again and again. Burying every inch of his cock inside me. And then stiffening, his body arching beneath me as he came.

He pulled me down against him once again. I lay with my head on his chest, listening to the thundering of his heart, while his hands stroked slowly over my back and we both struggled for breath. But, even then, even that soon afterwards, I could feel the anxiety rising within me.

Are you cold?" he asked as he reached for the sheet.

I shook my head. "No, I'm fine. Really." Kissing him lightly on the lips, I slid out of bed. I was shivering all right, but not from cold. Reaction was setting in, and all I wanted was to get out of here, to get away, to go home.

Frowning, he propped himself up on his elbow. "Wait, what are you doing?"

"I have to go," I said, grabbing my clothes from the floor.

"Now?"

"I uh, yes. I have things to do." I couldn't find my underwear, and didn't feel like searching for it. So, he'd have a souvenir of our time together. I could live with that.

"Just like that, huh?" Sounding vaguely disgruntled, he removed the used condom and tossed it into the waste basket. "Well...shit, at least give me your phone number, all right? So I can call you sometime?"

"Okay." My phone number. Sure. No problem with that, was there? I slid my feet into my shoes. "Or, you know what? Why don't you just give me yours, instead?"

His frown deepened. "Look, Angel, did I miss something in the last couple of minutes? Is anything wrong?"

I shook my head. "No." Nothing was wrong, nothing at all. Why should I remember my own phone number, anyway? It was early in the day, I'd just gotten up, my head ached and, besides, it's not like 1 made a habit of calling myself, right? "What could be wrong?"

"How would I know? But, it's obvious something's bothering you."

"Don't be silly. Of course there's nothing bothering me. I'm fine." I scanned the room impatiently. "Where's my purse?"

Reaching into the nightstand drawer, he extracted paper and pen. "You didn't bring one."

No purse? "Well, where's the rest of my stuff then?"

"What stuff is that?" he asked absently, scribbling away.

"You know, keys, money, a wallet?"

"I dunno. In your jacket maybe?" He gestured toward an armchair, just inside the door.

"My jacket. Right." As I lunged for the suede jacket draped over the back of the chair, he got out of bed and headed toward me; still naked and semi-erect. I tried not to stare.

"Here." He held out the slip of paper he'd been writing on.

I left off searching through my jacket pockets long enough to take it, smiling as I read what he'd written, not just his number, but his name and address, as well. *Thank God!* "Thanks, Zach. I'll call you." Probably I would, too, if only to explain why I wouldn't be seeing him again. I folded the paper and carefully stowed it in one of the pockets I'd already checked, then resumed my search.

"I thought we could at least have breakfast together," Zach complained, still sounding disgruntled. He stroked his hand down my arm. "C'mon, it's Saturday. Do you really have to rush off like this?"

I nodded. "I'm kind of in a hurry." Fingers trembling I checked inside the last pocket, it was as empty as the rest. My knees were shaking so hard now, I couldn't stand. "There's nothing in here," I muttered as I sank down in the chair, trying to think, trying not to think. I had no money, no keys, no license, no ID. But, maybe there was nothing odd about that. Maybe I didn't need a license, or a key. Maybe I didn't have a car. Maybe I lived with people who would let me in. What terrified me was the fact that I couldn't remember.

Zach crouched in front of me and took hold of my hands. "Hey, relax. Don't panic, okay? Probably your cousin has your purse, right?"

"My cousin?"

He nodded. "Yeah, it figures, doesn't it? You came into the bar with him, right? So probably you gave him your stuff to hold onto. Or maybe you left it in his car, or something, and just forgot."

I clung to his hands and his words and tried not to cry. "Okay. That makes sense, I guess."

"Sure it does." Rising, he crossed the room again and grabbed his phone. "Here. Why don't you give him a call and find out? It'll be cool. You'll see."

I shook my head. "I uh, I can't call. I don't remember his number."

"Oh." He returned the phone to its stand and then sighed. "Okay, well, still not a problem. I'll just get dressed and give you a ride over there. How's that sound?"

I wrapped my arms around myself and swallowed hard. It sounded great, except for one small detail. "I don't know where he lives."

"You don't?" His voice sounded skeptical, I didn't blame him. Surely, I should know where my own cousin lived, shouldn't I? He sighed. "Well, okay, scratch that plan, then. Where do *you* live? I'll just take you home and we can..."

"I don't know." My voice sounded so calm, so matter of fact, no one would ever guess that I was dying on the inside. But, something was wrong all right, and I'd just realized what. "I can't remember that either."

Zach gazed at me sternly. "Okay, very funny. Now, cut it out. I'm trying to help, you know."

"I know," I whispered hugging myself even tighter, feeling hollow and helpless and altogether wretched. "But I can't help it. And it's not funny at all. I don't remember anything." Including my name.

Chapter Two

This early in the day, Malibu Beach was deserted; a flat expanse of golden sand under a pale, blue sky. I stared through the window of Gladstone's restaurant, where Zach had taken me for breakfast, watching the waves roll in—ceaseless, never ending, like the questions in my mind—until his voice recalled me. "You figure out what you want to eat yet?"

Reluctantly, I turned away from the window and gazed at my menu, once more scanning disinterestedly through the list of breakfast items. "No. I don't know what I want. I don't know what I like. I can't even tell if I've eaten any of these things, or just heard about them." And I wasn't sure I cared. I had serious doubts about Zach's contention that I'd feel better after I ate something. Could a full stomach really compensate for an empty head?

"Order the pancakes," he suggested, smiling sweetly. "You can't go wrong with that, right? I mean, *nobody* doesn't like pancakes."

"Okay," I agreed, trying hard not to sound ungracious, trying even harder to hide my resentment over the fact that he could still smile and make jokes and be so cheerfully good humored at a time like this.

Our waitress returned with the drinks Zach had ordered when we first sat down: coffee for both of us, plus a large glass of orange juice for him.

"Are you sure you don't want any juice?" he asked now, as if we hadn't just had this conversation five minutes earlier. I shook my head.

As he ordered our meal, pancakes for me, something called a Hangtown Fry for himself, I picked up my coffee cup and sniffed the aroma, trying to determine if it was familiar.

Of course it's familiar, I realized after no more than a few seconds. I'd been smelling it for the past fifteen minutes, ever since we first stepped foot in the restaurant; I just hadn't known what it was. Sighing, I returned the cup to the table.

"Anything?" There was a trace of sympathy in Zach's voice.

I shrugged a little. "Not really."

"Try tasting it."

I lifted the cup to my lips. It was hotter than I'd expected, with a dark, bitter edge, a mellow undertone and a hint of something not quite sweet. "It's okay."

"Want some whipped cream to go with it? Sugar? How about some of these little chocolate chips they got here? Maybe you'll like it better that way."

I shook my head. "No, it's fine." I wasn't all that interested in the coffee. I had much bigger things to worry about.

"Look, this doesn't have to be so bad, you know."

"You think not? Maybe you should try it."

"I kind of wish I could," he said, and I could tell by the wistful look on his face that he really meant it. "It's gotta be like...well, like being a virgin all over again. Everything is brand new. You've got the whole world to discover."

"I don't want the whole world. At the moment, I'd be happy just to discover what my name is."

Zach sighed. "I already told you that, didn't I? Your name's Angel."

"Well, that's not very helpful, is it?" One name? One name was useless. Worse than useless, really, since this was LA where entirely too many people used stage names. For all I knew, I was one of them. "I just wish there was something I could *do*."

"Like what? We've been through this already. You didn't want to go to the hospital, which, hey, I completely understand."

"No." I shook my head. "No hospitals." What could they do for me in a hospital? There was nothing physically wrong with me, so far as I could tell. And the thought of getting trapped there— with no way to leave, and nowhere to go—was almost more frightening than anything else I could imagine.

"And, like I said, there's no sense in going to the police yet, since if anyone's going to file a missing person's report, they'll have to wait twenty four hours before they do it. Plus, it's a weekend, which means there's a good chance you won't even be missed until Monday."

I nodded my head and sipped more coffee, disguising the vague sense of uneasiness that gripped me every time Zach made that particular point. It couldn't be normal, not to be missed for days on end. Why was he so anxious for me to believe that it was?

"Besides, like I keep telling you, it's probably just temporary, anyway. You had a lot to drink last night. You hit your head. You'll probably wake up tomorrow morning remembering everything."

"I hope so," I murmured, clinging to the idea. And, if it turned out he was right, and I'd brought this on myself; if this amnesia was the result of nothing more than a night of too much partying? Then I was never going to take so much as a sip of anything alcoholic, ever again. "We're still going to check out that bar, though, right? The one where you say we met? Just in case I left my purse there, or my cousin left a message, or something?"

Zach nodded. "Sure. We'll swing by Zephyr right after breakfast. It won't be open yet, but they know me there. They'll let us in and we can take a look around. Who knows, maybe just being there'll be enough to bring your memory back?"

I sighed. "That would be nice." But I sure wasn't counting on it.

Our food arrived, accompanied by a hot blast of fragrance. I sniffed the air appreciatively. Everything smelled so good and I could feel a rumbling anticipation in my stomach. Perhaps Zach was right, after all. Maybe eating really would make me feel better.

I was digging into my pancakes when he stopped me. "Hold on," he said, picking up the little plastic tub that had accompanied my meal. "Can't forget the syrup, right?" His eyes were twinkling as he poured it over the contents of my plate. "There. Now try it."

I slid the first forkful into my mouth and felt my eyes widen in surprise as the soft, melting sweetness, the warm, creamy flavor hit my tongue.

"Good?" Zach asked, eyeing me curiously.

My mouth full, I nodded; and forked up another bite.

"Want to try some of mine?"

I glanced at his plate. According to the menu, his dish was a classic: oysters sautéed with bacon, onion and scrambled eggs. Which meant precisely nothing to me. "I don't know. How does it taste? Is it good?"

"Well, I think so. Here. Let's see what you think of oysters." He leaned across the table. The little blob at the end of his fork looked gray and unappealing, but I opened my mouth obligingly, just the same. One taste, however, and I immediately wished I hadn't been so trusting.

"Omigod," I mumbled, clasping my hand to my mouth. I don't know what I'd expected, but it wasn't this. The taste was dark—much darker than the coffee—intense, slightly salty, I swallowed it fast and then drank more coffee to wash it down.

"So? D'you like it?"

I shook my head. "Mm-mm." Sure, there was something faintly intriguing about the flavor, but it was much too strong.

"Oh." Zach looked vaguely crestfallen. "Probably more of

an acquired taste, I guess. We'll work on that later. Here, try some of this melon."

This time, a bright, orange square glistened on the end of his fork, I gazed at it doubtfully. "No, thanks. I think I'll stick to pancakes."

"Aw, c'mon," Zach urged. "Give it a try. What's life without a few risks?"

"Safe," I answered, taking another bite, hoping to deflect him. No such luck.

One of those hard to resist grins lit up his face. "C'mon, I promise, you're in no danger from this cantaloupe. Unless you're a diabetic, of course, in which case those pancakes you're eating will probably kill you."

Startled, I stopped eating and stared at him. "What?"

He shook his head. "Don't worry. You're not diabetic. You wouldn't have been out drinking last night, if you were."

I sighed in relief. "Don't scare me like that." He was still holding his fork out to me, and it was clear he had no intentions of backing down. "You don't take no for an answer, do you?"

That put the grin back on his face in a hurry. "Not if I can help it."

"Okay, fine. Let me have it."

Again he slid his fork into my open mouth. Melon was... nice, I decided. Not as nice as pancakes, but juicy, faintly sweet, vaguely musky. "Does all your food taste like you?" I asked, the words popping out of my mouth before I thought about how they'd sound.

Now it was Zach who looked startled. "Like me?"

I could feel my cheeks burning. "Well, no, not-not like *you*, exactly, but... you know...sort of..." Sort of like that tantalizing drop I'd licked off the tip of his penis this morning. Even the oyster, while too intense on its own, and not at all what I'd been expecting had had a salty, tangy musk to it that was almost... arousing.

"Interesting thought," Zach murmured, folding his arms on the table and gazing at me curiously.

The gravelly tone of his voice made my mouth go dry. Avoiding his eyes, I lunged for the coffee.

"So, I guess maybe the next thing we ought to do is to try and find some foods that taste like you." Leaning in close, he lowered his voice even more as he continued. "Of course, that'll mean going back to my place so I can get a real good taste of you first, won't it? You know, so I'll know exactly what flavor I'm looking for."

Oh, boy. I'd asked for that, hadn't I? Swallowing hard, I raised my gaze to his face. His smile was wicked. His eyes smoldered. I was in sooo much trouble.

"Well?"

"Maybe." Just the thought of his tongue sliding along my slit, teasing my lips apart, licking into me made my pussy wet all over again. I clamped my thighs together, but that only added to the hot, fluttering pressure. My clit throbbed as I imagined his hands prying my legs apart, his lips closing in on the tender nub, nibbling gently...

"Can I get you folks anything else?" our waitress asked, placing the check on the table.

Zach sat back slowly, his eyes still on my face. "I'm good. How about you?"

"Nothing else for me, thanks," I mumbled as, cheeks aflame, I dropped my gaze and dug back into my pancakes. From the corner of my eye, I watched Zach take his wallet from his pocket and place a credit card on top of the check and all the lust I was feeling dissolved in an instant as it occurred to me just how much I'd been taking for granted. Especially from someone I had only met the night before.

What was he up to, buying me breakfast, driving me around, giving me a place to stay? Was it just sex he wanted from me? Or was he after something else?

My appetite gone, I pushed my plate away. "Why are you doing this?"

Zach looked up in surprise. "Doing what?"

"All this." I gestured at the table. "Buying me breakfast and... well, everything, really."

He looked at me curiously. "What's the matter? Haven't you ever been on a date before? No, wait." He put up a hand to stop my reply. "Don't answer that. I know: You can't remember."

"No, I can't. But what's dating got to do with it?"

He sipped his coffee, then smiled. "It's simple. I'm sure you get asked out a lot. And I'll bet that, most of the time, whoever the lucky guy is, he pays. So, why should I be any different? Besides, what else do you expect me to do? Let you starve? You don't have any money, remember?"

I shook my head. "I'm not just talking about that. I mean, you must have had plans for the day, didn't you? And now..." I broke off when the waitress returned with Zach's credit card, and then I waited, impatiently, as he studied his receipt and added the tip.

"Sure I had plans," he answered at last, scrawling his name across the sales slip. "What I'd *planned* on doing was to spend some time with you. I thought we could hang out for a few hours, get to know each other better, have some fun. After the way you tried to run out on me this morning, I figure it's lucky for me that you *did* lose your memory. Otherwise, I'd have been eating breakfast alone right now, and then I'd have to think up some other way to spend the day."

"But, it's not just today we're talking about either," I pointed out, as anxiety set in again. "It's tomorrow, too, probably. And—and what if you're right? What if no one even notices I'm gone until Monday? Or even later? How long can I..."

"You worry too much." Reaching across the table, Zach took hold of my hand. "It's only been a few hours. Why are you worrying about what's going to happen on Monday? Let's just take things one day at a time, okay? Things will work out."

"How can you be so certain?"

"Same way I can tell you've probably been on lots of dates." He squeezed my hand reassuringly. "Trust me. You're not the kind of person who'd go unnoticed for long. Someone out there is going to miss you real soon, you'll see. And when they do, you'll get found. And then you'll be back home in no time Now why don't we just forget about the amnesia, for the time being, and pretend that we'd *both* planned on spending the weekend together. Let Monday worry about itself. All right?"

I nodded. "Okay." What choice did I have other than to go along with whatever he wanted? Like it or not, he was the one calling the shots, a state of affairs that didn't sit well with me, not at all.

"Good." He gave my hand a final squeeze, took a last sip of coffee and then slid from the booth. "Come on, let's get out of here. Let's go to Zephyr and see if we can't find something there that'll spark your memory."

** **

Hand in hand, we left the restaurant. As we were crossing the parking lot toward Zach's motorcycle, he veered suddenly toward the beach.

"Where are we going?" I asked, feeling faintly alarmed.

"Look around." He waved his hand, encompassing the entire

landscape. "It's a beautiful day. Let's go for a walk."

We stopped at the edge of the pavement and removed our shoes. I had to admit that the cool sand felt good between my toes and, despite everything that should be worrying me, I let myself relax.

Zach was right, it *was* a beautiful day. Puffy, white clouds floated in the blue sky, and there was just enough sunshine to warm away the morning chill. The beach itself was still mostly deserted, pristine except for the footprints and tire-tracks left by those who had been here before us. A handful of gulls circled overhead, waiting to see if we'd drop any food.

We walked down to the sea and stared out at the horizon, letting the cold water lap at our feet. A faint breeze ruffled our hair. The air smelled fresh and clean. I sighed contentedly, feeling happy just to be alive.

"That's better," Zach murmured as he swept me into his embrace. "It's nice to see you smiling again."

I closed my eyes as his lips met mine, clutching at his arms while tendrils of heat coiled in my belly. My breasts tingled as I pressed against him. I might not remember having been kissed by anyone else, but I was pretty certain it had not been like this.

How could it be? People kissed one another all the time without ever going further, without it ever leading anywhere. And, apparently, without it even meaning very much to them. If every kiss was this good, none of that would be possible. How could anyone resist this much temptation on a regular basis?

Which could only mean one thing. I was falling for this stranger, harder and more quickly than was wise.

Frightened by the realization, I pulled away, ducking my head when he tried to recapture my mouth. "My feet are cold," I murmured. Not really a lie; I *was* getting cold feet, just not literally.

Zach sighed. "Okay. Come on." And, hand in hand again, we headed back across the sand.

I looked around me as we walked, looking at everything, anything, but him. The empty beach as metaphor was even less comforting then before.

If the restless waves were like my thoughts, then the beach itself, blank and featureless, must represent my brain. And that was scary as hell. Because, just as the sand kept record of every footprint, so might my mind retain the imprint of whoever trod across it.

Chapter Three

Richie

George Venezuela was furious. "You did *what?*" he bellowed in his most stentorian tones as he paced around his office, eyes bulging, neck veins prominent, causing his only son to wince in pain.

"Papa, please." Slumped in a chair in front of his father's desk, Richie clutched his aching head. It wasn't enough, was it, that he'd had to spend all of last evening bouncing from bar to bar in an effort to establish the premise that April had been drinking heavily—and contracting the Mother of all Hangovers in the process. No, on top of that, he'd also been forced into performing a variety of criminal acts, into consuming too many revolting drinks, and now—Did he really have to endure his father's yelling at him, as well?

"You *lost* her?" his father continued, taking no notice of Richie's distress. "How is this possible? This is your *cousin* we're talking about, not some stray Chihuahua that slipped off its leash! How could you lose an entire person, someone you'd taken out for the evening? Explain this to me. From the beginning."

Richie sighed. "I already told you. It didn't work. The plan didn't work. I gave her the scopolamine, just like you said to do, and... nothing happened." The drug, which one of his father's friends had procured for him in Ecuador, was supposed to have rendered April temporarily docile and compliant; submissive enough to do whatever was asked of her. Under its influence, she was supposed to have willingly put her signature to whatever papers George needed her to sign—and then retain no memory of any of it ever happening. It had failed to affect her. "Compliant, my ass. I couldn't even get her to leave the bar."

"Then you administered it incorrectly," his father snapped, sinking into his own chair, and glaring at him. "Or she didn't ingest enough of it. Or you didn't wait for it to take effect."

"Or she found out what we were doing, and she only pretended to take it." Richie scowled at his father. "Which is what I told you would happen. You always underestimate her." The old man had a lot of nerve getting angry at him. It was Richie who'd be facing a prison term, if his suspicions about his cousin were correct. His father had, very wisely it appeared, kept his own hands clean.

"Bah," his father muttered, waving one of those clean hands dismissively. "How could she find out? The drug is colorless, odorless, tasteless. It is completely undetectable. Unless she watched you put it into her drink, or unless you told her what you were doing, she couldn't have known."

"She knew. That look on her face... I could tell."

George shook his head. "So, you decided it wasn't working. What then?"

Richie set his teeth. "I gave her the other drug."

"The chloral hydrate? *Madre del Dios*," his father groaned. "*Por qué*, Richie? Why would you do such a thing? It would have put her to sleep. Do people sign documents in their sleep? I do not think that they do."

The chloral hydrate was supposed to have been given to her later in the evening, after April had done what they wanted. It would have rendered her unconscious. At that point she was to have been photographed in some compromising position, in case it became necessary to either blackmail her or provide 'proof' that she had been acting on her own volition.

"But, she would *not* leave the bar!" Richie yelled in frustration. Pain knifed through his head and he lowered his voice as he continued, "I keep telling you that. What the fuck did you want me to do? I thought if she started feeling sleepy, she'd be more likely to go home. There would still have been time to get her to sign your papers before she passed out."

"I see." His father studied him through narrowed eyes. "So, this is why you're so worried that she discovered your plan, eh? You think she could taste it, don't you? And you'd be right!"

Richie glared at his father. Since when had this debacle become *his* plan? "Of course she tasted it. You think I wasn't prepared for that? But she had no idea it was a drug she was tasting. She thought the juice was sour—that's all. I'm not an idiot, Papa."

"*Ésa es su opinión*," his father muttered. "And then? Why did you not leave then?"

"Because that's when you called me, remember? And I went out to my car, so I could speak to you without being overheard. When I hung up the phone..." Richie shook his head. Just remembering the panic that had seized him the night before had him sweating all over his Armani reversible. "That's when I saw her—saw *them*—April and her… her accomplice. She must have contacted him right after I left. Suddenly, it all made perfect sense. They were in it together. That's why she wouldn't leave. That's why the drugs weren't affecting her. He must have slipped her an antidote, to counteract their effects."

George buried his head in his hands, muttering something that sounded suspiciously like, "*Mi hijo es un imbecile.*" My son is an imbecile. "What antidote? There *is* no antidote. And, again, how could this person—this stranger—know what we had planned? Was he here when we discussed it? Did you tell him?"

"Well, he must have found out somehow. And he must have given her something, because she wasn't passing out and she wasn't following orders and, my God, you should have seen the way she was kissing him! They were going at it in the alley like… like animals. Is it likely that April would be doing that? With someone she doesn't know, someone she'd only just met?"

George shrugged. "It wouldn't be the first time she'd been taken in. That she'd been made a fool of by some… man."

"Exactly. Which is why she must have had some reason for trusting him. I'm telling you, Papa, it was a set up."

"Maybe." George sighed. "And then? What did you do then?"

"Well, I-I left. I drove away." He'd panicked, that's what he'd done. He'd nearly run them both down in his hurry to get away before they saw him, before the police showed up to arrest him, before anything else could go wrong. But his father didn't need to know about that.

George's eyes were bulging once again. Richie prepared himself for more yelling. "You left your cousin, who was loaded with drugs, a fact that would shortly become noticeable to anybody who was with her, and you just…drove away? You left her in the hands of a stranger…"

"I'm telling you, he wasn't…"

"Fine then! With someone neither you or I know. And you did not see a problem with this? Eh, *mi hijo*? Have you lost your mind?"

"I only went around the block," Richie replied with a sigh, although it had actually been three or four blocks, and then another two while he thought up a convincing reason for why he'd been gone. "I just drove around the block and came right back, but they were gone."

"*Que?*" His father looked mystified. "Gone? What do you

mean, gone?"

"Gone. Nowhere in sight. They'd disappeared."

"In the time it took you to drive around the block? Did it not occur to you that, perhaps, they'd simply gone back inside?"

Richie nodded. "Sure it did. I checked. The bar was closed, and they wouldn't let me in, but I asked if she was there, if she'd left a note or a message. Nothing. No one even remembered seeing them leave." Which only proved that they were *all* lying, and likely in on April's little scheme, as well. Because the whole point of taking her around to a lot of different bars, the whole point of sitting in the spotlight, was to get her noticed, and remembered later.

"So what do we do?" Richie asked after the silence had stretched out for several minutes.

George shook his head. "I don't know. I have to think. Everything depends on how much of this your cousin has been able to piece together, how much she knows."

"I keep telling you. She knows everything! This is *her* game now, whatever it is. That's why she hasn't come home yet. She's out there, somewhere, playing with us, plotting her revenge. Don't you see that yet?"

George's eyes flashed. "Enough!" He glared coldly at his son. "You had better hope that is not the case. Or, no, what you had better do is to pray. Pray that you are mistaken. Pray hard."

Chapter Four

April

Zephyr was closed when we got there, as Zach predicted it would be; but, just as he'd promised, getting inside presented no problem. He parked his bike in the alley behind the bar, pounded loudly on the back door, and waited. Within minutes, the door was pushed open and a large man poked his head out. His somewhat forbidding expression quickly gave way to a pleased smile. "Zach? Good to see you, buddy. What are you doin' here in the middle of the day?"

Zach touched knuckles with the man. "Hey, Cuz. I'd like you to meet a friend of mine." Wrapping his arm around me, he propelled me forward. "Angel, say hello to Big Tony."

I hid my surprise at the sobriquet as best I could, smiling as I extended my hand. Big Tony was... well, big. That wasn't the source of my amazement. Rather, it was the realization that there were actually people in the world who answered to such names. Zach's acquaintance with one of them had me unsettled. It seemed to underscore the difference between us.

"Angel was here last night and we think she might have left her purse. Can we take a look around?"

"Sure, sure." Tony pushed the door open wider. "Come on in."

As we followed him inside, I grabbed hold of Zach's arm. "Is he really your cousin?" I whispered.

Grinning, he shook his head. "Nah, just a good friend. Now, come on, see if you recognize anything."

A pungent, not unpleasant fragrance tickled my nostrils as I looked around, but it elicited no clear memory. The bar was dark, cool, quiet and totally unremarkable with its wood paneling, black vinyl bar stools, neon beer signs and rows and rows of bottles. Look up unpretentious in any dictionary you care to consult, and this—or something close to it—is exactly what you'll find.

"Well?" Zach inquired.

I shook my head. "Nothing." Not only did I not remember this place, but every moment I spent here left me feeling more and more certain I was out of my element.

"Maybe you just need the right perspective." He gestured to a table right up front, near the small stage. "You were seated over there. Maybe things will look different if you sit down?"

I shrugged. "I guess it wouldn't hurt to try."

"Good." Zach nodded at Tony, who was rummaging behind the bar. "And while you're doing that, I'm gonna go give Tony a hand. See what we can find."

I headed for the table he'd indicated. "Sorry, bud," I heard Tony tell Zach. "But, it doesn't look like anything's been turned in."

"What about messages?" Zach asked.

"Nope. Not for anyone named Angel."

I seated myself at the table, facing the stage. A spotlight, set in the ceiling, seemed to cast its light directly on me. I looked around, trying to imagine the place filled with people, with noise, with music. Nothing. Feeling hopeless, I buried my face in my hands.

"Here," I heard Tony say. "On the house. Maybe it'll help cheer her up."

A minute later, Zach placed a large glass filled with foamy, amber liquid in front of me. He seated himself on the other side of the table and watched as I sniffed cautiously at the glass. Once again, a little of the fragrance mystery was resolved. Whatever this was, its aroma was heavy in the cool air. "What is this stuff?"

"Ale. Tony's answer to all life's problems." Zach grimaced slightly. "Look, I know it's early, but just try and drink a little of it, okay? Otherwise, you'll hurt his feelings."

I took a sip. It tasted cold, crisp, slightly yeasty. "Not bad. I like it."

"You like beer?" Looking almost as surprised as he was pleased, Zach leaned back in his seat and smiled at me. "Well, all right then. My kind of woman."

That smile of his had a way of messing me up, big time. From some hidden, inaccessible corner of my mind came the thought that I was not *his* kind of woman—not even close. But, ooh, when he smiled at me that way, I so wished I was. "What was I drinking last night?" I asked, partly out of curiosity, partly just to have something to say. But, man, was that ever the wrong question to ask!

My stomach did a funny little flip when his smile powered up another notch or three and turned wicked into the bargain. "Baby, all's I know is it had a straw. And the way you sucked that thing—damn."

"Oh." I felt my cheeks redden and dropped my gaze. It was a weird feeling, knowing I had done things with him I couldn't remember; it was like being naked in public. He was a stranger, yet he knew more about me than I knew about myself.

He sighed. "But I guess you don't remember any of that either, huh?"

I shook my head, not looking at him, tracing designs with my thumb in the moisture that coated the outside of my glass. "Why don't you tell me some of it? Tell me how we met."

"All right. Let's see...I was on stage when you arrived, we'd just started our last set. Ordinarily, I don't pay much attention to who's coming in or out, but I saw you the moment you walked through the door." His voice had turned reflective, and there was a dark, moody edge to it that I didn't understand. "You stood at the entrance and looked around, kind of checking the place out, and I thought to myself, *now there's a woman who knows who she is.*"

Startled, I glanced at him. Was he making fun of my memory loss? "What do you mean?"

His eyes had gone dreamy with remembering, it took a while before he refocused on my face. "I don't know how to explain it exactly. There was just... something about your expression, the way you surveyed the room. It wasn't like a lot of the people who come in here—always looking to see if anybody's noticed them yet. You looked like you couldn't care less about any of that. Like you didn't need anyone's approval." He smiled again, resting his arms on the table, leaning in. "I couldn't take my eyes off you. You looked so... confident, I guess. Self assured. It was sexy. It made me want to get to know you." He shrugged as he added, "I'd still like the chance to do that."

"Sorry to disappoint you," I mumbled swallowing more beer. Confident? Self assured? Was that really me?

He frowned. "What do you mean?"

I heaved an exasperated sigh. It wasn't obvious? And here I thought *I* was the only one with a lack of memory. Maybe I was wrong. Maybe it was endemic. "I mean, *getting to know me* is what I want, too. But it looks like we're both SOL. I'm as much in the dark as you are." Maybe more.

"Oh. That." Another slow smile curved Zach's lips. He looked curiously relieved.

"Yes, *that*," I snapped angrily. What the hell was he smiling about?

He shook his head. "Hey, it's like I told you at breakfast.

This doesn't have to be so bad. The fact that you can't remember... well, that just makes things more interesting, doesn't it?"

"Not really."

"Then maybe you're looking at it the wrong way. This is a once in a lifetime opportunity, a chance to discover who you really are—not your name or your address, but the important stuff. It's the perfect time to play, to experiment, to try things." He leaned in even closer, captured my hand and held it tight. "I want to watch as you experience that; as you learn about yourself. I want to help."

"How? How can you help? How can I..." *How can I even begin to learn... anything about myself.*

"Come back home with me," he urged. "Give me until Monday. I bet, by then, we can find out more about who you really are than you ever knew before."

My stomach fluttered nervously. Go home with him? But, wasn't that *already* the plan? I bit my lip, not really wanting to remind him I had nowhere else *to* go. With the light spilling down from the spot overhead gilding his golden blond curls, he looked like a fallen angel. Wicked. Depraved. Irresistible.

"What did you have in mind?" I asked, although I was pretty sure I already knew. There was no missing the heat that blazed in those sea green eyes.

My heart picked up speed when the sexy devil hit me again with that killer smile.

"Relax. There's nothing for you to be scared about. We'll just try things—whatever comes to mind. If you like it, we'll keep going. If you don't, or if anything makes you uncomfortable, you just say the word and we'll stop. How's that sound?"

It sounded too easy. And much too enticing. Lucifer, I thought wildly; that's who he is. Lucifer in the flesh, tempting me into sin... or into an even bigger mess.

"C'mon," he urged again. "Two days. Whaddaya got to lose?"

And wasn't that exactly what the devil always wanted you to think?

** **

The face that stared back at me in Zach's bathroom mirror should have been a familiar one. I think the fact that it wasn't scared me more than anything else so far. I'd escaped into the bathroom right after we got back to his apartment on the pretext of needing to take a shower. Really, I just needed some time alone.

I'd avoided looking at my reflection earlier today, but I knew I couldn't put it off forever. Now, as I studied my image, I was hoping something would spark a memory. So far, nothing had.

Dark brown hair, still slightly damp from the shower, fell in shining waves past my shoulders. My eyes were brown as well—large, wide set, with amber flecks that picked up the gold of the hoops in my ears and the chain around my neck—I thought they'd be pretty, if they weren't so worried looking.

The rest was fairly unremarkable. Dark brows. Long lashes. Straight nose. Generous mouth. Good teeth. It was an attractive enough face; not beautiful, but nothing that would make me want to stick a paper bag over my head either. I took a step back and checked out the rest of the package. I was a little shorter than average and more curvy than was fashionable; I suspected the tailored clothes I'd been wearing earlier had been chosen in an attempt to minimize those two factors. But they were both accentuated now, thanks to the short, clingy, satin robe Zach had pulled out of his closet for me to change into while my clothes were being washed.

I sniffed at the cuffs of the sleeves I'd rolled up. A trace of perfume still lingered in the pale pink fabric; a sweet, floral scent that made me think of blonde hair and blue eyes, and wonder anew who the robe belonged to.

"You almost done?" Zach stuck his head inside the door to ask. I glanced at him in the mirror. He'd removed both his shirt and his shoes, and was now wearing only jeans. He was tall, tanned, toned and I couldn't help but notice, all over again, how mouthwateringly delicious he looked. Just like I couldn't help noticing the way the soft, faded denim hugged him in all the right places. "What's taking so long? What have you been doing in here all by yourself, anyway?"

I shrugged, too overcome with lust to speak. The desire to strip him bare was just about overwhelming .

Crossing the room, Zach pulled me close, banding me to him as he bent to nuzzle my neck. I sucked in a quick breath as I felt the robe mold itself to my damp skin.

As his hands coasted slowly over my hips and then up again, fabric bunching between his fingers, I found myself canting my hips, pressing against him, urging him onward. "I mean, if you're just in here trying to make yourself beautiful, you're wasting your time."

"Oh. Thanks a lot." I have to admit his words stung, even

though it was no more than what I'd been thinking myself. But, did he really have to agree with me?

He chuckled softly. "No, silly, I mean you're *already* beautiful. In fact, I can think of only a few areas where there's any possible room for improvement at all."

Improvement? Heat pooled between my thighs as one of his hands slipped between the folds of the robe to touch bare flesh. *What does he mean improvement?* It dismayed me to realize that I still wanted him as much as ever. Surely any woman with an ounce of self respect would be halfway to the door by now, not standing docile in his arms, practically asking to be insulted again. My breath caught as his fingers probed my slit, bringing my attention to the wetness there. *More. Deeper. Now.* My pussy ached to feel those fingers inside me—to feel his cock inside me. I cleared my throat. "What kind of improvement are we talking about anyway?" I asked, hoping to sound detached and clinical, unaffected by his criticism. Unaffected by *him.*

Still chuckling, he withdrew his hand. "Well, let's see. For starters..." He gave the belt I'd knotted at my waist a tug and it came undone. I shivered as the robe fell open. "There. Now you're *absolutely* perfect." He slid the robe from my shoulder, leaned forward and kissed my cheek. "Do you like looking at yourself?"

"I don't know." I liked looking at *him.* Liked the smoky look in his eyes. Liked knowing I was its cause. *Really* liked knowing that he'd only been teasing me about needing improvement. It felt nice to be appreciated.

"Think about it," he insisted. "Because that's the whole point, remember? To find out what you like."

"How are we going to do that?" My voice sounded so pathetically whiny it made me cringe, but Zach didn't seem to notice.

Flashing me another grin, he slid a hand under one of my thighs, lifted it, and then braced my foot against the counter top. "I was thinking we should do things alphabetically."

"What's that mean?"

"You know. Like the alphabet." He took hold of my hand and ran my palm slowly up the inside of my thigh. "A, B, C..."

"I know what the word means, but how..." I broke off on a gasp as my fingers made contact with the slick folds of my dripping pussy. When had I gotten so wet?

Zach's hand guided mine in circles; around and around and

around. "Right. So I figure we'll start with A; with things like auto-eroticism, aphrodisiacs, a little audio-visual stimulation, some anal play..."

"No." I pulled my hand from his, took my foot from the counter and tried to wrench myself from his embrace. "I don't—Stop."

Zach's arms tightened around me. "Whoa, calm down. What's wrong?"

"No anal sex," I told him, finally managing to turn myself around so that we were face to face. "Forget it, Zach. I just—I don't—Just no. Okay?"

"Sure," he replied with a shrug. "Relax, okay? I told you we wouldn't do anything you didn't want to, didn't I?"

"Yes." I gulped for breath as I felt the panic recede, but I still held myself rigid in his arms. "You did. Thank you."

His lips quirked. "You're welcome. But do you mind telling me why not?"

Now it was my turn to shrug. "I don't know."

"Well, did you remember something? Did you try it before and not like it? Did someone hurt you? Or do you just not think you'd be interested? Because, if that's the case, then..."

"I said, I don't know!" I really didn't, either. But something about the idea caused my heart to race and all the nerves along the back of my neck tingled a warning. The same thing had happened in bed that morning when I'd felt the tip of his cock teasing my anus. Maybe I didn't like it. Maybe I liked it too much. Or maybe I just couldn't handle the thought of not being in control. The idea of lying face down on the bed, ass in the air, while Zach, or anyone..."I just don't want to, all right?" And I didn't want to talk about it, either.

"I already said it was, remember? What's going on here? You're acting... I dunno... spooked."

I made no answer. He was a stranger, a complete unknown—that's what was going on. And I was spooked because I had no idea how far I could trust him; or even if I should trust him at all. *I should leave, that's what I should do.* Even if I had no money and nowhere to go, I should still go... someplace.

Zach stared at me for another moment then bent and kissed me full on the lips. His kiss was all heat and passion, but it was also oddly reassuring. Comforting even. I felt myself relax again, finally, and slid one hand up to cup his face, reveling in the slight stubble that lined his cheek and chin.

"Better now?" he asked as he broke the kiss off.

"Mmm." I nodded, going up on my toes to kiss him again. The sprinkling of hair on his chest tickled my nipples as I slid against him. I concentrated on the delicious sensation, and on the silky feel of the hair at the back of his neck, as I pulled his head down to mine, and pushed all my fears to the back of my mind. I just wouldn't think about any of that right now, that's all. I'd think about this, instead.

Zach seemed to hesitate for a moment, until my tongue slid out and teased his lips. Then a low growl sounded in his throat and his arms tightened around me, pressing me close as his mouth ravaged mine.

Much better, I thought, as I tangled the fingers of both hands in his hair. The way he kissed me left me with no doubt that he was as hot for me as I was for him. I was comfortable with that. It was simple, straightforward, safe. And completely equitable. As long as we kept things on that level—both of us focused on enjoying ourselves and making each other feel good—I was pretty sure we would be okay; and that, when my memory returned, I could walk away from this with no hard feelings on either side.

"What about the rest of it?" Zach was breathing hard as he tore his mouth away from mine again.

"The rest of...?"

"Yeah. All the other stuff I mentioned. Was there a problem with anything else?"

I couldn't really remember what else he'd mentioned, but I shook my head.

"Good." A wicked smile curved his lips. "Then turn your sexy self around, put your foot back up on the counter and let's get busy." Despite the smile, his words still sounded like an order. Anticipation twisted knots in my gut, making me shiver. "Well?" he prompted, raising an eyebrow when I didn't move fast enough. "What are you waiting for?"

Cheeks flaming, I spun around and planted my heel on the edge of the faux marble countertop. He slid one of his legs between mine, nudging the foot I was standing on aside, forcing my legs farther apart. I grabbed his arm and leaned into his chest for balance.

"Good," he murmured, wrapping one arm around my waist for support. With his other hand he clutched my upraised thigh and pressed it open. "I like that. That's very nice. Don't you think so?"

Shifting my gaze, I studied myself in the mirror once again. My lips were swollen now, from his kisses. My skin was flushed with heat. I was all pink, pink, pink except for the thatch of dark hair that covered my mound. I looked voluptuous wrapped up in his arms with my head thrown back and my breasts jutting forward, tipped with more pink. I looked scandalous, round and ready, my legs spread wide, the glistening lips of my pussy exposed to his view. I looked... fuckable. That was really the only word that came to mind. But it was the sight of his fingers splayed on my flesh that really turned me on; that and the strength I could sense in his grip. I moved against him just to feel his hold on me tighten. I was wet, I was waiting, and if he didn't take me soon, I'd go out of my mind.

"Tell me," he prompted again, apparently unmindful of my growing desperation. "I want to know everything you're thinking. Tell me what you like."

"I like pleasing you," I answered, as startled by the words that popped out of my mouth as I was by the slight tremor that ran through all his muscles. Surely, that wasn't true? I'd already turned down one request. How eager to please could I be? I half expected him to point that out, but he didn't. He just stared at my reflection, with a hot, disquieting look in his eyes, 'til I felt like his gaze would burn my skin. "Zach. Please..." The words were a whimper, a whisper, a plea. *Hurry!*

"Touch yourself," he said, at last, in a voice even thicker and smokier than before. My clit throbbed in response.

I shook my head. "No. You."

"Oh, I will, baby," he promised. "Before we're done, I'm gonna have my hands all over every hot inch of you. But first things first. Right now I want to watch as you get yourself off."

I stifled a groan. Well, I'd asked for it, hadn't I? I'd said I wanted to please him, so how could I keep saying no? Curbing my impatience as best I could, I slid one hand between my legs. "Like this?" I asked as my fingers massaged the swollen lips of my sex.

"Is that how you like it? Show me."

But I didn't know how I liked it and didn't want to waste time finding out. Besides, experimenting like that in front of him seemed altogether too revealing, more intimate than anything else we'd done. "Tell me what to do," I begged, appalled by the breathy, little girl sound of my voice.

A dimple appeared in Zach's cheek, green fire flashed in his eyes. "What are you saying? You want me to talk dirty to you?"

That wasn't exactly what I'd said—or what I meant—but his breath was warm against my skin and his voice, so deep, so dark, sent a delicious little shiver racing down my spine. "Oh, God, yes." Who cared what I meant? He could talk however he wanted, just as long as he used that voice!

"All right." His tongue flicked out and traced the curve of my ear. "Give me your hand."

Startled by his request, I did as he asked. He took hold of my wrist and brought my hand to his mouth, quickly laving my fingertips with his tongue. "Now, stroke your clit for me," he told me as he released my hand. "Pretend your fingers are my tongue and I'm licking you."

He watched me in the mirror as I followed his instructions. "That's it. Imagine how good it's gonna feel when I take you with my mouth."

I could imagine it, all right; maybe too well. I moaned loudly, pressing harder on the little nub, circling faster.

"Slow down," Zach cautioned. "Not so fast. When I lick your pussy I'm gonna do it sloooowly front to back, back to font, over and over, until you're bucking beneath me and begging me to put my cock inside you. I'm gonna hold you still and rim your sweet clit with my tongue and when I feel it start to swell I'm gonna take it between my lips and suck on it 'til you're just about ripe to explode. Then, when you think you can't stand any more, I'm gonna stick my tongue deep in your creaming, hot hole and lap up all your juices."

"Now," I groaned as my fingers, mimicking his tongue, plunged into my heat. *It's not enough. It's not nearly enough.* His voice was a river of sound; I'd half closed my eyes, the better to hear him. Now, I was aware of another river running—this one between my thighs. "I want all of that now." *I need it!*

"Soon enough," Zach murmured, chuckling wickedly. "But first... give me your hand again. I want to taste your wetness."

I pulled my fingers free of my pussy and lifted my hand toward his face. He leaned forward and my womb seized as his lips closed on my fingers. It seized again as his hands crept upward to caress my breasts.

My legs had started to shake by now and I could have come right then and there. I probably would have, too, if I could have just gotten my other hand anywhere near my clit, but it was pinned by his arm.

"Mmm," he mumbled around my fingers. "Good."

I wriggled my shoulder, hoping he'd take the hint and move his arm out of the way and let me get my hand free, but he appeared not to notice. "Move," I told him, wriggling harder. "Let me go."

He left off sucking my fingers and looked at me. "What's wrong?"

"N-nothing," I said as the hand he'd just released crept south. "I just... I just... I need..."

"Whoa." Laughing, he grabbed hold of my wrist. "Where do you think you're going with that hand?"

"Let go," I repeated.

He shook his head. "I don't think so."

"Please." I closed my eyes and swallowed hard. "Enough games. Let me touch myself."

"I'll tell you when it's enough," he said in a voice filled with laughter. "Right now, we're not even close."

"Hey!" I opened my eyes and glared at him, but the look on his face disarmed me. "Come on, you're not playing fair."

"How's that?" he asked as his guileless green eyes met mine. "You asked me to tell you what to do, didn't you? And that's just what I'm doing. Besides, I want more cream. Give it to me."

"Zach, please..." I begged again, tugging against his grip. "I can't stand it. I'll die if I don't come soon."

He bent his head to nuzzle my neck. "More. Cream. Now. Say, 'yes, Zach, anything you want'."

I groaned. *Anything. I'll say anything just to get some relief.* "Yes," I whispered in surrender, then held my breath waiting for my chance, waiting for him to release my hand, knowing that all it would take was a single touch and I would go over.

Could he be on to me? Apparently so. Keeping his grip on my wrist, Zach guided my fingers past my aching clit and thrust them all too briefly inside me. Moisture immediately flooded my hand. Muscles clenching, I tilted my hips, hoping to prolong the contact, but he was already pulling my hand away and moving it back toward his mouth.

"Now, don't move," he ordered as he positioned my hand in front of his face and let go. A tiny mewl escaped my lips as both of his hands covered my breasts once more. His fingers teased the turgid peaks and I inhaled sharply, but I didn't move. I couldn't. He was killing me, but complying with his demands was also making me hotter than everything else combined.

Slowly, Zach slid his tongue up the first of my fingers. "After I make you come with my mouth, then it will be time for *these*." Again he rolled my nipples between his fingers; this time, my whole body spasmed.

"Zach!" His name emerged as a strangled squeak.

"Go ahead," he chuckled as his tongue laved my second finger. "Scream if you want to. I won't mind."

"Mm-mm." I clamped my lips together and shook my head. There were limits, after all. No matter how long he tortured me, I was *not* going to scream.

"You will you know," he said as he sucked the next finger into his mouth. "Before I'm done, you will *definitely* scream."

"Not happening," I said, gritting my teeth, .although, truth be told, I wasn't so sure.

"You'll see," he promised, pinching my nipples again, even harder than before. "Cause after I finish giving your tits all the attention they deserve, then I'm gonna fuck you. And, baby, if that doesn't make you scream then I guess..." He paused for a moment, obviously trying to think of something good, while I battled to hold down the scream that was already trying to work its way out of my throat. "Well, I guess then I'll just have to let you have your way with me, won't I?"

"Yessss." The thought I could have him at my mercy; be free to drive him crazy, like he was doing to me, was intoxicating. And I would show him no mercy. None.

Zach chuckled once again. "Never gonna happen though, 'cause I'm not gonna just fuck you once, I'm gonna fuck you all over. I want to come with my cock in your pussy, your mouth, sandwiched between your tits. I want to flip you over and give it to your ass."

"No," I whispered, trembling harder.

"Shhh," Zach murmured as he brushed a kiss across my cheek. "I know. It's off limits. But knowing I can't have something's never made me stop wanting it yet." He took his hands from my breasts and squeezed my ass. "And, honey, I want to fuck this sweet ass of yours more than I've wanted anything in a long, long time." He lowered his voice until it was the faintest of whispers. "I'd do just about anything to get a piece of this."

Blood thundered in my ears as my gaze met Zach's in the mirror. The look in his eyes left me with no doubt he meant exactly what he said. And even though I wasn't even tempted to give in to that particular desire, just knowing he wanted me like that had me shaking with need. I was breathing so hard now, I could barely talk. "Need. To come. Now."

He nodded and dropped a kiss on my shoulder. "I know, baby." His hands slid lower, spreading my labia wide; then he slipped two fingers into my streaming pussy. "But I need to see and feel it when you do."

With trembling fingers I stroked my clit. In no time at all, I went off like a rocket. And as I felt my muscles tighten around Zach's fingers, milking them for all they were worth, I shrieked.

"Oh, my God," I murmured, knowing I was lost. I was already screaming and we hadn't even begun to fuck.

Chapter Five

The spicy aroma of pizza tickled my nose when Zach flipped the box open to hand me a second slice.

"Mmm." I reached for it greedily. "Thank you." Pizza was delicious, I decided, as I took a big bite.

The late afternoon sun moved slowly across Zach's living room, gilding everything in its path with its warm, golden light. We lay on the couch; each of us propped up against one of the sofa's arms; our legs entwined with one another along the seat. I took another bite and considered my situation. I felt a mass of contradictions at the moment; exhausted yet animated, happy and scared. I was lost. I was found. I was sated and spent. I was starving for more. What I should have been was sleepy—but I was too wound up to sleep.

After we'd finished in the bathroom, Zach had carried me into his bedroom, where he'd laid me on his bed and proceeded to make me scream several more times. By rights, I should have been depressed about that. At this rate, I was never going to make him my love slave.

You were never going to anyway, a tiny voice, way in the back of my mind, sneered at the very thought.

But, I didn't *know* that. And, right now. I hoped the voice was wrong. I really hoped that, when I found out who I was, I would learn that I *did* belong in Zach's strange world. That I *was* 'his kind of woman'. And that I *would* find a way to make him my slave... at least part of the time.

Because, despite all the weirdness and uncertainty, despite having a lifetime memory that stretched back for all of about ten hours, at this precise instant, what I felt most of all was an underlying contentment. Some inner sense was telling me I hadn't known too many moments like that in my life.

But I didn't want to think about that. There was nothing I could do about it right now, anyhow. And, since that same inner sense was also saying this golden moment was not likely to last very long, I was determined to make the most of it while it was here. I took another bite of pizza and let everything else fall away.

Pizza, I thought, had to be the most perfect food ever invented, although, admittedly, my experience, at present, wasn't all that wide. And pizza and beer together—now that was surely an unbeatable combination.

"What do you call this stuff again?" I asked, picking a small, white blob off the top of my slice and popping it in my mouth. Creamy and warm with a distinct salt tang, I loved the way it melted on my tongue.

Zach smiled. "That's Feta cheese. You like it?"

"Mmm." It reminded me of sex. "And the green stuff underneath?"

"Pesto. Basil, garlic, olive oil…I don't know what else."

"It's good." Pesto tasted earthy and pungent. It reminded me of sex, too.

"Yep," Zach sighed, sounding pretty content, himself. "Green pizza and red beer. It doesn't get much better than that."

Nodding agreement, I leaned down and retrieved my bottle from the floor. After taking a sip I smacked my lips. "Delicious." But it was better than that; really. It was refreshing in a dark, vibrant, exciting sort of way; like a cool, wet, never-ending kiss…

Come to think of it, everything reminded me of sex just now, even the soft cheese that was layered beneath the pesto. Soft, stretchy, springy; it brought to mind the tender sac that held Zach's balls.

I moved my foot a little, stretching my leg as far as it would reach, until my sole was pressed against the bulge at Zach's crotch. I rubbed him with my heel, back and forth in a little semi-circle, testing to see how much of that soft springiness I could feel through the denim of his jeans.

"Hey." Zach swatted at my foot. "Cut it out. Stop that."

He looked amused, however, rather than annoyed, so I decided not to take him seriously. I scrunched up my toes and pressed harder. "Stop what?"

Mischief gleaming in his eyes, he swallowed the last bite of his pizza and put down his bottle. "You're really asking for it, aren't you?"

Was I? I nibbled at the edge of my own pizza while I considered the matter. Truth was, I was feeling a little tired. "Not just right now, thanks. Maybe later."

"That's what you think." Shifting backwards suddenly, so that he was out of my foot's reach, Zach swung his legs over mine.

I sucked in a quick breath when his big toe nudged my pussy. I was pinned beneath his legs, naked under the pink robe. A thin layer of satin was all that separated my most sensitive flesh from his marauding foot. Heat spread through me at the thought, along with a faint trace of alarm. "Zach, don't."

"Don't... what?" he mocked, using his other foot to spread my legs apart.

Tears stung my eyes as laughter competed with nerves. I still wasn't completely sure I could trust him, after all, and with pizza in one hand, beer in the other, what could I use to defend myself if things turned rough? My elbows? Ha. But, even so, desire curled in my belly. My nipples peaked. I felt anxious, vulnerable... and almost more excited than I could stand. "Please..."

"You know I like it when you beg," Zach murmured as his toe massaged my clit. Then his smile widened. His eyes met mine and breathing became that much harder, I could tell he was feeling the same thing I was: my juices soaking through the satin. "You like it too, don't you?"

His voice alone made my clit throb, so intense it was almost painful, reminding me I was feeling more than a little sore. I shook my head. "No."

"No?" All movement stopped. Zach froze, looking startled.

My sex pulsed, mourning the loss of his heat, already missing his toe's tormenting pressure. Screw the soreness. I rocked my hips, trying to rub myself against his foot.

Laughter rumbled from his throat; low, sexy, triumphant. "Liar." Still laughing, he lifted his legs from mine and pulled away from me completely.

"Pig," I muttered, feeling bereft, abandoned, frustrated. My chest heaved and I briefly considered which one to hurl at his head—the pizza or the beer—until Zach solved the problem for me by removing both from my hands and then pulling me down on top of him.

"You are such a nut," he murmured holding me still so he could kiss me.

"Takes one to know one," I replied straddling his legs and stretching out on top of him. No question about it, I liked being on top; liked the feel of his body, broad and strong, laid out beneath me; liked the feel of his big hands cupping my head, his fingers tangling in my hair.

His lips were warm. He tasted of beer and pizza and male. Did all guys taste this good, or was it just him? I sank my teeth into his bottom lip, frustrated by the fact that there didn't seem to be any way to get enough of him.

"Ow." Zach's hands closed on my shoulders. "What'd you

do that for?" He held me away from him while his tongue snaked out to explore the damage to his lower lip.

"I like the way you taste," I explained, feeling completely unapologetic as I braced my hands on his chest and gazed down at him. It was his own fault, after all. He didn't *have* to taste that good.

A startled smile curved his lips. "You do, huh?"

I nodded and lied. "Yes, I do. Almost as much as pizza."

"That much?" Releasing my shoulders, he slid his hands slowly down the length of my back until they were cupping my ass. "Wow. I'm flattered. What else do you like?"

"Beer."

"And...?"

"Sex. Definitely." *With you.*

"Good to know. So...do you like this too?" His hands tightened on my butt. Pressing my hips to his, he ground his hot cock against my mound.

I nodded. "Mm-hm."

"And how about... this?" Curling up suddenly, he took a nipple between his teeth and bit down gently.

"Unh!" The air left my lungs in a rush.

"Was that a *yes?*" he asked as his tongue lashed the tender peak. Heat zinged, like an electric shock, from nipple to clit, robbing me of speech.

He glanced up at me, eyes flashing wickedness. "Well?"

I nodded again, still struggling for breath. "Yes."

"Anything else you like?"

"Um, like what?" I asked feigning innocence. *You, perhaps?* I held my breath, wondering if he'd ask; wondering what I should say, if he did.

He gazed at me expectantly for a moment, then his smile softened. "I don't know," he said, taking hold of my shoulders and easing me down on top of him again. "Maybe that's enough for now."

"Yep," I murmured, feeling relieved, but also disappointed.

"I like you, too, you know," he said as he tucked my head beneath his chin. "*More* than pizza."

I smiled at that, plucking absently at the hair on his chest. Too content to talk, I wanted to stay like this, wrapped up in his arms, for a good, long time. Maybe even the rest of the night.

"So, I guess I was right."

Puzzled, I craned my neck to glance up at him. "Right about what?"

"Learning things about yourself. Finding out what you like and don't like. It was easier than you thought it'd be, wasn't it?"

"Oh." I nodded, thinking about it. "I guess it was." I didn't know much, yet, but it was more than I'd known this morning. And it helped. I felt safer somehow, more grounded, less frightened. "Thank you."

"My pleasure," he replied, hugging me tight for a moment.

I nodded again thinking, *yeah, it probably was.* But that was okay. He deserved to get something out of this, too. I just wished I knew more about *him*, as well. Things like, how come he wasn't already taken? From what I could see he was pretty much perfect, other than maybe not having a lot of money. Why hadn't someone grabbed him by now?

"Do you surf?" I asked, propping myself up on my elbows so I could see his face.

His eyes widened. "Do I surf? We're in LA. Doesn't everyone?"

I shook my head. "No. I mean, is that what you do? Is that how you spend your time? Are you a surfer?"

A puzzled frown creased his brow. "No. I'm a musician. We talked about that, remember?"

"Yeah, but... so that's your job then? That's what you do for money?"

Zach shrugged. "Mostly. I do some other stuff too, you know."

"Like what?"

"Oh, I don't know. Construction, sometimes. Tony's uncle's a contractor; he gives me work from time to time. That's how Tony and I met, in fact."

"Oh." Interesting as that was, it was getting us nowhere. "And you live alone?"

He cocked his head to the side and gazed at me curiously. "Well, you've been here most of the day. Have you seen anyone else living here?"

I shook my head.

"Then, I guess it's just me."

"What about girlfriends?"

A disbelieving smile curled his lips. "What about 'em?"

"Do you have one?"

His smile widened. "What do you think?"

"I don't know. That's why I'm asking."

He sighed. "Okay, look, I'm not saying that I have a problem with casual sex, 'cause obviously I don't. But, when I *am* in a relationship... well, I don't go around picking up girls, that's all. Not even when they're as hot as you."

"You think I'm hot?" It wasn't anything I'd planned on asking, but he surprised me and I couldn't help myself.

"Oh, man." His eyes crinkled up as he laughed. "Is *that* what this is about? You know, if you were just looking for compliments, all you had to do was say so. What do you want to hear? That you're stunning and sexy and..."

"No, that's not—I'm just curious. *Why* don't you have a girlfriend?"

"I dunno." The laughter faded from his eyes leaving him looking a little bit wistful. "Just not commitment material, I guess. That's what most of the women I've been with lately have been looking for; someone they can settle down with. And me... I'm not that guy."

"Oh." Well, that answered that question, didn't it? I sat up and grabbed another piece of pizza, hoping to hide my disappointment. It answered a lot of questions, actually. I'd been right all along. I wasn't his type of woman. If he even had a type.

Even with no memory, I could tell I wouldn't be satisfied for very long with the kind of relationship he was offering. Temporary. Casual. Uncommitted. Who the hell needed that?

A small smile flickered about his face as he watched me eat. "So, is that it? No more questions?"

"Just one. Where are these aphrodisiacs you mentioned?" I might be disappointed with him, but that didn't mean I still wasn't going to make the best of things. He could make me mindless with pleasure until I passed out from exhaustion. And then, when I woke up tomorrow, maybe I'd remember enough to go home.

Zach chuckled. "We might have to leave those for tomorrow. They're not exactly the kind of thing I have on hand. Unless you wanna get dressed and go shopping?"

"Not really." My clothes were washed and dried, by now, but I didn't feel like dressing. "I don't want to move from this couch all night."

He nodded. "That works for me."

"So, I guess it's time to move on to B?"

"Not quite." Zach gestured at the end of the couch. "Why don't you sit back down over there."

Wondering what he had in mind, I picked up my beer and

scooted back to where I'd been seated earlier. I watched with interest as he picked up his guitar. "Are you going to serenade me?"

He smiled slyly. "You'll see."

He hadn't been playing for more than a couple of minutes before I realized a few things. First thing I realized was how good he was. Damn good, I thought, even if I had nothing to compare it to. I could tell how much it meant to him, too—that was the second thing that hit me. His eyes were half closed and there was a dreamy, abstracted look on his face. I'd have bet anything that he could hear the music in his head, before he'd even played a note. I loved the intensity, the passion, on his face.

The third thing I realized was how much his music was affecting me—and I'm not talking emotionally, either.

It was a physical thing. I could feel each of the notes he played as it resonated inside me. My pussy responded as if it were my actual flesh he was strumming, rather than guitar strings. "How are you doing that?"

The sexy smile he flashed told me that he knew exactly what I meant. "Like it?"

I nodded. "Yes. But, how..."

"It's called a vibrato. Or a tremolo—either one. And, if you do it just right, it's supposed to stimulate something known as the vaginal frequency."

"You're kidding?"

"Sounds crazy, I know. But, that's what some of the old timers say. You tell me."

His fingers caressed the strings until I had to clench my thighs together in an attempt to ease the pressure. Much more of this and I'd have to jump him.

"Well?"

I managed a casual shrug. "I'd say they're right."

Green eyes glinted as he smiled at me. "Yeah, that's what you seemed to think last night, too."

"Last night?"

He nodded. "In the bar."

My jaw dropped. "You did this to me in a room full of people?" I'd never be able to show my face there again!

"Oh, don't act so scandalized. You gave back as good as you got."

"How'd I do that?"

He arched one eyebrow and gazed at me ruefully. "Those lips, those eyes, that body... I didn't stop to think what it was going to do to me watching as you got turned on. You don't take any prisoners, do you?"

But why was he asking me that—how would I know what I did or didn't do? "Why would you do something like that?"

He stopped playing then, and looked at me, resting his hands lightly on his guitar. "Remember how I told you I'd seen you come in the door?"

Puzzled, I nodded.

"I thought you were different. Special. But then you came and sat at that table, in the spotlight, and I thought maybe I'd gotten the wrong impression."

I thought back to earlier this afternoon, trying to recall the table in question. "It's very bright there, isn't it?"

Laughter sparked in Zach's green eyes. "Yeah, it is. See, that particular light got jostled out of place during an earthquake and nobody's gotten around to fixing it. It used to point at the stage. Most of the time, when people pick that table it's 'cause they want to be seen. I guess I was kind of disappointed that I'd been wrong about you. So, I thought I'd have a little fun."

"At my expense, you mean?" Well, there was something else I could not like about him, I thought, feeling hurt.

He nodded. "It didn't take me long to realize that I'd made a mistake. I'd been right the first time; you really didn't care if anyone was looking. Other than me. I think you were getting turned on more by how hot you were making me than you were by the music."

That surprised me. And if it turned out I wasn't the only one who'd been affected, well that would go a long way toward making me feel better, too. "So how hot were you?"

His laugh was low and rueful. "I could have driven nails with my dick. Meanwhile, I thought the guy you were with was your date and I just knew I'd be looking at one very long, lonely night. That's why, as soon as I saw he'd left you alone, I made my move. I figured, even if you told me to get lost, I had nothing to lose."

I nodded thoughtfully. He'd given me a lot to think about. "You must have made one hell of a pitch to get me to come home with you after that."

Zach sighed. "Yeah, that's what I was thinking too. I figured I'd be doing good just to get your phone number." Then he smiled at me and I knew right then his pitch probably hadn't mattered in the slightest. He wouldn't have had to say a word. All he'd have had to do was flash that smile. "I can't tell you how happy I was to be proved wrong about that, too."

I swallowed the last of my beer, put the bottle down and then leaned back against the couch. "Okay, so then show me."

"What's that?" he asked, looking puzzled.

I let my legs fall open a bit, knowing he would get just a glimpse of my pussy; happy in the realization that we were in this mess together, both of us slaves to our own desires, helpless to resist the attraction we each felt for one other. At least for now. "If you can't tell me how happy you are, why don't you come over here and show me?"

Heat flared in his eyes and flushed his cheeks. I think he even groaned. Still, I have to give him credit for trying. He shook his head and motioned at the guitar. "I wasn't finished playing."

But I was. I also had a desperate need to exert a little control over the situation. "Later for that. Right now I want you over here. I need that nail-driving cock of yours inside me. Now."

And that was all it took. He set the guitar aside and swarmed on top of me. His body was still broad and strong and it felt just as nice when I was pinned beneath it.

Chapter Six

Zach

Pale sunlight shone through Zach's bedroom window the next morning, illuminating the face of the girl who lay sleeping there. He propped himself up on one elbow to watch her as she slept. She had curled away from him during the night and now lay face down with her butt in the air. She looked pretty, with her cheeks flushed and her eyes closed, her lips just slightly parted, as though waiting for his kiss.

She looked trusting, submissive, defenseless and willing. And even though he knew it to be a fantasy, at least in part, it was still a dick hardening combination. Especially given the way the sheet had molded itself to her body. Not to mention the fact that he knew her to be buck naked under said sheet.

"No wonder they named you Angel," he murmured as he slowly slid the sheet away from her naked form. She had a heavenly body, if he'd ever seen one. He paused and held his breath when she stirred a little. He didn't want her waking up yet, he wanted a few minutes first, to look at her. He *needed* to look at her. That ass of hers was breaking his heart.

Ah, baby, he thought, sliding the sheet down over her thighs, *what I could do to you, if you'd let me...*

He knew she'd like it, too. He'd make sure she did. No matter how long it took to bring her around... but that was precisely the problem, wasn't it? Given the resistance she'd already shown to the idea, what were the odds he could keep her around long enough to change her mind? Not good, if past experience was anything to go by.

Assuming she didn't disappear within minutes of recovering her memory, he might reasonably expect a four month window. Four months, maybe less. That's how long it usually took a woman to decide there was no future with him.

Like he'd told her last night, it was something he'd heard repeatedly from just about all the women he'd dated: he was nice, good company, sexy, he was a great lay and one helluva guitar player. But no matter how much they liked him, loved him, enjoyed spending time with him; he just wasn't the kind of guy any one of them would ever choose to settle down with.

Peter Pan had been referenced. Several times, as he recalled.

As well as his fondness for games and lack of a steady paycheck.

He couldn't support a family with his music; that seemed to be the general consensus. And even if he could, even if he found a way to prove them wrong on that count, as the wife of a musician, what kind of life would they lead?

A lonely one, stuck at home with the kids while he was off on the road. An unpredictable one, given the fickleness of fame, the preponderance of drugs, the ubiquity of groupies. A thankless, unfulfilled one, a life lived in his shadow—*and, honestly, Zach, who would want that?*

It had long since ceased to bother him, however. Life was good, women were plentiful, he had his music and, if honesty was really what they wanted to hear, he'd yet to meet the woman he'd be willing to give that up for.

Maybe someday he would, but, in the meantime, he wasn't going to lose any sleep over it. Not while he had an Angel in his bed. And a sexy, naked angel at that.

He'd dropped the sheet when he'd bared her to the knees, and wrapped his hand around his cock. Pre-cum leaked from the tip now as he stroked himself, his gaze glued to her ass, his mind lost in a fantasy...

He'd have her on her knees: chest down, ass up, legs spread. The curve of her back was a thing of beauty. He'd coast one hand down her spine just to feel it; and to feel her shiver at his touch.

"Zach, please," she'd pant. "I have to have it now. Don't make me wait any longer." And, because it was a fantasy, he'd have no trouble making out the words. He'd have no trouble seeing her face, either. Her eyes would be dark with heat. Her lips would tremble as she ran her tongue over them, until they were just as wet, just as red, just as soft, slick and swollen as her pussy.

Because it was a fantasy, he wouldn't have to bother with things like condoms or lubricants. He'd just thrust his naked cock into her slippery, hot bush and coat himself with her juices.

"Don't stop, don't stop," she'd beg when he pulled out of her.

"Shh," he'd whisper soothingly. Then he'd spread her ass cheeks for his first good look at her puckered hole. "Is this where you want it?" he'd ask, leaning in to rim her with his tongue. "Are you ready for me now?" The musky scent of her would almost be his undoing. But he wouldn't let himself lose it yet. He'd hold it together, determined to give her the ride of her life.

"Yes, Zach, yes," she'd murmur, wriggling her ass in his face, tempting him beyond any man's endurance.

"Then open up for me, baby," he'd tell her, lining the tip of his cock up with her anus, pushing gently, slowly, until just his head was inside. Patiently stretching her, pausing for as long as she needed him to, waiting for her muscles to adjust to the pressure.

He'd be shuddering by then; sweating with the effort he'd be making to stay in control, to hold back, to wait for her. He'd be loving the wait. He'd be intoxicated with every torturous second.

"Oh, God, that's good," she'd say, panting again, the words barely audible. She'd push back with her hips, impaling herself on his cock, crying out, just a little, when impatience made her hurry beyond her limits.

"Easy," he'd caution, holding her still, stroking her hips and thighs until her muscles relaxed. "I don't want to hurt you." The desire, no, the *need*, to protect her, to care for her, to love her, would give him the strength to resist, to hold back, to wait until she was really ready.

Then he'd rock into her. Slowly, at first, and then, when he sensed she could take it, faster, harder, deeper. Until she was swallowing every inch. Until he was buried balls deep inside her. Until they were rocking together, sweating together, breathing hard. Together.

With one hand tangled in her hair, one hand grasping her hip, he'd ride her, guide her, send her soaring into ecstasy.

A scream would burst from her lips. Cream would gush from her pussy. Her ass would squeeze and squeeze and squeeze his cock until—

"Ah, shit," Zach muttered as he lunged for the box of tissues. He'd nearly lost it. He'd nearly shot his load all over her back—which would have suited him just fine, but which would probably have pissed her off no end.

He lay on his back, still sweating, still breathing hard, while he waited for the thundering of his heart to subside. He turned his head to watch her, grateful that she was still asleep. He'd never understood the objection some women had to being fantasized over. Any woman of his acquaintance was welcome to use him as the object of her fantasy. Any time, any place.

Welcome twice over, in fact, if she was willing to let him watch while she did it.

As he continued to gaze at her, melodies and stray scraps of song lyrics wended their way through his mind. A not uncommon occurrence.

Maybe he'd write a song about her some day. Not that it would *really* be about her, of course. This particular woman would leave, as they all did. But, even when she did, even when she took her fine ass and sashayed from his life, the idea of her would still remain; would be forever his.

And it was that woman, that mythic, elusive *She* about whom he'd write. She was his inspiration. The love of his life. Though she might wear a thousand different faces or answer to a thousand different names, there was really only one. His woman. His muse.

Too bad he'd never really find her. Sighing, just a little sadly, Zach rolled over on his side and pulled the sheets back up around her.

He pressed the briefest, lightest, softest kiss against her shoulder; thanking her for pleasures she'd never even know she'd given him.

I wish you'd stay, he told her silently, tracing a finger down the curve of her cheek. But those were words he'd never say aloud. He'd become the master of the graceful exit in the last few years. He'd let her go with a smile, as he'd done with all the rest. With a kiss. With well wishes for the future and a fond good-bye.

It would be easy. Even though she was a heartbreaker—no question there—she wouldn't break *his* heart. He was too slick for that. Too old. Too practiced. Too careful. He'd been there, he'd done that, and he was *not* going down that road again.

So, careful not to wake her, he slid out of bed. It was time to plan her next lesson in love. They had a busy day ahead of them.

Chapter Seven

April

"Wake up."

The words were whispered softly in my ear and my eyes shot open at the shock of hearing a man's voice at so close a proximity. *What the hell?*

I scrambled to my knees; heart pounding, brain immediately registering the fact that I was naked, that this wasn't my bed or my room, and...*omigod*... Who was this guy perched on the edge of the bed with a tray of food in his hands? Why was he here? And what did he think he was doing—staring, smiling, ogling. Was this some new form of room service—breakfast with a leer? Not that this room looked like any hotel I'd want to be found dead in.

I sagged in relief as recognition finally dawned. "Oh." Right. "Zach. It's you."

"Hey, are you okay?" he asked, the smile fading from his face. "What's wrong?"

I felt my eyes flash in fury. "What do you *think* is wrong?" I snapped, then cringed at my own bitchiness. Why should I expect him to understand that I'd been surprised to see him here? I wasn't entirely clear about it myself. This was *his* room, *his* bed and I was lucky he'd asked me to share it for a second night. But for a split second I'd forgotten all of that and remembered... everything else. All of it. All the memories. All the information. All the details of my former life. Everything that I needed to make sense of things had been right there at the edge of my consciousness...

Now it was gone again, beyond my grasp.

"Sorry," I mumbled rubbing my temples, wiping the sleep from my eyes, trying to resist the urge to throw myself face down on the bed and cry my eyes out—I was that close to despair. "I just—Oh, never mind. You startled me, that's all. I forgot where I was for a minute and, and..."

"C'mere," he sighed, putting down the tray and opening his arms. I was happy to crawl over to where he was seated and rest my head against his chest; happy to feel his arms close around me. It felt nice. Comforting. Not half as nice as it would have been to have remembered my name, or where I lived; but it was still nothing I was in a hurry to give up.

"I didn't mean to scare you," he said as he cuddled me close.

"Should I have let you sleep longer? I just thought that you'd like breakfast in bed and I didn't want your omelet to get cold."

"It's okay. Thanks." I was touched by his thoughtfulness, though I was a little disappointed that food should be the first thing on his mind this morning—had I become that boring? Already? But, come to think of it, I was pretty hungry myself. I gestured at the tray. "What's all that?"

One of those quiet, sexy laughs I'd come to love rumbled out of his throat. "Those are some of the aphrodisiacs you were asking about. I got up early and went shopping." He pulled the tray closer and pointed at each of the items in turn. "I got you fresh strawberries, champagne, anise seed biscotti, coffee, an asparagus and white truffle omelet and, for dessert, marzipan fruit."

I leaned away from him to study the tray. The coffee I recognized. And what he'd called fruit appeared to be some kind of luridly colored candy. "You really know a lot about aphrodisiacs, huh?" I have to admit I was impressed.

Zach shrugged. "Not really. Luckily, I ran into one of my neighbors in the elevator this morning. A lot of these were her suggestions."

"You told your neighbors about us?" But what was it that surprised me more? The fact that he was on such intimate terms with them, or that I merited any mention at all? I thought he'd made things pretty plain last night. I was someone he'd picked up while he was in between relationships. Temporary, casual, uncommitted relationships, at that. As such, I hardly seemed discussion-worthy.

"Not exactly." Zach looked surprised, as well. "Gabby and I are friends. Besides, she's really smart about this kind of stuff. Trust me, you're getting a much better breakfast than you would have if I'd tried to figure it out on my own."

I shook my head. "Oh, I'm not complaining. I'm just..." Happy, actually. Maybe this thing between us wasn't quite as meaningless as he'd led me to believe. I reached for the tray, but he pulled it away from me. I sat back on my heels and looked at him questioningly. "Can't I have my food now?"

"In a minute," he said, pulling a long, black scarf from his back pocket.

I looked at it dubiously. "What's that?"

His eyes twinkled and there was that dimple again, but his words caught me totally by surprise. "This is a blindfold."

"A what?"

"A blindfold. You know, it starts with a B?"

"I heard you the first time. But... you've got to be kidding?"

He shook his head. "Nope. It's a blind taste test, see? I've shown you what everything looks like, now you get to taste it and see if you can match the flavors and the textures with how it all looks."

My gaze shifted from him to the tray and back again. "And...*why* are we doing this?"

Zach's eyebrows rose. "For fun, why else?"

"I see. So, what's the fun part? The part where I can't see what you're up to, or the part where you shove potentially disgusting things into my mouth?"

"You ought to be more trusting," he said, shaking his head sadly. "First of all, I already told you we wouldn't do anything you don't want to do, so stop worrying about what I'm up to. Second, none of this is disgusting, so that's also a non-issue. And third..."

"That's what you said about the oysters," I reminded him. "Just because you think something tastes good, that doesn't mean I'm going to think so too."

He nodded. "Okay, point taken. But how're you going to know what you like unless you try things?"

"I don't know." To tell the truth, I didn't really care, either. It seemed a little early in the day to be playing games.

"What if I promise to be really slow and gentle, to only give you tiny little bites and you don't have to swallow anything unless you want to. Would that work?"

Lovely. He could delicately place things in my mouth and I could blindly spit them back out if I didn't like them. That would be attractive. "Why can't we skip the blindfold? Why can't I just eat what I want, leave the rest and be done with it?"

"I could give you a reward for every right answer," he offered. "Now are you interested?"

The look in his eyes *was* intriguing. "Maybe. What kind of reward are we talking about?"

He smiled triumphantly, as though he knew he had me. "Anything you want."

"Anything?"

"As long as it's within reason, yes."

Since most of what I wanted seemed totally reasonable to me, I agreed. "Okay. You're on." What could I lose?

A moment later, as he secured the blindfold around my head,

I wasn't so sure. As my bare breasts brushed against the front of his shirt I felt my nipples pucker up on contact. I inhaled sharply.

"Sorry," he murmured placing a brief kiss on my lips. Too brief, I thought, clutching his arms and drawing him back in for a better one. He seemed happy to oblige me, but as his hands cupped my face I really had to wonder what I was doing. I was naked. Blindfolded. In bed with a fully dressed man I still hardly knew, but who seemed fully capable of kissing me into total submission whenever it suited him to do so.

All of that struck me as being much more erotic than I ever would have believed.

"Can't we just skip the guessing and move straight on to the reward?" I asked, moving against him in what I hoped was a persuasive manner as I slid my arms up and around his shoulders.

"No." Removing my hands from his neck, he set me gently but firmly away from him. "Now, open up."

I knew he meant my mouth but I was tempted—so tempted—to spread my legs instead. I didn't, because it wouldn't have been nearly as much fun if I couldn't see his reaction, but, *someday*, I silently promised us both.

"Bite down," Zach instructed as something brushed against my lips. True to his word, he'd placed just the tiniest taste of food within my mouth.

I bit into something soft, juicy, sweet... it had to be fruit. And, since I'd already determined that what he was calling fruit really wasn't..."Strawberry?"

"Good answer," he murmured, trailing the rest of the berry over my chin and down my throat, his mouth following closely behind—licking up the juice, I imagined.

I gasped as he ran the fruit in circles around my breast's taut peak. "What are you doing?"

His voice held a deep, delicious sounding huskiness. "Rewarding you," he said just before his hot mouth closed around my nipple.

"Nice."

"Very." He gave my breast a final flick with his tongue. "So did you like it?"

"Mmm." I reached for him, hoping for more, but he eluded my grasp.

He chuckled. "I meant the strawberry."

I nodded. "That too."

"Okay, let's move on," he said. "Here. Take a sip."

I felt the smooth, rounded edge of a glass press against my lip as something cold and bubbly, not quite sweet, just a little bit sharp, slid into my mouth. *Too easy*, I thought, hiding a smile as I pretended to consider the matter. There were only two liquids on the tray, and since this wasn't coffee... "Could it be... Champagne?"

"Ooh, right again."

I did smile then, licking my lips in anticipation of my reward as I heard him return the glass to the tray. He swept me into his arms with an almost startling swiftness and I all but moaned with pleasure and surprise. He must have swallowed some of the wine as well because his lips were cool as they closed over mine and his mouth carried the same taste I'd just sampled. Champagne had just become my new, favorite flavor, I decided, as I thrust my tongue between his teeth in search of more.

"I think we're getting sidetracked," he said, breaking away again.

"Good." Sidetracked was good. Startled was good. Rewards were good. As for the rest... "You know, Zach, if you're still looking for suggestions, I bet I could think of an aphrodisiac or two that aren't on that tray. Want me to show you what I'm talking about? I think you'd like it."

"No," he said and it sounded like he was grinning again. "Never mind that now. We're supposed to be figuring out what kinds of things *you* like, remember? So do you like Champagne?"

"Love Champagne," I replied as I licked my lips once more.

Zach chuckled. "Okay, open up again."

"Oh, don't tempt me."

He used a fork this time to slide something warm and soft onto my tongue. It had an odd, pungent taste, vaguely reminiscent of oysters. I'd have had no clue what it was except for the temperature. He hadn't wanted my omelet to get cold—that's what he'd said, right? Which could only mean...

"Omelet?"

"Right again."

"How come you're the one with all the choices?" I asked as he picked up one of my hands and brought it to his mouth. "You pick what I get to taste, how I get rewarded..."

"Are you complaining?" he asked, gently kissing each of my fingers in turn.

Thrills of pleasure raced up my arm when his lips moved to

my palm. "Not exactly, but..."

"Good." He kept his hold on my hand, but the kissing had stopped. I could hear him fumbling with something on the tray. "Try this."

A warm, slippery cylinder, about the diameter of his little finger, slipped into my mouth. I began to bite into it and then froze. It was firm, but not too firm, fleshy in fact; and I twirled my tongue around it experimentally, wanting to make sure that I didn't bite anything off that shouldn't be bitten. I sucked on it thoughtfully, puzzled by the taste.

"Well? Any guesses?"

"Not a one."

His breath was warm against my ear when he leaned in to whisper, "How can I give you your reward, if you won't even try?"

"Marzipan?" I guessed wildly, "Biscotti?" I knew it wasn't coffee.

"Ohh, too bad, wrong answer."

"Which one?" I asked, impatiently.

I was startled when he answered, "Both."

"What do you mean both?" I shoved the blindfold off my head and glared at him. "What else could it be? There's nothing else on the tray!"

He looked at me, eyebrows raised in surprise. "You think I'm cheating? It was an asparagus from the omelet."

"What? That's not fair! You can't pick things apart and—besides, I'd already guessed right on the omelet."

"Not *fair*?" Smiling in disbelief, Zach set the tray aside and then turned on me, plucking the scarf from my hand. "Sounds like someone's being a sore loser."

"So what if I am?" I answered, falling back against the pillows as he loomed over me. "I didn't want to play this game in the first place, you know."

"That's true," he said as he knotted the scarf around one of my wrists, the twinkle in his eyes a clear-cut warning he was up to no good. "Maybe you'll like this one better."

When he slipped the scarf through the rails of the headboard, I balked. "Hold on a minute," I said, planting my other hand dead center in his chest and pushing. "What do you think you're doing?"

He kissed the tip of my nose and grinned. "Bondage. It's another B word. Don't tell me you're going to say *no* to this too? I think it would really help you to work through some of your trust issues."

"I don't *have* trust issues," I told him. "And I don't have a problem with bondage either. But why am *I* the one getting tied up?"

"What d'you mean? You think you should be tying me up instead?"

"Why not? I bet I'd like that a lot. I think you'd make a good slave. I'm seeing a leather collar, maybe some chains..."

"A collar, huh?" He laughed at that. "I dunno. I wouldn't get my heart too set on that, if I were you."

"I could make you like it," I promised, not altogether certain that was true, but more than willing to give it a try.

"You know what I'd like even more?"

I shook my head.

"You. In my bed. Helpless to resist me."

But he already had that, didn't he? "I thought this weekend was about figuring out what *I* like?" I asked, pouting just a little, playing the pity card for all it was worth, feeling only the slightest bit guilty when Zach's smile faded.

"I tell you what," he said as he untied my wrist and sat up. "Why don't we make it a contest? We'll choose an activity where neither of us has an advantage, and whoever wins gets to tie the other up first."

"What kind of activity?" I asked, taking the tray as he handed it to me.

"You'll see. I have an idea. So hurry up and eat your breakfast. We have some shopping to do."

I sipped my coffee; it was good, hot, bracing, exactly what I needed to clear the clouds of lust from my mind. "What kind of shopping?"

"Well, clothes shopping, for one thing. For what I have in mind, you'll want something a little more casual than the one outfit you have. And for another..."

"Zach...no. I can't have you buying clothes for me." I was in his debt enough already. I could rationalize it to an extent, as he had at breakfast the previous day, by likening it to a very long date. But, if things went much farther, I'd really start to owe him... more than I could easily repay.

He waved away my objections. "Why not? I'm not talking about an entire wardrobe, just a couple of outfits. Besides, I'm pretty sure I'll have to buy them for you, you know. Even as lovely as you are, I still don't know of any stores likely to give you clothes for free just 'cause of your good looks and charm."

Lovely, huh? I nibbled on another strawberry and considered everything I'd learned about myself so far, starting with the fact I was clearly a sucker for flattery. According to Zach I was lovely, hot, self assured, confident—pretty much irresistible. He was such a sweet talker! And I was pretty sure I could be falling for him because of that alone. In a way, I hoped that was all it was. Better to be in love with a string of honeyed words than to actually lose my heart to someone who was gorgeous, sweet, sexy, patient, thoughtful, inventive, generous to a fault, playful, funny, kind... and totally averse to commitment.

I swallowed the berry and nodded. "Okay, but on one condition. After we figure out who I am, you let me pay you back."

"Fine," he said as he smiled at me. It was one of those gorgeous, sweet, sexy, patient smiles I was doing my best to ignore. "If it makes you feel better, you can pay for whatever you want."

** **

The noise inside the *Lucky Strike Lanes* bowling alley was deafening. Balls clattered and whirred along the alleys, pins crashed and tumbled as they were swept away. I ran my tongue nervously over lips that were suddenly dry, aware of every jittering, jarring vibration as it echoed deep inside me.

I arched an eyebrow at Zach. "*This* is your idea for how to settle the bondage issue? We're going bowling?"

He smiled. "Why not? It's simple, uncomplicated, it begins with a B. It'll be fun."

"Fun, huh?" There was that word again. "How do I know this isn't a trick? How do I know that you're not an expert bowler?"

Zach gazed at me sadly. "You have a very suspicious mind. I'm not an expert bowler. You'll just have to take my word for that. I'm guessing you're not one either. But I figure, since just about everyone's bowled at least a few times, we're probably even. Neither of us has an obvious advantage. If you can think of something more fair than that, I'm all ears."

"I suppose you have a point," I admitted grudgingly. But, just then, another ball hit the boards. Fluttering waves of sensation washed through me and I realized Zach's point, if he had one, was moot. Either he was mistaken or he was lying, because, thanks to the little gift he'd presented me with after one of our earlier stops, one of us had a very big advantage right now—and it wasn't me.

We'd gone clothes shopping first, at *Beverly Center*, where I'd picked out several outfits to tide me over for the next few days— just in case. Then we took Melrose east to La Brea, to a place called *Babeland*, where, while I checked out a cherry-red mini-whip and matching cuffs, Zach purchased a variety of goodies, including a pair of Ben Wa balls...

"I'm supposed to put these where?" I asked, staring at the surprisingly heavy gold balls nestled on their red velvet bed.

"You put them inside you," he repeated, flashing that rogue dimple once again. "See, these gold balls are hollow. There are smaller, solid balls inside of them. If you shake them, you can feel them rolling around in there. They do that when you're wearing them and it feels really good. Or so I've been told. I thought you might like to give them a try."

If I were even half as suspicious-minded as Zach claimed I was, I would probably have guessed, right then, that something was up. But I didn't. Not even on the ride over here, though the throbbing of the motorcycle's engine seemed hugely, and pleasantly magnified, thanks to the spherical weights lodged in my pussy.

They felt nice, if distracting, and I hadn't thought anything of the way he'd urged me to immediately try them out, until we arrived here. Now, I'd bet anything Zach had counted on his gift making me too distracted to win this little contest. Talk about sore losers! If this didn't count as cheating... well, it certainly should have.

There had to be a way for me to even the odds. But how?

I pondered the question while we waited for shoes and then for a lane; as Zach helped me choose a ball, and as he explained the basics of scoring. But it wasn't until he was showing me proper form—instructing me on arm-swing and all the finer points of good delivery—that the solution appeared.

It felt nice to have him stand so close behind me, one hand grasping my wrist, the other snug around my waist. I already would have had a hard time concentrating on anything else under those circumstances, but it was at that point the player on the next lane over made his approach and when his ball made contact with the maple I gasped, rocking back on my heels.

"Are you okay?" Zach asked as he steadied me.

"Yeah, I'm fine. I just, um..." And that's when it hit me. I could tell by the way my cheeks were flaming a flush had spread up my chest to my face. When I noticed how Zach's gaze kept sliding south, to where my peaked nipples strained against the new draped top he'd bought me, I knew just what I had to do.

It might not have been entirely fair, and it was certainly not completely honest, but it was nothing I was going to apologize for, either. I really *needed* to win this contest!

"Wow," I murmured softly, allowing my lashes to fan my cheeks as I let out a slow, shaky breath. "I'm fine," I repeated, smiling just a little as I extricated myself from his arms.

"It's like this, right?" I asked, mentally reciting the instructions in my mind; *step, step, step, slide...*

The ball left my hand and rolled slowly down the lane to connect with the head pin. Several pins clattered to the floor and I allowed myself a dramatic little shudder.

Smiling, I turned to look at Zach. "Not bad, huh?"

"Not bad at all," he agreed. "But are you planning on doing that little shimmy thing every time?"

"Maybe. I just can't help myself." Walking over to where he stood, I pressed my body close to his, loving the way his hands automatically clutched my hips. "These balls you got me are driving me crazy," I whispered in his ear.

His fingers bit into my flesh. "Are they?"

"Mm-hm. It's incredible. I can feel..." I broke off when our neighbor in the next lane released a cranker. "*Oh, God...*" I licked my lips in anticipation and moaned softly when the pins went flying. "I can feel *everything*. It's like wearing an internal vibrator."

"Damn." Zach sounded stunned.

"I know." I brushed a chaste, little kiss on his cheek. "I'm *so* turned on right now I can barely see straight." To be honest, I'd been much more turned on by his guitar playing last night. And, even right now, the touch of his hands, the smell of his skin, the heat that flared in his eyes when I smiled at him—they were all doing so much more for me than any vibrator ever could.

But he didn't have to know that, did he?

"Come on, let's play," I said brightly, stepping away from him again and heading for the ball return; hiding my smile when I heard him mutter, "I don't believe this."

Believe it, I thought, laughing quietly to myself. He might have been the one to start this game, but I was gonna take him down, just the same.

I played pretty well, all things considered, but at the seventh frame Zach was ahead by a few points and I decided it was time to get serious.

I fanned myself vigorously with both hands as I returned to my seat. "Is it hot in here, or is it just me?"

"You," Zach said as he snagged my wrist and pulled me down onto his lap. "Definitely you."

"Oh." I smiled as he raised his face to mine and fell into his kiss with a happy little sigh.

"I need you to do something for me," I murmured a few minutes later, when we came up for air.

He nodded. "Anything."

I snuggled closer—close enough to ensure that my hip nudged against his erection. "I need you to bowl a strike."

Zach's expression turned curious. "I'm already ahead of you. Are you saying you want me to win?"

I bit my lip and squirmed a little more. "I don't really care about that right now. I just *need* you to knock down all ten pins at once."

"How come?"

"Because it feels...so...unbelievably...*good*," I breathed.

Zach groaned. "You know you're killing me, don't you?"

Damn right I knew. I had to struggle to keep from laughing. "*Please?*" My lashes fluttered rapidly. "I really need this, Zach."

"Well, I'll certainly try," he promised, easing me off his lap and getting to his feet.

I leaned back into him and whispered in his ear, "Try really *hard*."

And that was pretty much all it took. Zach's next four balls ended up in the gutter.

"It's not your fault," I murmured as I watched him set up to throw his last two balls. "It's just that the channel is sooo slick."

He turned and looked at me, his expression startled. "What?"

"The channel," I repeated, pointing at the gutter. "Isn't that what you call that thing your balls keep trying to bury themselves in? I think that's the problem right there. It's just so slick and smooth and tight and..."

"Could you not talk about this any more right now?" he asked.

"Of course." I slid my hands between my legs and tightened my thighs around them. "I'll do whatever you want me to do, Zach."

He gazed at me wordlessly as I bounced impatiently in place. Shaking his head, he turned back to the pins. "Good. Try and remember that."

But I think we both knew it was over.

"Does this mean I win?" I asked when he turned back around a few minutes later, having once more failed to knock down a single pin.

"Did you ever doubt it for an instant?"

I thought about that. "No. Not really." I got to my feet and threw my arms around his neck. "You're mine now," I whispered in his ear. "I own you."

"You think so?" He pulled a way a little—just far enough for me to see the smile on his face, the gleam in his eyes.

I nodded, surprised by the thrill the idea gave me. Perhaps, when I rediscovered who I was, I'd learn I was a dominatrix. "I know so. Take me home and I'll prove it to you."

Zach shook his head. "Food first. I have a feeling I'm gonna need all the nourishment I can get."

I was feeling hungry again too, now that I thought of it. All that acting was hard work. "All right," I agreed, frowning sternly. "One stop, but that's all. And it better not take too long either. If you make me wait, I'll make you sorry."

Zach's grin stretched wider. "You're evil, you know that? Pure evil."

"Yep," I said, not bothering to hide my own grin this time. "And I'm gonna make you love it, too."

Chapter Eight

There was a stiff breeze blowing when we left the bowling alley. Warm and dry, I could feel it buffeting my skin in a way that left me feeling instantly impatient. "Where are we eating?" I asked Zach as I took the helmet he offered me and eased it over my head.

"I'm taking you to *The Pig*," he answered. "You'll love it. It's got some of the best barbecue in the Southland."

The Pig? My nose wrinkled as I considered the name. "How come? How do you even know I'll like barbecue? Why can't we have pizza again, instead?"

Zach paused for a moment with his own helmet still in his hands. He looked tall and sexy with the wind blowing in his hair and the sunlight glinting on the gold stubble of his beard. He hadn't shaved in the two days we'd been together and I loved the way he looked now, with the coarse hair framing his lips, showcasing their softness, making me yearn for his kiss. His green eyes sparkled mischievously. "You know what? I'll bet you anything you want to come up with—anything at all—that you're going to love barbecue."

"Anything, huh?" I knew a challenge when I heard one, but there was no way I was taking this one. For one thing, he looked entirely too sure of himself. "You must think you know me pretty well to make a bet like that?"

"I think so. Still not as well as I'd like to, but... well enough for right now. So what's it gonna be? What're we betting?"

"Nothing."

"What?"

"Forget it. No bet."

"How come? You chicken?"

I shook my head. "No, just smart enough to quit while I'm ahead."

"C'mon," he urged. "I'll give you anything you want. Double or nothing. How can you resist those odds?"

"Easy. Besides, I'm already getting what I want." Him. At my mercy. Was he trying to weasel out of our deal? Fat chance I'd let that happen! "Did bowling teach you nothing?"

Zach's laugh was low and sexy. "Sure it did. It taught me I can't trust you to play fair."

"Right back atcha," I told him, pulling the chin strap tight and straddling the bike. "You and your Ben Wa balls. What was so fair about that?"

"Well, I guess you have a point," he replied, slipping into the seat in front of me.

"Damn right I do," I muttered, feeling instantly short of breath when he turned on the engine and the vibrations started up again. I felt my nipples straining against the scratchy lace of my new bra. My labia spasmed as the metal spheres slipped lower in my pussy. I had to wrap my legs around Zach's hips and squeeze for all I was worth just to keep those damn balls from popping out.

"Yeah." He turned his head to grin at me, just before pulling out into traffic. "But it's fun, isn't it?"

* * * *

"What's with the wind?" I asked a short while later, gnawing on a sauce covered rib, feeling smarter than ever for not taking Zach's bet. The taste and the texture were doing a good job of making me forget all about pizza. But the wind was irritating the hell out of me.

"It's the Santa Anas," Zach replied, slowly drawing a bone between his lips, licking every last drop of sauce away, and starting a nice little fantasy scene rolling in my mind...

If only we were alone. I'd 'accidentally' dump the extra sauce in my lap. After removing my new jeans, I'd be all dismayed to find that the sauce had soaked through to my skin; I'd have to ask for his help in cleaning up the mess I'd made. I could just imagine how good his lips and tongue, even his teeth, would feel against my tender flesh.

"It tends to make people uptight and edgy," Zach said, sucking noisily. "Lot a fights break out when it blows like that."

I frowned, puzzled. I'd lost my place in the conversation. "What are you talking about?"

"The winds. They're predicting them to last all week. That's why you'll want to be extra careful if you decide to come with me to Zephyr tomorrow night."

"Oh. Okay." I was still feeling confused, but for different reasons now. *If* I came to Zephyr with him? Was there something else he imagined I'd be busy doing tomorrow night? Was he that sure I'd be found before then? Or was this his not-so-subtle way of saying he didn't want me there?

"Are you ready to go?" I asked, although I could tell he wasn't. "Or are you trying to see how long you can stall?"

"Me? Stall?" Zach's eyes widened into an expression of innocent surprise. He scraped another bone through his teeth—even more slowly this time—his lips curving into a wicked smile as he studied my face. "Now, baby, why would I wanna go and do something like that, when I'm looking forward to this even more than you are?"

"You suggested we stop here," I reminded him, feeling even more confused. Since when had he wanted me to win?

"Yeah, I did." He nodded. "But only 'cause I didn't want either of us passing out from hunger before we're done. You have a history of doing that, you know."

"Do I?"

"Mm-hm. Friday night."

"I thought that was because I'd had too much to drink?" Wasn't that what he told me? "Now you're saying it was because I didn't eat enough?"

Zach shrugged. "Too much to drink, too little too eat, who the hell knows? And not that you didn't look real cute all curled up, fast asleep like you were, but, damn, I thought I'd just about die of frustration. I'd rather not do that again, if you don't mind."

"Oh."

"Now come on," he said, smiling as he got to his feet. "If you're all done, let's get going. I can't wait to see what you've got planned for me."

* * * *

True to his word, Zach wasted no time once we returned to his apartment. He was stripped and waiting for me within minutes of our arrival; watching from the bed as I took my time undressing.

Stretched out like he was, naked, with his arms folded behind his head, he would have looked totally relaxed if it weren't for the way his stiff cock bobbed against his belly with every article of clothing I removed.

I pretended not to notice as I took my time undoing the clasp of my bra. I wiggled one shoulder a couple of times until the strap slid partway down my arm. The cup sagged. Zach's cock twitched again. I hid my smile.

"Want some help with that?" he asked hopefully.

I shot him a stern look. "You just stay right where you are and be quiet. I'll deal with you when I'm good and ready."

He raised an eyebrow. An amused smile curved his lips. "Whatever you say."

I released the clasp, but held the bra in place with a hand

against my chest while I slipped first one arm, then the other, free of the straps. When I finally eased the lacy garment away from my breasts it was with excruciating slowness, eliciting a deep, appreciative sigh from Zach, along with a muttered, "Nice."

Gratifying though his admiration was, I managed a reproving frown as I tossed the bra aside. "I thought I told you to be quiet," I said, turning my back to him and starting in on my panties. Still moving at a languid pace I rolled them deliberately down over my butt and then down, down, down my legs, bending slowly forward as I did, giving him a nice view of my ass, smiling at the groan that rumbled up his throat.

I turned my head to look at him over my shoulder. "Oh, you like that?"

He nodded. "Come over here and I'll show you how much."

"All in good time." I rose leisurely back up to my full height, then turned around again to face him once more.

Zach's eyes widened as I planted the sole of one foot on the arm of his chair and splayed my legs wide, in preparation for removing the Ben Wa balls. "I could do that for you," he offered, tilting his head for a better view.

Doing my best to ignore the slick heat his suggestion created, I glared at him coldly. "What part of *keep quiet* didn't you understand?"

"I could use my tongue. I could slip my tongue deep inside your pussy and scoop those balls out one at a time. Slowly. Very slowly. Might take all night."

The idea of that—of his nimble fingers prying my labia apart so that his teasing tongue could lick inside me—released a fresh flood of cream. I ignored it, too. "You're not getting this are you?"

Zach grinned. "Oh, but I'd like to get it. C'mon, give my mouth something to do, that'll keep me quiet."

"I'll think about it," I told him, moving away from the chair, leaving the balls in place for now. "Maybe, if you're good, I'll let you do that as part of your reward."

"Oh, I will," he promised. "I'll be *real* good."

"We'll see about that."

The pretty, new bondage kit he'd bought earlier today— probably when he still thought he'd be tying me up tonight, instead of the other way around—was waiting on the nightstand. "Up until now you've been a very bad boy," I said, picking up one of the creamy white, vanilla silk straps and pulling it so that it snapped.

"And now I'm afraid I'm going to have to punish you."

"Careful," Zach warned, eyes sparkling with amusement. "You could hurt someone with that thing."

I took hold of one of his arms and started winding the silk around his wrist. "Maybe you should have thought about that before you were so naughty."

He snorted with laughter. "So that's what this is supposed to be? Some kind of punishment? Baby, have you got a lot to learn."

"You're not going to take this seriously, are you?" I glanced again at the kit, wondering if it included a gag.

"Sure I will," he replied, still smirking. "I'll take it any way I can get it. Seriously, not seriously..."

"Zach."

"Okay," he sighed. "I'll try and be more serious, if that's what you want. But I gotta warn you, I've never been real good at serious. And this is a side of you I haven't seen before. It might take me a little while to get used to it."

It was a side of me I couldn't remember seeing before, either. But I was liking it a lot. "Don't know me as well as you thought you did, do you?"

"I told you before. Not as well as I'd like to."

I nodded. He *had* said that before. Several times. I was beginning to wonder what he meant by it. "And how well is that?"

He didn't answer for a moment, but as I lifted his arm above his head, leaning forward so I could thread the strap through the headboard, he took his free hand from behind his head and reached out to touch my face.

"Hey!" I reared back, scowling at him with mock annoyance. "Did I say you could move?"

He froze; a slight frown on his face. "Angel, come on, I just..."

"Put your arm back over your head," I ordered. "And leave it there." Was he having second thoughts? Was he going to ask me to stop? Oh, I hoped he wouldn't. If he would just continue to play along, I'd make it good for him, I'd make sure he wasn't disappointed. I held his gaze for a long moment, hoping he could read the silent promise in my eyes.

Sighing, he returned his hand to the bed, but he still looked faintly annoyed. "You're the one who wanted to be serious. You asked me a question. I was trying to answer it."

"Okay, fine." Hiding my relief that he hadn't decided to call a halt to our game, I climbed onto the bed and straddled him;

enjoying the slight heaving of his flanks between my legs, the quivering response of my pussy to the smooth slide of his skin beneath me. I tamped down the urge to rub myself against him and quickly wrapped the loose end of the tie around his other wrist. "So answer, already."

He hesitated, saying nothing at first; and then he shrugged. "As well as you'll let me, I guess."

Which was no kind of answer at all. I knew I shouldn't allow myself to feel disappointed, given everything he'd said last night about not being commitment material, but it was hard not to. It would have been so nice if he could have answered the question directly. But, on the other hand, maybe it was better this way. Maybe this was neither the time nor the place for that kind of discussion.

His wrists secure, I glanced down at his face, wondering how he was taking it. A tiny smile had curved his lips. The expression in his eyes was open, gentle, maybe a little wistful. And trusting.

A lot more trusting than I thought I'd be, if the situation was reversed. And I think that's what did it for me. I felt my heart melt on the spot. I wanted that trust, that openness. I wanted a relationship where that kind of emotion ran deep, and in both directions. The only problem was, I wanted it with Zach.

Unable to stop myself I bent my head and kissed him, reveling in the way he surrendered to me, kissing me back without reservation. Following my lead, his lips parted allowing my tongue access. I cupped his face between my hands and made love to his mouth, immediately regretting that I'd tied him up, missing the feel of his arms around me—and kissing him all the harder because of that.

A few minutes later, a tiny whimper forced its way up my throat and I realized I was losing myself in his kiss. I took stock of the situation. I was stretched out on top of him, pressed chest to chest, my elbows braced on either side of his head, my hands tangled in his hair. His mouth was now as insistent as my own and it was a struggle just to pull back, break off the kiss and grab hold of the headboard.

I was breathing hard as I got my knees under me. Leaning both hands on the headboard I lowered my left breast to within inches of Zach's mouth. "Suck me," I commanded.

A faint flush had stained his cheeks and his eyes were slumberous with heat. He looked at me for a moment, unmoving, and I was just about to repeat the command when his tongue snaked out and lashed my nipple several times before swirling lazily around the swollen peak. It was delicious, but not what I'd asked for—as I was certain he knew. I was just about to complain about his inability to follow direction when his teeth closed gently on my wet flesh, teasing it to new hardness before finally taking it into his mouth. I gritted my own teeth to keep from moaning as I felt the heat travel from tit to clit with lightning speed.

"That's enough," I gasped after no more than a few minutes. "Now the other one."

Speculation gleamed in Zach's eyes when they opened, and he took his time transferring his attentions to my other breast.

My clit was throbbing and I could feel the steady flow of warm juices dribbling out of my pussy—more with every pull of Zach's lips—when I finally made him stop. I was pretty sure he could feel it too; warm and wet, forming a small pool on his midriff where I was pressed against him.

"Now you're gonna get what's coming to you," I whispered in his ear before coasting slowly down his body. I took my time about it; stopping first to suck and tweak his nipples and then, again, to plunge my tongue into his navel; swirling it inside the little crevice in imitation of the way his tongue had teased my nipple. He groaned and arched his back as I moved on, obviously wanting me to continue, but I ignored him and slid between his legs.

"That's better," I murmured as I pushed his legs wide. Lightly, I scored his thighs with my nails. My gaze was locked on his cock, which rose tall and proud from the thatch of sand colored hair. The bead of fluid trembling at the tip had me licking my lips in anticipation.

"You can do more than just look, you know," Zach said, his voice tight.

"I know." Reaching out one finger I trailed my nail along the underside of his shaft, then used the pad of my fingertip to spread the pre-cum over the head of his cock. A second drop oozed out of the tiny slit, and then a third. Zach's gaze was riveted on my finger's progress as it circled around and around.

And then I stopped. Withdrawing my finger, I sucked it into my mouth. "Mmm."

"More," Zach growled, hips straining.

"You better lie still," I admonished. "Or I'll have to tie up your ankles, as well."

Zach tried to laugh, but it ended in a groan. "Would you

please quit fooling around and blow me? Either that or untie me, I'm dying here."

I shook my head. "You don't have much patience for this, do you?" Opening my mouth wide, I leaned in toward him; stopping when I was only inches away. Then I pursed my lips and blew a stream of cool air over the flesh I'd just dampened. "Like that d'you mean?"

"Suck me," he begged. "Fuck me with your mouth, or, shit, fuck me with your hand—fuck me with something—anything you want."

I knew it was mean, but I couldn't stop myself from laughing. "*Anything*, Zach? There's a scary thought." Relenting, I leaned in again, rapidly flicking my tongue back and forth across his frenulum and down his shaft; following the route my nail had sketched there, in reverse; ending at his balls which I sucked gently, one by one, into my mouth. "Still think I have a lot to learn about punishing you?"

"Nothing," Zach half laughed, half groaned again. "Not a thing. You're the Torture Queen. Why don't you let me go now and I'll bow at your feet and worship you?"

"Hmm." I pretended to think about it as I licked my way back up his cock. Bow down and worship me? Yeah, right. More likely he'd throw me down and ram himself into me—not a bad option if he were already wearing a condom but as it was, no freakin' way. "Tempting, but no."

Still, if the rock hard condition of his cock, with its pulsing veins and weeping tip, was any indication, it was time I put him out of his misery. I scooted forward, cupped his balls gently in one hand, wrapped my other hand around the base, and slowly eased his cock into my mouth; sucking deeply, sliding my mouth up and down for several minutes.

Finally, I sat back on my heels. "Where do you want to come?"

His eyes slitted open. "Huh?"

I continued to pump him with my hand as I listed the options. "In my mouth, on my face, on my tits, or do you just want me to hold you and let you spurt all over?"

Eyes glazed, he stared at me uncomprehending for a moment, and then gruffly answered. "Yes."

I blinked in surprise. "Yes, what?" I snapped, the words coming out more sharply than I'd intended. But, come on, the way his balls were drawn so tight I knew the question was about to become moot—and what the hell did 'yes' mean?

"Ah, shit," Zach groaned, a long, tortured sigh. "Yes...*please!*"

Oh. I took him in my mouth quickly; ducking my head, hoping to hide my smile since this was, obviously, no laughing matter. But that *wasn't* the answer I'd been expecting either, and I couldn't *not* laugh.

In no time at all, however, I forgot completely about laughing as Zach went stiff all over and flooded my mouth with hot, salty cum. I continued to suck greedily on his pulsing cock until it finally stopped.

"Mmm," I murmured as I sat up using my tongue first to wipe the last leaking drips from his cock, and then to lick my lips. "Good?"

He nodded, breathing hard. "The best."

Pleased, I slid up alongside him and untied his wrists. I wasn't surprised when he immediately rolled toward me, strap in hand, reaching for my wrist. But I also wasn't in the mood to indulge that particular fantasy right now. "Stop," I said, shaking free of his grasp.

"What?" Zach's eyes widened. "But it's my turn."

I shook my head. "I know. But later, maybe, okay? Right now I just want to hold you."

He paused, eyeing me curiously, looking not at all convinced.

"Please." I laid a hand against his chest and rubbed softly, enjoying the crisp tickle of hair, the warm smoothness of skin, the gentle beating of his heart. "I missed having your arms around me when we kissed. I need to touch you now. I need to feel your skin beneath my fingers when we make love. This was fun, but please..."

Nodding, Zach tossed the strap aside and pulled me close. "You make it hard to argue."

"Good." Smiling, I snuggled against his chest. "Then don't."

"Something else you should know," he whispered as he held me tight. "You're gonna make it damn hard to say good-bye."

Right back atcha, I thought; but I said nothing this time. I just nodded and snuggled closer. Good-bye was the last thing I wanted to think about right now. The very last thing.

Chapter Nine

George

Monday morning found George Valenzuela standing in front of the large, leaded-glass window behind his desk. Staring unseeing at the estate grounds, he let his coffee grow cold while he pondered what his next move should be. His niece was still missing and the reasons for her continued absence remained a mystery. An unpleasant one, at that.

At least she hasn't been kidnapped, he thought, anxiously tapping the toe of one *Berluti* loafer against the plush silk of his *Isfahan* carpet. Despite Richie's claims that April had chosen to stay away as part of some plot against them, George had considered kidnapping to be both the likeliest and the most logical explanation for her disappearance. April was wealthy—thanks to the combined short-sightedness of her father and grandfather—and this would not have been the first time someone had tried to separate her from her wealth. That was not the only reason he'd put off alerting the police to her disappearance, but it was one of them.

Kidnappings had a way of turning ugly when the police got involved. All their petty concerns regarding legalities and procedures tended to interfere with what was, at heart, a simple business transaction; an exchange of currency for... an item of value.

Given their rather single-minded preoccupation with catching and incarcerating anyone they considered to be law-breakers and evil-doers, the police could hardly be trusted—or even expected—to stand by and allow George to deal with the criminals in his own fashion, or to recover his niece on his own terms.

And so he had waited. But two days had passed and no demands for a ransom had arrived. Reluctantly, he scratched kidnapping from the list of possibilities.

"Maybe she's dead," Richie suggested.

George didn't know whether the emotion vibrating in his son's voice was dread or hope. He didn't want to know. Some things were better left a mystery. He shook his head. "I don't think she's dead."

Although logically, in the absence of a ransom note, abduction for some other, even more sinister purpose should be the frontrunner in the possibility stakes, George had reasons of his own for not believing this to be the case.

For the last few nights, his late brother's ghost had haunted his dreams. Surely, if Eduardo's daughter was really dead, his specter would do more than glare balefully at his brother with that scornful look of disapproval George remembered all too well.

"Well, then, where is she?" Richie demanded, sounding angry and scared—two emotions George found most distressful, under the circumstances.

"I don't know," he sighed as he quietly resumed his seat. For a moment, he said nothing more. He studied his son in silence, while absently drumming the fingers of one manicured hand against the olive burl surface of his *Kittinger* desk. It was clearly useless to remind Richie that if he'd done as he'd been told on Friday night, none of this would have happened. Worse than useless. Because now, besides having to determine how best to deal with April's absence, and his own, worsening financial problems, George had also to keep a close eye on his son. If Richie's emotions got the best of him he might say or do something rash or ill-advised; something that would further implicate them in...whatever was going on.

"She can't still be with that... that man," Richie exclaimed. "I mean, can she? Does that seem logical to you?"

"Logical?" George shrugged. Were women ever truly logical? Especially one caught up in the throes of lust? It did seem unlikely, however, particularly in this case. April's taste in men had often struck George as being... regrettable. But, as Richie had pointed out on Saturday, lately she had seemed to have changed her ways.

Even if she were backsliding it did not seem credible she would voluntarily stay gone this long. A night, two nights, certainly. But for his niece to willingly go any longer than that without a change of clothes, without access to her money, without her feather bed, her *Sferra* sheets, seemed very unlikely indeed.

"Perhaps you were mistaken about his identity. Are you sure he was no one... that we would know?" Someone wealthy—that's what he meant to say—someone who traveled in the same social circles as they. Things might be different if that were the case. April might very well be on a yacht right now, or a private island—where she would have no need of clothes or funds or IDs. If her lover were rich enough he'd have his own soft sheets and her temporary lack of the rest would hardly be a cause for concern to either of them.

"I told you," Richie gritted. "He's no one."

"Ah, well, then perhaps she is dead." George squeezed the bridge of his nose and tried to think. Because, if, on the other hand, this man—this mythical guitar player/accomplice/seducer of heiresses whom Richie insisted had captivated April and spirited her away—was not rich, then April would have surely returned by now. April's less savory assignations seldom lasted longer than a single night, after all, and generally left her in the same, foul mood: edgy, angry, depressed, frustrated. And even more bitchy than usual.

And, if that's the case, if she is dead because of that, then it's your fault, Eduardo, not mine, George addressed his brother silently. *It was you who spoiled the girl, after her mother died. You made her what she is. Was. No, is!*

"No." Richie shook his head vehemently. "No, you're right. She's not dead. She just wants us to think that. She's playing with us."

George looked at his son wearily. "How, *mi hijo?* How is she playing? She is doing *nothing.* That is not playing. That is..."

"It is, I tell you. Why else would that bartender have claimed to know nothing about the man she was with? I offered him five hundred dollars last night, for information, and he turned me down. First he claimed he hadn't worked on Friday—which I'm almost sure is a lie. Next he told me the guitarist that night had been a last minute replacement—that he was from out-of-town and had already returned to Canada. That he'd been paid in cash. That no one knew who he was, where he was, how to reach him. April's behind this. She must be. She's hiding on purpose—to make us wonder."

"Perhaps you're right," George murmured, not really believing it for an instant. One thing was certain. Richie could not withstand police questioning at this point. So however he dealt with this, George knew he could not let on that April's absence was anything other than voluntary and easily explainable.

There had to be some other way to deal with this; a way to flush April, or her abductors, if that was the case, out of hiding.

"What if we leaked word of this to the media?" George said, thinking aloud. "We could claim she's become infatuated with some man we hardly know. That she's run off because I would not approve of him. We could tell them she's eloped with this man who, we believe, is only after her money."

"Are you crazy?" Richie stared at him in alarm. "Do you know how fucking pissed she'll be if you do something like that?"

George frowned. "Richie, please, your language." But then he nodded and allowed himself a small smile because, yes, he knew just how 'pissed' and embarrassed and humiliated his niece would be by such a story. The last thing April wanted was to look like a naive, gullible fool. "She will be very angry, I'm sure. Angry enough to return and put all the rumors to rest."

Richie's eyes grew wide. "You're right. This could work."

George nodded again. "It had better." Because, if it didn't, he had no idea what to do next.

Chapter Ten

April

Zach was tense and quiet Monday morning. There were no jokes, no games, no breakfast in bed. Distant and preoccupied, he didn't even look particularly happy to see me. Was it the wind? Was it grating on his nerves, as it was on mine? Or was it something else?

Maybe he'd had bad dreams. Mine had been unsettling, filled with people I didn't know, places I'd never seen, but which, for all of that, still seemed totally familiar.

Maybe sharing his space with someone else was wearing on him, though it sure hadn't seemed to bother him last night, when we had made love again and again. I'd dressed in the clothes I'd been wearing Friday night, wanting to look as much like myself as possible for our visit to the police station, then I took a long look around the apartment, wondering if it was the last time I'd ever see it. Turning back, I caught such a look of apprehension on Zach's face, it left me stunned. Was he that afraid he'd never get rid of me? Perhaps, despite all his brave words on Saturday, he was more worried then he'd let on that I wouldn't be claimed anytime soon.

That still seemed like the best guess. When we left the police station, just before noon, after a very unproductive visit. Zach appeared even more thoughtful, more quiet. It had to be disappointment, didn't it? Because, contrary to his earlier assurances my absence wouldn't go unnoticed for long, it seemed nobody had missed me yet.

"Maybe no one wants me back," I joked as we stood in the parking lot by his bike. Sure, I wasn't too happy about the lack of progress either, but, at that particular moment, what I wanted most of all was to lighten the mood between us. I wanted to tease at least one small smile onto Zach's face.

Frowning, he turned to me. "What?"

I shrugged. "Yeah, you know. Maybe, wherever I'm supposed to be, they've noticed I'm missing and they're thinking, 'thank God!'."

Well, I got my smile then, but it was not what I expected. Sweet and tender it only seemed to magnify the sadness in his eyes. When he reached for me, my first instinct was to push him away. I didn't want or need sympathy—it was about time I started standing on my own two feet. The last thing I needed was to become any more dependent than I already was on the warmth of his embrace.

"No one would ever say that," Zach murmured softly, pulling me close, stroking my hair, sending a shiver of longing running through me. "It's still early, we'll check back later, if you want. Plus they have my number—they'll call if anything comes up. And there could be tons of reasons why no one's reported you missing yet. Maybe you're supposed to be on vacation this week, or something. Don't worry, things will work out."

That was easy to say, but who was he kidding? He had to realize, just as I did, that we couldn't go on like this forever. One way or another, I'd have to make some hard decisions soon. This illusion of *belonging*—always stronger when he held me like this— only made things more difficult. It made me too reluctant to leave, made it all too easy not to think about the future, or to think of anything that lay beyond the circle of his arms.

Forcing a smile, I eased myself away from him. "Do I look worried? I just want to know where you're taking me for lunch. What's a good 'C' food, anyway?"

And with that, the last wisp of Zach's smile faded from his eyes. Frowning again, he sighed. "Actually, I have to work this afternoon. Just for a few hours but... will you be all right at home by yourself? We can stop for a burger, or something, on the way back, if you're hungry, but then I have to go. I'll make it up to you tonight. I'll buy you some chocolates. Or maybe we can have Chinese for dinner."

My heart clutched—either at his casual reference to *home*, or at the realization that he really *didn't* want me going with him to the bar. "You're working now? I thought you didn't have to be at Zephyr 'til later?"

"I don't." Zach looked puzzled for a moment, then his face cleared. "I'm *playing* there tonight. This afternoon I'm doing a job for Tony's uncle."

"Oh." There really didn't seem anything else to say, so I nodded. "Okay, sure. Let's go."

* * * *

We stopped in the lobby of Zach's apartment building so he could check his mail. On our way to the elevators, he glanced through the windows and abruptly changed course.

"Where are we going?" I asked as he grabbed my hand and headed for the glass doors leading to the courtyard.

"Shh," he cautioned, mischief gleaming in his eyes. "Quiet. There's someone I want you to meet."

The courtyard was deserted, except for a lone blonde, seated at the edge of the pool. Zach dropped my hand and crept noiselessly up behind her.

"Watch out!" he shouted, grabbing hold of her shoulders and giving them a shake.

"Zach!" she shrieked, arms flailing. "Shit. What are you doing?"

Laughing, he leaned over and kissed her cheek. "Just checking up on you. Making sure your heart's getting a regular work-out. How're you doin' today, Mama?"

Mama? What's up with that? Whoever this girl was she was certainly *not* old enough to be called Mama—not by Zach, anyhow.

"I was doing just fine until you scared the crap out of me," she grumbled, sounding not all that upset as she pushed the hair out of her face. Smiling, she half turned to face him and I got my first good look at the swell of her belly. Suddenly, calling her Mama made perfect sense, she was significantly pregnant. "What's got into you all of a sudden, anyway?" Her blue eyes slid past him, widening as they focused on me. A look of purely feminine speculation sharpened her features. "Oh. Hi."

"Gabby, this is Angel," Zach said gesturing at me but not, as he had done when I met Tony, using the introduction as an excuse to draw me close.

"Ohhh." Gabby's smile widened into a knowing grin as she extended her hand. "Right. Aphrodisiac girl. Nice to meet you."

"You too," I replied, my eyes widening a little at my new nickname. I recognized her name, too, from yesterday's conversation. I couldn't help but wonder how much Zach had told her about me.

Gabby's gaze swept over me curiously, stalling when it reached my feet. "Oh, hey, now those are some *seriously* great slingbacks. *Ferragamo*, right?"

"Oh, I uh, I guess," I stammered, staring cluelessly at my feet.

"Trust you to know that, Gabe," Zach chuckled. "Not every woman is as obsessed with footwear as you are."

Gabby shot him a withering look. "Sure they are. They just don't admit it. Besides, those stacked cork heels are practically a signature." She turned back to me with a comradely smile. "Am I right?"

Before I had the chance to mumble something incoherent, Zach jumped into the conversation again. "So, how's Derek doing these days?" he asked. "He still taking care of that foot fetish for you?"

Gabby gaped in surprise. "Yes, thank you, he is." Blushing prettily, she dropped her gaze and fell silent, paddling her feet in the water, staring at her pink-polished toes. I'd caught just a glimpse of her face before she'd ducked her head. A tiny smile curled her lips. She had the happy look of someone recalling slightly guilty pleasures.

My gaze darted back to Zach's face. He was wearing his own happily reminiscent expression too—minus the guilt. "Glad to hear it," he murmured softly, his eyes trained on her feet as well. I'm not sure if it was shock or stubbornness that kept me locked in place, that kept me from giving into the urge to tiptoe quietly away, and leave the two of them to their memories.

Finally Zach stirred and something seemed to harden in his gaze. He turned his attention back to me. "Okay, well, I have to go to work now. Are you coming upstairs or do you want to hang out down here for a while?"

"Oh, stay here," Gabby urged, smiling warmly. "We'll have some girl talk."

Which meant she'd grill me about Zach, I surmised. Still, that could work both ways. There was a lot I'd like to know, too. "Okay," I agreed slowly. "That sounds like fun."

"You have everything you need?" Zach asked.

He'd already given me his spare key and I couldn't think of anything else—other than the obvious. Money. A memory. A plan for the future. "I think so."

"Good." He was still smiling, but there was a tenseness in his jaw, a bleakness in his eyes that had me unsettled. Something fluttered in my midsection—a sensation like butterflies, only colder.

I nodded, wordlessly.

"Okay, then." Zach shrugged. "So... I guess I'll be going." He reached out a hand and I thought he meant to draw me in for a kiss, but he merely skimmed his fingers lightly down my arm, then turned and left, walking quickly across the courtyard.

I watched him go, feeling lonely and lost, then turned back to Gabby, surprised to find her watching me with a look of shrewd assessment in her narrowed eyes.

"Zach's a great guy," she said after a moment, her voice oddly insistent, defensive, and just a little colder than before. "A real sweetheart."

I nodded again. "I know." Feeling as if I needed to reassure her about something, I tried to smile, but the sense of isolation that had gripped me made that impossible. Why did I feel like neither Zach or Gabby was saying what they really meant today? It was as if the whole world was suddenly united in a conspiracy to keep secrets from me.

* * * *

"So how long were you and Gabby together?" I asked Zach later that evening as we were in the elevator heading down to the garage where his bike was parked.

He glanced at me, his expression curious. "Is that what you two talked about? Why? What'd she say?"

"Nothing. She didn't have to. You think I didn't see the way you two looked at each other? Not to mention that whole foot fetish nonsense."

"Nonsense, is it?" A wicked smile lit up his face. "Just wait 'til we get to 'F'. Could be you'll end up with a foot fetish, too."

I snorted. "*If* we get to 'F' you mean. I might decide to call it quits at 'D'."

"D?" Zach stared at me in surprise. "Why D?"

I shrugged. "Why not D?" D stood for domination, after all, and I could see us playing that game for a good, long time.

"Hmph." Frowning, Zach leaned back against the wall of the elevator, his hands shoved deep into the pockets of his jacket as he lapsed into a thoughtful silence.

And now, it was my turn to be surprised. Was it my imagination or had the temperature just dropped by several degrees?

The car stopped, the door slid open and Zach pushed away from the wall exiting the elevator without a glance in my direction.

"So?" I asked again, following him out of the elevator. The patter of footsteps echoed off the cement walls of the parking garage as I hurried to keep up. "Are you going to tell me? How long were you two together?"

"Not long," he answered, not bothering to turn around. "A couple of days."

Just like us. Feeling the cold flutter of wings in my stomach once more, I wrapped my sweater more tightly around me. Maybe *a couple of days* was all the shelf life any woman had with him. "How come?" Stung, curious, I had to know: "Were you in-between relationships then, too?"

"*I* was. Unfortunately, *she* wasn't."

"Oh." I supposed the fact that he could remain friends with a former lover, especially one who'd clearly hurt him, should be encouraging, but it wasn't really; not when I couldn't see myself taking things in such casual stride.

As he bent over the bike to unlock the helmets, I sneaked a peek at his face. He looked grim, distant. It suddenly occurred to me that perhaps I'd been reading him all wrong. If his current expression was anything to judge by, I'd been treading on sensitive ground.

"Sorry," I mumbled, embarrassed by my lack of tact. "I didn't mean to pry. I didn't realize it was a touchy subject."

"It's not," he said, his voice clipped and cold. But he tossed the helmet at me, whereas before he'd always put it in my hands, and once we were both seated on the bike he took off without a backwards glance, where up until now he'd always checked first, to see that I was ready. And I couldn't help but think that, *yes, damn it, it is*: a lot more touchy than he wanted to let on.

* * * *

Other than being noisier and more crowded than it had been Saturday morning, Zephyr was pretty much as I remembered it, which would have been a comfort if it weren't for the look I got from Tony when we arrived.

He'd returned Zach's greeting with a casual nod, but then his gaze zeroed in on me. His eyes narrowed, their expression dark, appraising, glacially cold. I glanced at Zach, curious to see what he made of the change, but he gave no indication that he'd noticed anything amiss.

At least *his* mood had improved on the ride over. I was as grateful for that as I was for the arm he kept wrapped around my shoulders, and his steady stream of banter, as he introduced me to the other band members—all of whom, it seemed, remembered me very well from Friday night.

Up until then, I had never questioned that it would be nice to remember some of what I'd done here that first night, but after a few minutes of good natured teasing I was beginning to wonder if I wasn't better off not knowing.

"Come on over here, Angel," Zach said, finally, placing a hand on my back and guiding me away toward the tables, "we've got to get started now, so why don't you take a seat?"

I dug in my heels when I saw where he was leading me—to the same overly-bright table where we'd sat Saturday morning. "No, not here. Please. Let me find someplace less noticeable."

"Come on," he urged. "It'll be okay. I want you to sit here. I have a surprise for you and I want to be able to see your face."

A surprise? Yeah, I'll bet. What was he planning on doing to me tonight? I could feel my stomach bottom out with nerves and I gazed at him, appealingly, thinking, *please, Zach. No more games.* But there was neither malice or mischief in his eyes and I wanted to be able to trust him, as he'd trusted me last night, so, reluctantly, I agreed.

"Great." Kissing me swiftly on the cheek, he peeled off his leather jacket and dropped it on the back of an empty chair. "And, listen, go ahead and order whatever you want to drink. Just tell Tony to put it on my tab."

Tony? I glanced back toward the bar, caught a glimpse of the big man's forbidding demeanor and knew there wasn't a chance in hell I'd be asking him for anything tonight. Turning back to Zach I flashed my brightest smile. "Don't worry about me. I'll be fine."

My resolve not to drink anything lasted through the band's first set. It wasn't all that hard, really. To be honest, I found it difficult to think of anything but Zach. He looked god-like in the spotlight; lean and muscular in snug jeans and a T-shirt that did nothing to hide any of what nature had given him.

Any woman could be excused for drooling over that, I thought. But, it was worse for me. Because as good as he looked up there on that stage, I couldn't stop picturing him naked. In bed. In me.

As well as on me, under me, and in every other way that I could imagine having him!

It could have been the effect of his music again, I suppose, but I don't think it was. He could have been playing air guitar and his hands would still be making my skin itch with the need to feel them all over me once again.

Caught up in the rhythm, I leaned my elbows on the table and rocked in my seat; my legs pressed tight together, to ease the throbbing of my clit; my arms pressed even tighter against my tingling nipples.

I wished like hell I'd thought to bring the Ben Wa balls with me tonight.

When the band stopped for a break, Zach hopped off the

stage and headed in my direction. My stomach flipped at the sight of him coming toward me, a wicked sparkle in his eyes, and in the back of my mind something shifted, flickered, nudged. It was nothing so clear as a memory, just a vague, vague feeling of familiarity. Or maybe I was imagining it. Maybe it was just anticipation I was feeling.

"So? What'd you think?" he asked brushing a quick kiss on my lips before dropping into the chair beside me.

"Awesome. You guys are great."

Soon the rest of the guys had pulled up chairs and joined us, bringing mugs of beer and plates full of food. Nachos might not begin with a 'C', but, being mostly chips, I decided to let it count. In any case, they were good; hot and spicy, temptingly delicious.

They were, however, not half as delicious as it felt to sit next to Zach; with his arm stretched casually across the back of my chair, with his fingers tangling idly in my hair, or tracing random, abstract patterns on my back. And nowhere near as hot and tempted as I got whenever he turned that slow, sweet smile of his in my direction. As badly as I wanted to jump his bones, right then and there, I figured it for a good thing I wasn't drinking tonight, even though I took a lot of kidding about that fact. I guess everyone thought I was abstaining in reaction to Friday.

When the band went back on stage they left their glasses and a large portion of nachos behind. Between the fragrance of the beer and the saltiness of the chips, I soon had a raging thirst.

I fought it for as long as I could, but it wasn't going to go away on its own and not even drooling over Zach was going to be enough to wet my throat now. Finally, I turned in my seat and glanced at the bar. Tony was chatting with several customers and though it was a little hard to be certain from this distance, there didn't appear to be anything particularly ominous about his expression. Since no one else had mentioned anything about him being in a weird mood I was beginning to think perhaps I'd been imagining the whole thing.

Deciding to risk it, I made my way over to the bar. Tony took one look in my direction and his expression frosted over. Obviously, I'd been right the first time.

"Can I help you with something?" he asked coldly.

"C-could I get an, an ale, please?" I stammered.

He nodded once, then went back to his conversation, leaving me waiting for over a minute before deliberately—and very slowly—working his way over to where I stood.

His expression grim, he leaned into the bar, rested his arms on the shiny surface and fixed me with a steely gaze. I dug my nails into my fists and resisted the urge to back away.

"So, your name's Angel—isn't that what Zach said?"

I nodded, surprised as much by his question as I was by his tone.

"Just wanted to make sure I had that straight." He glanced towards the stage, then back at me. "So, tell me something, Angel, what are you doing with my boy Zach anyway?"

Doing with him? "I-I don't know," I answered, stammering again. "I'm not sure what you mean."

Tony studied my face for a moment. "Zach's a good guy," he said at last, which sounded so eerily like what Gabby had told me earlier today that it left me mentally shaking my head at the irony. For a woman with very few memories I was racking up an awful lot of *been here, done this* moments.

"A real good guy," Tony continued. "But, sometimes, he rushes into things without thinking them all the way through. He gets in over his head, hooks up with the wrong people. That's a good way to get yourself in trouble, especially a guy like him. Know what I mean?"

I shook my head.

He sighed. "Look, Zach and me are like family, and I don't like it when people try and take advantage of my family."

I felt my eyes widen. "You think *I'm* taking advantage of Zach?"

Tony said nothing, just looked at me as if he thought I was stupid.

"I'm not. I, I wouldn't. I just..." I glanced towards the stage, gaze softening as my eyes focused on Zach. "He's helping me out of a jam, that's all. *I'm* the one who's in trouble. I—I don't know how I'd have made it through the weekend without him." I didn't know how I'd make it through tomorrow without him, either. Or any day in the future.

Shit. Maybe Tony had a point; I *was* stupid. If anyone was in something over their heads, it was me.

Sighing, I turned back to Tony. He studied my face for another moment and then nodded. "You know something? You're all right."

Startled, I watched as he turned and took a pint glass down from the shelf behind him. He poured out an ale, and then slid the glass across the bar to me. "You said an ale, right?"

I nodded, licking my lips as the thirst I'd almost forgotten about returned. I had said ale and I really, really wanted this one, but I was a little reluctant to touch the glass just yet. "Zach said to put it on his tab," I told him, cringing a little inside as I waited for his response.

"Oh, he did, huh?" Tony snorted, shaking his head. "Nice try, sweetheart, but I don't think so." Then he smiled. "Your drinks are on me tonight. You tell him I said that."

"Thanks, Tony," I said, feeling unexpectedly touched; but still confused as hell, and emotionally wrung out by our encounter. I took a sip. It tasted as good as I remembered, maybe even a little better, on account of my thirst. I still didn't understand what Tony thought I'd planned on doing to Zach, but considering how suspicious he'd seemed of me initially, I was surprised at how quickly he'd appeared to change his mind about it.

"You better get back to your seat now," Tony said with a nod of his head. "I think he's looking for you."

I glanced around, surprised to realize the music had stopped. Zach was standing in front of the microphone, scanning the room. He smiled when his eyes found me.

"This is gonna be our last song," he announced as I threaded my way across the room toward my table. "This is 'Lucky', by Melissa Etheridge, and I'd like to dedicate it to a very special lady who just happens to be here with me tonight."

Heart pounding, I sat down quickly, afraid my knees might give way. I glanced up at the stage, and found myself staring straight into Zach's eyes. Heat flared in my cheeks when he winked at me. His mouth curved up in a small smile as he said, "This is for you, Angel."

I took a quick sip of beer, then I held my breath, not knowing what to expect. As the band started playing I kept my gaze glued to Zach's face. His dimple re-surfaced as he started to sing and, after that, I couldn't have taken my eyes off him if I tried.

I didn't know what he was trying to say with the song. Did he mean it to be about me? Or about him? Maybe he wasn't saying anything at all; maybe he just liked the song. But, it didn't matter. All I know is when he hit the line in the chorus that goes, '*I want to ride with my Angel and live shockingly*,' I suddenly knew that's what I wanted, as well; to ride with Zach as far as I could, as far as he'd let me.

I found myself almost hoping I never found out about my

old life. What if it was filled with people I'd have to go back to? Maybe there was a reason why I couldn't remember anything—a good reason, one I'd never even considered until now. Maybe I'd forgotten it all on purpose.

At the moment, I was almost willing to bet that was the case. I was almost ready to wipe the past clean, stop searching for answers, look at tomorrow as the beginning of a whole new life. Almost.

Was that shocking? I couldn't tell, but, even more important, I didn't care.

This time, I was on my feet as soon as the music ended. By the time Zach hopped off the stage I was right there to meet him.

I looped my arms around his neck and gave him a big hug. "Thank you."

Chuckling, he hugged me back. "Does this mean you've changed your mind about quitting at D?"

D? I pulled pack to look at him. Forget D, I wanted to skip straight to Z. Z for Zach. I already knew how I felt about him, but there was still so much more I wanted to explore. "Take me home," I told him, smiling into those shining green eyes. "And let's see how lucky we get."

Chapter Eleven

The wind was rattling the windows when I woke up Tuesday morning. Eyes squeezed shut, I groaned as the noise pulled me from a peaceful sleep. I slid my hand across to Zach's side of the bed surprised and disappointed to find it empty. *Where has he gone*, I wondered, stretching a little on the cool sheets. I loved the delicious ache in all my muscles, the faint pulsing in my sex. The flood of hot memories from last night made my nipples peak and caused me to shudder with remembered pleasure. *When's he coming back?*

I pulled a pillow over my head, in an attempt to drown out the noise, and let my mind drift back to last night...

We couldn't find a Chinese restaurant that was still open, so Zach took me to Canters, instead, and ordered me a Chinese Chicken Salad from a surprisingly rude waitress. It was good, I guess, but I barely tasted it. As I shoveled it into my mouth, all I could think about was getting done, getting out of there, getting back to Zach's apartment. I couldn't wait to get naked with him again; to feel his body pressed against mine, skin to skin.

"You're awfully quiet tonight," he observed between bites of his Reuben sandwich. "How come?"

I looked at him, startled. I was just about to protest that it wasn't so, when it occurred to me that maybe he was right. "Sorry. I guess I've just been thinking about stuff."

He cocked his head to the side and looked at me curiously "What kind of stuff?"

Stuff like getting you into bed again. Like fucking you so good, you beg me to spend the rest of my life with you.

Definitely not the kind of thing you said to someone who was commitment-phobic. I pushed my plate away. "I don't know." I shrugged. "Look, I'm tired. Can we just go back to your place now?" Suddenly, I could no longer bear to sit there with the width of the table between us, I needed to wrap myself around him, to hold him close and never let go.

"Don't worry so much about it," he murmured, surprising me with the seriousness of his tone.

"What?"

"I know you're disappointed we haven't learned anything yet, but it won't be much longer. I promise."

"Zach, you can't possibly promise something like that," I pointed out, wondering what he'd say if I told him what I was really worried about—about losing this, us, him, when I learned about my past life. Because that's what it

seemed like it was now—another lifetime, something I'd outgrown, or no longer fit into.

And maybe it really was. Maybe I'd died when I hit my head that night, maybe I wasn't meant to remember what had gone before, or maybe... maybe I was just deluding myself. About everything.

"You're right," Zach sighed. "I can't promise that. But I can promise that it will be okay. Whatever happens, we'll deal with it. We'll just take things one day at a time. I just don't..."

He broke off then, but I could guess what he was thinking. He probably didn't want to think about the future any more than I did.

"Look, I don't want to talk about this now either. Can we just go home please?"

The rattling of the wind shook me back to the present. It was even louder now, interspersed with an odd, prolonged buzzing. It took a long, long moment before I recognized it for what it really was; the sound of someone pounding on Zach's front door and ringing his bell.

Maybe he's locked himself out? Jumping out of bed, I grabbed the pink robe I'd almost come to think of as mine, and raced to let him in. My eyes widened when I looked through the peek hole and saw who was standing there.

"Gabby, hi. What're you doing here?"

"Have you seen it?" she demanded as she stormed into the apartment. "Turn on the TV."

I followed her into the living room. She looked flushed, furious, and I couldn't understand the look she'd just given me. I glanced down at myself, and then at her, taking note of her height, her build, her coloring, comparing it with the robe I was wearing. *Hers?*

"I can't believe this shit," she muttered grabbing the TV control and quickly punching buttons. A perky blonde newscaster appeared on the screen wearing a too-somber expression, one she didn't come close to pulling off. Gabby dropped onto the couch. I sank down beside her, still trying to wake up properly, reluctantly turning my attention to whatever the blonde on TV had to say.

"Sources close to the reclusive heiress' family say April Valenzuela was last seen Friday night with a man described only as a drifter. Amid rumors of a weekend wedding, the family is reportedly very anxious to discover the young woman's whereabouts.

"'They just want to know that she's all right,' a spokesman for the

family said, '*that she hasn't been harmed in any way and that she's in no immediate danger.*'

"Although very few details have yet to be released, kidnapping has not been ruled out. According to reports, her family had previously received information suggesting April's companion has a history of mental illness, drug abuse and violence.

"The heiress, described by relatives as somewhat sheltered and naive, left the Bel Aire mansion where she lives with her uncle and cousin, sometime Friday evening, after they'd urged her to end the affair with the as yet unnamed man.

"This isn't the first time fortune hunters have tried to get their hands on the Valenzuela estate, the same source claims, citing another such attempt earlier this year..."

The screen abruptly went black as Gabby savagely punched the controls again. "Well?" she demanded turning to face me. "Did you know about this? Did you know what they were going to say? What the hell do you think you're doing?"

"I don't understand," I said, feeling mystified. Obviously, Gabby was upset and, given her condition, it couldn't be good for her to be getting this worked up. But, what did she want me to say? What did any of this have to do with me?

"That's *Zach* they're talking about," she snapped. "Zach, a fortune hunter! Of all the ridiculous— And, mental illness? Violence? Please, like he'd ever hurt a fly."

"Gabby, how could they be talking about Zach? Zach's been here with me all weekend, how could he be off getting married to some... some idiot on TV?"

For a moment, Gabby's eyes bulged like they were getting ready to pop right out of her head. "Because *you're* the idiot."

"Excuse me?"

"You. You're her—April Valenzuela." She took a deep breath and then continued, speaking slowly, clearly, angrily. "Sheltered innocent. Self described idiot. Heir to... some sort of empire, apparently. With a mansion in Bel Aire, a family of morons, millions—or maybe billions—of dollars, and a hell of a lot of nerve to sit here acting so damn dumb. You're not even blonde!"

"Impossible," I whispered. "Why would you think that?"

"Didn't you see the picture?"

I shook my head. "No. What picture?"

Grumbling something beneath her breath, Gabby snapped the TV back on, flipping quickly through the channels 'til she found what she wanted. "There. See that? Now what do you have to say for yourself?"

I stared at the screen. Different blonde, same story with one crucial difference. In the upper right-hand corner of the screen there was a photo of a somewhat sullen, unhappy looking woman. *Me?* I felt the blood rush to my face. "I-I don't understand."

"What's not to understand, *April?*" Gabby's voice dripped with disdain. "Your family's bad mouthing Zach—who hasn't done *anything* to deserve it, by the way—all over the air waves. And what I want to know is, what are you going to do about it?"

I have no idea what answer I would have made, but the rattle of a key in the lock caught our attention, had us turning our heads in tandem to face the door. "Hey," Zach greeted us, smile fading, eyebrows rising as his gaze shifted back and forth between us. "What's up? Is everything okay?"

"You tell him," Gabby whispered fiercely, pushing herself off the couch. "And you *fix* this."

"I was just leaving," she told Zach as she crossed to the door. She rested a hand on his arm. "Call me if you need to talk," she urged quietly. Then she was gone.

Zach shook his head as he set the paper bag he'd been carrying down on the table. "This pregnancy is playing hell with her moods," he said as he came and sat on the couch beside me. "What's she worked up about this time?"

Hardly aware of what I was doing, I gestured at the screen where the story was being repeated. "Did you know about this?"

"Know about what?" he asked as he turned his attention toward the TV. His eyebrows rose. "Hey, that's you!" Then his mouth fell open, his eyes widened further, the color drained from his face. "Holy shit."

I felt sick. "Excuse me," I murmured as I fled to the bathroom. "I have to get out of here."

* * * *

With shaking hands I splashed cold water on my face, then stared at myself in the mirror. I guess I was in shock because, for the life of me, I couldn't figure out how I was feeling. I had a name now—it meant nothing to me. I had a family, a home to go back to, and a whole lot of money. All good things, under normal circumstances. But finding out about it like this only left me with more questions than I'd had before.

Not wanting to look at myself in that robe anymore, I

dressed quickly, and rejoined Zach in the living room.

He hadn't moved from the couch. He looked up at me when I entered the room. There was an odd look on his face. Cold, distant, suspicious, subdued, I didn't know what to make of it, but it stopped me in my tracks.

"Don't look at me like that," I pleaded.

"Like what?" he asked in a voice that perfectly matched his expression—I hated them both.

"Like you don't know who I am."

Zach shrugged. "Obviously I don't."

"Yes, you do," I said, starting towards him again, but my steps ground to a halt again when he leaped from the couch and stalked to the window, putting even more space between us.

"Oh, please. *'Do you know about this?'*" Turning, he practically spat the words at me. "Why would you ask me something like that? What the hell is that supposed to mean?"

I blinked in surprise. "I d-don't know." It was the same question Gabby had asked me and, frankly, I didn't know what either of us had meant by it—probably nothing. It was just something to say. I knew he didn't know about it. He couldn't possibly have known unless... unless he had. Unless the TV was right and he *was* just after my money.

Was it possible? I hated the idea, but I had to admit that, on some level, it resonated with me, almost as if it wasn't the first time I'd had the thought. It made sense, didn't it? At the moment, it felt like the only thing that did.

Suddenly, all the conversations I'd had in the last few days came back to haunt me. *Zach's a good guy*—that's what everyone had insisted—but one who made bad decisions from time to time, who got into trouble when he trusted the wrong people, who jumped into situations without thinking them through.

But why the insistence? It was obvious, wasn't it? So then why had they tried so hard to convince me?

I remembered the sneer in Tony's voice last night, "*So, your name's Angel—isn't that what Zach said?*"

No wonder he'd looked at me as if I was stupid because, no, actually, it wasn't my name, after all! "Why'd you tell everyone my name was Angel?" I blurted.

"Because that's what *you* told me it was."

"But, why? Why would I do that?"

Zach threw his hands in the air. "Why ask me? How would I know what you're thinking? Maybe you wanted to go slumming.

Maybe this weekend was your idea of a joke. Maybe you never had a problem with your memory at all."

Well, that was ridiculous. Besides, this weekend had been *his* idea, hadn't it? I'd opened my mouth to tell him just that when another memory surfaced.

"Any messages?" I recalled Zach asking Tony on Saturday, and, *"Not for anyone named Angel,"* he'd replied. I felt my stomach lurch again.

Had there been messages left for someone else—for April, perhaps? If only Zach had asked who the messages had been left for—but maybe he didn't want to. Maybe he already knew.

Had it all been a scam? All of it?

"Tell me you really didn't know who I was all along," I begged. "Tell me you're just as surprised by all of this as I am."

"Surprised?" Zach shook his head. "Baby, I think I left surprised outside in the hallway somewhere. I can't fucking believe any of this shit."

Which wasn't, *"Yes, of course, I'm surprised."* Which wasn't, *"I swear I didn't know."* I had asked a simple enough question, I thought. Why couldn't he give me a straightforward answer? Unless he just didn't want to.

"Maybe you should go now," he said quietly.

"Go? Go where?"

"Go home. Isn't that what you've been whining about all weekend? No point in hanging around here any more, now that you know where you belong. Besides, I wouldn't want anyone to think I was holding you against your will."

"But, how? I don't know where it is. I..."

"I'm sure the police can help you out, or the TV station. Hell, just take a cab. You're a celebrity, April. They probably have your address on one of those maps they sell to tourists."

"That's not funny," I snapped, feeling more frightened than I had any time since Saturday. I still didn't know who I was, now Zach was a stranger, as well. "And, even if you're right, just how do you expect me to pay for this cab? I still don't have any money, you know."

"Oh, right." Shaking his head, Zach reached into his pocket and took out his wallet. "And isn't that a joke? Shit, and they say *I'm* the one who likes to play games."

Too stunned to react, I watched in disbelief as he counted out several twenties.

"Here," he said, holding them out to me. "Take it all. This should be enough to get you wherever you need to go."

I shook my head. "Stop it, Zach. I don't..."

"What's the matter?" he asked, grabbing hold of my wrist, pushing the money into my palm, closing my fingers around it. Forcing me to take it. Forcing me to leave. "Afraid I can't afford it? Well, hell, don't start worrying about me now, I'll be fine."

"Since when was *that* ever a question?" I snapped, scowling furiously as I pulled my wrist from his grasp.

He didn't even answer, just turned his face away. I stood there for an instant longer, waiting; feeling even more like an idiot—what did I expect him to say, after all? What did I imagine he was going to do? Change his mind, beg me to stay?

I think we both knew that would never happen.

I shoved the money he'd given me into my jeans pocket, turned and left, pausing only to grab my jacket from the hook by the door.

I didn't even care that I was leaving the rest of my stuff behind—the clothes I'd been wearing Friday night, the *Ferragamo* shoes Gabby had admired so much. There was only one thing I was leaving that meant anything to me, only one thing that mattered.

No, I thought angrily, *scratch that*. I wasn't leaving anything behind. Not anything at all.

Chapter Twelve

Zach

Zach had turned away from April, so he wouldn't have to watch as she walked away, but the slamming of his front door hit him like a fist.

"Fuck," he muttered as his shoulders sagged and he felt the anger he'd been using to console himself waver. He fisted his hands again, hurriedly pushing back the despair that threatened to overtake him, closing his ears to the urging of his heart which was telling him to go after her. *What the hell for?*

His eyes fell on the small, paper bag he'd brought home with him. Snatching it up he turned and flung it, as hard as he could, at the door. It connected with a satisfying smash and he smiled grimly at the thought of the contents shattering, irreparably, into crumbs, into dust, into garbage. *Another fucking waste.*

Good. It served him right for being so stupid. He only wished they'd cost more. He deserved to lose a whole lot more than the small amount he'd spent on a pint of chocolate covered fortune cookies with custom fortunes tucked inside: *You are special. You are beautiful. You are sexy. You are unpredictable. You are breathtaking. You are inspiring. You are loved.*

Those were just some of the fortunes he'd had printed; all variations on the same basic theme, except for one. The last one. Wrapped separately in cellophane, that one was still secure, for now, in his pocket. Its message destined to go unread forever: *Stay with me?*

"Stay with me. Riiiight. You dumb ass. Maybe she'll give up her mansion and move in here." Sighing, he sat down on his couch, pulled the cookie from his pocket, looked at it for a moment, and then tucked it back away. He knew he should go ahead and toss it. And he would. He'd get around to it. Sometime. He just didn't have the heart to do it now.

"Fuck," he muttered again, resting his elbows on his knees and fisting his hands in his hair. He could not believe how she'd managed to get to him in such a short time—just a handful of days. Hardly any longer than his affair with Gabby had lasted, and yet the aftermath couldn't have been more different.

He and Gabby had separated with no hurt feelings on either

side. Watching April walk away shouldn't have been any more painful. But it was. Oh, God, was it painful.

He'd been so sure yesterday morning that the police would have information and that she'd be gone before noon—whisked away by friends or family.

When that hadn't happened, he'd been embarrassed by how relieved he felt. He could tell how disappointed she was, even though she had tried to pass it off with a joke. *Maybe they don't want me back.*

Yeah, right. It sure looked that way now, didn't it?

Four days—that's how long he'd known her—less than four days, really. That was nothing. But no matter how he tried to convince himself of that, his heart knew otherwise and it wouldn't be fooled.

He thought of all the stern lectures he'd given himself over the last few days; all the warnings. Damn it, he should have known better. Come to think of it, she'd warned him too, hadn't she? *"Who says we'll get to F? Maybe I'll quit at D."* Except she hadn't even waited for D. She'd quit a whole day early.

Lifting his head, Zach stared into space for several seconds, recalling all the things he had planned, all the things they'd never get to do now. Maybe it was just as well she was gone already. Hell, it had to be, didn't it? If it was this hard now, what would four weeks have been like? Or four months? Better not to know. Much better.

He took a deep breath, sat up straight and nodded to himself. There were a lot of questions in his mind—thoughts of what he could have done differently, and whether any of it would have mattered—but he wouldn't think about that now. None of it made a difference anyway. Sooner or later she would have gone. So it was sooner. So what?

Whenever she'd left, it would have been the same. He'd still have been stuck with the problem of having to get over her. And he would. He'd get over her because he had to. What other choice was there?

Chapter Thirteen

April

Whoever said 'you can't go home again' obviously never lived in Bel Aire. Going home was surprisingly easy. Everyone was amazingly eager to help me, once I told them my name. By mid-afternoon I was back where I belonged, in the house I'd inherited from my grandfather, the house I'd grown up in—or so I'd been told.

I wish I could have said it looked familiar, but it didn't. The most I could say for it was that it didn't look *un*familiar, in the sense that I didn't find myself thinking 'this can't be right'.

No, it all felt *right* enough I suppose. It just didn't feel like home.

"So, you're saying you can't remember anything that happened Friday night?" the man who'd identified himself as my cousin Richie asked—for what had to be the third or fourth time. "Nothing at all?"

"Stop badgering your cousin," Richie's father—my Uncle George, apparently—snapped at his son. "She's already answered that, hasn't she?" We were seated in George's office—a room so large Zach's whole apartment could almost have fit inside it.

I glanced at my cousin wearily. "Not Friday night, and nothing before Friday night. I don't remember anything before Saturday morning."

"That's not right," Richie muttered, fisting and unfisting his hands on the arms of his chair. "That can't be right. Have you seen a doctor? What did the police say about it?"

"Enough!" George slammed his palm against the desktop, making us both jump. Then he turned to me, smiling gently. "Perhaps, if you're still not feeling well tomorrow, we'll call the doctor and..."

"No." I shook my head. "No doctors."

"Just to make sure you're all right," George said soothingly.

"I'm fine," I told him. "Really."

"Fine?" Richie glared. "How can you be fine? What makes you think you even know what fine is? This is a disaster!"

"Richie!" George glared at his son, then turned again to me. "I'm sure you *are* fine, April. But, just the same, you must have questions about your condition—as do we all. And we still need to make certain you haven't been... harmed in any way."

Harmed. What did they think had happened to me? I felt a twinge of conscience remembering the anger in Gabby's eyes this morning. This was about Zach, wasn't it? "Uncle George, you have to do something. That stuff they said on TV, about Zach—They have to take it back. They have to tell everyone they made a mistake."

"Zach?" Richie glanced back and forth between his father and me, his expression mystified. "TV? What's she talking about?"

"My dear girl." George's smile was tight, grim, ironic. "What is it you expect me to do? You overestimate my influence with the press if you think I can get them to run some kind of retraction."

"Retraction?" Richie frowned at his father. "What are you talking about? *Who* are you talking about?" This time, we both ignored him.

"But that's not fair!" I said, leaning forward angrily, digging my nails into the arms of my chair, not caring if I scarred the surface. It was my chair, wasn't it? "They can't just say things like that—that he was after my money, or that he's violent or-It isn't true!"

"How do you know that?" George asked, tempering his challenge with a small smile. "Because he told you so?"

"Yes. And because I trust him." Why hadn't I told *him* that, I wondered, remembering the angry look in Zach's eyes this morning. Would it have made a difference if I had? Or would we still have been over?

"Am I talking to myself?" Richie growled, throwing his hands in the air. "Trust who, damn it?"

"Zach," I murmured, to quiet him down, then cringed at the sound of George's soft laughter.

"Trust? Some stranger you can't even remember meeting? A man who claims to have picked you up in a bar? While you were drunk? The kind of man who would take advantage of a girl with no memory?"

"He didn't take advantage of me," I insisted. "He was only trying to help."

George shook his head sadly. "My dear, I'm afraid you still have a lot to learn about the ways of the world. It's very lucky you found your way home to us before anything more serious happened to you."

Richie heaved a deep sigh. "Who is Zach?"

"No one," I said, heart breaking at the lie. "A-a friend." Then I raised my eyes to meet my uncle's gaze, daring him to disagree. But he didn't have to say a word. His smile said it all and I found myself, suddenly, closer to tears than I'd been all week. "I'm tired. Can someone please tell me where my room is?"

"Of course," my uncle said smoothly. "I'll call one of the maids to take you there."

"No," Richie said, getting to his feet. "I'll show her where it is."

"Richie," his father said, warningly. "Not a word."

Richie shook his head. "I know. I won't say anything to upset her."

"Thanks." I smiled gratefully at my cousin and stood, allowing him to take hold of my elbow and guide me out of the room.

"So, tell me something," Richie said, as he led me up the stairs. "This man you keep talking about—Zach—what does he look like?"

I thought about that as we climbed the stairs, as we headed down the upstairs hallway. How does one answer a question like that? Simply cataloguing his features wouldn't do it. There were so many things I could have said, yet none of them seemed right.

"I don't know," I said, finally, when he paused outside a door I could only assume led to my bedroom. I looked up at Richie and shrugged. "Like an angel," I told him at last. "He looks like an angel."

Richie sighed. "Well, that's helpful," he murmured as he pushed the door open.

"No, it really isn't," I agreed, but then I stopped, too surprised to continue. The room before me was lovely, but impossibly big; more like a whole apartment, really—less a kitchen. There was a bed, a couch, a couple of chairs, a fireplace, a desk... "This is all mine?" I asked, taking a few steps into the room and gazing around.

Richie gave an angry sounding snort and muttered something beneath his breath. I turned and eyed him questioningly. "Yes," he snapped. "All yours. Just like everything else."

Embarrassed, I turned away again. I made a show of exploring my surroundings, pretending to take no notice of the way my cousin continued to stand in the doorway, watching me coldly.

"You don't like me very much, do you?" I finally gathered the courage to ask.

"That's not—I didn't—I wouldn't say that."

No, I thought. *Maybe not to my face. But it's true just the same.* "Why? Am I hard to get along with?"

Richie shrugged. "How am I supposed to answer that?"

"Honestly?"

"You're my cousin. We're family. But... yeah, sure, you could say that, I guess. Who isn't difficult some of the time? Runs in the family, right?"

"I wouldn't know. Does it?"

"Look, it's just... well, things lately..." He stopped again, running his fingers through his hair. "It's been an adjustment, that's all. For all of us. And everyone... everyone probably did stuff they'd rather not remember, or think too much about. Why don't we just leave it at that, all right?"

I wished I could. But I couldn't leave it at that. There was too much I needed to know. I opened the drawer in the table next to my bed, spotted the large box of condoms and a new thought occurred. "Do I have a boyfriend?"

"Good question," Richie responded. "Why don't you tell me?"

I frowned at him crossly. "Because I can't. I don't remember."

He looked indecisive, as if he wanted to say something, but didn't know how. Maybe it wasn't that he was keeping things from me. He'd promised his father he wouldn't say anything to upset me. Maybe this was a touchy subject?

"Please," I said quietly. "I just need to know."

For a moment, Richie's face lost the guarded look he always seemed to wear. He looked at me... almost sadly. "You don't tell us everything, you know. But, as far as I'm aware of... no. Not currently."

"Right," I sighed as I closed the drawer. I wasn't sure if I was relieved...or even more depressed. "So, what was he like then?"

"What was who like?"

"The boyfriend I don't have anymore."

"I don't know," Richie replied wearily. I looked at him in surprise. "*They* never stuck around long enough for me to get to know any of them."

Well, that was something to think about, wasn't it? Maybe Zach and I both had commitment issues. Or maybe I was only attracted to men with really short attention spans. "How come?"

"Because your taste in men sucks. Because they were only after one thing."

"Sex?"

"No. Money."

"Even better." I could not believe how badly I'd messed up. Still, at least now I knew where the idea that Zach was after my money had come from. "Could you leave me alone now? I'm not feeling very well."

"Why don't you take a bath?" Richie suggested. "You always said they made you feel better."

"Okay." *I liked baths. Good to know.* "Maybe I will."

"Good." Richie paused for a moment, with his hand on the door knob, studying me uncertainly. "What really happened to you this weekend?" he asked at last. "You seem... different."

I looked at him curiously. "Different? How?"

"I don't know. Weird. Softer. More like you used to be. Not such a..." He stopped suddenly, looking uncomfortable, looking guilty.

"Go on," I prompted.

"Look," he blurted at last. "I'm sorry, okay? About...well, about everything. No matter what you did, or how you acted, you still didn't... well, you didn't deserve this. You know?"

I didn't know. And I couldn't even guess what he was talking about. But, right now, it didn't even matter. I was too tired, too depressed. I just wanted to be alone. "Yeah," I murmured softly. "I know."

* * * *

I'd only taken showers at Zach's place, so I hadn't realized how much I missed baths. My muscles were certainly remembering it now. As I lay submerged up to my neck in the softly roiling water of my very own whirlpool tub, my muscles were remembering it, loving it, and trying their damnedest to dissolve into mush, I think. Too bad my mind wasn't as easily distracted.

An angel. Why had I said that? What did it even mean? I couldn't ignore the coincidence that it was what Zach had called me, too. Maybe...

Somewhere in the back of my mind a thought struggled to take flight... but then it was gone again, shot down by the depressing realization that maybe no one would ever call me Angel again. That maybe no one would ever sing to me again, either, or

163

look at me the way Zach had, his sea green eyes flashing heat.

I wanted to scream at life's unfairness. Here I'd finally met a man who wasn't after my money... and I'd accused him of it anyway. *Brilliant job, April. Way to go.*

I closed my eyes and tried to clear my mind, tried to focus on the jets of water pummeling my flesh. But memories of Zach's face kept intruding. The tub was as big as the bed we'd shared these last few nights, how I wished he was here to share this bath with me now.

Thoughts of his wicked smile made my pussy throb and I slid one hand between my legs to rub my aching clit; all the while remembering last Saturday, in his bathroom, when I'd played with myself for him. I remembered how his eyes had held mine in the mirror, and all the hot words that fell from his lips...

I'm gonna take your clit between my lips and suck....I'm gonna stick my tongue deep in your creaming, hot hole and lap up all your juices...

It wasn't long before I'd brought myself to climax, hot cum mixing with the cooling water, tears leaking from my eyes because he wasn't here to hold me through the after-shocks.

I climbed from the tub and wrapped myself in one of the fluffy white bath sheets that were stacked on the shelf. Then I padded back into my bedroom and curled up, just as I was—damp, drained, disappointed—on the soft, cotton sheets.

It wasn't that late, but I was exhausted both physically and mentally by the events of the day and I couldn't bear the thought of staying awake another hour. Even so, I did think, briefly, about getting up and going downstairs, about finding something to eat. But how could I even know what I wanted, without Zach there to make suggestions?

In the end, I just piled all the pillows in the center of the bed and nestled my back against them, pretending it wasn't just me here tonight, pretending I was back where I really belonged. Then I closed my eyes and fell into a dream...

Chapter Fourteen

I dreamed I was at Zephyr again, sitting at the same table I always seemed to wind up at, watching Zach play.

"Who do you think you're looking at?" my cousin Richie inquired, sounding annoyed.

"That's Zach," I said as I turned to face him.

"Don't be ridiculous." Richie pushed a glass across the table toward me. "You don't know who anyone is. Now, finish your drink and let's go. It's time you went home."

"But I don't want to go home," I told him as I picked up the glass. "I want to stay here. With Zach."

"Finish your drink," Richie repeated as I put the glass to my lips. "I don't even know who you're talking about."

Suddenly there was a roaring in my ears as Zach leaped from the stage and lunged at me. "Noooo," he yelled as he grabbed my shoulders and pushed me backwards. "Don't drink that! Don't you know it's been poisoned?"

I awoke with a start, heart pounding, surprised to find myself lying on my back in bed. It was daylight. Outside my windows, tree branches, whipped by the wind, swayed back and forth. It took me a while to get my bearings.

I looked around. My room looked just as it had the day before; still furnished with the same massive, white-painted, gold trimmed furniture—tables, dressers, armoire, desk—along with the gold-and-blue upholstered couch and chairs that matched both the bedding and the drapes that I'd forgotten to draw across my windows. I felt like I was looking at everything through two sets of eyes—neither of which were in focus.

I knew my name, but it still meant nothing. I knew where I was, but it still didn't feel like home. I knew I missed Zach, and I wondered how many days would have to pass before he wasn't the first thing on my mind when I opened my eyes in the morning, or the last thing I thought about before falling asleep.

Too depressed to even think about taking another bath, I got dressed and went downstairs, following the scent of coffee until I found my way into the dining room.

"How are you feeling this morning?" my uncle greeted me from the end of the table. "Did you sleep well?"

I shrugged as I took my place along one of the table's long

sides, across from my cousin. "I guess."

"I'm sure it must have been a relief, wasn't it, to be back in your own bed again?"

"Yeah," I sighed. "A relief." A maid in a crisply starched, peach and white uniform poured coffee into my waiting cup. "Thank you," I murmured, smiling gratefully. *I have maids. Amazing. I guess I really do own people.*

I sipped my coffee for a minute or so, while I tried to decide what I felt like eating. Finally I gave up. I looked up again, glancing at my family as I asked. "What do I like for breakfast?"

Richie put down the newspaper he'd been hiding behind and frowned at me. "You still can't remember anything?"

I shook my head.

His mouth compressed. He looked at his father, then back at me. "Eat some toast," he said, at last, reaching for a basket piled high with toast points and various pastries, and shoving it across the table.

"I spoke to the head gardener for you this morning, April," my uncle said. "Apparently, one of the trees on the east side of the estate was badly damaged by the winds. He's going to have to remove several limbs, but if the damage is severe enough, I think it might be better to take it down altogether."

I nodded, took a bite of toast, thought about that. *I have trees and a head gardener now too? Well, yay, me.* "Whatever."

Silence settled over the table and it occurred to me I wasn't acting very nicely. It was probably the wind that was making me so grumpy, but still—I glanced up at my uncle and smiled apologetically. "Sorry, Uncle George. Thank you for all your help."

"You're welcome," he replied, inclining his head. He gazed at me for a moment, his eyes hooded. Then he stood. "I'll leave you to your breakfast."

I watched him go, then turned back to find Richie eyeing me suspiciously.

"Something wrong?" I asked, but he just shook his head and retreated behind his paper once more.

I sighed. Maybe he thought I was acting weird again. Maybe I was. I felt weird. That much was certain. I glanced at the glass of orange juice that had been set beside my plate, recognizing it from Saturday, when Zach had ordered it at *Gladstone's*. At the time, I hadn't wanted to try it, now I wondered what it would taste like. Would I like it? Would it remind me of Zach? *Doesn't everything?* I took a tiny sip and almost gagged.

Hurriedly, I returned the glass to the table, feeling like my lips had been burned. It wasn't that it tasted bad, exactly, but it left me with an unpleasant feeling in the back of my mind. I could feel my heart skipping uneasily in my chest. Like an echo of the panic I'd felt in my dream.

"Did your orange juice taste all right?" I asked Richie, whose own glass was empty.

He stared at me over the top of his paper. "What did you say?"

I pointed at his glass. "Your orange juice. Did you notice anything funny about the taste of it?"

He stared at me for another moment, color flared on his cheeks then he ducked behind his paper again. "No. It tasted fine."

I propped my elbows on the table, wondering what to do next. Not surprisingly, my thoughts circled back to Zach. I needed closure, I decided at last. The way it had ended was wrong. All wrong. I couldn't leave things like that, could I? I didn't want there to be bad feelings between us. I had to do...something. Before I could put this past weekend behind me, I had to find some way to settle things, to make things right.

"How much do you suppose it costs to support someone?" I asked Richie. Paying Zach back for all the money he'd laid out wouldn't be enough, of course, but it was a good place to start.

Richie lowered the paper more slowly this time. "What are you talking about? Support who? Where? Are you talking about an... institution of some sort?"

"No, nothing like that," I said. "I'm just curious. If you were going to put someone up for a few days, if you had to pay for all their meals and buy them clothes, entertain them—how much would you be likely to spend?"

"Clothes? What kind of clothes?" Richie's eyes narrowed suspiciously again. "Work clothes? Uniforms? Are you sure you're not talking about... about incarcerating someone?"

"No! Of course not. Just... I don't know. A couple of outfits. Nothing fancy. Just... some pants, dresses, shoes—that sort of thing."

"How many days?" Richie asked still looking uncomfortable. "And where, exactly, would they be staying?"

"Four days. And, just...never mind where; it doesn't matter. Pretend it's here."

"Okay." He studied me in silence and then asked, "One

person? What about food? Are you eating all your meals out...or in?"

"Out."

"For four days?"

I nodded.

"Good food?"

"Very good."

"Drinks too?"

"Yes."

Richie shrugged. "Five thousand?"

"Five thousand dollars?" I thought about that. Considering I had millions—or more—that didn't sound like very much. "Is that all?"

"Maybe a little more. Why?"

"No reason," I said, taking refuge in my coffee cup. I didn't want to tell him what I was planning. This was between me and Zach, after all. "Do I have a checkbook?"

"Sure." Richie replied, frowning suspiciously again. "Upstairs in your room. In your desk."

"Great." I downed my coffee and stood. "Thanks Richie."

* * * *

I found the checkbook, right where Richie had said it would be, along with stationery printed with my name and address. Perfect. I wrote the check out quickly then glanced around.

My jacket was still on the chair where I'd dropped it the day before. My hands were shaking as I unzipped the pocket. What if I'd lost the paper with Zach's address on it? What if it was no longer there?

I knew there were other ways I could locate him—I could always go to Zephyr, for example, and face Tony down again—but, all the same, I breathed a sigh of relief when my hand closed around the paper. *Yes!* It would be so much better this way. Easier. Simpler. Quicker.

I wrote Zach's name and address on the envelope and sealed it. Then I headed downstairs, almost running into Richie who was crossing the foyer.

"How can I get something delivered to someone?" I asked him.

"What are you up to?" He reached for the envelope, but I held it away from him. "Come on, let me see that. What are you doing? Who are you sending things to? I thought you couldn't remember anything?"

"I can't," I told him. "This is something different. It's private. It's nothing you need to know about. I just need to get it delivered today."

"Would you like me to call a messenger for you, Miss April?" the maid who'd served me coffee this morning asked.

"Yes," I said, sighing in relief as I shoved the envelope into her hands. "Thank you. Right away, please."

Richie and I watched as she hurried away, taking the envelope with her. "I don't know what game you're playing," Richie muttered angrily.

"I'm not," I said, shaking my head. "I'm not playing any games." I was just trying to find a way to make things right. The question was, would it work?

Chapter Fifteen

Zach

Zach groaned softly. The beeping of his microwave sounded excruciatingly loud this morning. His head was pounding. He'd had too much to drink last night, now he was paying the price for it.

He opened the microwave, wincing a little as his hand closed around the hot porcelain of his coffee mug. It wasn't supposed to be hot, but it was. The coffee wasn't supposed to taste so bitter, either, but it did.

Nothing was supposed to be the way it was this morning—it was all supposed to have looked better, to have felt better. He was supposed to be over her by now, to have put it all behind him. But he hadn't put anything behind him and as for being over her—he wasn't even close.

It had occurred to him, somewhere in the middle of the long, sleepless night, that maybe he'd been overly hasty in sending her away. Maybe if he'd sat down with her, instead, and explained how he felt—But could he convince her that he'd felt that way all along? Or would she insist that it was only her money he was interested in?

His doorbell rang suddenly and he jumped, spilling coffee on his hand. Maybe she'd come back? Maybe it had all been a mistake? He felt his hopes rise and his heart speed up, and cursed himself for being such an asshole. He knew better than to get his hopes up, didn't he?

"Can I help you?" he asked as he opened the door.

"Delivery. Sign here." The messenger replied in disinterested tones.

Sighing, Zach scribbled his name on the receipt. His eyes widened in wonder, however, when he caught sight of the return address. Maybe he hadn't been wrong after all? Shoving the door closed with his foot, Zach peeled open the envelope, aware that his mouth had gone dry.

A single slip of paper fell out and fluttered to the floor. He picked it up, turned it over and felt his mouth drop open, felt his heart falter in his chest. His head began to pound in earnest as he felt his blood pressure spike.

"Fuck, fuck, fuck, fuck, *fuck*!" Disbelief knifed through him. He crumpled the envelope in his fist, feeling impotent, hollow, furious. He closed his eyes, leaned his head back against the wall and growled. "Sonofabitch. You gotta be kidding me."

Chapter Sixteen

April

I don't know what I'd been expecting. Probably that Zach would call right away. He didn't, of course. It could be he was out and just hadn't gotten my check yet. Or maybe he had and he just didn't care.

I couldn't decide what to do next. Should I call him, just to let him know that I'd been thinking about him? That seemed fairly pathetic. Besides, the fact that I'd remembered my promise to repay him was proof of that, wasn't it?

I wandered around the house, feeling restless, listless and bored. It was a large, rambling, hacienda of a place; two story with a stucco facade and a ceramic tile roof. The long drive leading up to the house was bordered by terraced gardens on either side, and bisected by fountains and a reflecting pool. There was a garage, of course, set discreetly around toward the back, yet a couple of cars had been left parked in the front courtyard, as though on display—among them the Porsche with which Richie had picked me up from the police station.

It was a nice place—don't get me wrong. I wasn't complaining. It's just that my head was starting to hurt from all the tears I wouldn't cry. Cry? Now? After all the times this weekend that I'd whined about going home? I don't think so.

I was lucky to be here, and I knew it. But, at the moment, I'd still have traded it all away to be back in Zach's bed. He'd been right all along. Last weekend had been the chance of a lifetime. Now it was over.

I finally curled up on a sofa—one of several—in a room overlooking the back lawn, picked up a magazine and tried to read. I told myself I wasn't listening for the sound of his bike roaring up the driveway—but who was I kidding? Not that it made any difference what I told myself. The glass in the windows was so thick, I couldn't even hear the wind.

"Miss April?" one of the maids addressed me, tentatively.

I lifted my head. "Yes?" One of these days I was going to have to re-learn their names. And maybe see if I couldn't convince them to call me something else.

"Your uncle asked me to let you know that he's expecting a visitor, soon, to see you."

"To see me?" Zach?

The maid nodded. "If you'd like to join them in his office, he and your cousin are waiting for you."

"Of course." I threw down the magazine and raced from the room. My steps sounded loud on the marble floor of the foyer, but not as loud as the beating of my heart.

I pushed the door open and glanced around the room still holding my breath in anticipation, hopes dimming when I realized that George and Richie were the room's only occupants.

"Ah, April, there you are," my uncle smiled genially at me. "Come in. Close the door."

"What's going on?" I asked, closing the door behind me and then leaning my back against it, reluctant to move any farther into the room. My gaze traveled back and forth between George, seated at his desk, and Richie, standing by the window looking out. "You said someone's coming to see me? Who?"

"Now, now, don't be upset," George replied soothingly. "We just need to talk about some things, that's all." Then he gestured at the two chairs arrayed in front of his desk. "Here. Sit. Please."

"I don't want to sit," I protested, still keeping my back glued to the door—staying as close to the exit as I could get. Is it just me, or is there something inherently upsetting about being told *not* to be upset? "What's happening? Talk about what? Who's coming to see me?"

"Look," Richie turned suddenly to glare at me. "Why don't you just go over there and sign the papers, April, okay? Trust me, you'll save yourself a lot of trouble that way."

Confused, I transferred my gaze to my cousin. "What papers? Who's coming?"

"A doctor. All right? That's who's coming. He's called a doctor for you. Is that what you want?"

A doctor? Oh, hell, no. "Uncle George, I told you. I *don't* want to see a doctor."

George held up a hand. "I merely asked a friend of mine..." he began, breaking off to glare reprovingly at his son. "Who, yes, happens to be a doctor—if he wouldn't mind stopping by today to talk to you, April, that's all. And, perhaps, to... prescribe some medication. For your nerves."

"No." I shook my head, still trying to make sense of things. "My nerves are fine. It's just—What papers?"

George sighed. "April, you must realize that you're not quite...

173

yourself... at the moment. And yet this estate needs to be maintained, does it not? There are bills to be paid, decisions to be made and, frankly, my dear, I'm not so certain that you're qualified, right now, to make them."

"Go on," I said cautiously. So far, he hadn't said anything I didn't agree with. Make decisions regarding this house, when I could barely determine what I wanted to eat? No, I wasn't qualified for that.

"So, in view of that, I've had our lawyers draw up some papers today granting me temporary power of attorney."

"That's it?" I asked. "Those are the papers you want me to sign?"

"Yes," George replied quietly. "It's nothing more alarming than that."

I nodded. "Okay. That sounds reasonable enough." Just then, the sound of someone pounding loudly and insistently on the front door filtered into the room. "But no doctors," I added, quickly. "And no meds, Uncle George. I don't want..."

Out in the foyer, a voice was raised. A loud, familiar voice. I stopped in mid sentence to listen.

"Where is she? I want to see her. Now!"

Zach? Breathless with anticipation, I turned, pulled the door behind me open and stuck my head out into the foyer. "What are you doing here?"

At the sound of my voice, Zach left off arguing with the maid who'd opened the door for him and glared in my direction. For a moment, relief mingled with the anger on his face. Then the anger won. "There you are. I need to talk to you."

Since *what are you doing here* had to rank among the world's stupidest questions to ask just then, I wasn't surprised that he'd ignored it.

"April?" my uncle inquired. "What's going on? Who's here?"

"Just give me a minute, Uncle George," I said as I stepped into the foyer. "I'll be right back." Closing the door on my uncle and cousin, I turned to face Zach who was striding across the foyer, unzipping his leather jacket along the way.

"What in the hell is this?" he demanded, thrusting his hand into the inside pocket of his jacket and pulling out the check I'd sent him just that morning. Another great question. One I couldn't imagine he was expecting an answer to, either.

"What's the matter? It's not enough?"

"Enough?" Zach's mouth dropped open. I watched in

surprise as he skidded to a stop right in front of me. "Enough for *what?*"

God, he was gorgeous. It was all I could do to control my elation at seeing him again. But he was angry, I had to focus on that. Smiling was clearly not indicated. "I-I told you the other day that I wanted to pay you back for the clothes you bought me and... and... everything. And, well, you said that was okay, didn't you?"

"Clothes?" Zach's voice rose an octave. "This—This...is...for *clothes?* I bought you a pair of jeans! And, and sneakers and a couple of shirts."

I nodded. "And some underwear. I know. I was there. Isn't it enough?"

"Oh, jeez." Zach's eyes fell shut for an instant. Leaning the heel of one hand on the door frame, almost as though he needed support, he shook his head. "Yes, it's enough. It's about *ten times* enough."

"Oh." Crap. I felt my cheeks flush as I stared at him, horrified. Had I just made things worse? "I-I didn't know."

"Yeah." A small, small smile curved his lips. But at least it *was* a smile. "I got that. I guess I shoulda figured it out sooner, huh?" He held the check out to me. "Baby, I can't take this."

I nodded, taking the check from his hands, knowing better than to ask him if I could give him one for a smaller amount. Not now. Not when I'd already insulted him once. "I'm sorry," I whispered, biting my lip and trying not to cry. This was *not* how things were supposed to turn out.

"Me, too," he murmured, leaning toward me; fingers toying with a strand of my hair, knuckles brushing against my face. I tried to resist the urge to rest my cheek against his hand, but I couldn't quite.

"I didn't mean what I said yesterday," I told him, meeting his gaze again. "I know you didn't know about... any of this. I was just surprised and, and, and..."

"Shh." He laid a finger against my lips. "I know. I'm sorry too. I should have been a whole lot nicer about everything." He glanced around. "But I guess you made it home okay, huh?"

I nodded.

Regret seemed to gleam in his eyes. "Yeah." He sighed again and straightened up. "Well. I better go."

"What?" I stared at him, dismayed.

He gestured at the check in my hand. "That's all I really came here for; to give you that back. So... now that I have... I should leave."

"But why?" I whispered, reaching out a trembling hand to just touch the front of his jacket, all the while trying my damnedest to think up some excuse, anything that I could say to make him stay. "Why now? Why..."

"Because." He still had one hand clenched on the door jam and his gaze was focused on my mouth. Regret burned even brighter in his eyes. He shook his head. "I want to kiss you so badly right now that if I stay even another five minutes, I won't be able to help myself."

"Oh." I reached for him with both hands then. My fingers tightened on the leather of his jacket and I smiled. "Well, in that case, I guess you'll have to stay *at least* five minutes, won't you?"

His answering smile was sweet but sad. "Will I?"

"Yes. Please?" I closed my eyes as he leaned in close, sighing in relief as his lips brushed mine. I slid my arms around his neck, loving the way he held me, his fingers splayed on my back, urging me closer.

Just one hand, though. His other hand stayed where it had been all along, clutching the molding that surrounded the door; as though he were holding a part of himself in check. But why?

It took me a moment to make the connection. It was the commitment thing, wasn't it? It had to be. And it was hard to be angry or fault him too much for that. Not when he'd made himself clear, right from the start. I didn't have to like it much, but I did have to respect it.

"Mm, nice," I murmured, as I pulled away ending the kiss before either of us were ready.

Zach sighed heavily as he opened his eyes. "Okay. Now I *really* have to leave."

"I know." At least we'd opened the door, we'd broken the ice, and maybe—

"You could call me up sometime, you know," Zach suggested. "I mean, if you wanted to. And we could, maybe, I dunno... get together, do something fun?"

I smiled. "I'd like that."

"Good." He dropped his hand from the doorframe then, and smiled. "You take care of yourself." Then he turned and walked away.

I watched him go, taking deep breaths so I wouldn't do anything stupid—like run after him, or call him back, or just burst into tears. It would be okay. I would call him. He'd *asked* me to call him. He *wanted* me to call.

"Or, you know what," he said, stopping suddenly and pivoting back to face me. "You left a lot of stuff back at my place. I could maybe pack it up and bring it over here sometime. If that's okay with you?"

Yes! "Sure," I said, smiling widely. "Whenever you want. That would be great." He could come here. To this house. Where my uncle and cousin and a thousand maids would be looking on. Where we would never be alone. Where I could never tell him how I felt and we could be just as stilted and awkward and stiff with each other as we were right now. "Or maybe I can pick them up at your place? I could come over sometime, when you're not too busy and..." And maybe spend the night?

"Yeah." Zach nodded, smiling back at me—just as if the same thought had occurred to him too. "Good idea. We can do that." Then his gaze shifted. He glanced at the foyer around us, his smile fading. He shook his head. "No, we can't."

I felt my heart skip a beat. "What?"

"Look around you," he said spreading his arms. "This is never gonna work out. One of these days you're gonna regain your memory, and then you'll figure out that you don't belong with me. Then what'll I do, huh? Forget it. It's better to end it now."

No, no, no. I stared at him in dismay. *No, please...* "It's just a house, Zach."

"Yeah." He nodded. "You're right. It's just a house. And you're just a girl, I'm just a guy and all this stuff..." He glanced around again. "Is a whole lot bigger than both of us."

I shrugged, trying to make a joke of it. Trying to make it *not* be happening, *not* be real. "It wouldn't be much of a house, would it, if it wasn't just a little bit bigger than the people who have to fit inside it."

Zach smiled. "True."

I held my breath for a moment, hoping—

But then he shook his head. "Good-bye, April. It's been fun."

Then he turned and left. For real this time.

I had time to draw just one shaky breath before the door to my uncle's office swung open. *Oh, hell. Not now!* I bit my lip, dug my nails into my palms, and did everything else I could think of to keep myself from crying or screaming...or maybe hurting someone. I wanted to hurt someone. I wanted the whole world to hurt as much as I did right now. Except for Zach.

"April?" My uncle's voice held only the thinnest pretense of patience. "We're waiting."

"Coming," I replied, swallowing my anger, avoiding his eyes, as I slipped past him and into the office. I crossed to one of the chairs George had indicated earlier and sat down, ignoring the wary look of alarm on Richie's face.

"Okay, what am I signing?" I sighed as I picked up the papers that had been laid out on the desk. I took another deep breath and began to read. I didn't get very far; the words kept trying to swim off the page. After spending several minutes trying to get past the first page, I gave up. Not that it mattered. I'd read enough.

"Maybe we can do this tomorrow?" I suggested as I put the document back on the desk and massaged my aching temples. It was all too much to deal with, at the moment, and it hurt too much to think. I felt trapped; like I was in a hole that I'd never, ever be able to dig out of.

"Richie. Get your cousin a drink," my uncle ordered.

"What?" Richie stared at his father in alarm. "Why? She said she'd sign them tomorrow. What's the rush?"

"Please. Just some water, maybe?" I murmured, feeling frightened. Would another day really make a difference? Would tomorrow be any better than today? Would the next day? Or any day from now until... forever?

Still grumbling Richie crossed to the sideboard and splashed some water into a glass. "Here." Returning, he slammed the tumbler down on the desk in front of me, glaring at his father as he did so. "Water. Just water."

I was reaching for the glass when the office door burst open. Startled, I spun around to face it. Zach filled the doorway. He was breathing hard, looking twice as angry as he had before. "You're back," I gasped, not caring for any of that, hardly daring to believe my eyes.

"Whose Porsche is that in the driveway?" he demanded.

"Papa, call the police!" Richie urged, sidling towards the French doors that led out to the terrace. "Hurry!"

"No," I said as I scrambled out of my chair. "It's all right, Uncle George. We don't need the police." I felt almost speechless with surprise. Hope fluttered to life once again as I gazed at Zach. Had he changed his mind? "What are you doing here? I thought you'd left?"

"I did. I mean, I was," Zach replied, sounding distracted. "But then I saw that car and, and..." He broke off as his gaze zeroed in on Richie. "Wait a minute, I *know* you. You're the jerk who tried to run us down!"

"What?" Eyes bulging nearly out of his head, George froze. He put the phone back down and glared at his son. "Richie? What's he talking about?"

Richie squirmed. "It's nothing, Papa."

"Nothing? Bullshit." Zach took hold of my shoulders. "Listen to me. I know what I saw. That car outside is the same one that nearly hit us in the alley behind Zephyr Friday night."

"Richie?" George demanded again, still staring at Richie as if he'd never seen him before. "Are you insane? When were you going to tell me about this?"

Zach nodded at Richie. "He was there, April. At Zephyr. That's the guy you were with. The same guy who was driving the car. I knew he looked familiar at the time, I just never put two and two together until now."

"It was an accident," Richie insisted, spreading his hands wide, gazing at me appealingly. "My foot slipped. I panicked."

"I'll bet," Zach growled, his eyes still sparking fury.

"What else might you have neglected to mention about that night?" George asked coldly.

"What?" Richie turned and glared back at his father. "Oh, no, you don't. You are *not* making this my fault. This whole mess was your plan—not mine."

"Plan?" I mumbled, feeling shocked, confused and lost...or almost lost. Now that Zach was here everything seemed so much more manageable, somehow—even a mess like this.

"Oh, fuck, no." Zach's arms closed protectively around me. "That's it. We're getting out of here. I'm taking you home with me now."

"Wait." I patted his chest soothingly. "Hold on. Not yet." As wonderful as the idea of going home with him sounded, this was my life we were talking about and I'd lost almost a week of it already. It was time I took control of the situation.

"Wait for *what?*" Zach loosened his hold on me to point at my cousin. "Baby, that bastard tried to *kill* you! And I'll bet anything these two are to blame for your memory loss. What'd you do?" he jeered at Richie. "You slip something into her drink? That's it, isn't it?"

Richie blanched. He glanced first at his father and then at me.

"It wasn't supposed to be like this. It was only supposed to last a little while."

"A little while?" Zach's jaw clenched. "I'll show you a little while, you son of a bitch."

"Stop!" I ordered. "Let me think."

"What's there to think about? Call the police—just like he wanted. I bet they'll be very interested in all of this."

"In all of what?" George murmured softly. "It would be just your word against ours, you know."

"No one's calling the police," I said, glaring at all of them. "I want everyone to sit down. Now!"

Richie was the first to comply, stumbling backwards and all but falling into an armchair by the window.

I tugged Zach over to the chair I'd been sitting in earlier and motioned to the one beside it. He gave me a sour look as he dropped grumpily into it. "I'm not happy about this," he muttered.

"I know," I murmured, flashing him a small smile as I sat down too. "I'll make it up to you later."

Then I looked at my uncle. "Uncle George?"

"Oh, very well," he sighed, regally lowering himself into his desk chair. "Not that I have any idea what this is all about."

"Let's start at the beginning," I suggested, turning to my cousin. "Richie... you drugged me?"

"It was only supposed to last a couple of hours," he said, tossing a nervous glance at Zach. "And it wasn't supposed to take your memory away—not like it did. It was just supposed to make you... submissive."

Zach snorted. "This is your family?" He arched one eyebrow at me. "They sure don't know you very well, do they?"

"Shh," I hushed, frowning reprovingly. That look in his eyes had my thoughts trending in all the most inappropriate directions. "Not now."

I turned to my uncle. "But why?"

George's mouth compressed but he said nothing.

"Because you wouldn't lend him the money he needed to keep his business from going under," Richie explained. "Why do you think? He asked, but you said no. Like all of a sudden you know so much about how things should be done. Who do you think has kept this place going all these years? It sure wasn't you!"

I felt my eyes widen. This was about money? I guess I should have figured that, but, somehow...

"It's always been the family's money," Richie continued.

"And everybody got along and we never had any of these problems. But now... now you act like it's all yours!"

"Hey!" Zach snapped, turning in his seat to glare at my cousin. "Get a clue. If it was left to her, then it *is* hers. Tough shit, pal. For you *and* your old man."

I looked at my uncle. "You need money, Uncle George?"

George waved one hand in a negligent gesture. "I have some... business ventures... that would benefit from a fresh influx of cash," he allowed.

"And this would take care of it?" I asked, reaching for the document he'd wanted me to sign.

He looked at me for a moment, then nodded. "Yes. It would."

I turned to Zach. "Would you hand me a pen, please?"

His eyes narrowed, he stared suspiciously at the pages in my hand. "What are you doing? What are those?"

"These are papers giving my uncle temporary power of attorney so he can handle my estate for me."

Zach pointed at my uncle. "Is that what *he* told you?"

I nodded. "Yes."

"And you believed him? Well, forget it, April. They're the bad guys, remember? You can't trust what they say. If you sign that, you'll probably be signing away everything you own."

I nodded again. "I know."

"You *know?*"

"I'm not an idiot, Zach."

"Then why are you doing this?"

I sighed. How could I make him understand? So far, having money had caused me nothing but trouble. I was having a hard time believing I wouldn't be a whole lot better off without it. "Tell me something, Zach. Did you have any objections to our seeing one another before this money thing came up?"

"What's that got to do with anything? Don't make this about us—because it's not."

"Just answer the question."

"No. Of course not. But I'm still not going to let you sign that paper."

"See, Papa?" Richie glared at his father. "You see? What did I tell you? He's been behind this the whole time. Ask him," he said, turning to me. "Ask him how long he's known you. Ask him when you two met. He's the one who's after your money."

"I never intended to hurt you, April," my uncle said quietly, "despite what you may think; or to leave you penniless. Your cousin and I had your best interests in mind, as well as our own. And this young man does not sound quite like the disinterested party he'd have you think." He shook his head sadly. "He's after something. I'm afraid this isn't the first time it's happened, you know."

"The first time?" Richie scoffed. "It's not even the second or third time it's happened!"

I looked at Zach. "Well?"

He gazed at me tiredly. "I don't know what the hell is going on here. What do you want me to tell you—that I just met you Friday? You already know that. I don't know why you're even bothering with these people, after everything they've done. But if I want your money so damn badly then tell me why I gave you back your check?"

It was a very small check, all things considered. He could have been holding out for more, for all of it, even. But I knew he wasn't. Still, for clarity's sake, I had to ask. "So if you don't want my money then why do you care if I give it away?"

"Ahh, that's a good one," Richie crowed. "Let's see him answer that!"

Anger flared briefly in Zach's eyes, anger and hurt. "I *don't* care—it's got nothing to do with me. But it's like I told you before; one of these days you'll get your memory back. If you want to give all your money away at that point, then go for it. But don't do it now. Not when you can't possibly know if it's something you'll end up regretting."

"Very admirable sentiments," George murmured softly. "And, I've no doubt, you're hoping that the person she gives it all away to is you."

Zach shook his head. "Sorry to disappoint you, asshole. I'm not that delusional. I know the odds. I'll likely I'll be history, by then. So, I've got nothing to gain from this situation."

"But if, as you claim, you've known my niece for less than a week, why should she take your word for anything? You're very quick to tell her what she should think, who she should trust. Why should she believe you?"

This time, when Zach opened his mouth to answer, I stopped him. "No, Zach," I said, reaching over and clasping his hand. "Don't bother." I turned to my uncle. "Sorry, Uncle George. But, 'why' is none of your business. The bottom line is, I do believe him. And I trust him. Thanks to you and Richie he's the only one I feel like I do know or can trust right now. I'd take his word over... well, pretty much anyone else's. So that's that." Leaning forward, I placed the papers, still unsigned, back on the desk. "There has to be another way to deal with this situation. What if I gave you the loan you'd wanted originally. Would that help?"

"Oh, that's great," Zach grumbled. "Reward him. Why don't you just ask them to drug you again? Or, I know, the car's still outside. Maybe..."

"Do you have a better idea?" I asked, turning to him with a smile.

"Yeah," he snapped. "Call the police."

I shook my head. "No." I didn't want to do that. I didn't want a lengthy court battle. I didn't want to see my picture splashed all over the TV again, or watch as Zach's name got dragged through more mud. Like it or not, this was my family. If I hadn't kicked George or Richie out before now, maybe I'd had a reason for letting them stay. And, come to think of it, despite everything they'd tried to do, I had a pretty good reason for keeping them here now, too. I still needed someone to run the estate for me, and where would I find anyone with a more vested interest in the place?

"Look Zach, I'm just doing what you told me to do. Until I know what's what, I don't want to do anything I might regret. Besides, you said it yourself: This is a big place. I figure it's big enough for all of us."

"That's not what I meant and you know it."

I nodded. "Yeah, I know. But it's true, just the same." I glanced at my uncle as I got to my feet. "Okay, Uncle George. You can have the money, but here are my conditions. First of all, I want a controlling interest in the company. I'm not going to loan you the money, since I really don't want to risk finding out how far you'll go to keep from having to pay it back. Instead I want a piece of the pie—big enough so that it's in both your best interests to make sure that nothing happens to me. Because, if anything does happen, you're both gonna end up losing. Big time. Is that clear?"

George nodded. "Go on."

"Number two, I need both of you to promise that you'll *never* do anything like this again."

"That'll work," Zach grumbled. "Since when are you so trusting, anyway?"

"Shh," I murmured. Taking the others' silence for consent, I continued. "Finally, you have to agree to stay on and run this place for me for as long as I need you to. Is it a deal?"

"Do we have a choice?" Richie asked, sounding bitter.

I shook my head. "Not really. But, on the other hand, how much are you really losing? You get to keep your clothes, your room, your car..."

"Oh, yeah, can't let him lose that," Zach grumbled again

"And whatever else you have," I continued, smiling sadly at Richie. "Besides, those orange jumpsuits they give you to wear in prison? Not a good look for you."

"No," Richie sighed. "I don't believe I'd care for the cuisine, either."

"So, do we have a deal?"

Richie nodded. "Deal."

"Uncle George?"

My uncle looked at me for a moment in silence. Then he nodded as well. "Very well, April. I accept your terms."

"Good." I smiled at Zach. "See? That wasn't so hard, was it? Now, come on, I have something I need to show you."

I took hold of his hand and led him out of the room, breathing a sigh of relief when the office door closed behind us and we were back in the foyer, alone.

"Wait," Zach protested as I headed for the stairs and I almost laughed at the look of trepidation on his face. "Where are we going?"

"I'm kidnapping you," I teased. Then, remembering that he had a problem with the whole commitment thing, I turned my head to smile reassuringly. "But don't worry. It's only temporary."

Chapter Seventeen

"Wow." Zach stopped dead in his tracks just inside my bedroom door, staring at the room, taking it all in.

"It's nice isn't it?" I asked as I crossed to the bed.

"Yeah. Sure. Real nice."

Frankly, up until that moment, I thought it was. Once the initial shock had worn off, I thought I liked the room's opulent elegance, but if it was going to put that expression on Zach's face—one of defeat, depression, and I-don't-know-what-else—then I hated it. And I was damn sure going to have the whole place remodeled to within an inch of its pretentious, gilt-and-lacquered life. Still, I pretended not to notice his discomfort as I took things from the night table drawer, making sure I had everything I needed and arranging them on the table top.

Returning to where he stood, hands jammed in his pockets, I went up on my toes and kissed him. His hands closed on my waist, which was nice enough, but he kissed me back like he had downstairs, with his new, reserved manner and none of his usual exuberance. I couldn't help but suspect that, if the kiss went on too long, he'd put an end to it by using that same grip on my waist to push me away.

"What's going on?" he sighed, not quite protesting, but not helping much either, as I struggled to remove his jacket. "I thought you needed to show me something?"

I nodded. "I do."

I needed to show him just how much I trusted him, how much I cared. I still owed him—for so many things. It was clear now that he was never going to let me repay him with money, but there were other things I could give him, weren't there? Things I wanted to give him, needed to give him.

Now. While I had the chance. And before I lost my nerve.

Something in the jacket's inside pocket crackled when I finally wrestled the garment from his arms, eliciting a look of concern and a softly muttered, "Shit. Be careful with that."

Tossing the jacket aside I slid my hands up his arms and around his neck. I couldn't stop looking at him, touching him. It felt like so much longer than a single day had passed since I'd last

185

seen him.

"April," he murmured my name softly, his eyes half closed. "What are you doing to me?"

I shrugged. "Nothing." Yet.

I just loved the way he looked in his T-shirt and jeans. True, I hadn't seen him dressed in anything else, other than nothing— and nothing was damn nice, too—but the look worked for him. His clothes caressed his muscles and hugged him tight as though they loved him as much as I did. I wanted to do the same. I wanted to spend the rest of my life doing nothing else.

"I should leave," he said.

I shook my head. "No, you should stay. I haven't had a chance to thank you properly yet."

"Thank me?" His eyes opened at that. "For what?"

"Well, for rescuing me. For being my hero and saving me from the bad guys."

A frown creased his brows. "I'm not real happy about that, you know. You shouldn't have let them off so easily. I'm really worried about you being here alone with them."

I nodded. Well, that was easily solved, wasn't it? He could move in here and protect me. Night and day. But, of course I couldn't say that. "So, maybe I'll get myself a couple of dogs. Two of those Doberman Pinschers ought to do it."

"A couple of guns would be better," he muttered.

"Mm, yeah." I slid my hands over his biceps again. "A couple of big guns. That would definitely work for me." If he caught my meaning, he ignored it. I suppressed a sigh of disappointment. I knew that nothing had changed in the last half hour. I knew the odds were better than good that he'd be leaving again soon; walking away without a backward glance. But not just yet.

"Look, Zach, one day won't really make all that much difference, will it?" I asked.

He looked at me curiously. "What do you mean?"

"There are all those letters we're never gonna get to and I guess I can live with that. But, one more day, you can spare me that much, can't you?"

"You don't know how unfair this is," he moaned. "I can't." But the heat in his eyes told me otherwise.

"Please?"

A low groan broke from his throat and I knew I had him. He pulled me against him suddenly, lips closing on mine in the kind of kiss I'd been longing for; the kind that felt as though he'd put his entire heart and soul into it.

My lips parted to receive his tongue. My hands clasped his face as I kissed him back greedily, loving the tingling of my nipples, the pulsing of my sex, the fire that kindled low in my belly then traveled South to become a liquid flow of heat between my thighs.

Zach's hands slipped under my shirt and roved across my back, so feverishly hot I thought he must be trying to brand me with his touch. When his fingers slid into the gap at the back of my jeans and squeezed my ass I arched against him. When his mouth moved down to claim my neck I clasped his head in my hands and murmured, "Yes, Zach, yes."

I lifted my arms to help him when he tugged my shirt over my head; and then I left them there, with my forearms still tangled in the sleeves of my shirt, my crossed wrists resting on my head. As he dragged the cups of my bra away from my breasts and began to suckle I raised up on my toes to meet him, holding myself immobile, available, his.

Can't you see the love I feel for you? I begged silently. *Don't you know I'd deny you nothing if you'd just tell me you feel the same?*

But I said nothing, not until he'd lifted me in his arms and was headed for the bed. Then I stopped him with a hand against his chest.

"No. Not there."

He stopped and looked at me in surprise as I slid from his arms and took hold of his hand. "Where are we going?"

"You'll see," I said as I led him toward the bathroom.

"So, we're still working on C, right?" he asked, with a tired sounding sigh.

I shook my head. "Nope. D." Still pulling him along, I pushed open the door leading into the bathroom.

"D?" he whined in protest. "But I wasn't finished with C yet."

Amused by his tone, I glanced back at him. His face was flushed. His eyes glowed darkly. "Well, maybe we can come back to it, if you can spare the time," I told him. "But, as of right now, we're definitely on D." Then, smiling, I touched the light switch on the wall.

"Holy shit." His eyes widened as he stared at the tub, with its white marble surround and gold plated taps, set amid a jungle of green plants in a shining glass-and-mirror alcove.

"I know," I agreed, turning on the water and the jets and adding a healthy dose of Lime-Patchouli bath oil. "Get in."

"We're taking a bath?"

His eyes met mine in the mirror and I smiled. "Of course. Do you really think I'd let this thing go to waste?" I felt a tiny stab of pain as I said it. I'd have the tub for as long as I wanted. But he would be here for so short a time. Still, he was here now and I was determined to make the most of it.

He toed off his boots reluctantly, then peeled off his shirt, then his pants. His socks followed. "What am I missing?" he asked as he climbed into the tub and settled himself on his back on the broad, sloped surface. "Where's the D in all this?"

"Well..." I climbed in after, straddling his waist, smiling slyly. "You see, we're kind of working our way up to that."

"We are?"

"Mm-hmm." Donning a bath-mitt I began to stroke over his chest and arms. "The thing is, we need to wash up first. We need to get each other really, really...clean."

"Clean? That sounds like C, to me." His voice was husky and low. His eyes feasted on my breasts as I worked.

"Well, it's not," I said, admiring the way his wet skin gleamed; loving the way his hands tightened on my hips when I raised myself up on my knees and leaned in close. Close enough to whisper in his ear. "Because I'm feeling extra dirty tonight. That's dirty with a capital D."

"You are, huh?" He smiled up at me as his hands slid down my ass; fingers skimming along the crack until they were teasing the plump lips of my pussy.

I nodded. "Yes. And I hope you're ready for it, because it's only gonna get worse."

* * * *

Water foamed and bubbled around us as I kissed him. It seemed like I couldn't stop moaning. First when his fingers invaded my slick channel, stroking deeply. Then again when his other hand curled up to cup my breast, tugging the already taut peak to new hardness, then drawing it to his mouth.

"I need to touch you, too," I murmured, pulling away from him at last. I raised up slightly. Reaching between my legs, my hand found his hard cock and grasped it firmly.

"Condom," he gritted, eyes widening in alarm as I fitted the tip of his shaft to my waiting sex and lowered myself onto him. "April, wait!"

Nodding, I bent my lips to his again as I rode him slowly. "I know. It'll be all right. Just give me a minute; it feels so good like this, doesn't it?"

He nodded, his eyes squeezing shut, his muscles trembling, his hands poised to push me away. "April, please," he begged. "I can't last this way."

Neither could I. I forced myself to stop. I rose to my feet and smiled down at him. "Well, come on then. Let's go."

"Go?" he muttered in confusion, watching as I stepped from the tub and wrapped myself in one of the bath sheets—just to blot up the extra water, no one likes a wet bed, after all. "Go where?"

"Back to my bedroom, of course." My body was thrumming with desire. I was so hot for him I could barely see straight. But my muscles were warm and relaxed and I hoped that would help. I hoped that I could handle what was coming, or at least that it wouldn't be as bad as I feared. These few days with him had been so good, I would hate to ruin it all at the end.

But I had to do this. I had to try.

"Your bedroom?" Zach was looking at me as if I'd lost my mind. "Baby, that's practically in the next Zip code. You really expect me to walk that far like this?" He was still lying in the tub, clasping his cock in his hand.

I couldn't help smiling. "Well, you'd better. Because I sure can't carry you."

"I don't think you realize how painful this is," he murmured, still complaining as he climbed slowly out of the tub. I gave him a towel and watched as he wrapped it awkwardly around himself. His bulging erection seemed to be making the process a slow and difficult one.

"I'll make it up to you," I promised as I led the way back into the bedroom. I gathered my supplies from the bedside table and handed them to him. Massage oil, lubricant and the box of condoms I'd noticed the day before.

He looked at the box, and then at me. I shrugged. "What can I tell you? Apparently I buy in bulk." Why, I still didn't know since, from what I could tell, my love life could not possibly have been all that exciting.

With a playful tug, I pulled the towel from around his waist and let it drop to the floor. I dropped my own as well, then I turned and crawled up on the bed, arranging myself on all fours, feeling conspicuous, ridiculous, exposed. My stomach fluttered nervously and I had to take a deep breath before I could manage to toss a casual smile over my shoulder. "Well? What are you waiting for?"

Zach's cock stirred as he looked at me. "I don't know. What are we doing?"

"Why, Zach," I said with mock surprise. "I'm shocked. You mean you've never heard of doggie-style?"

Laughter glimmered in his eyes, putting me instantly at ease. "Ah, I get it. D, right?"

"Took you long enough."

Nodding, he tossed the condoms and the massage oil on the bed, and then sat on the edge of the mattress. "So what are you giving me this for?" he asked, waving the tube of lubricant at me as he slipped his other hand between my legs and stroked along the slick length of my slit. "You really think we're gonna need this stuff?"

"Yes," I murmured huskily, rocking against his hand as he fingered my clit. "But not there."

His hand stilled. "What?"

I cleared my throat and tried again. "I said, that's not where I need it."

"Then where?" he asked cautiously.

I felt the blood rush to my cheeks as I pushed back with my hips, wiggling my ass practically in his face. "Come on, Zach. I don't have to draw you a map, do I?"

His hand dropped to the bed. "I thought you said no?"

It was becoming impossible to continue the conversation while craning my neck around at that angle, to say nothing of embarrassing. Sighing, I plopped down on the bed and sat facing him. "I did. But that was days ago. Now I'm saying yes."

"Why?"

A simple question. I probably should have answered with an equally simple lie. Instead, I went with the truth. Sort of. "Because you want to, don't you? And I... I want to do this for you. I want to give you this." *I want to give you everything.* "I want to give you what you want."

His gaze softened. "Baby... that's not much of a reason. I told you, we don't have to do anything you don't want to do."

I looked away, feeling stung. *Not much of a reason?* Well, I thought it was a damn good one, myself. "Look, Zach, we talked about this, remember? We talked about all the things we wanted to do. This sounded like it was at the top of your list—am I wrong?"

More than I've wanted anything in a long, long time. That's what he'd told me. That's what he'd said. "Have you changed your mind?"

He shook his head. "No. But..."

"Then think of it as a going away present."

"Oh, that's even better," he murmured, sarcasm dripping from his tongue. "Thanks."

"Well, you haven't changed your mind about that either, have you?" I asked hopefully. "About what you said downstairs in the foyer—about breaking things off now?"

Sighing, he shook his head again. "No. It's for the best."

Right. Somehow, I managed a smile. "I really do want to do this with you, Zach. You're not going to make me beg, are you?"

His dimple peeked out at me, suddenly, from the corner of his own very tiny smile. "Well, no. Not unless you wanted to beg?"

"I don't. Not this time."

"C'mere," he said, sighing again as he stood up and held out his hands to me. I slid to my feet and took hold of them, and let him pull me into his arms. He kissed me softly, sweetly, far too briefly. "Let me make a few adjustments," he murmured as he let me go and began to gather pillows together, stacking several on the end of the bed.

I watched, breathing deep, trying not to pass out or give in to the nervous twisting in my gut.

Then he turned and reached for me, drawing me close, patting the pile of pillows he'd just made, urging me face down with a gentle hand on my back. I felt even more exposed now, especially when he moved one leg so that I was straddling the corner of the bed, and then lifted and bent the other so that my thigh rested on the pillows, right next to my hip. This new position forced my head and chest flat on the mattress. My ass was elevated, my legs were spread wide and my throbbing pussy was fully visible. If I was with anyone else but Zach, I was sure I'd be wearing twenty different shades of embarrassed blush. But I loved the touch of his hands on me, manipulating my limbs, positioning me just the way he wanted. I loved the idea that I was giving him something he'd been craving, something we'd both remember for a long time. So I concentrated on that, and let the rest go.

Standing between my thighs he poured a river of oil down my spine, then coasted his hand along it. "Just relax," he murmured in soothing tones.

I took a deep breath, but it didn't really help. It's only my

191

opinion, of course, but *just relax* is right up there with *don't be upset*, when it comes to increasing tension. But I held my tongue about that. I doubted Zach would appreciate any comparisons to my uncle.

Besides, it really was hard to stay tense while his gentle hands massaged my back and legs. He ran his oil coated fingers over my ass; squeezing, stroking, circling my pussy with feather-light touches that teased and probed and tormented; exciting me to the point where my whole attention was focused on just those few, small inches of aching, throbbing flesh.

"Now, Zach, please," I murmured desperately after he'd brought me to the brink again and again, never letting me go over. "I need it now." My fingers clutched at the bedspread. I'd almost forgotten how skilled he was at prolonging this kind of torture.

I felt him reach for the condoms with one hand, while, with the other, he continued to stroke my slit. Then he withdrew that hand, too, and I stiffened in anticipation.

Gently parting my lips, he slid his cock along the swollen folds of my pussy once, twice and again; then thrust slickly inside. I moaned in pleased surprise. "Oh, yes. There. That feels so good." *Has he changed his mind*, I wondered hopefully.

But, no such luck. His hands parted my ass cheeks next and as he thrust again with his cock he pushed one lubed finger partly into the tight bud of my anus. And then out again. Alternating the strokes of his cock and his finger, he kept me dangling in suspense, never knowing which to expect from him next.

Unable to keep still, I rocked my hips against him. "More," I chanted hoarsely. "Give me more."

"I will, baby," Zach promised, his own voice just as strained. Continuing to grind inside me, he slipped his other hand between my legs to fondle my clit. "I will."

"Zach, please," I begged at last when I could stand no more, when I had to come—now!

He stopped suddenly, and pulled out. Muscles trembling with tension, skin slick with sweat, he leaned forward, bending over my back to whisper, almost in my ear, "Tell me what you want."

"Fuck me," I panted. *Please, please...* "Fuck me. Fuck me now!"

"Where?" he murmured, gulping for breath. "Tell me where."

I almost chickened out then. I almost said, "my pussy, please." But I didn't. I dug my nails even deeper into the bedspread and whispered, "My ass. Fuck my ass."

I felt the shudder that ran through him as he straightened,

heard the shaky intake of his breath as he spread my cheeks, carefully fitting his cock-head against my ass.

I thought it would hurt, but I guess I should have known better. He rocked forward slowly, gently, an inch at a time, until almost his whole length was buried inside me. I was amazed by the feeling, amazed by my clit's throbbing response to the fullness.

I could feel an orgasm building inside me like a gathering storm, or a mountainous wave. But I was suddenly in no hurry to get to the peak. Eyes closed I arched into each stroke, wishing the ride could go on forever.

"Oh, God, Zach," I sobbed, almost beyond words. I pulled my leg closer to my chest, canting my hips higher, granting him even more access. I wanted to take all of him inside me, wanted to feel every inch. I wanted to own and be owned.

I thought I'd feel helpless, but I didn't. And the strangled noises that broke from his lips let me know that his own control was mostly facade. We were both trapped, driven by torturous need to give ourselves over and over and over again.

Zach's breathing was harsh, uneven, shattered, as he reached one hand between my labia again. He thrust his thumb into my weeping sex, his fingers pressing, caressing my swollen clit, until the pressure inside me at last exploded and I came in great crashing waves. His fingers tightened on my hips then. Writhing, I clawed at the mattress as he pulled me against his thrusting hips, shoving into me with hard, sharp strokes that prolonged and heightened the sensations I was feeling, until they were almost unbearable.

"Zach, please!" I begged, unable to stand any more. Then he broke, too, grunting as he shoved himself inside me one last time. I could feel us both pulsing around and within each other, as though our bodies were echoing one another's rhythms.

"How was that," he panted a few minutes later, as his hands stroked slowly over my legs.

"Incredible," I mumbled, barely able to get the word out. I was only sorry it was over. *Want to do it again?* I almost asked, but I didn't. I was pretty sure it would kill us both to climax again right now and I didn't want his death on my conscience.

"Good," he breathed, pulling out slowly. Then he leaned forward once more, kissing my cheek, my shoulder, and all the way down my back.

I smiled sleepily. "Mm, nice. Thank you."

"Don't move," he said as he straightened. "I'll be right back."

Move? I turned the word over in my mind, considering it from all angles. *Not likely.* I didn't think I'd ever move again. Not that I wanted to, exactly, although I suppose I could've wished for a slightly more dignified position to be found dead in.

Zach was back in a minute with a warm, wet washcloth. I sighed in pleasure as he wiped around my pussy, working back toward my ass, cleaning and caressing; mopping up my juices, I supposed, along with the lubricants and oils.

"Are you trying to repair some of the damage you've done?" I teased softly.

His hand stilled. "Damage?"

"Mm-hm." Damage. Another D word. And a not-too-bad description of how I was feeling at the moment: totally wrecked in a completely wonderful way.

"Are you saying I hurt you?"

The concern in his voice made me smile, and I couldn't help laughing. "Yeah. You made me hurt sooo good."

Zach snorted and playfully swatted my rear with the washcloth. "Shit, woman, you scare me like that again and I'll make you sorry."

"Hmph." Where was the joke in that, I wondered. It wasn't likely I'd ever get the chance to scare him again, was it? And for that I was already sorry.

* * * *

I guess Zach finally figured out that I was incapable of moving on my own. So he picked me up and tucked me into bed. I opened my arms and reached for him, holding his gaze, wordlessly asking him to stay; so afraid he wouldn't, that he'd kiss me one last time and walk away.

"I'll really miss this," he murmured, after he'd climbed into bed and taken me into his arms. He ran his fingers down my back, pressed a soft kiss against my hair. "I'll miss *you*."

Lips trembling, I nodded. I didn't trust myself to speak.

Then he hugged me. Tight. Squeezing me so hard I almost couldn't breathe. "You're killing me," he whispered, so low I almost didn't catch it.

"What?" Startled, I raised my head to look at him, shocked by the pain in his eyes. "What's wrong?"

"Nothing," he murmured rolling onto his back, draping an arm across his face as though to close me out.

"Zach? What's going on?"

I tried to sit up, but he pulled me down against him, wrapping his other arm around my shoulders. "Shh, it's okay. It was just a joke." A minute passed in silence. Finally Zach heaved a long, shaky sigh. "Shit. I should go."

"Not yet." Maybe I could talk him into waiting until I fell asleep? At least that way I wouldn't have to watch him walk away.

"Baby..."

"Just a little while longer."

He sighed. "Well, I can't stay too long, you know. Your uncle probably thinks I've killed you by now, as it is."

"You mean he hopes so, don't you? Anyway, he'd be a fine one to talk." I was still disgusted at the thought of George and Richie and their stupid plan. But without that plan I'd probably never have met Zach. Another reason I should cut them some slack, I supposed. On the other hand, maybe I should take a leaf from the family book and come up with a stupid plan of my own; one to kidnap Zach and chain him to my bed. That sounded doable, didn't it?

"What are you thinking about?" he asked quietly.

"Chains," I told him. Chains, ropes, leather straps—whatever it took. "And maybe some rings."

"Rings?"

"Yeah." I walked my fingers across his chest. "A pretty, little gold one, right... about... here." Then I caught his nipple between my nails and pinched it. Hard. I was back to feeling like I wanted to hurt someone, and this time I wasn't making any exceptions.

"Ouch!" He grabbed my hand and pulled it away. But then he folded his own around it and held it tight. He looked at me. "Shit, what did you do that for?"

I shrugged, but said nothing. What was there to say, after all? More time passed.

"So, you're into nipple piercings, huh?"

Not in general, but on him it would be cute. I sighed a little as I thought about teasing his nipple with my tongue, taking the ring between my teeth and tugging gently. "Yep." It could have been fun, all right.

Zach chuckled softly. "Well, you know something? For you, I'd do it."

Surprised, I glanced up at him. "You would?"

"Sure." A tiny smile glimmered on his lips. "I'd do pretty much anything for you. Don't you know that?"

Misery tightened in my chest and I ducked my head, not

wanting him to read the pain in my eyes. Damn him for saying something so sweet when he had one foot already out the door! And, no, as a matter of fact, I did *not* know anything of the kind. "Anything, huh?"

He released the hand he'd been holding and ran his fingers lightly up and down my arm. "Pretty much."

Well, that was interesting. "And would anything happen to include... moving in here so you could protect me from my big, bad uncle and cousin?"

Zach's arms tightened around me. "That's no joke, April. I told you before. I'm really worried about leaving you here with those two."

Mentally crossing my fingers I took a deep breath and shrugged. "So then don't."

"Come on," he said quietly. "You know I can't do that."

It seemed there were a lot of things I was supposed to know about that I didn't. Here was another. "Why not?"

He sighed. "Well, for one thing, how would you know that's why I'm doing it? How would you know I wasn't just after your money, like they said I was?"

I pulled away from him and sat up. "Because I know you're not! Damn it, Zach, you should realize by now how much I trust you. Or did you think I was lying when I told my uncle that I'd take your word over his?"

He met my gaze for just a moment, then his own slid away. "I dunno. Maybe. I was."

"You were what? Lying?" I really didn't want things to end like this, with us sniping at each other. But it was either that or burst into tears and, if those were my only choices, I'd go with anger.

"Hell, yeah," he snorted, sounding angry, too. "Do you think *I* meant it when I said none of it mattered to me, that there was nothing for me to gain from this? That was bullshit. I have plenty to gain. It's just... I've got even more to lose."

"Like what?" I asked, gazing at him in hopeless confusion. What was going on? I was the loser here, not him. But it was hard to stay angry in the face of the bleak, bitter look in Zach's eyes when he met my gaze this time.

"Like you. Like my heart." Then his face changed. An angry sneer curled his lips once more. He rolled his eyes and smacked himself on the head. "Oh, wait, what am I saying? I've already lost that, haven't I?"

I thought I was confused before, but that was nothing. I stared at him, not knowing what to say. He'd lost his heart? To whom?

Zach stared right back at me, looking angry and miserable. Then the anger faded from his face, leaving him looking unbearably sad. "Baby, don't you know I'm so deep in love with you I can't see straight? It's killing me knowing I have to say good-bye."

In love with me? No, I hadn't known that either. And, now that I did, I couldn't even take very much pleasure in the fact because he was still talking about good-bye. "But, why, Zach? Why say good-bye at all? Are you that afraid of commitment?"

His eyebrows rose and he gazed at me in disbelief. "Afraid? Of what? Of being too happy? Of loving you too much? Of having you again and again every night for years, for decades, until we're so old we've *both* forgotten our names? Then having really hot senior sex with you until I finally drop dead from exhaustion? Yeah, that would really suck. I'm terrified of any of *that* happening. Shit." He shook his head, turning serious again. "Sure I'd like to have that kind of life with you, April. But who am I kidding? I'm not the kind of guy women want for that sort of thing."

"Oh, yeah," I said softly, tears swimming in my eyes as I smiled. "I can see why that would be. I can tell you'd be really bad at it."

He nodded. "I would be. I'm not gonna grow up, cut my hair, get a real job, give up my music and go all corporate, be home for dinner every night at six, support you in the lifestyle you deserve, give you babies and a white picket fence. That's not me and I can't change that." He glanced away again, sighing softly, speaking almost to himself. "I don't know. Maybe I'm wrong. Maybe I could be that kind of guy. I could try, I guess. Maybe."

My hand was shaking as I reached out and touched his cheek, gently turning his face back to me. "Zach, I don't want you to be that kind of guy, either. I love you, too, you know. Just the way you are."

He smiled softly. "Yeah, but?"

But? "But what?" I asked, feeling angry and hurt all over again. *What's that supposed to mean?*

He shrugged, looking tired and sad. "I don't know. You tell me. All's I know is there's always a but after a statement like that. *I love you but...I can't be happy that way. I love you but... I need something more. I love you but...it's never gonna last..."*

I nodded slowly as understanding finally dawned. I blamed exhaustion for why it took me so long to get here. And next time we went to *Babeland* I was definitely buying him a gag. Because sometimes the man talked entirely too much.

"How about this, Zach? *I love you but nothing.* I don't want you to give up your music. I don't want you to do anything you don't want to do. And I don't exactly need you to support me, either. I mean... have you seen this place?"

He looked at me for a moment, eyes widening in surprise. Then a glimmer of something else replaced the surprise. Hope, maybe. Or relief. Along with something that looked suspiciously like tears. His lips quirked as he glanced at the room around us. "Yeah, I guess you've pretty much got that part covered, don't you?"

I ignored the sheepish blush that had spread over his cheeks. "Uh-huh. And while I'm still a little sketchy on some of the details, I'm pretty sure that, if I really wanted them, I could probably afford to buy myself a couple of acres worth of fences too. Don't you think?"

Laughing, he pulled me back down against his chest. "Hell, yeah. If you sold this place you'd probably rake in enough to buy yourself a coupla small states."

I blinked back the tears that were trying to leak from my eyes and smiled up at him. "Well, I could do that, I suppose, if you think that's something you'd like. They'd have to be states with really good music industries though."

"Good idea." He smiled back. "So, I guess we're thinking what, Nashville and Memphis? Oh, wait, those aren't states, are they?"

I shook my head. "Why are you asking me? You know I can't remember that stuff yet."

A thread of worry appeared in Zach's eyes as his smile disappeared once again.

I sighed impatiently. "What now?"

"Well, that's the other thing, isn't it? We still don't really know what you're going to think about any of this once you get your memory back. Maybe you'll decide there is a *but* lurking around out there after all."

"No, I won't." Pulling his face down to mine, I silenced him with a kiss. "Stop worrying. There are no *buts* lurking anywhere in our future. I promise."

"How can you promise something like that?" he asked softly, but he was smiling as he said it, love gleaming in his eyes. It was a look I'd seen there several times in the last few days; finally I could recognize it for what it was.

"Easy. It's like pizza and bowling and Champagne and nice sheets—and all the really important things in life. There are some things you always know, Zach, no matter what. You taught me that, remember? Some things—and some people—are too deep in your heart to ever be forgotten."

Epilogue

It was another Friday night at Zephyr, and April Valenzuela was seated at her usual table, watching her boyfriend's band perform. Zach was looking especially hot tonight, she thought as she rested her crossed arms on the table, pressing her breasts against them, surreptitiously fingering her nipple ring—the twin of the one she'd gotten him—through her blouse.

It was hard to believe they'd known each other for so short a time, hard to believe she hadn't known him all her life. And, especially now that her memories had begun to filter back into her conscious mind, it was hard to believe she'd survived all those empty years without him. Without beer or bowling. Without true love.

To be sure, some of those memories had been easier to handle than others. April wasn't entirely happy with the person she had been. She was still struggling with that, and with the anger she felt toward her uncle and cousin. They hadn't always been nice to her younger self, but, then again, she hadn't been very nice to them, either. Though she knew it hadn't been their intention, they'd done her a great big favor by making her forget the woman she used to be.

She'd remembered enough about that April, her pre-Zach self, to know that she probably wasn't all that different from a lot of the women Zach had dated. Cynical and distrustful, she, too, would have viewed him as no more that a temporary playmate; sexy, exciting and fun, but no one to take seriously, and certainly no one she would risk giving her heart to. She never would have bothered, or dared, to look beneath the surface, and she never would have found the gentle man within.

So, despite her anger, she'd forgiven George and Richie. She'd allowed them to stay on at the mansion and she'd been happy—more than happy—to allow George to continue running things.

Keeping her uncle busy was the best way she could think of to ensure he didn't have the time to dream up any more plans.

She glanced up in surprise when a blended margarita, improbably garnished with a bright green flexible straw, was placed on the table in front of her.

"Here you go, sweetheart," Tony said cheerfully. "Drink up."

She shook her head. "I didn't order this. What's going on?"

The big man shrugged. "Don't ask me, I don't know nuthin'.

Some guy sent it over."

Some guy? "Well, send it back," she told him, staring at it in alarm. "Tell him I don't want it. Tell him I'm not interested." She knew she was overreacting. If Tony had mixed it for her, the odds of something being wrong with the drink were astronomically low. But did it really pay to take chances?

"Calm down," Tony said, with a wink and a subtle nod in the direction of the stage. "Maybe you just wanna play along, right?"

Understanding dawned and April had to bite her lip to keep from smiling. *What's he up to this time?* she wondered. "Okay, Tony, sure. Thanks."

Tony returned her smile. "No problem. But, uh, better use the straw. Know what I mean? I wouldn't want you to choke or anything."

April nodded. So, there was something hidden in her drink, was there? Her mind boggled as she considered what that something might turn out to be. Given the size of the glass, and her knowledge of just how broad Zach's definition of *fun* tended to be, she knew it could be almost anything. A waterproof bullet vibe. A new anal plug. Ben Wa balls painted to look like eyes. Or a fortune cookie dipped in bronze—a reminder of the chocolate covered one he'd finally gotten around to giving her...

"I was sure you'd leave at the first opportunity," she remembered him telling her, that first night at her place, as they sat cross legged on her bed. "I was actually happy the police couldn't help you right away. I thought 'if I just have enough time, maybe I can convince her to stay, to give us a chance'."

April thought back to that day by the pool with Gabby. "Funny, you sure didn't look happy."

Zach smiled sheepishly. "Well, that's 'cause I felt kind of guilty about it too. I knew how disappointed you must be, how much you wanted to go home. Then you and Gabby got to talking about shoes and I thought, 'maybe I'll get her a pair of Ruby Slippers, tell her they'll take her home whenever she's ready, tell her maybe she just isn't ready yet'."

"That would have been cute," April mumbled, dropping her gaze to her lap, to his jacket, which covered her bare legs, to the little cellophane wrapper and the shattered remains of her fortune cookie. She was almost sorry she'd broken it open. She would have liked to have kept it whole and treasured it always, but then she never would have found the true treasure, which was hidden inside. "So why'd you change your mind about the slippers?"

Zach laughed. "Who says I did? We haven't gotten to F yet. I haven't even started on your feet." He reached out and grabbed one ankle as he spoke.

April fell backwards, propping herself on her elbows and smiling as he lifted her foot to his mouth and nipped at her toe.

"But, I dunno," Zach mused, kissing his way along her instep. "F was still a few days away, I might have thought of something else by then. I was kinda worried about those slippers anyway. What if they worked?"

April was a little more than halfway finished with her drink when something glittery at the bottom of the glass caught her eye. She fished it out, nearly bursting into laughter when she spied the tiny gold and diamond ring hanging from the end of her straw.

She rinsed it in her water glass and studied it more closely. *Only Zach would think of something like this,* she thought, admiring the trinket—a gold captive ring for her new piercing, with a diamond encrusted, heart-shaped dangle. Perfect.

"You didn't really lose your heart, did you?" she'd teased him that night in her room, hoping to challenge him into proving he had. "I bet you were lying about that, too."

"You're right," he agreed as he stretched out on top of her, clasping her hands in his own, giving her no chance to get away. "I was." He bent his head and flicked her nipple with his tongue, again and again, until she writhed beneath him. Then he lifted his head and smiled, gazing deep into her eyes. "It didn't get lost at all. I knew just what I did with it. I gave it to you."

Glancing up at the stage, April caught Zach smiling at her. *Just wait 'til I get you home tonight,* she thought, as she returned the heated look he flashed in her direction. She couldn't wait for that herself, come to think of it. She couldn't wait to find out what else he might have planned for them both.

They were working their way through the alphabet yet again. Smiling, she let her mind play with all the possibilities...

Let Me Count the Ways

As the owner of The Body Electric, LA's hottest new exercise studio, sexy, former film star Claire Calhoun has her pick of studly young men eager to do her bidding. Small wonder she's used to calling the shots, both in and out of bed. But everything changes the night the actress-turned-entrepreneur has one mojito too many at a party and decides it would be fun to pick up her accountant, Mike Sherman. She's thinking fling. He's thinking forever.

Claire has been Mike's fantasy since the first time he saw her bare it all for the camera. Now, she's in his bed and he'll do whatever's necessary to keep her there. But he's not a stalker, right? He's just a devoted fan.

Prologue

Mike

I guess you could say I fell for Claire Calhoun the first time I saw her up there on the big silver screen. I don't know what it was about her that affected me so strongly. Maybe it was the Titian hair. The sultry shimmer in those hazel, hellcat eyes. The curve of her lips when she turned and smiled right at the camera—right at *me*. Whatever it was, it was simply... stunning. Literally. It hit me hard and low and just wouldn't quit.

She looked like an angel with all that California sunshine spilling down around her; like sweet, lust-inducing innocence dipped in honey. A vision straight from some Garden of Earthly Delights.

But if her face was made for heaven, everything south of that had been built with a far different destination in mind. Her body was sinful enough to tempt even a saint into straying. Happily. Right through the gates of Hell. And I'm far from being a saint.

Despite my on-going fascination with the woman, I'd just like to state for the record that I never deluded myself into believing we had a relationship. Claire could have been as fictional as any of the characters she played for all the good I figured it was ever going to do me. There had to be at least a million other guys in the world who wanted her as badly as I did and I knew any number of them were more likely than I to even meet her. Not that it stopped me from dreaming, of course. But dreaming, fantasizing, collecting memorabilia—along with copies of every one of her films I could get my hands on—that's as far as it went.

For a while, Claire's name was box office magic. Everything she touched turned golden. But then a string of unsuccessful movies and even less successful relationships caused her star to plummet. These days, her screen appearances are mostly limited to round-ups subtitled '*Where Are They Now?*'

To me, however, Claire would always be a major star, a full blown fantasy, a lush and lovely dream come true. Which is why I could scarcely believe my eyes the day she walked into my office hoping to secure my services as accountant to her new exercise studio, The Body Electric.

To say I was star-struck in her presence is to understate the case by a very, very wide margin. I was hopelessly tongue-tied, socially inept, and all but physically impaired by the kind of hard-on most men my age have given up expecting to achieve without pharmaceutical assistance. It still surprises me that we both made it through that first meeting; that I didn't embarrass myself any worse than I had; that she didn't bolt for the door after spending less than five minutes in my bumbling presence.

Luckily for me, I had come highly recommended by Claire's attorney, Dave Gillen. Dave, who'd recently extricated Claire from marriage number six and brokered the deal that allowed her to walk away with enough money to start her business in the first place, was also one of my oldest clients.

Claire trusted Dave, Dave trusted me, and the rest, as they say, is history...

Chapter One

Claire

Yoga is not easy, so the Bhagavad Gita warns, *for those whose minds are not subdued.* But I can tell you, it's pretty damn hard for any of us. Especially after forty.

I suppose I shouldn't say such things. After all, Yoga did save my life. I turned to it in much the same way Tina turned to Buddhism after Ike. Married to a cruel, emotionally distant man, my career, my health, my looks, my self esteem had all hit the skids. Yoga offered me a way out, a way back. It offered sanity, peace of mind, discipline, and the courage I needed to pick myself up and turn my life around.

That's why I used the money I got in my divorce settlement to open The Body Electric. I wanted to give something back, to share the blessings I'd received, to support myself by working at something I could still believe in. Still, as the Gita says, it's not easy. Of course, the same can be said of pretty much anything; business, relationships, life itself. There are days, and today was definitely one of them, when it all seems damn near impossible.

Standing in front of the floor-to-ceiling smoked glass that lined one entire wall of my second-floor office, I watched the class working out in the studio below me. A dozen and a half youthful beauties—mostly female—twisted their bodies into pretzels. Willingly. Eagerly. Effortlessly.

The first two were something I could completely understand and totally empathize with, given that their instructor was Derek Novello. Derek has some of the most beautiful musculature I've ever seen. And I've seen a lot. What woman wouldn't be eager to give her all for a piece of that? But the effortless part—now, that's where they had me beat. That's what had me feeling every last year of my age today.

How many years, you wonder? Well, sorry to disappoint you, but there are some things I just don't share. Age is nothing but a number, you know, and a girl's entitled to keep a few secrets.

Derek is the most popular teacher we have here, which is saying rather a lot. Especially when you consider that his classes are also among the hardest we offer. He's tough enough to challenge the men to push themselves to their limits, charming enough to make the women want to melt—into those same willing pretzels I've mentioned.

Tireless, talented, passionate, intense. Derek brings everything he has to his teaching. For almost five months, he brought most of it to our lovemaking, too. All but his heart. That, I suppose, was par for the course, and frankly I wasn't expecting anything more. These older woman/younger man things rarely last long and are almost never about love. I knew the moment it was over. Probably before he did. I could tell right away that Derek's heart had been lost to a pretty blonde pretzel.

Still, I really can't complain. I've been dumped before, but never so discreetly. To the casual observer I'm sure it appeared that I'd tired of him, rather than the other way around. I think even the pretzel was confused. And, in the months since our affair ended, I'd discovered another reason to be thankful. I no longer have to take even one of his classes. I can't tell you what a relief that's been!

At least I still look fit, I thought, taking a step back so that I could see my reflection in the glass. I sucked in my tummy, tucked in my buns, pivoted from side to side. "Not bad," I murmured as I thrust back my shoulders and studied my breasts, wondering how much longer I could get away without having them lifted. "But you're not what you used to be, that's for sure." *Still, things could be worse, and no doubt they will be, in time.*

"Nonsense," a male voice insisted from somewhere behind me. "You're as beautiful as ever."

I spun around, startled to find Mike Sherman watching from the doorway—which just goes to show you the kind of funk I'd been in all day. I'd totally forgotten his standing, bi-monthly appointment to go over the books, three p.m. every other Thursday.

"Sorry," he mumbled, his face flaming. "I didn't mean to intrude."

"Don't be silly." Calling on all my training to hide my own embarrassment, I rolled my eyes and grimaced slightly. "Actors, you know." I waved my hand in a negligent gesture as I seated myself—not in my chair but on the edge of my desk—where my crossed legs would appear to their best advantage. "We're always so focused on appearances." *And ain't that the truth?*

"Well, you have to be, don't you? The same way singers have to take care of their voices." He looked so sincere as he said it too. As if he really might mean it.

"What a nice way of putting it." I beamed at him as he crossed the room to his own desk. "How are things with you, Mike? How's your day going?"

He didn't answer right away. A small smile played over his lips as he slid his briefcase beneath the desk and seated himself. Then he glanced up at me, his eyes twinkling. "It's always a good day when I know I'm going to see you, Claire. Don't you know that?"

"Flatterer." Laughing, I leaned forward a little, just enough to flash some cleavage in his direction. Call it a reward, if you will. "You have all the right answers today, don't you?"

If they ever make a movie of my life, no doubt they'll get someone like Danny DeVito to play the part of Mike, which will be a shame. Don't get me wrong, I think Danny is a fine actor and he's got the bald head, the soulful brown eyes and the teddy bear physique the part calls for. He'll do a fine job of catching the nervous, slightly awkward exuberance Mike exhibited when we first met. But there's so much more to the role than that.

For starters, Mike is big. Brian Denehy big. With Denehy's surprising gracefulness—when he's not acting all nervous. Mike, I mean. Then there's his impeccably trimmed beard, the wicked twinkle in his eye and his rare and wondrous smile, all of which bring Sean Connery to mind.

But, even though Sean would be a dream to work with, if I were casting for the part I'd go for something different. I'd pick someone like a young James Earl Jones, for example. For his eyes and his smile and his size. For his astonishing ability to shift from fearful to fierce, from stern to boyish, from gentle to regal to commanding to jovial—or back again, or all at once. But, more than anything else, for his voice. For that deep, dark, delicious river of sound that could never be anything but male and can't help but leave you wondering, *why all the fuss about Tenors?*

"It doesn't count as flattery if it's fact," Mike replied in that lovely, low rumble of his.

"Oh, fact, is it?" I couldn't help but smile as I recalled my recent conversation with Dave, my lawyer, over tapas and drinks. Dave had been pleased I'd taken his advice and gone to see Mike, but he'd seemed shocked by the deal we'd worked out...

"He's handling it himself?" Dave asked, looking up from his seared tuna, clearly having trouble coming to grips with the idea. "Didn't he assign you to one of the people who works for him? You don't have to bring your paperwork there? He just shows up at your office—himself—every month?"

"No, twice a month," I corrected, nibbling at the celery stalk that had come in my michelada. "Why? Isn't that what you told me to do—to hire someone reputable? Someone I could trust? You said he was the best."

"I know I did, but, damn it, Claire, he doesn't even do that for me anymore, and I was one of his very first clients! How much is he charging you, anyway?"

Surprised, I told him.

"Oh, hell, no," Dave replied, sounding almost insulted. "That's nothing!"

I sipped my drink and refrained from pointing out that, in my current financial state, it hadn't seemed quite like nothing to me. Then again, neither had Dave's fees. You get what you pay for, I suppose.

Dave's gaze had turned speculative. If he were anyone else, I know exactly what he'd have been thinking—that I must be giving Mike some additional form of compensation. Entirely too many people still confuse the terms 'actress' and 'prostitute'.

"He's a fan, Dave," I tried to explain. "It's not that uncommon." Although, these days, I'm afraid it really is.

But Dave had his own ideas. "You know what I think it is? He probably knows your business is too small to afford his usual rates yet. Probably he figures he can afford to give you a break because he's banking on the fact he can use your name to attract other Hollywood types."

"Well, that would be foolish," I sighed. I knew just how far my name would take him in Hollywood, even if Dave didn't. It wouldn't even take him as far as it takes me. Which is close to nowhere anymore. "Maybe he's just being nice."

"Nice is no way to stay in business," Dave grumbled, which only made me laugh because Dave is one of the nicest people I know. "He probably doesn't want to pay one of his employees to work on an account he's not making any money on. I bet that's why he's doing it himself."

"I'm sure you're right," I murmured. One thing I've learned over the years is that there's no arguing with a man who's made up his mind about something. So why bother trying? Reason and logic are no match for sheer, pig-headed, male determination. And, when it turns out you were right all along, that'll just prove to him that you're a bitch. Directors are especially good at making that connection.

"It is," Mike insisted now. "Absolutely fact."

And I wasn't about to argue with him, either. Not just because he's a man. Not just because I didn't want him to re-think the great deal he was giving me, or assign my account to someone else. No, I had an even better reason than those.

Mike's a fan, no matter that Dave doesn't see it that way, and you never, ever argue with your fans. That's rule number one of being a celebrity. Fans are the lifeblood of our business. They're why we do what we do. They're the customer. They're always right. And you *never* want to run the risk of their turning into Kathy Bates

* * * *

Mike

Amusement shimmered in Claire's eyes. "Whatever you say, Mike," she murmured as she slid off her desk. She stood there for a moment, staring absently, running her hands up and down her thighs in a way that couldn't help but focus my attention there.

All sorts of inappropriate thoughts followed. I had to clear my throat to relieve the tension there.

Claire started and smiled. "Well, I guess I'd better stop wasting your time and let you get to work, huh?"

Her voice was tinged with regret as she said it. As though she really *was* sorry. As though she'd like nothing better than to spend the rest of the day chatting with me. I loved that. Even though I knew it was an act, I loved the tinge and the implication that went with it. And I loved her all the more for that small gift of pretense. For taking the trouble to sound like that for me. For allowing me the tiny pleasure of pretending right along with her.

I nodded with mock gravity. "Yes, well, you know what they say. *Time is money.*" And was rewarded again when she flashed a swift smile in my direction before she turned and slipped into her seat.

Silence settled over the room as we both settled into our work.

I'm good at what I do. That's not bragging, it's just a fact. And Claire's account is simple, straightforward—boring work really—nothing I can't do... well, pretty much in my sleep at this point. Which was lucky for both of us since, with the best will in the world, I still could not manage to keep my mind completely focused on what I was doing. Not with Claire seated in the same room with me, constantly re-igniting every fantasy I'd ever had about her.

She'd caught me off-guard with her question about my day. Since taking her on as a client, my life had become a surreal, slightly pathetic routine of counting. Every morning when I got up I automatically counted the days until I'd see her again. When every other Thursday rolled around, I counted the hours, and then the minutes. Finally, I counted the blocks I had to drive to get to her studio, the stairs I had to climb to reach her office.

And then there were most of my evenings. Nights when I could find no better way to occupy my time than to spend them conversing with her shadow in my mind. Or replaying our actual conversations. Remembering in detail each word, each look, each nuance. Weaving her every gesture into the fantasies I'd already spent years honing.

Well, what did you expect? I said it was pathetic, didn't I?

But I couldn't help it. I reveled in the knowledge that when she spoke my name, when she turned her head and saw me and smiled in greeting—her eyes shining, her whole face lighting up—that it was really me she was talking to and smiling at.

She hadn't been smiling when I arrived today, however. Her face, reflected in the glass, looked sad, vulnerable. I was pretty sure I knew why. It was him. Derek. Her former lover. The... kid... she'd recently broken up with. Or who'd broken up with her, if my suspicions were correct.

Which is not to say she didn't put on a great act, just like always, but I'd seen the way she looked at him—the way she was looking at him today through the windows in her office. I know what it's like to watch and want and worship from afar; to long for something you can never have. He'd moved on—that's how I read it—and Claire was putting the best face on it that she could. But it was all for show When she thought no one was looking, when she was alone, unobserved, that's when she let down her guard. That's when her real feelings shone though.

I would have liked to have said something more to comfort her, but what could I have said? Should I have told her it was all for the best? That she should have known better? He was too young for her. She was too good for him. It was doomed from the start. All true, but hardly likely to make her feel any better.

I could have told her that a woman like her shouldn't have to waste her time playing with boys. Not when there was a man around who could understand what she wants, what she needs...

But, no, what was I thinking? A woman *like* Claire? Impossible. Such a creature doesn't exist. There's *no one* like Claire. She's an original. She's in a class all her own.

"Are you doing anything later this evening?" Claire's voice broke into my reverie.

Startled, and pretty certain I was hearing things, I glanced at her. "I'm sorry... what did you say?"

"I was wondering if you were busy tonight?" she said and then shook her head and smiled. "Sorry. I guess I'm thinking aloud again. It's just that a friend of mine has a new gallery. They're having an opening party tonight. She's sent me a bunch of invitations and I was wondering if you would be interested in attending?"

"A gallery opening? Tonight? Will you be there?"

Claire nodded. "I try to attend as many of these things as I can. This seems like a nice one... cocktails, hors d'oeuvres, live music. But, it's short notice. You probably have other plans..."

"No, actually, I don't." The only thing I had going tonight was the start of a new countdown. Fourteen long days until the next time I'd see her. Or thirteen days, twenty-one hours and change, if you want to be exact. But so what? It would feel like a long time, that much I knew. Why would I not want to shave even a few hours off that total? "I'd love to go."

Chapter Two

Claire

The gallery was crowded. The music was loud and not to my liking. And although some of the art on display was interesting enough, let's face it; I wasn't in the market for any more investments. I'd sunk almost everything I had into The Body Electric, which was still in its 'hot new thing' phase. Sure, business was good—for now. But who knew how long that would last?

Still, the evening wasn't a total loss. The drinks were complimentary and the bartender was to die for. I sipped my mojito and looked him over once again.

He caught my look and smiled. "How is everything?" he asked, meaning my drink.

"Just delicious," I replied, making sure he knew I didn't.

Could I just say right here that I love men? For, oh, so many reasons. Just the sheer *maleness* of them. Even the sight of a five o'clock shadow on a rugged, square chin can turn me on. Can make my skin burn. Can make my fingers itch with the urge to touch and make me quiver as I imagine soft, sandpapery warmth in all my most sensitive places. Then there's the strength in their hands, their fingers. The softness of their lips. The musk of their sweat. I swear those veins that stand out on their arms when they flex their muscles are enough, sometimes, to make me crazy. Not to mention the muscles themselves.

The bartender had it all going on—including a killer smile and a soulful, sweet expression beneath a pair of jet black brows. He was an actor, of course. Just like everyone in this town. At least, everyone under twenty-five. That seems to be the cut-off. By twenty-six you know if you stand the ghost of a chance or are just marking time. If you're still in the business at twenty-eight it's because you've either tasted success or figured out that there's nothing else you're suited for.

When I was twenty-five, I thought I was Money. I had it made. It didn't last. I wonder, sometimes, if it wouldn't have been better—for me—if it hadn't ever happened at all. Sure, I wouldn't have been famous, but maybe I'd have been happy instead.

Some days it feels like I gave up a lot to get here. Others, it feels like I gave up too much. Still, even on those other days, fame does have its perks. Maybe especially on those days. I'm a name.

I'm a face. And I could still recall how the game was played.

"What's your name, sweetie?" I asked, getting into the role.

The bartender's eyes lit up. "Javier," he replied, with another deadly smile.

I pushed my glass across the bar and returned his smile with one of my own; every bit as lethal. "Well, Javier, the ice in my drink has begun to melt. Why don't you be a darling and see if you can't find a way to freshen it up for me, okay?"

His smile disappeared. "Right away, Miss Calhoun," he said as he hustled away.

"Claire," I murmured watching him run. Have I mentioned he had a nice butt, too? "Call me Claire."

Would Javier sweetie really be quite so attentive if I was just a washed-up, not quite middle-aged, no-one-in-particular? Not bloody likely. But even tarnished stars still have some shine. No doubt he thought I could open doors for him. That I knew people who knew people who would give him a break. And maybe I did. Maybe I would. For a price.

Cold? Possibly. But don't expect me to shed any tears over yet another aspiring Adonis. This town is full of them. And, male or female, we all have to pay our dues. There's only one real difference between Javier and me and it's this: when I was in his shoes I was wearing heels.

In less than a minute, he was back with a fresh new mojito. I smiled my thanks.

"So, Claire, what are you doing after the party tonight?" he leaned in to ask, ambition gleaming brightly in those sweet brown eyes. No doubt he'd checked out the room while he was re-filling my drink. He'd obviously concluded that I was either the biggest name here or the easiest to hit on. Maybe both. The next move was mine.

Before I had a chance to make it, however... "Red wine, please," a man's deep voice ordered sharply.

Startled, Javier scrambled back to work. I turned to find Mike looming menacingly behind me. He looked quite resplendent tonight, if a little grim, dressed in charcoal pin-stripes paired with an olive silk shirt.

"Nice suit," I said, as I took it all in. "Fioravanti?"

Mike snorted in amusement. "Don't I wish. No. Dolce and Gabbana."

"Also nice." I continued to study him, idly twirling the straw around in my glass. "You clean up good."

"Thank you," Mike said, shooting another stern glance in Javier's direction. The slight clenching of his jaw drew my attention higher, to the small, brownish gold stone shining in his left ear lobe.

"Is this new?" I asked, reaching up to touch it, my fingers grazing his cheek as I did.

Mike's eyes widened into an astonished expression. His gaze flew to my face.

"Oops." I grinned. "Sorry. I guess my fingers are cold, huh?"

Mike shook his head. "No. Not at all." Red stained his cheekbones. His skin felt very warm against my fingers.

"Liar." Clucking my tongue, I withdrew my hand. My eyes, however, stayed locked with his and a familiar thrill ran through me. I love being desired. Who doesn't? I love that flash of heat that flares in a man's eyes when he wants you. I could see it in Mike's eyes now and it made it hard to look away.

"Your wine, sir," Javier murmured from somewhere far away. We both ignored him.

"You don't wear that all the time, do you?" I asked.

"Not very often. Just special occasions."

"Oh? So is this a special occasion?"

Mike nodded gravely. "Yes. Most definitely."

I dropped my gaze then, and sipped my drink. "Well I think it's a waste to save it for something like that. It looks good on you. You should wear it all the time."

"Maybe I will."

Behind me, I could hear Javier moving away to help someone else. "But what's all this?" I asked, gesturing at Mike's suit again. "You've been holding out on me. I had no idea you had such exquisite taste. Don't tell me. I bet you keep an entire wardrobe locked up in your office in case of last minute invitations from thoughtless clients. Don't you?"

He smiled. "No. And you're certainly not thoughtless. I went home to change."

"Oh? Where's home?"

"Topanga Canyon."

Now it was my turn to be surprised. "Wow. That's quite a drive."

"It can be," he agreed. "But it's worth it. It's like living in another world out there. In a matter of minutes, you can be at the beach. And in another few minutes, you're back in town. Or not—

depending on the traffic, of course."

Mostly not, I thought, nodding. "I haven't been in years. But I remember thinking it was beautiful there. I shot a few pictures out that way."

"I know. I've seen them."

"Have you?" I sincerely hoped not! The films I shot in Topanga Canyon fell squarely in the dues-I'd-paid-when-I-was-too-young-to-know-any-better category. Definitely *not* the kind of thing I'd want associated with my name today. I shouldn't even have mentioned them. "So, tell me about your home," I said, just to change the subject. "Big place? New?"

Mike sipped his wine and shook his head. I snagged a lavender and goat cheese empanada from one of the trays that were being circulated.

"No, actually, it's very small," Mike said. "Just two bedrooms, not quite half an acre. But it's just me, after all, so I don't need much space. And I had a hand in designing it, so I'm partial to it."

"You design houses?" I asked around a mouthful of pastry.

"Well, no. Just the one. Architecture has always been a passion of mine. And, besides, it was years ago."

He was full of surprises tonight, but my mouth was full and before I could learn more, we were interrupted by some of my staff from work, including Derek along with his new friend, coming up to say hello. When I turned back to continue our conversation, Mike was gone.

"Can I freshen that drink for you, Claire?" Javier asked hopefully. But I was no longer in the mood.

I flashed a smile. "Sorry, sweetie. Not tonight." Then I stuffed some bills into the tip glass and slipped into the crowd.

I planned on making one more circle around the room before I left. There was only one thing I wanted this evening, and I was damned unlikely to get it. I knew now what was making me feel so out of sorts, and could only wonder why I hadn't figured it out sooner. It'd had been months since I had anyone to warm my bed. Months! I was horny. Worse yet, I was *lonely*. Auto-eroticism might be the safest sex there is, but it can also be the most boring. The best vibrator in the world is still nothing you're gonna be thrilled to wake up beside in the morning. My mood was only going to be improved by one thing. A fling. An affair. A good, old fashioned shag-fest with a real live human being.

But, who? Ah, now, that was the question.

My lovers, over the years, have pretty much fallen into two basic categories—powerful, influential older men or those who were young, hot and hungry. Lately there hadn't been many of the older ones and, frankly, I didn't miss them. I'd long since tired of being used as a prop. Something to bolster their sagging egos, their flagging careers, their diminished mental acuity. Or anything else that had gone soft on them.

But, to be honest, I wasn't in the mood for someone like Javier tonight, either.

Young men... well, sometimes they're just too damn *young*. It's tiring. Trying to impress them, trying to keep up with them, trying not to mother them—who needs it?

The plain truth was, both young and old, most men would want something from me tonight that I didn't want to give: A performance. I didn't want to act young or adoring or impressed tonight. I didn't want to act innocent or worldly. I didn't want to act at all. All I wanted was sex—hot, sweaty and satisfying—with a man who wanted the same exact thing. And who wanted me just for myself.

But where would I find someone like that? Nowhere in this room, that was certain. Probably nowhere in this town.

I swept the crowd with a glance, taking in all the players— and they were *all* players, weren't they? But no, scratch that. Not all. My eyes settled on Mike, studying one of the paintings on display with every appearance of interest. My heart began to beat a little faster and I smiled.

He'd made no excuses for his presence here. No pretense of a last minute cancellation, a coincidental meeting in the neighborhood, prior plans to be here anyway. He'd made it clear he'd gone out of his way to come here tonight and for no other reason than because I'd invited him.

He was interesting, honest, refreshingly direct in a town where high concept was the official language; where every story had a spin and every conversation was a pitch.

My decision made, I cut short my circuit of the room and headed in his direction.

* * * *

Mike

The touch on my arm was soft but insistent. I turned reluctantly from the painting I'd been examining to find Claire smiling at me. Her eyes were wide and luminous and, as often seemed to happen, the sight of her left me tongue-tied.

"I'd like you to take me home tonight," she said. There was a flush on her cheeks and a strange catch in her voice.

It took a moment for the words to register. When they did, they brought a slight sense of alarm. Obviously, she must have decided she was too drunk to drive herself home. But, surely there were others closer to her that she could have asked for a ride: friends, former lovers, hangers-on, employees. *Why me?*

Maybe it was more than just drink? *Has someone been bothering her? Upsetting her? Hurting her?* Someone like Derek, perhaps, flaunting his latest conquest in her face. Or that bartender...

Thinking about it brought a rush of anger that rendered me even more speechless than usual. The urge to protect her was not so much unexpected as it was illogical because, again, there were plenty of others here who'd be better suited for that, as well.

"Mike?"

I shook myself out of my stupor. She'd chosen me—why really didn't matter—and there could be no question as to how I'd respond. "Yes, of course. Certainly. Did you mean now?"

Looking vaguely surprised, Claire nodded. "Well, yes, sure. Unless you'd rather stay?"

"No, not at all," I assured her. "I'm ready when you are."

"Good to know." Her smile peeked out once again. "So then what are we waiting for?"

* * * *

"Where to?" I asked as I pulled away from the gallery entrance.

Claire didn't answer right away. She seemed distracted—as she had ever since the valet pulled the Jag up to the curb. "Well... I don't know." Her gaze was thoughtful as she glanced around at the car's interior. "How would you feel about taking a drive along Mulholland first to get some air? Maybe stop for a moment to see the lights?"

"Air?" *She mustn't be feeling well,* I thought and groaned inwardly. *Shit. Isn't that great?* I'm really not overly anal when it comes to my possessions, but I happen to love my car—a classic Jaguar, built in the years before all the electrical problems; before the company was taken over by GM. I really hated the idea of anyone getting sick all over the upholstery. Even Claire. If a little fresh air was going to prevent that, "Mulholland it is."

Neither of us said anything as we sped along the mostly deserted streets. I was just praying that the winding road wouldn't make her even more sick.

The turnout that you always see in movies is all the way at the western end of the highway, close to where the pavement stops. I was pretty certain she wouldn't want to drive that far, but there are plenty of places to stop along the way to admire the view. I pulled into the first likely spot and turned off the ignition.

Claire removed her seatbelt but she made no move to open the door, which I took to be a good sign.

"How are you feeling now?" I asked, watching as she stared at the lights below us.

She laughed a little, as though I'd said something funny. "You know, I used to drive up here all the time, when I was younger, when I was new to LA and depressed about my career. Somehow, it always seemed to help me put things in perspective. I'd sit up here and listen to the radio and try to remember why I was putting myself through all that misery. So, I guess... compared to then... I'm feeling pretty good right now. How about you?"

"Me?" I thought about that. There I was, in the middle of a clear, star-studded night, parked atop the Hollywood Hills, with Claire Calhoun in the passenger seat of my Jaguar. I didn't really see how things could get much better than that. But, at a time when I should be feeling like the king of the world, what was the main thing on my mind? Something I never thought I'd be worried about. Carpet cleaner. Un-fucking-believable. I shook my head, pushed all thoughts of cleaning products from my mind and smiled. "I'm fantastic."

"Are you?" She slanted me an amused glance, then looked away again, running the fingers of her right hand along the wood of the dash. "So, tell me about your car. It's a Jaguar, right? I can't believe..."

"What?" I asked, mesmerized by her fingers, wondering if she could possibly have been reading my mind. Or did she just think it an unlikely vehicle for an accountant to drive?

"Nothing." She shook her head and prompted. "The car?"

I shrugged. "Not that much to tell, really. I just always... well, I'd seen this exact car in a showroom years ago—this model, I mean—back when it was new. It was love at first sight. I must've gone back there oh, a dozen or so times, just to sit in it. Never even took it out for a test drive. I think I was afraid to. Afraid I wouldn't want to bring it back. I was young then, just starting out, couldn't come close to affording it. I mean... it wasn't even in the realm of possibility, at that point. It was just... a dream, you know?"

"So what happened?" she asked quietly.

I sighed. "Nothing happened. After a couple of weeks, I gave in to the inevitable and bought something else. It was damned hard having to settle for something—for anything—less when my heart was set on this, but what could I do? I told myself 'some day' but, then, later, when I had a little more money, there were always other things that seemed more pressing, more important, more practical. I found a piece of land I fell in love with, built a house; that took money. Plus, the newer Jags... well, they just weren't the same. So, I guess I just put it from my mind. But then, a couple of years ago, I was in the market for a new car, once again, and I came across an ad for this one—used, in need of a little work, selling for a song. It's not what I'd been looking for. In fact, by then, I'd pretty much given up on the dream entirely. But, when it came right down to it, it was *My Car*. How could I resist? I had to buy it."

Claire was looking at me strangely when I finished talking. "That is a very romantic story."

"You think so?"

"Mm-hm. And it's a beautiful car."

Well, that part I agreed with. "It is. It's a classic. Beautiful, elegant, it can't ever really go out of style. And it handles... well, like I always knew it would." Suddenly, I remembered that she wasn't feeling well. "I'm sorry, I shouldn't have gone on so long. You must be bored."

Claire shook her head. "Not a bit. And don't be sorry. I asked, remember?" Then she flashed that wonderful smile at me again. "Why don't we get going now?"

I nodded, feeling just a little sorry because this was a moment I knew wouldn't likely come again. It would have been nice to stretch it out a little longer.

If only she were feeling better. If only I'd thought to pack a picnic, a blanket, a bottle of wine. But, given the circumstances—really not a good idea. I'd started the car when I remembered, "I still don't know where you live."

"That's all right," she said as she re-fastened her seatbelt. "I don't want to go there anyway."

My eyebrows rose. "Well, then, where are we going?"

Her hands stilled on the buckle. She looked at me

questioningly. "I thought... your house. No?"

"*My* house?"

She nodded. "Mm-hm. You know, the one you said you helped design? I'm intrigued. I'd really like to see it."

"But... that's... that's all the way out in Topanga Canyon." Surely she didn't expect me to drive all the way out there, then back here, then back out there again? All in one night? Or was she so drunk the idea seemed reasonable?

Claire's lips quirked. "I know where it is. Is there a problem?"

I sighed. That would be a *Yes* on the drunk question, wouldn't it? "Look, Claire, that's a little far for a joy ride, don't you think?" I hinted, as gently as I could.

"Weren't you planning on going home tonight anyway?"

"Yes. Once. But not... not two or three times." Not that the idea of spending all that time alone with her wasn't heavenly but... well, no, damn it, this was not quite what I'd had in mind. "I know I said the drive back into town only takes a matter of minutes but, even so, those minutes do add up. And I've driven out there and back once tonight already. Besides, it's getting a little late. Wouldn't you rather I just take you home now?"

Claire was staring at me fixedly, as though attempting to puzzle something out. Finally, "Michael, I thought you understood? When I asked you to take me home I meant I wanted to spend the night with you."

This time, I knew for certain I was hearing things. I shook my head, hoping to clear it. "Spend the night?"

She nodded. "With you. Yes. Is something wrong?"

The only thing wrong was the way the blood had left my skull, headed straight for my dick. Somehow, I'd have thought that would make my brain feel clearer, but it didn't. "Just—Jesus, how much did you have to drink back there anyhow?"

Laughing, Claire slipped her seatbelt off again. She leaned in close and lifted one of her hands to frame my face. Her fingers felt as cool as they had before; but this was even better than before because this time she was touching me on purpose. Her eyes were dark, her smile was sultry and her voice and her words were something out of a dream. "You're a very sweet man, Mike. You shouldn't sell yourself short." Then she kissed me.

For a moment, I think I forgot who either of us was. We were simply Man and Woman and *nothing* had ever felt more right. Her lips were soft, her scent was sweet and everything male in me responded. *Mine.* Fierce and insistent, the instinct to claim her, to take her as my own—now, tonight, forever—overrode everything else.

I kissed her back, tugging her hard against me, my tongue coaxing hers into play. Touching everything I could get my hands on, I practically tore the material of her dress as I sought for the zipper. Then my hands registered the feel of the sequined gown they were coasting over—the same glimmering garment I'd been trying, all evening, not to stare at. Suddenly, I remembered where I was and who I was with.

"Claire. Oh, my God. I'm sorry, I—"

She opened her eyes. Something dark flickered in their depths—heat and passion and something else. Alarm, maybe?

"Wow." Her voice emerged hoarse and breathless. "Mike. You *really* shouldn't sell yourself short."

A relieved laugh burst from my lips. I'd been half expecting her to slap me, never mind that she'd started it. "I think that 'wow' just made my night. Thank you." I took a deep breath. Resting my forehead against hers, I forced myself to take control. "But, please tell me where you live so I can drive you home."

"What?" Claire pulled away from me. "I already told you. I *don't* want to go there."

I nodded. "I know you did. But, come on, you've been drinking. Even if I thought you actually meant it, I still can't take advantage of you like this."

"Is *that* what's bothering you?" She shook her head, gazing at me in disbelief. "So I've been drinking, Mike. So what? It's not exactly the first time that's happened you know. And, besides, isn't that really the reason most people drink to begin with? So they can loosen up, release their inhibitions, forget about the rules they don't want to follow?"

"Sleep with people they wouldn't otherwise in a million years?"

"That too." Laughter sparkled suddenly in her eyes. "Which is not always a bad thing, you know. And, besides..." Leaning in, she ran one hand up my chest. Her lips were only inches from mine; her voice husky and low. "I want you. If you're trying to imply that's only because I'm drunk, it's not true."

My heart was hammering in my chest. If I wanted to remain sane, I needed some space. Now. I pushed her away a little. "Claire. Stop kidding around. You *know* it's true."

"It's not! Not even a little."

"Oh, it isn't? Really? I've known you for months. How come this is the first time it's come up then?"

"Well, I mean," Grinning, she peeked up at me through her lashes. "I don't *always* sleep with everyone I meet within minutes of meeting them either, you know. Besides... a million years, Mike? That's a *really* long time."

"I know how long it is." And I figured it was maybe half as long as it was gonna take me to forget that kiss. Or to stop wanting to kiss her again. Right now. But, want it or not, it *wasn't* going to happen.

A petulant frown creased Claire's brow. "You can't *possibly* believe I'm so drunk I don't know what I'm doing? Or do you think I'm gonna wake up tomorrow morning and wonder, *what the hell was I thinking last night?*"

That was *exactly* what I thought. I felt my jaw clench. "You might."

She shook her head. "I won't"

"Your address," I repeated stubbornly.

Uttering an exasperated sigh, Claire collapsed against the car door. Arms folded, she glared at me. "You know, Mike, a little hesitation is endearing, too much feels like rejection. No woman likes that. And I can assure you I'm not anywhere *near* as drunk as I'd have to be to forget about this. Is that really what you want me to remember when I wake up tomorrow morning? That I asked you to take me to bed and you turned me down? Because I can promise you, I'm not gonna like it any better then."

"Claire, I am *not* turning you down. I wouldn't *ever* do that."

"Oh, you're not?"

"No! I—I... shit." What the hell was I saying? Of course I was turning her down. What the fuck was wrong with me?

I couldn't believe this conversation. And, as bad as the one I was having with her, it had nothing on the internal one I had going on with myself. It was like one of those old cartoons, where I had an angel on one shoulder and a devil on the other; both urging me on, both sounding incredibly convincing. Only one of them could be right and, as usual, that would be the one telling you what you didn't want to hear.

"Look, I don't want you waking up tomorrow and remembering I took advantage of you while you were drunk." That would be the worst. I was pretty sure that would be worse than any of the alternatives. Wouldn't it?

"Why don't we let me worry about how I'm going to feel about things in the morning, hmm?" Claire arched an eyebrow, clearly waiting for me to give in.

I said nothing.

"Oh, for God's sake," she fumed. "It's just *sex*, Mike. It's fun. It feels good. It's supposed to be enjoyable. If you're looking for something you can feel guilty about, I suggest you run a few stop signs on the way home."

"Claire..."

She shook her head sadly, shoulders sagging, and I could tell I'd finally worn her down. Winning had never left me feeling so shitty. But I was wrong. She wasn't done. Not quite yet.

Taking a deep breath, Claire raised her head and fixed me with a steely gaze. Her voice, when she spoke, was clear, quiet, sad. But not the voice of someone who was intoxicated. Not even a little. "There have been a few things in my life I've regretted doing, Mike. If I live long enough, I'm sure there'll be more. Sleeping with you tonight would *not* have been one of them. Can you say the same, if you turn me down?"

And, no, God help me, I couldn't say that. Without another word, I put the car in gear and floored the gas. What else was there to say, after all?

"Now, that's more like it," Claire murmured happily, settling back in her seat and snapping her seatbelt back into place.

A man can only withstand so much temptation. And, when the choice is one of being damned if you do, damned if you don't, well, that's really not much of a choice now, is it?

Chapter Three

Claire

The air in the canyon was warm, fragrant; drier and grittier than the air in town had been, but clearer, too, and what looked like a billion stars were shining overhead.

"Well, here we are," Mike announced as he pulled into his drive. I couldn't decide if he sounded nervous or excited or both. His house was small, just as he'd described it, but it looked cozy. Even in the dark, I could see that the grounds were impeccably kept.

As I opened the car door the smell of lemons and moss greeted me, along with the fainter scents of bay laurel and chaparral. Mike was out of the car ahead of me. Before I'd put so much as a foot on the ground, he was right there, extending a hand to help me out. I smiled at him as I stood, coming to my feet with only scant inches between us. I thought that would have been a great time for him to kiss me again, in the soft air and the starlight, but he didn't. He just reached around me to push the door shut, then put his hand on my back and guided me up the path toward the house. Frankly, I was a little disappointed.

That kiss we'd shared in the car had seemed nothing short of amazing and I was eager for a repeat. But, maybe I'd been imagining things? Maybe I'd been looking for something—an excuse to continue in the face of his reluctance, a reason to convince him, or maybe to convince us both, that this was a good idea, that we wouldn't just be wasting our time tonight.

He'd certainly seemed eager enough—then. But now? Now he seemed distant, remote, and I'd had more than enough of that in my last marriage. Of course, it could be he was just tired. But, on a night when I was hoping for heat or, failing that, a little warmth; at a time when I longed for the honest passion of an honest man, it struck the wrong note entirely.

A couple of steps led up to the front entry. Two wide, porcelain bowls, jade green and filled with water, stood at the top, delicate water lilies floating inside. The double doors of the front entry, also jade green, were unadorned, save for the round windows in each one. Made of thick, wavy discs of blown glass forming concentric rings, they looked like water that had frozen in mid-ripple.

Mike unlocked the door and pushed it open. "After you," he murmured.

I smiled as I slipped past him into the house, but said nothing.

Inside, the house was a comfortable, timeless blending of old and new. Hardwood floors in the living room, wooden vigas on the ceiling, a distressed-brick fireplace that seemed to take up one entire wall. Mission Oak furniture. A Mondrian-style carpet. Arts and Crafts lampshades.

A set of whimsical, wrought-iron fireplace tools graced the hearth, their spiral design echoed in the iron pot rack that hung above the stove. The terracotta kitchen floor wore the kind of shiny, rich patina that only comes with age and care. An earthenware water jug sat atop the mosaic tiled counter and next to it, a heavy tumbler of Mexican glass. Beyond that was the dining room: Danish teak beneath a copper and mica chandelier.

The back wall, which faced the softly burbling creek, was mostly louvered glass. With all its narrow frosted panes angled open, as they were now, it was like a solid wall of night. Through it, all the sounds and smells that rose on the evening air flowed, unchecked, into the house.

"It's lovely," I murmured politely. It *was* lovely, and unusual and different, but I hadn't really come here for the house.

"Thank you," Mike replied, making no move to join me. He'd tossed his jacket over the back of the couch when we entered, but after that, he'd seemed to be almost frozen in place, moving just enough to keep me in sight. "Would you like something to drink?" he asked at last.

Seriously? "Uh, no," I said, trying hard not to laugh. "I think I'm okay for now." He already thought I was drunk, didn't he? He must be more nervous than I thought, if he was offering me more. Or maybe he was looking to get me completely plastered?

"Coffee? Tea? Something to eat, then? Cheese and crackers, perhaps? Or..."

"Nothing. Thanks."

I continued exploring. Berber carpeting in the bedroom. More glass. Another fireplace—this one framed in river rock. The bed was a huge four-poster; walnut and wrought iron.

"I can see you really have a thing for iron," I observed, turning toward the doorway where Mike was propping up the doorframe. "Another passion?"

He shrugged. "Not really. There's an artist—up near Pismo. I was at a fair... oh, several years ago now... I saw his work and... well, I was redecorating, anyway, so..." His voice trailed away. We stared at each other with the length of the room between us.

Finally, he dropped his gaze. "Help me out, Claire. I'm lost. I don't know what to do here."

Well, at least he was honest. And wasn't that what I said I wanted? I felt my lips quirk. "Well... you *could* start by kissing me again."

I think I was expecting him to hesitate, maybe even argue with me again. But he didn't. He was across the room in an instant, caging my face between his hands, lowering his mouth to mine.

Oh, yes. I hadn't been mistaken. Mike's kiss was a heady mix of persuasion and demand. Gentle yet insistent with a deliciously dominant edge—something that had been missing from most of my relationships, ever since my third husband—an abusive sonofabitch if there ever was one—had taught me to fear strong men.

This was just what I wanted, just what I'd been hoping for—for so long I'd almost given up on ever finding it. I leaned into him eagerly, flattening my hands on his chest, content to follow his lead, giving him free rein with my mouth and with anything else he cared to try for.

After a long, luscious moment, Mike lifted his head, then appeared to change his mind. His fingers tightened on my face again and he kissed me twice more, very quickly. "God, Claire." His voice, husky and even deeper than usual, rumbled out of his chest. "Are you really serious about this?"

I sighed contentedly. "About what?"

"About this. Us. Tonight. Everything."

Still? "Oh, Mike." Shaking my head, I pushed away from him, took a few steps back, unzipped my dress and let it fall to the ground. I kicked it aside. Heat flared in his eyes.

"Does this answer your question?" I asked as I stood before him, hands on my hips, wearing only a few scraps of lace—panties, bra, garter belt—stockings and heels.

He swallowed hard and nodded. "I guess so."

"Good." Smiling, I stepped back into his arms. He grabbed me as soon as I came within reach, pulling me close. The look on his face, just before I kissed him, was one of unabashed relief.

Finally, I thought as I felt his hesitation dissolve; as he speared both hands into my hair, wrestling with the clip that held it in place finally freeing it to tumble loose around my shoulders. Then, with one hand firmly cupping the back of my head, the other one framing my face, he slanted my head to the side and took control again.

My skin tingled as his fingers trailed down my cheek, my throat, my chest. My nipples beaded hard and tight in anticipation of his touch. I pressed myself closer. But he ignored the invitation. His hand curved only briefly around my breast and continued onward; gliding warmly over my ribs, to my hip; sliding over my butt to grasp the top of my thigh. He lifted my leg and wrapped it around his waist. Then he slipped his fingers beneath the flimsy lace of my panties to pet my slit. He teased my clit, brushing lightly all around it, circling, circling, circling, coming tantalizingly close, and then moving away.

As his fingers probed my opening, a rush of fluid from my pussy coated his hand. I could feel my own slickness in the silken gliding of his fingers as he continued his exploration; moving even further back now, to tease my anus. I rocked my hips against the motion of his hand, eager for more; shuddering as my sex suddenly spasmed. The leg I was standing on trembled and Mike adjusted his hold on me, trapping me ever more tightly against him, curtailing my movements—and sending another tremor rocketing through me.

I was going to come in no time at all if he kept this up, which was not what I wanted. Not here, not now, not yet. All-night sex is a young man's game—at least that's how it's always seemed to me—unless drugs are involved. I figured Mike and I were good for one round tonight, or maybe two. So, wasting it all now was not any part of my game plan. I was hoping we could make things last a little longer than that!

Wrenching my mouth away from his I murmured, "Take off your clothes."

Mike gazed blankly at me for an instant, and then dragged me back in for another kiss.

"Your clothes," I repeated, pushing him away again.

"What about 'em?"

"Take them off."

Half closed eyes glittered darkly. Mike's fingers, still tight on my flesh but unmoving now, seemed hot enough to almost sear my skin.

The look on his face set my heart racing. I had to swallow hard before I could add a whispered, "please," to my request.

"All right," he muttered as he released me. "Just give me a minute. And don't move."

Don't move? What's that about? Curious, I widened my stance a little, clasped my hands behind my back and waited.

As I watched, Mike struggled to unbutton his shirt and then remove his cufflinks. His chest was broad and lightly furred. He was more muscular than I'd expected, thick and solid around the middle. Not fat, as I'd first thought, but without either the burnished, bronze skin or six-pack abs I'd grown so used to after dating younger men. He caught me looking and averted his eyes from my face. I'd swear he was blushing. I bit back a smile as he began to swear softly at the cufflink that was giving him so much trouble.

Finally, he prevailed over the recalcitrant bit of metal. Sighing with relief, Mike peeled off his shirt. Then he tossed it and the cufflinks on top of his dresser and grabbed hold of my arm.

"Wait," I protested as he all but dragged me across the room. "What are you doing?"

He glanced at me quizzically. "What do you mean, 'what am I doing'? I'm getting undressed. That's what you wanted, right?"

Surprised, I nodded.

"All right then." He dropped my arm when I was about a foot from the bed. "So, just... just... ah, shit. Just stand there, okay? Right where I can see you."

Ahh. I felt my eyebrows rise as the implication hit home. *I get it now. He likes to watch.* "Okay, Mike, sure. Whatever you say."

Nodding, Mike sat down on the bed and began to remove his shoes.

"So, what is it you want to see?" Smiling archly, I slid one hand down over my belly, playfully covering my mound, while my other hand lightly cupped one breast. "Do you want to watch me touch myself? Or would you rather have me strip for you?"

For an instant, Mike's mouth gaped open. Then he shook his head, chuckling softly. "What a question. I dunno, both maybe? But later, okay?" He removed his other shoe muttering, "Oh, man, I do not *believe* this is happening." Then he looked at me and added a hopeful, "I know, could you maybe lose the bra?"

"I could," I purred, as I slowly slipped the straps off my shoulders. I reached behind me to release the catch and then whipped the bra away from my chest, striking a pose with my legs apart and one hand on my hip. The other arm, the one holding the bra, I held out to the side at shoulder height. Lace dangled from my finger tips. A smile lingered on my lips. "Better?"

Mike nodded. "Come here."

Dropping the garment to the floor, I cat-walked over to where he sat. He reached for my waist and pulled me closer, until I was standing trapped between his legs, the fronts of my thighs nearly brushing against the bulge in his trousers.

"God, they're even more beautiful in person," he murmured, his gaze riveted on my breasts; dusky, distended nipples poking straight at his face. A shudder of apprehension rippled through me, one that owed nothing to his gaze.

It had been quite a while since I'd bared my breasts for the camera. I'd thought, or hoped, that most of those pictures had gotten lost in the intervening years. Once again I found myself wondering how much Mike had seen. And when. And where. But then he ran the fingers of one hand almost reverently across the swollen tips, causing them to harden even more, and I stopped thinking, stopped caring, stopped worrying. For now.

Mike's eyes shifted upwards to lock with mine. "You're so beautiful. More beautiful than I'd ever dreamed."

And you're sooo scoring points with that, I thought, smiling encouragingly. "Don't stop."

"Never."

There's a type of gentleness that comes from weakness, from hesitancy or uncertainty, or even disinterest. But, there's another type that speaks of quiet strength, control, authority, of banked fires held deliberately in check. Mike's touch was definitely the second type. He stroked my flesh with slow certainty, first with his fingers, then with his tongue. The soft, teasing touches soon put me right back on the edge of orgasm and left me moaning. "More. Now."

"Shhh," Mike hushed, pausing to lave the tip of one nipple with his tongue. "This is much too good to hurry." It was clear that he intended to thoroughly enjoy himself—no matter how long it took.

I know I'd said that's what I wanted as well; to take things slow, to prolong this as much as possible, but I've always had extraordinarily sensitive nipples and the sensations his gentle touch was eliciting were zinging straight to my groin with the speed of a falling elevator. I could feel my labia swelling, throbbing, aching for relief. Enough was enough.

Grabbing Mike's head between my hands, I forced his face

upward, lowered my mouth to his and kissed him. Then I was straddling his lap, and grinding my damp crotch against his erection.

Groaning, Mike fell backward onto the bed, palming my breasts in his hands, kissing me back, seemingly acquiescent for maybe half a minute. Then, without warning, he rolled and I was beneath him, wrists pinned to the bed on either side of my head.

Flat on my back, I stared up into his face.

Mike's eyes were fierce in the low light. "You're friggin' killing me here. I'm gonna have to fuck you right the hell now. Is that what you want?"

I gasped, surprised by his words, still surprised to find myself suddenly helpless, at his mercy. I was almost dizzy with all the lust the scene was evoking. "Yes," I whispered. "Please."

"Fine." Letting go of one of my wrists, Mike unzipped his pants, freeing his erection. Here too, he was more solid than I'd expected. Not overly large, but thick and hard and definitely ready. "Then that's just what you're gonna get."

"Yes." I licked my lips, already imagining how good that cock was going to feel thrusting against the walls of my pussy, filling me, stretching me.

"Ah, shit," Mike groaned as his penis jerked once, twice, three times; like an overeager race horse kicking at the gate. And, each kick caused an answering throb deep inside me. "I don't believe this. I'm about ready to go off in your face."

"Well, if that's what you want..." *Mmm. Yum.* Mouth watering at the thought, I was about ready to start begging for a taste.

"No." Mike closed his eyes and wrapped his hand around his shaft. He looked as though he were trying to will himself calm. I wriggled impatiently. *Let's go already!* After a moment he sighed, opened his eyes, released his cock, and reached toward the night table.

"What now?" I moaned fretfully. Good lord, what was taking so long?

"Condom," he rasped in reply, fingers scrabbling for the drawer handle.

I shook my head. "Don't bother. IUD. We're good."

With his hand in mid-reach, Mike froze. He gazed at me inquiringly. "We are?"

"I'm okay if you are," I told him.

He nodded. "I'm okay." Then he hooked a finger into the crotch of my panties and pulled them aside. "So sweet," he murmured, flexing his hips until the tip of his cock nudged my pussy. His hand re-captured my wrists as he pushed forward slowly, stretching and filling me, until he'd seated himself fully inside me. "So fucking sweet."

"Mmm," I answered, head thrashing from side to side. "Mmm—more. More."

"You got it," he growled, leaning down to kiss my lips once, harshly, briefly, and then he was pounding into me hard, fast, unstoppable. "Open up. Let me in and I'll give you all you want."

I planted my heels on the bed, spread my thighs wider, canted my hips upwards and that was all it took. Mike's next stroke hit my sweet spot so perfectly that I came right then bucking beneath him, again and again. The muscles of my vagina spasmed as they tried to close around his cock; squeezing tighter, tighter, tighter.

"No, damn it," Mike gritted through clenched teeth. "Not. Yet. Shit!" His fingers tightened on my wrists as he came; hot cum spurting high inside me while the aftershocks rocked us both.

In the next instant, he'd rolled off of me to lie on his back. His expression was strained as he gazed at the ceiling. He appeared to be in shock. Then he turned his head to look at me. We stared at each other in silence until I'd gathered the strength to move. Finally, smiling weakly, I slid my hand the couple of inches necessary to stroke his cheek. "Nice one," I murmured.

He turned his head a tiny bit more—enough so that my fingers grazed his lips. Softly, he kissed each one. "You're really something, you know that?"

"Yeah." I smiled wider. "Tired." Reluctantly, I pulled my hand away so I could cover my own mouth as I yawned. "I'm really tired." There'd been a time when I'd have been insulted if a man had behaved as I was doing now—pleading exhaustion after just one screw—but tonight, the shoe was on the other foot. I'd just had what was possibly the best quickie of my life, and I was content. All I wanted was a soft bed, sound sleep and a warm body to curl up against.

I didn't even want to muster up the energy to finish undressing. I just kicked off my shoes rolled onto my side and closed my eyes. Maybe I'd get lucky and he'd take the hint, roll up next to me and—

"What're you doing?" he asked instead, sounding vaguely alarmed.

"Resting," I murmured. *God, I hope he's not gonna turn all chatty on me now.*

"Oh. Good idea." Levering himself up on his elbow, Mike dropped a kiss on my shoulder and got out of bed. "You rest for a minute. I'll be back."

"Yes, Governor. Whatever you say." A minute? Ha! A minute wasn't gonna begin to cover it, not that it mattered. I didn't know where he was going, but I knew exactly where I'd be by the time he got back: fast asleep and out for the count.

Chapter Four

Mike

I tucked my dick back into my trousers, tugged up the zipper, then turned again to look at Claire. She looked stunningly sexy lying there mostly naked and mostly asleep. Much as I hated losing the view, I hated the thought of her getting cold while I was gone even more. I took a spare comforter from the closet and tossed it over her before heading to the kitchen.

I was feeling both elated and appalled and I was having a hard time coming to terms with the evening's events. I'd just fucked Claire Calhoun. The thought made me wince, even as it put a great big smile on my face. This was *Claire*, for God's sake, and part of me was embarrassed to even think anything so crude. But, facts were facts, and it was a little late in the game to start sugar-coating the situation. Having just exhibited all the control and staying power of an over-eager teenager, combined with the courtesy and finesse of a drunken goat, I could hardly claim to have made love to her.

No, I'd fucked her, sure enough, and probably myself, as well. Now, I could only hope she really *was* too drunk to remember what had gone on here tonight. Maybe, if she slept it off for a little while, I could find a way to redeem myself.

What are you worrying for? my imaginary Claire asked in soothing tones, as she followed me into the kitchen, wearing the same diaphanous gown she'd worn in *Love of a Werewolf*—before it was torn to shreds by the pack. *You'll fix things. Don't you always?*

"This is different," I muttered, carefully placing half a dozen river rocks into a pot of water and putting it on the stove to boil. Reality was, predictably enough, proving to be a good deal trickier to manage than any fantasy. Which is not to suggest I was feeling at all let down. Far from it. Not even my hottest dreams had been *this* hot.

Tell me that, phantom Claire suggested, drifting closer. *Maybe I'll be flattered to know how much you've thought about this, how often you've fantasized about being with me.*

"Maybe." Or maybe not—depending on how awkwardly I blurted it out. I could end up sounding like a dangerously perverted stalker and, this time, she probably *would* run for the door.

Michael, my dream woman cooed reproachfully. *Run? From you? How could you think it? You know I want you. Could I have been any more obvious about it?*

I sighed. Claire had been obvious, all right. She'd been up-front, forthright and honest but I'd be feeling a lot more confident if I had even the faintest idea what it was all about. *Why me? Why tonight? How did I get so lucky, all of a sudden?*

But maybe her original reasons didn't even apply anymore. After experiencing my underwhelming charm firsthand, would she want me again? Would *any* woman choose such a crude and inconsiderate lover, especially when she could have her pick of pretty much anyone she wanted?

Make me want you again, my fantasy urged in a hopeful voice as I turned the heat off on the stove, slid two oven mitts on my hands and picked up the steaming pot. *Show me how much better you can be. You can do that, can't you, Mike?*

I could only hope.

* * * *

Back in the bedroom, Claire was snoring softly—not something I would have expected of her. What was even more surprising, however, was the fact that I found it charming. It made her seem that much more human, that much more *real.* I put the pot down on the floor near the bed and then hung up her dress and her bra before gathering the rest of what I'd need from the bathroom. When I was ready, I stripped out of my pants and pulled the covers away from her.

Her shoes were still on the bed, I grabbed them and set them on the floor in front of the night table. I sat down beside her and slipped my fingers into the top of one of her stockings, at the front of her thigh, and released the first clip.

Claire stirred. Her eyes slitted open and she turned her head to look at me. "Hi," she murmured sleepily. "What's up?"

"Nothing. I'm just trying to get the rest of these clothes off you."

"Oh." Closing her eyes again she snuggled back into the pillow. "Thanks, but not necessary."

"Actually, it is," I insisted. "I'm giving you a massage so, unless you want your underwear covered in oil, these clothes have to go."

"A massage, huh?"

I nodded. "I've noticed you've been looking tense lately; I figured this might help relax you."

"Tense?" That got her eyes open wide. She rolled over on her back, propped herself up on her elbows and gazed skeptically at me. "I look *tense* to you?"

I couldn't help but grin. "Well, no, not *now* you don't. But, speaking in general, over the last few months? Yeah, you have."

She stared at me a moment longer, then shrugged. "Perhaps you're right."

Well, I already *knew* I was right, but it seemed less than diplomatic to say so. I gestured at her leg. "So? May I continue?"

Without answering, she bent her leg at the knee, giving me access to the clip at the back of her thigh. I took that as a yes and slid my hand there, reveling in the warmth and softness of her skin.

Eyes hooded, she continued to watch me as I un-did the clasp and then carefully rolled the stocking down her leg. With her foot in my hand I paused just long enough to press a brief kiss against the tops of her toes. Then I tossed her stocking aside and repeated the process with her other leg, trying not to stare too openly at the rise and fall of her chest, at her lush, round breasts with their hard, rosy peaks. Not that I altogether restrained myself either, of course. I mean, why the hell would I do that? Chances like this didn't come along every day. I'd be a fool not to take full advantage of one when it did.

When the second stocking had joined the first, Claire lifted her hips in mute invitation. I hooked my fingers into the lace at either side and pulled garter and panties away from her. Her bare mound came into view, taking me somewhat by surprise. The total lack of pubic hair hadn't really registered during the brief glimpse I'd gotten earlier and not even her movies had prepared me for the sight I'd just uncovered. My blood boiled as her legs fell open wider. I found myself staring, mesmerized by the sight, by the pretty pink folds of flesh that glistened so temptingly.

"I believe you said something about a massage?" Claire murmured in teasing tones.

"Hmm?" I wrenched my eyes away with difficulty. My gaze drifted up towards her face, taking the slow, scenic route past all her naked glory. "What?"

Claire arched one eyebrow. "My massage?"

Crap. So much for repairing the damage I'd done with my earlier performance. Here I was, acting like an ass all over again.

"Right." Standing, I gathered up her clothes. "Why don't you roll over on your stomach and I'll get started.

Averting my eyes as she repositioned herself on the bed, I dropped Claire's stockings and garter on top of her shoes. Her panties I let fall in the space between the table and the bed where I hoped they'd go unnoticed.

Inexcusable, I know, but given how badly I was screwing up, I suspected this was likely to be a one time event. That being the case, I knew I'd need something with which to console myself in the years ahead.

I lifted the bottle of massage oil from the pot of water, where I'd put it to warm up, and poured some into my palm. The heady sweet scents of almond, honey amber and musk filled the air as I rubbed my hands together. Using a light effleurage stroke I quickly covered Claire's back with the oil, and then coated her arms and legs as well. Then I turned away to remove the first rock from the pot.

"Well, that was very nice," Claire said as she started to get up. "Thank you."

I glanced at her over my shoulder and frowned. "No you don't. Where do you think you're going? Lie back down. We're just getting started."

She looked surprised, but she did as I said. I squirted oil over the stone in my hand and then turned back to her.

"*That* was not the massage," I said as I brushed the hair away from her neck and then began to gently rub the stone in small circles down her neck and across her shoulder. "*That* was just getting you ready. Are you always this impatient?"

"Yes," she replied, biting the word out sharply, and I couldn't decide whether her tone was teasing or annoyed. "Actors have very short attention spans. Are *you* always so bossy?"

I sighed. "Probably. I've been running my own company for a long time now. I guess I've gotten used to it."

"Hmph," she muttered darkly. "You have an answer for everything, don't you?" And then we both fell silent. The muscles at the back of her neck were knotted. I rubbed harder. I'd been right about the tension. For an instant, I actually considered telling her that. Luckily, I reconsidered the impulse. Being right was a lot like being boss. Invaluable in business but, more often than not, a complication everywhere else.

"Omigod," Claire murmured a moment later. "What *is* that? Whatever you're doing, it feels wonderful."

"Haven't you ever had a hot stone massage? The heat is supposed to help relax the muscles and the pressure is different from what you can get using just your hands."

"I see. I guess you must do this sort of thing often."

I switched hands and went to work on the other side of her neck. "Well, no, I wouldn't say often. Occasionally though."

"So... you just happened to have everything you needed on hand? Is that what you're telling me?"

"It doesn't take much, you know. Just massage oil. Rocks. A pot to heat them up in. It's really pretty simple."

"Simple. Right." Claire shook her head. "Amazing. Fashion. Architecture. Decorating. Classic cars. Hot stone massage. Next thing you'll tell me is that you mix your own massage oil too."

My hand faltered. "Well, yeah, actually, I—I did."

"Unbelievable. Mike, are you *sure* you're an accountant?"

I laughed. "I guess you'd better hope I am, huh?"

"I guess so," she muttered. "Jeez. You're full of surprises tonight."

"Good surprises, I hope?" I quipped lightly.

Claire sighed and it was a moment before she answered. "Very good. Just very... unexpected."

I suppose that sigh, and the pause that followed it, should have worried me more than it did, but I was too focused on what I was doing to think that much about anything else. Taking a fresh rock from the water I massaged her arms and hands before changing rocks again and continuing down her back.

I mixed things up a little as I went along. In places I used one rock, other places two, and sometimes I used just my hands. When the urge arose to trail hot kisses down her spine, to caress the small of her back with my lips and tongue, I had to struggle to restrain myself. Once I started down that path, I knew I'd never be able to stop.

I gently plucked and pummeled the flesh of her butt cheeks and then stroked lightly along her crease with the backs of my fingers; longing to do more. I longed to take her flawless, creamy flesh between my teeth; to suck and nip until I'd marked her as my own. I wanted to slide my fingers inside her wet channel and test her warmth; wanted to spread her legs wide, pry open her lips, taste her juices on my tongue. Instead, I moved on. I massaged her legs—first one, then the other—slowly stroking and kneading all the way to her feet.

"Flip over and let me do you from the front," I said as I reached for a fresh rock.

A soft, sultry laugh purled up Claire's throat as she rolled onto her back and propped herself up, once again on her elbows. "You do know how dirty that sounded, don't you?"

Dirty? I turned to face her and my gaze drifted hungrily over her body. As I said, up until now I'd been holding back; using mostly relaxing touches and strokes. But I'd paid the price for my manners. My balls were aching with unconsummated lust. "Not nearly as dirty as I could make it feel, if I weren't trying to be such a gentleman."

"A gentleman?" Claire's eyes lit up at that. "Is that so?"

"Yes." I smiled back at her. "It is. Why? Don't believe me?"

"I'd never say that," she murmured, lowering her eyes demurely. "Although, I must admit, I've never really thought being a gentleman was all it's cracked up to be." I waited, hoping she'd say more. Finally she shrugged. "So, if it's dirty you want... why not just go for it?"

Which was all the encouragement I needed. Dropping the rock back into the pot, I picked up the bottle of massage oil, placed a finger beneath Claire's chin and tipped her head back.

"Unh," she gasped in surprise as the warm oil streamed over her, coating her neck, her chest, cascading between her breasts, flowing over her belly, all the way to her mound. I knew the bedcovers would be forever stained with the oil, but I couldn't have cared less. Tossing the bottle aside, I straddled her hips.

I could feel her heart pounding as I skated my hands through the oil; up the center of her chest, up and around her neck; until they were buried in the hair at the back of her head. As my fingers massaged her scalp and the lobes and rims of her ears, I lowered my mouth to hers, and kissed her deeply.

"How's that?" I finally lifted my head to ask.

Claire's eyes fluttered open. "Don't you dare stop now."

"I won't," I promised, as I rubbed slow circles along her forehead and over her temples. "Now close your eyes again and lie back."

"Yes, Mike." She complied immediately.

"Good girl," I murmured, rewarding her with soft kisses on her eyelids.

Pressing gently, my fingers slowly traced the shape of her eye-sockets and then the bridge of her nose. Then they moved down to her jaw line, to her throat, to her shoulders. And, all the while, I studied her face, searching for clues about what was going on inside her head. Her sudden show of submission had taken me by surprise. It wasn't what I'd been expecting. Not that I really knew what to expect at this point. The whole evening had been one surprise after another. About the only thing that wasn't surprising me was my own response.

The dominant side of my nature was something I'd long ago recognized. I'd told her I was used to being the boss, and that was certainly true. But what I hadn't said was that the trait had never been confined to business. Command was something that had always come naturally to me. I liked it, felt comfortable with it, was good at it. Wanted it.

In the bedroom, however, it was something I generally tried to suppress. Claire's every action tonight was making that less and less possible.

Unable to completely resist the impulse, I slid my hands down her arms and took hold of her wrists. Claire gasped in surprise as I swept her arms up behind her head "Grab hold of the headboard," I whispered against her ear. "Keep your eyes closed and don't move again until I tell you to."

I told myself I did it mainly to test her. But I might have been lying to myself. I might have done it purely for the thrill it gave me. In either case, I knew I was safe. At this point I could still pass it off as a joke, if I had to. As it turned out, however, no such subterfuge was necessary.

A red flush stained Claire's cheeks as she twined her fingers willingly through the wrought iron bars. Then she held herself motionless, seeming scarcely to breathe.

Dick throbbing at the sight of her tightly curled fists, I stared at her uneasily. Just how badly were the events of the night affecting my judgment? On one hand, I *knew* this was what we both wanted. On the other... what the hell made me think I knew *anything* about what Claire might want? She was an actress! This could all be part of an act, couldn't it? Maybe I was imagining things—seeing only what I wanted to see. Maybe Claire had intuited my needs and was merely playing along, humoring me.

I stroked my hands down her arms again, taking comfort in the shivers that coursed through her, from the tiny smile that played across her lips. She could be acting, I supposed, but why would she do that? What was in it for her? A laugh at my expense? If that was all she was after, she was taking the joke a little far.

Her closed eyes made me bolder than I might have been otherwise. Bold enough to tell her what I was thinking. "I guess it's no secret how I feel about you," I said as my hands moved slowly over the top of her slick, oil-coated chest, gently kneading the muscles there, trying to proceed as planned with her massage. "You must have known it all along."

A slight frown creased Claire's forehead. "I'm not sure I— Known what?"

"How big a fan I've always been. The fact that I've loved you for years. You knew that, right?"

"Oh." Her lips quirked. "Well, you, um, did sort of mention being a fan when we met." She opened her eyes and gazed at me steadily. "I hope you know that's got nothing to do with why I'm here tonight, Mike. Much as I appreciate my fans, I really don't go around sleeping with all of them, either, you know."

"I certainly hope not," I replied, dropping my gaze. It was insane, I know, but I couldn't help feeling just a little bit jealous at the thought. Sure, she *said* that wasn't the reason she was with me now, but how did I know for certain? How could I separate the woman from the actress? Maybe that was *exactly* why she was here. Sex with an adoring fan—that would have to be a gigantic boost to anyone's ego. Who wouldn't want that from time to time?

My hands swept outward along her chest, curving down and around her breasts and then in again over her midriff, until my thumbs met in the center of her rib cage. "That would be a very bad idea," I cautioned. "You'd only end up completely exhausting yourself if you tried doing that."

Claire's body shook with laughter. "Well, yeah, exactly. Besides, with so many of them, how could I fit them all in?"

How indeed?

"I mean, I'd have to double up, or something. Take 'em two or three at a time."

Images appeared in my mind, conjured by her words, and my body flooded with lust and adrenaline. My hands stilled. I schooled my features into neutrality, glanced up at her face and frowned. "Did I tell you to open your eyes?"

"What?" Her eyes widened in surprise. She stared at me. I stared back.

"Close them."

For the space of maybe three seconds we continued to stare at each other. Then she breathed out a shuddery little sigh, and did as she'd been told.

My hands went back into motion; slowly smoothing across her ribs and up her sides, retracing their previous movement.

"These last months, working with you, I've been like some little boy with his nose pressed up against the candy store window; admiring all that lusciousness, coveting it, but never expecting to actually have it. Never even expecting to get any closer to it than I was. Until tonight."

My fingers met each other again, in the center of her chest, and then parted, sweeping outward once more and then down and around. "Tonight, you opened the door. You let me come inside. You should have known what would happen if you did that, Claire."

"What?" she asked again, breathlessly.

Although I hadn't so much as touched her breasts, her nipples were hard and had been so almost since I'd started. Now, as I bent close and blew alternating currents of warm and cool air across the tips, she shivered in response. "You should have realized I'd have to taste every last piece of candy. That I'd never be satisfied until I'd sampled everything you had to offer. That, even then, I'd want to sneak back in when you weren't looking and go for seconds on all my favorites."

Claire's throat worked for a moment. "Mike?"

"Yes?"

"I'm not looking now, am I?"

I felt myself smile. "No, you're not." Leaning forward, I pressed a single kiss against her stomach, right below the notch of her ribs. "So, I guess there's nothing to stop me from taking everything I want. Is there?"

She didn't answer right away, but she was breathing hard and I could see her lower lip trembling.

"Is there?" I repeated softly. "Claire? Is there anything stopping me from having everything I want tonight? From taking the whole store?"

"No," she said at last, in a voice even more breathless than before. "Nothing."

"Good." Abandoning any further attempts at massage, I slid down her body, leaving kisses in my wake, pre-cum leaking from the tip of my cock to mix with the oil. "Spread your legs," I said, not really waiting for her to oblige, inserting first one and then the other of my own knees in the space between her thighs, gently forcing them apart. I could smell the scent of her arousal even as my hands slid up the insides of her thighs. Even before I pried her lips apart I knew I would find her wet and ready. "Yes. Like that."

I stretched out on the bed between her legs, doing my best to ignore the urging of my cock, which wanted nothing more than to pump into her. To take her hard and fast, just like last time. *No. Not happening.*

This time I was determined to stay in control. I pressed my forearms into her thighs, urging her to open them wider. I leaned in close. Close enough to feel myself surrounded by her soft flesh and musky scent. Close enough to slide my tongue up and down along the length of her dripping slit, learning her taste by heart.

Claire moaned and bucked her hips as I continued the caress. I tightened my grip on her legs and held her still, methodically laving every inch, over and over again, until her breathing had become a series of ragged sobs. Finally, I sighted in on her swollen clit and dove. Taking the whole of the tender nub between my lips, I lashed furiously at the tip with my tongue.

Claire jerked and cried out, a little too sharply. Alarmed, I pulled back again and looked at her. "What is it? What's wrong?"

"N-nothing," she gulped, seeming to force the word out. Her face was flaming. Her chest heaved with each breath.

"Claire?"

"It's nothing. Your beard. I, I..."

My beard? Shit. What had I done now? My glance went to the bare skin of her mound, where I'd just had my face buried. Was it too red? Too sore? Had I been rougher than I'd intended? "Too scratchy? I didn't hurt you, did I?" *Oh, God, please say no...*

"Mm-mm." She shook her head, but her expression remained clouded. "No. That's not what I meant."

"Claire..."

"Look, forget it," she insisted, wriggling restlessly. "Everything's fine."

"That's not how it looks to me."

Sighing, she opened her eyes. "Well, looks can be deceiving, Mike. Haven't you ever heard that?"

"Claire."

"Okay, maybe my arms are getting a little stiff in this position, but that's it. Really."

I could barely suppress my own sigh of frustration. "Then put them down, Claire. This was only ever a game, you know. It stops whenever you want it to."

For a moment, she said nothing. Then, very softly, "I don't want to stop."

Well, I didn't want to stop either, but I certainly didn't intend to make her suffer. There's pain and there's good pain; and the latter was the only kind I was interested in causing. I thought for an instant. "Give me your hands," I said at last.

Claire's lips compressed. She looked like she wanted to protest. I held her gaze. Arching one eyebrow imperiously, I waited. Finally, she sighed and reluctantly lowered her arms. I took hold of her hands and brought them to her crotch. "Here. Now, spread your lips for me," I instructed, watching as heat, and maybe a trace of relief, flared in her eyes. Her breathing picked up.

"Like this?" she asked, almost shyly; fingers trembling, once or twice losing their purchase on her slick flesh.

"Yes. Just like that." I gazed hungrily at her exposed clit. "That's very good." It was fucking gorgeous is what it was, and, even better, her hands were perfectly placed to protect her more sensitive flesh from my beard—just in case it really was too rough. Another thought occurred just as I was about to dip my head. I glanced at Claire's face and met her gaze. "Do you want to watch?"

I saw the realization hit her: I hadn't told her she could open her eyes this time, either, had I? Her lips curved. Excitement darkened her eyes. Her voice shook a little as she answered, "Please, may I?"

I nodded. "All right." I let my gaze sweep over her one more time, before returning to her face. "I'm going to go down on you now. I'm going to take you with my mouth and you're gonna come on my tongue. Understood?"

Her mouth opened on a soft gasp. Her tongue made a brief appearance and then retreated, riveting my attention. I could no more tear my gaze away from those moist, trembling, red lips than I could fly.

I was on the verge of changing my mind, ordering her to take my cock in her mouth instead, when she nodded again and murmured, even more softly, "Yes."

It was a struggle trying to think back far enough to recall what it was she was agreeing to. *Later,* I promised my aching, impatient cock; *you'll have your turn, just not now.*

I didn't exactly trust myself to speak, either. Who knows what I might have said at that point? So, I said nothing. I merely nodded and lowered my head.

The scent of her musk, the sweet taste of her cream, these were things no picture, no movie could ever capture. Until tonight, they were things I could only wonder about and imagine. Now, they were mine. Mine to sample and explore. Mine to revel and delight in.

It was like touching heaven when I thrust my tongue into her pussy and began to lap up her juices. When the first soft moan broke from her lips, it put me into sensory overload. I licked harder. Twisting my head to the side, I delved deeper. My fingers bit into her flesh as I took hold of her thighs and laid her pussy open. *Mine. All mine.* I wanted everything. I wanted to devour her. And I couldn't, couldn't, couldn't get enough.

Claire. Oh, Claire. Oh, Claire!

I still couldn't believe she was really here, that this was really happening. I was overcome with emotion, with the need to show my gratitude. I would have done anything she wanted, given her anything she asked for.

Maybe my being a fan *was* all the reason she needed for being with me tonight. Who was I to judge her motives anyway? It's not like I could lay claim to any moral high ground. I knew she'd been drinking. I knew this was, most likely, no more than a whim on her part. I'd still caved.

And, come to think of it, why shouldn't I have? Show me the man who wouldn't jump at the chance to bed the woman of his dreams—for any reason, or none at all.

Claire's legs were trembling when I moved up to take her clit. She gasped again, but not as sharply as before and, this time, I resisted the impulse to ask if she was okay. I had to trust her to tell me if I was hurting her. I had to believe that she was enjoying this as much as I hoped she was. As much as I was enjoying her.

Curving my fingers into her heat, I stroked the bundle of nerves that lay just inside her entrance. When I felt her muscles start to tighten, I lifted my head. I wanted to watch her come. I wanted to see it in her face.

Claire's eyes, dark, hooded, glazed, met mine and satisfaction filled me. I knew that look. I'd seen her in the throes of passion so many times before—But I hadn't really, had I? Not like this. Not in person. Not when I was the one doing her; putting that flush on her cheeks, making her moan, making her cream, making her come. *Oh, God.* I slid another finger into her heat and pumped faster, harder. *Yes. Like that. Give it to me.*

Claire moaned again, louder this time, and her eyes rolled back. I couldn't help smiling. "That's right. That's what I like." *All of you. I want all of you.* "Now."

As the first spasm shook her, I felt my heart swell with

something very much like pleasure, very much like pride. Very much like love. *Oh, Claire...*

Suddenly, watching wasn't enough. Pulling my fingers away, I surged on top of her. Claire's fingers dug into my shoulders as I mounted her. Her eyes met mine.

"Don't stop coming," I said as I rocked into her.

She gasped and her fingers tightened their grip. "Mike, I..."

"Don't stop," I repeated urgently.

She murmured something incoherent as she wrapped her legs around me.

The hot, velvet slide of her skin on mine made me groan with pleasure. "God, yes. Like that."

Dipping my head I kissed her; a quick, bruising brush of my lips against hers, to thank her. Then I leaned lower still to take a nipple with my mouth.

She cried out, her body arching against me as a new set of contractions seized her.

Her muscles milked my cock relentlessly. I threw back my head, eyes closed, teeth gritted, and tried to maintain control, to stretch things out as long as I could. I didn't want to come yet. Not yet. I wanted the ride to go on forever.

But Claire's grasp on my shoulders weakened suddenly. Her nails raked down my arms and that was all it took to push me over the edge. Chills raced down my spine. My balls tightened and I broke. Pumping my seed into her. Jerking hard against her. Mindless and blind with pleasure.

When I could think again, I realized my arms were shaking with the effort to keep from collapsing on top of her.

"Oh, my God," Claire murmured beneath me. "Oh, my God, Mike, that was... What was that?"

I couldn't answer right away. I was so drained I was surprised I was still conscious. I pulled away slowly, barely able to move. "That was what you asked for."

I lay down beside her. I was sweating and breathing hard. So was she.

She stared at me. "What I asked for?"

"Yeah." I smiled faintly. "In the car, remember? 'It's fun. It feels good.' That's what you said you wanted, right?"

"Right." She sighed and shook her head. "I must have been out of my mind."

I gazed at her worriedly. "It wasn't good?"

"What?" Claire frowned at me. "Mike—Of course it was good! What are you talking about? It was... amazing."

"Well, what are *you* talking about? You said you were out of your mind."

"Yes! For thinking I needed to convince you. Obviously, you already had things figured out on your own."

"Oh." I chuckled in relief. "That's okay. I'm yours to convince. Convince me of anything you want."

"You're that easy, huh?"

"For you? Always." Yawning, I reached beyond her, blindly seeking for the comforter. I knew it had to be there, somewhere. "But tomorrow, okay? I'm too tired right now." Finally, my fingers found what they were searching for. I pulled the comforter over us both and tugged her closer.

"G'night, Claire," I murmured, as I wrapped my arm around her. If she made any answer, I didn't hear it. I was already asleep.

Chapter Five

Claire

I should *never* have quit all my exercise classes after Derek and I split up. That might not have been my very first thought upon waking up the next morning, but it was definitely the most coherent. My body had that deliciously decadent 'well-used' feeling that only really good lovemaking leaves in its wake but, oh, my God, I could barely move! It was obvious that the personal work-out regimen I'd been following was just not strenuous enough.

I lay still for a while and took stock of my surroundings. Sunlight streamed through the window. Birdsong filtered in from the canyon. Emptiness radiated from Mike's side of the bed.

I felt both disappointed and relieved about that. Disappointed because one of the things I'd been looking forward to was waking up to a warm body in the bed beside me. Relieved because, to be honest, I was feeling a little ambivalent this morning.

Mike had gotten too close last night. Somehow, he'd tapped into a facet of my personality that I hadn't shared with anyone in...

Well, actually, come to think of it, I hadn't shared it with anyone *ever*.

When I was young and sex was new, I'd been too naive to appreciate or even understand the subtle pleasures of power exchange. By the time I was older, wiser and more jaded I'd learned to protect myself, to protect my vulnerability, to protect my heart. I'd also learned how to act. I'd have liked to pretend that's what I was doing last night. Acting. Playing along with the scene he'd created. But that wasn't the case and I was pretty sure we both knew it.

Mike had caught me off-guard last night. Somehow, he'd seen the me behind the mask. He'd intuited things about me that, quite frankly, I wasn't altogether certain I wanted him to know. He'd disarmed me with his shyness, with his lack of pretension, his undisguised adulation. He'd let me think I was the one calling the shots. Then he'd turned the tables on me. By the time he was done, I'd have gone down on my knees, licked his balls and begged him for... anything, really. Whatever he wanted me to. Whatever he *told* me to beg for.

The thought was disturbing enough to get me out of bed,

despite the protests of my more-than-pleasantly-sore muscles, and into the shower.

The bathroom—now, there was another eye opener. More glass in the form of the tinted panels that made up the ceiling and the frosted walls that surrounded the tub/shower and which, apparently, could be retracted if one wished to bathe *al fresco*. A glass tile mosaic covered most of the remaining walls, I refused to look at it too closely. I was sure, if I did, I'd find Mike's signature there somewhere, worked into the design.

Was there nothing the man hadn't thought to try his hand at?

Somehow, I'd imagined an accountant would be more... conventional. Methodical, practical, traditional, even a little boring; that's really what I'd been expecting. But Mike, it appeared, was none of those. That should have been a good thing. And yet...

He was intriguing. There was no denying that. Unfortunately, I wasn't looking to be that intrigued by a casual lover. He was interesting, unusual, captivating. I wasn't looking to be captivated either. Not by anyone.

Claire Calhoun was damned good in bed, whether or not there were cameras rolling. She might play a submissive onscreen, if that's what the role called for. She might even tease a lover into thinking she was there to fulfill his every desire, rather than the other way around. But, at the end of the day—when the cameras stopped rolling, when the grunting and sweating were over—everyone knew it had just been an act. At least for the most part.

I stepped beneath the shower's powerful spray hoping to clear the confusion from my head. The warm water felt wonderful as it pounded at my sore muscles. It brought to mind the massage Mike had given me the night before. It brought to mind his hands and his mouth, his cock, his voice. Before I knew it, my hand had slipped down to finger my pussy, to rub my clit; already swollen, already aching. I groaned with the need I felt building within me.

Getting myself off would only relieve some of the tension. If I were really going to do the job right I'd need an assist. And, for that, I wanted Mike. I wanted him inside me now. I had half a mind to open the door and call for him. I wanted him to join me in the shower. To push me up against the wall and—

No. I snatched my hand away, turned off the water and stepped out of the shower. Sex would just have to wait. Right now, it was time to leave. I had a busy day ahead of me. I'm sure I had all sorts of appointments I was forgetting about.

I dressed quickly. Not willing to wait a moment longer than

necessary, I gave up searching for my panties, slipped bare feet into my heels, stuffed my stockings and garter into my purse and used the phone by Mike's bed to call for a cab.

* * * *

Mike was in the kitchen, scrambling eggs in a bowl, when I found him. The little tiger-eye stud still glittered in his ear lobe. I'd thought it looked sexy paired with a suit. It looked even better juxtaposed against the burgundy velour robe he was wearing this morning. His eyebrows rose as he looked me over. "You're dressed already?" He sounded disappointed. "I was going to bring you breakfast in bed."

He's really very sweet. I smiled, intending to tell him so, but before I got a word out, my attention was captured by the large mango-colored bird perched on the back of one of the dining room chairs, feeding itself from a bowl of fruit.

"Oh, my God." Changing course, I made a bee line for the bird who had stopped eating and was looking at me curiously. "Hello, there, gorgeous. Where did you come from? I didn't see you last night."

The macaw cocked her head to the side and murmured inquisitively.

"She was asleep when we got in," Mike said. "I keep her cage in the spare bedroom because, you know, she can be kind of loud at times."

"I'll bet." Maui Sunset Macaws are *very* talkative birds. They're also a very rare hybrid. Most people have never even seen a picture of one. The only reason I knew anything at all about them was because I'd worked with one in a movie years ago. And this one here, with her marmalade-shaded front, faded-olive back and tail, and the almost iridescent sheen on her wings, was a dead ringer for that other bird. They both resembled golden parrot idols come to life. Which was exactly what the bird in the film was supposed to have been.

Smiling, I stroked the soft plumage that covered her breast. "What's her name?"

There was a slight pause before Mike answered. "Zoe."

At the sound of her name, Zoe turned her gaze away from me to look at Mike. She croaked softly.

"Oh." I forced myself to show no emotion but chills were running down my spine. Zoe. Same name as the bird I'd worked with; same voice, same coloration. Coincidence? Imagination? So

249

not likely.

Turning back to Mike, I smiled brightly. "It's amazing how much she looks like the bird I worked with in *Inca Gold.*"

Mike dropped two pieces of bread in the toaster and nodded. "She is."

"She is what?" I replied, blinking innocently, pretending not to understand. Sidling away from the table, I mentally gauged the distance between the dining room and the front door.

"She's the same bird. Her handlers retired about eight years ago. They were selling off some of their... inventory. So I bought her."

"Ahh." I was wearing heels. That might slow me down if I made a run for it. On the other hand, Mike was probably bare foot, so the heels might be an asset in that way. "That, ah... that's a little creepy, don't you think?"

"Creepy?" Mike stared at me. "No. Why would you say that? Zoe's very sociable. She'd be miserable if she were locked in a cage in some pet shop somewhere or in a zoo. Or, worse yet, if she were sold to a breeder. She was hand raised. She loves being around people."

I nodded. "I know. I remember." I'd been very fond of Zoe. She was the most honestly affectionate female co-star I'd ever had. If I'd have known she was in danger of being sent to a zoo or anything else, I'd have bought her myself. That wasn't the point. "It's just that I feel a little uncomfortable with the thought of you collecting things that are... connected to me in some fashion. It feels kind of... I dunno... stalkery."

Mike's cheeks flamed red. "Claire, I—That's..." He swallowed hard and tried again. "Be fair. This was *years* ago. At the time... I had *no* idea I'd ever actually meet you. Never mind that I'd..." He fisted his hands on the counter and stared at me with a troubled expression. "It's not like... it's not like I follow you home. I don't loiter in alleys, picking things out of your garbage. Hell, how many months have I worked for you? And I still don't even know where you live! How can you suggest that I—And, anyway, you came to me, remember?"

"I know."

"I knew Dave was your lawyer. I never so much as hinted to him about... about anything! It was all his idea that you hire me. I never—"

I nodded. "I know that too." Although, actually, it had been my idea, not Dave's.

"And Zoe—I'd always wanted a macaw, all right? I don't know why, but I did. Maui's are beautiful. Everyone knows they have great temperaments and there aren't that many of them, either. And, yeah, it was neat knowing she was *connected* to you. I won't lie and say that wasn't part of the appeal. Sure it was. But there was nothing, nothing sinister about it."

"Maybe." He'd always wanted a macaw? Right. Just like he'd always wanted a classic Jaguar. I was seeing a pattern here. And yet, improbable as it seemed, it had to be coincidence. Because he couldn't *possibly* have known about the car...

The producer of several of my earliest films—including most of the ones I'd made here, in Topanga Canyon—had owned a similar make and model. Same color too, I think. I'd lost my innocence in that car.

Oh, not in a sexual sense, although the Jag's back seat was certainly cushy enough for pretty much anything along those lines that you might want to try. No, my moment of truth had occurred in the front passenger seat. That's where I'd come of age, so to speak. That's where I learned about the dark, seedy underside of the movie business. Where I learned all about the dues I'd be paying. About the crucial difference between acting in movies and performing on film.

I'd nearly given up that night. I'd nearly packed my bags and fled LA. And, even now, I could still recall exactly how I'd felt. The shock. The sick feeling in the pit of my stomach. The despair.

Can I live with myself if I do this? Is it worth it? How badly do I want this career? Isn't there any other way?

There was another way, of course, but I didn't know it then. I was told that this was the way things worked, the only way I'd ever get my foot in the door. I was young enough, and stupid enough, to believe it. By the time I learned the truth, by the time I realized I'd been lied to, manipulated, used, it was too late.

Last night, when the valet had pulled that Jag up to the front of the gallery, I'd nearly changed my mind. It had been years since I'd given any thought to that long ago night, but the sight of that car brought it all back. I didn't want to go anywhere with the man who owned it.

I'd been on the verge of faking a headache and asking Mike to take me home when I hit on the idea of driving up to Mulholland as a way to buy us both some time. I was glad now that I had. And I wasn't regretting anything this morning. But I *did* want to get away.

I smiled. "Maybe you're right."

"I *am* right." The toast popped out of the toaster, he ignored it. "People *do* collect celebrity memorabilia, Claire. It's a business as well as a hobby for some folks. And I'm not saying it's either of those for me. But, as a public figure, you should understand that. I'm sure you've donated personal items for charity auctions and other things, from time to time. Haven't you? Who'd you think was buying that stuff? Fans, for the most part."

"Okay, fine. You're right." Leaving my purse on the table I walked over to where he was standing. He turned to face me, still looking troubled. I slid my arms up around his neck. "You're definitely right. I concede the point. Can we please stop arguing now?"

"We're not..." He broke off, looking even more unhappy. "I'm not trying to argue with you, Claire. I'm just trying to make you understand. There's a difference between being a fan; between admiring someone, even having a crush on them, and... and stalking them. We're not all deranged, you know."

"I know that." I pressed myself against him deliberately as I leaned in to kiss him. Mike inhaled sharply, his skin heating on contact, just as it had the night before, back at the gallery, when I first touched his face. "And, I'm sorry. I didn't mean to suggest you were deranged, Mike."

If anyone was deranged, it was likely me. Because in spite of all my good intentions, all the stern lectures I'd given myself while I'd dressed, just that one kiss was enough to make my pussy wet. My nipples were tingling. The thought of getting naked again with him—right now—was almost irresistible.

"Claire..."

"Shh." I backed away quickly, before he could pull me close or deepen the kiss. Before I could go down on my knees and wrap my lips around the erection tenting the front of his robe. "You've made your point. There's a difference. I get that. Now... is that coffee I smell?"

"Uh—Yes." Still red-faced, Mike lunged for the coffee maker and quickly poured out a mug. "Here. How do you take it? Cream? Sugar?"

"Just black, please," I replied. My fingers grazed his as I reached to take the mug from his hand. He jerked and the mug nearly slipped to the floor. Luckily, I caught it in time.

I sipped my coffee and tried hard not to let my eyes drift

south, tried hard to hide my smile. I liked it when he got flustered. I liked the sense of control it brought. *This* was the way things between us were supposed to be, wasn't it? I wondered if it had anything to do with the fact that I was dressed and he wasn't? Maybe, next time we made love, I should keep my clothes on?

Mike cleared his throat. "So. How about breakfast? How does a *fine herbes* omelet sound?"

"It sounds lovely," I said, feeling regretful. "But I don't think I'll have time."

Mike looked puzzled. "What do you mean?"

A car horn sounded from outside. I gulped a last swallow of coffee and put my mug on the counter. "I mean I have to leave. My ride's here."

"Your ride?"

"Mm. I called a cab while I was dressing."

"But, why?"

"Because, silly, I have to go to work." I slipped my arms back around his neck and pressed myself against him one more time. "Thank you for a lovely evening."

"I would have been happy to drive you back to town," he replied stubbornly, ignoring the compliment, seemingly unaffected by my smile.

I kissed him anyway. "Thank you. But I didn't want to put you to any more trouble."

"It wouldn't have been any trouble." He eyed me glumly, then blurted, "Am I ever gonna see you again?"

He sounded so tragic, it was all I could do to keep from laughing. "Well, of course you will. Unless you decide to drop me as a client, I'll see you in two weeks, right?"

"I'm not talking about that," he growled. "I meant... socially."

Framing his face with my hand, I looked deep into his eyes and smiled. "I'd like that." I kissed him again then turned away quickly. Grabbing my purse from the table where I'd left it, I headed for the door.

"Claire." Mike's voice stopped me before I was halfway across the living room.

I turned back to face him. "Yes?"

"Have I done something to upset you? Is that—Is that why you're leaving so soon?"

I shook my head. "No. Of course not." I glanced back at the

table. "And I'm sorry if I overreacted about Zoe. I'm glad you bought her, Mike. Really. She's lucky to have you."

Mike continued to stare at me doubtfully. "You didn't have to call a cab."

"I know." Claire Calhoun never *had* to do anything. She *chose* to do the things she did. Always. I smiled and blew him a kiss. "I'll see you, okay?" And then I left, even though a part of me was wishing he'd call me back and make me stay.

* * * *

Mike

I stood where I was, unable to move from the spot I'd occupied since Claire had first appeared this morning, and watched her walk away. I couldn't think straight. The click of her heels against the hardwood floor resounded in my head. Each step was like another nail pounded into my heart. I guess it was shock that kept me rooted in place. A good thing, too. Otherwise I might have stormed outside after her. I might have dismissed the cab, might have demanded that she allow me to drive her back to town. Might have acted like a Neanderthal. Wouldn't that have been smooth?

I would like to have claimed that my self control is what prevented me from doing any such thing, but that's simply not true. Where Claire was concerned, my self control had never been good. This morning, it was at zero. I had nothing left. What little there'd been had dissolved overnight and there was no way of telling it I'd ever recover it.

To be honest, I didn't want to have to. I loved that we were lovers now. This was a new phase in our relationship and I wanted it to continue, to lead someplace. Maybe not to marriage, maybe not to a life-long commitment, but I wasn't some kid, happy for a one night stand with anything female.

Maybe that's all she wanted. Maybe I should have been content. Maybe I would have been—once. But not any more.

I was a grown man and I was looking for an adult relationship. Last night had meant something to me. And, damn it, I wanted it to mean something to her too, even if I had no idea how to accomplish that.

Maybe Claire would solve the problem for me. Maybe she'd take the initiative and call. But maybe she wouldn't. And, if she didn't? Well, I wasn't about to call her, that was for sure. Not until I had some vague idea just what in the hell she was thinking.

The sound of the cab pulling out of my drive dragged me

from my thoughts. I picked up the mug Claire had been using. Resisting the urge to hurl it across the room, I managed to dredge up enough restraint to set it gently in the sink. But only just.

I felt angry and disappointed. I felt like a fool. I'd already called into my office to say I was taking the day off. Why couldn't she have done the same?

Zoe must have sensed my distress because she launched herself into the air, landing on the counter in front of me. I lifted her to my shoulder automatically and then broke off a piece of toast and handed it to her. She crunched on it loudly and I winced a little at the sound, but it was better than having her nibble on my ear. That's something she's particularly fond of doing, and one of the main reasons I'd more or less stopped wearing my ear stud.

Even with all her little quirks, I wouldn't have traded Zoe for anything. Affectionate, intelligent, beautiful and generally self-sufficient, she was the perfect pet. The fact that she had a connection to Claire was, quite honestly, something I rarely even thought about anymore.

Which only made Claire's reaction to her, this morning, even more absurd. Stalking? Where the fuck had that come from?

But thinking about that would only make me angrier, and I was mad enough already. Not to mention frustrated beyond belief.

Normally, after a night like last night, I'd have woken up satisfied. But, waking up with Claire beside me had been a dream come true. I wanted her so badly, I knew I could do only one of two things: either get the hell out of bed or roll her over and go at it again.

Thinking it would be more thoughtful, and a whole lot more polite, if I at least let her get her eyes open before I jumped her, I'd opted for getting out of bed.

Big fucking mistake.

If I'd known she was going to call a cab and be gone before I had a chance to do more than kiss her, if I'd known I wouldn't even get a straight answer to my question about seeing her again, I'd have damned sure re-thought that decision.

To hell with behaving like a gentleman. Hadn't she warned me about that last night? I couldn't believe I'd passed up the chance to make love to her this morning. Who knew if the opportunity would ever come again?

"I should have fucking screwed her senseless," I muttered angrily.

"Should have fucking screwed her senseless," Zoe recited flawlessly.

Great job. I groaned inwardly. Wasn't *that* just perfect?

Not only did my words sound even worse repeated back at me, but, the way my luck was running, I could probably count on hearing them again and again. And at all the most inopportune times, as well. Much as I loved Zoe I had to admit that, sometimes, owning a pet with a talent for mimicry is not without its disadvantages.

Chapter Six

Claire

Two weeks passed with excruciating slowness. I lost count of how many times I found myself reaching for the phone to call Mike. I missed his voice, but I was afraid he'd read more into it than that, afraid he'd think I wanted more than friendship and occasional sex. That wouldn't be fair to either of us. He didn't call me either, so maybe he was thinking the same thing.

But not calling didn't stop me from thinking about him and it certainly didn't deter me from fantasizing. Night after night, I imagined Mike's face, Mike's voice, Mike's hands and mouth and cock as I brought myself to orgasm all alone in my bed.

It wasn't bad, as fantasies went, but by the time the second Thursday rolled around I was ready for the real thing. More than ready. And, by Thursday afternoon, I was in such a state of anticipation, I could no longer sit still. So, I headed downstairs hoping I could find a way to work off some of the erotic energy that was once again building inside me. I'd been throwing myself into exercise with a vengeance these last two weeks, sitting in on whichever classes struck my fancy.

All but Derek's.

I wasn't ready, yet, for that much torture. I was just looking for a way to take the edge off my craving.

As luck would have it, Derek was teaching in the main studio, but even if I'd been feeling up to it, I couldn't have joined in. Class was already in session and he's always been a stickler for promptness. Not even the fact I pay his salary would save me from being disciplined for my infraction if I tried to slip in late.

Fortunately, there was another option available to me. Damien and Raul were working out in the small exercise room just off the reception area. The pair had been trying, for several weeks now, to convince me to add a Capoeria class to the schedule. This seemed as good a time as any to allow them to give me a demonstration.

While Damien guided me through the movements, Raul kept the rhythm on something called an *Agogo*. I have to admit I was impressed. It was fun, fast paced and a lot more strenuous than I'd thought it would be. I was so absorbed in what we were doing, however, that I nearly missed Mike's arrival.

"Mike." I called out, a little breathlessly, as he passed by the open door. "Hi."

He swept the room with a glance, and nodded curtly. "Hello," he murmured as he continued up the stairs to my office.

I felt rebuffed. That was it? One word? My heart had actually skipped a beat when I saw him. I couldn't even remember the last time *that* had happened! And he couldn't spare me a smile? A second glance? A complete sentence? Not wanting to let my disappointment show, I kept the guys busy for almost fifteen minutes more before I pleaded exhaustion and escaped.

* * * *

Mike appeared to be absorbed in his work when I breezed into my office, vigorously fanning my face with one hand. "Whew, that was fun." I was glad I could blame the flush on my cheeks and the breathlessness in my voice on the exercise. When Mike's eyes met mine, I was even more glad he was too far away to notice the pounding of my heart.

Then he dropped his gaze and refocused on the papers in front of him, without so much as a single word.

Silence filled the room. Feigning indifference, I hopped on my desk, uncapped the bottle of water I'd taken from the refrigerator downstairs and gulped half of it down. I was now annoyed as well as disappointed. If I had any sense at all, Mike's present disinterest would have had a chilling effect on my libido, but, apparently, I'd learned nothing from my last marriage.

"Have you ever tried Capoeria, Mike?" I asked when I could think of nothing else to say. I was just trying to make conversation although, given Mike's wide range of interests, I wouldn't have been surprised to learn he used to teach it.

"No," he answered shortly.

"Oh, you should. It's so much fun."

"So you've said."

More silence. Dead air. God damn it. Why should I even bother? If Mike was no longer interested, I should just find someone who was. How hard could it be? He wasn't all that, after all. He was older, mostly bald, hardly in the best of shape. And, at the moment, he was as cranky and out of sorts as an entire cast of sleep-deprived, PMS-positive Divas in the midst of a chocolate famine. *Never* a good look for a man. And, yet... it was still all I could do to keep from launching an ambush, shoving his chair away from the desk, straddling his lap, unzipping his fly...

Maybe he wouldn't be ready for me, but so what? I knew

how to get him there quick.

But was it worth it? Did I want to have to work that hard for any man's attention?

Well, maybe. Just remembering how hot we'd been together was enough to start me creaming. One night wasn't enough. I wanted more of what we'd had. I wanted to be naked under him now. And, like a moth drawn to his particular brand of fire, no other candle was going to do it for me.

Groaning in disgust at my own weakness, I let my head fall back and slowly trailed the cool plastic cylinder down my throat, hoping it would slow my racing pulse. Capoeria might be great exercise, but it had obviously done *nothing* to diminish the horniness I was feeling. I was tempted to slide the bottle between my thighs, to rub its frigid surface against my heated flesh and maybe ease the fluttering pressure in my sex. Would Mike even notice if I did? I raised my head and caught him staring, eyes dark with what could only be lust. *Oh, yeah, he'd notice.* Good. I felt my mood lift. So much for disinterest.

Bracing my hands on the edge of the desk, I leaned forward. "So what's going on here, Mike? I don't even get a greeting now? What's up with that?"

He frowned, the heat in his gaze diminishing as his eyes narrowed. "What are you talking about?"

"I'm talking about when you first got here today. I said hi and you totally blew me off."

"Claire, I did not blow you off."

"You did. You completely ignored me."

"How? I said hello, didn't I?"

I snorted. "Barely."

"Well, you were occupied."

"Oh, please. What kind of excuse is that?"

"I didn't want to interrupt."

"Hmph." I thought about that as Mike once again focused on his work. It was plausible, I supposed. And really very considerate, if looked at in just the right way. I still felt slighted. "Very thoughtful. But hardly necessary. We were just fooling around."

"Yes, that would have been my impression too. It's a mystery to me why you do it."

"What does that mean?"

Mike sighed. "It means I don't understand why you waste

your time with these... with these young guys in their... beachwear."

Beachwear? "This is about clothing? What's wrong with the way they were dressed?"

"Nothing. Forget it."

Damien and Raul had been dressed appropriately, I'd thought, in white tanks, bearing the studio's logo, over black Lycra shorts. It was a look that was only slightly more casual than my own apparel, a lime colored, cap sleeve, scoop neck T and matching yoga pants. Mike, in comparison, was almost overdressed in khaki pants and a sage-green linen shirt. The stud I'd admired last time was once again glittering in his ear and a two-toned Rolex Oyster was clasped around his wrist. I had to admit he looked good. Attractive. Moderately affluent. Mature. Respectable. And angry.

But why? "What are you so angry about?"

"I'm not angry."

Right. Not much. Once again, I considered Mike's appearance, contrasting it with that of Damien and Raul. I recalled their hard sculpted bodies, their gleaming, oiled muscles, their... Oh. The corners of my mouth quirked upward. "Mike... are you jealous?"

"No." He continued to work steadily, but the heightened color in his cheeks and the grim set of his jaw gave him away. "Of course not."

"Mike..."

When he glanced up again, the scowl on his face wiped the smile from mine in a hurry. "Is that what you wanted Claire? Were you hoping I'd make a scene in front of your boys? Sorry to disappoint you."

I could feel my cheeks flaming. "No, that's not what I..."

"Excuse me. I have a lot of work to do."

"Mike!"

He ignored me. Frustrated, I blew out an exasperated breath. I tried hard to hold on to my sense of outrage, he was acting like an ass. But it was impossible for me to stay angry with him. There was an odd tightness in my chest that wouldn't allow it. I couldn't help but recall my own reaction, two weeks ago, to Derek and his class full of pretzels. How welcome Mike's admiration had been to me then.

I cleared my throat. "For what it's worth, I was *not* trying to make you jealous."

Mike nodded. "Glad to hear it."

"But, just in case you are feeling that way—"

"I'm *not*," he growled through clenched teeth. "I told you that already."

"Right. But if you *were* ever to, there's something you should know."

He was quiet for an instant and then, "What's that?"

"The truth is I find you maddeningly attractive."

He said nothing. If I didn't know better I might have thought he wasn't listening. But the slight trembling in his fingers gave him away.

"And very sexy."

Still nothing.

"In fact it's really quite distracting."

He continued working.

"Mike?"

"Thank you," he murmured, his voice subdued.

"Do you know you're blushing?"

"I'm not... blushing," he muttered, even more quietly.

But he was. To the tips of his ears he'd gone completely pink. I think even the top of his bald head was rosier than usual.

"Mike?"

Another silence. Then, finally, "Yes?"

"Would you like to kiss and make up now?"

His hand clenched hard on the pen he was holding. Any harder, and I think it might have snapped in two. He raised his eyes to mine.

I smiled and batted my eyes a time or two. "Unless you're too busy working?"

I'd forgotten how quickly he could move. I'd almost forgotten how well he could kiss. But the moment he clasped my face in his hands, the moment his lips touched mine, it all came rushing back. *Oh, yes.* I locked my hands behind his head and fell into his kiss. My only regret was that he couldn't talk and kiss at the same time. There aren't many ways in which fantasy is superior to reality, but that's definitely one of them.

When he finally raised his head, I locked eyes with him and smiled. "God, I've missed your mouth."

"Claire." Mike groaned in response. He pulled me close once more, muttering between kisses, "You don't know what it does when you say those things. These last weeks have been hell. I couldn't eat, couldn't sleep, couldn't think straight."

Huh? Bracing my hands against his chest, I pushed him away

a little. "Why's that?"

"Because! I didn't know where I stood with you, or what you wanted. You were so vague when I asked about seeing you again. And you left so quickly."

What the hell? "Mike, I was perfectly clear. I said it would be nice, didn't I? Or something to that effect."

He groaned again. "That's just what I mean. Too vague. Too polite. I wanted a simple yes or no."

Amused now, I couldn't help but murmur, "Really? You'd rather I'd said *no?*"

Mike frowned. "Don't play with me, Claire. You know how I feel. I've always been honest about my feelings for you."

"And I haven't been? I was not vague!"

"Maybe not intentionally," Mike conceded. "But it felt vague to me. And then when you didn't call..."

I held my tongue. It would have been easy to say, *well, you didn't call me, either*, but would that accomplish? All this conversation was taking us into murky territory. I didn't want a relationship with him. Not the kind where feelings could be hurt if someone didn't call. "Why are we talking about this now? Don't we have better things we could be doing?"

"Wh—what?" A frown furrowed Mike's brow as he glanced around the room, his expression stuck somewhere between eager and doubtful. "D'you mean here?"

I felt my eyes widen as his meaning hit home. No, that was *not* what I meant."

Or was it?

After all, it wouldn't be the first time. I'd seduced Derek in this room once, although it hadn't been easy. If there's one thing that man prides himself on it's his iron self-control. Something told me Mike would be a whole lot easier to bend.

I smiled. "Well, now that you mention it, sure. Why not? Unless you'd rather wait for some other time?"

"No." Mike's voice was flat and final. "That's one mistake I'll never make again."

Mistake? *What's he talking about?* Before I could ask, he'd pulled me in for another kiss. His hand tangled in the hair at the back of my head and he used it to lower me onto my back. From the sound, I think he must have used his other hand to clear my desk.

For just an instant, I thought about reminding him the office door wasn't locked. Even muffled by carpet, the thud of that many objects hitting the floor at once could attract attention. But, if he wasn't worried, why should I be? I could pretty much guarantee I'd been observed having sex more times than he and had long since learned to tune out an audience. Besides, by then, he'd already shoved both my shirt and my sports bra over my head and it was fair to say I was feeling a bit distracted.

Quickly, Mike pushed both garments up my arms, stopping when he reached my wrists. I shivered a little at the sudden exposure and then gasped when he gathered the material together in one hand. One twist of his fist and I was effectively trapped with my arms stretched out above my head. Heat rushed to my pussy as he trailed the fingers of his free hand down my arm, making me squirm. My nipples beaded tight, a clear invitation to touch, one I hoped he wouldn't ignore.

"Yes," I whispered, watching his face, watching desire light up his eyes. "Do it." My breath caught in my throat when his hand curved around my breast and it was all I could do to release it. But what did I care? At that point, I wanted his mouth on my chest more than I wanted to breathe again anyway. Squeezing my eyes shut, I arched into him. Offering. Asking. Aching. "Mike..."

Wet and warm, his mouth closed over one puckered nipple. He rolled the other between thumb and forefinger; his touch gentle, but not too gentle. Just perfect, in fact. I cried out softly in mindless pleasure.

I don't know how long it went on. I only know I was writhing by the time he released me from the sweet torture. Tears were leaking from the corners of my eyes and my breathing was too labored, too uneven to allow for speech.

Mike gave the bonds that held my wrists immobile a little tug. The added tension sent shivers racing across my skin. I inhaled sharply, arching upward again, whimpering delightedly as his hand slid down along my belly and into the waistband of my pants.

"You're so wet," he murmured hoarsely as he probed my slick, swollen flesh, fingering my clit, bringing me right to the edge. And then he stopped. "I have to see."

I groaned as his hand was withdrawn. *Noooo. Don't stop now. Not now!*

He didn't say, *don't move*, but I couldn't have anyway, even after he let go of my wrists. I was panting, partly in an effort to keep from screaming at him, *keep going—faster, faster*. As his hands slowly coaxed my pants off, a voice in my head was chanting, *do it*, *do it, do it...*

Mike went down on his knees and spread my thighs wide. I opened for him eagerly. The first swipe of his tongue set fire to my nerves. I went off in seconds. I'm not sure which of us was more surprised.

"Thank you for this," he murmured pressing a kiss against my thigh.

He's thanking me? Shaking my head in disbelief, I freed my hands and sat up. Stiffly. "Don't thank me yet," I told him as I nudged his shoulder with my foot, forcing him to get up, to get out of my way so I could stand.

Once we were both on our feet, I backed him around the desk and pushed him into my chair. Then I dropped to my knees on the floor between his legs and unzipped his fly.

Mike's breath gusted out as I took his erection into my hand, intending to give him the best head of his life, but then I inhaled his scent and memories from two weeks ago filled my head. My nipples pebbled up instantly. My pussy throbbed. Serious fellatio would have to wait . I was too needy to be so generous today.

Instead, I played the tease; circling his crown with my tongue, cradling his sac in one hand and pumping slowly with the other. Lowering my head, I nibbled my way along his shaft with just enough pressure to make him moan. When he did, I took it as my cue.

"Pussy wants filled," I murmured as I straddled his lap and nuzzled his neck. Knees pressed tight around his thighs, I lowered myself on top of him.

"Bring it here," Mike growled, fingers closing on me instantly, digging into my waist as he flexed his hips and thrust inside me. "All of it, Claire. I want all of you. Now."

Heat engulfed me; white hot, it left me writhing in Mike's arms. His teeth nipped at my shoulder as he held me to him and continued thrusting, impaling me over and over until I gave him what he wanted: All of me. Now.

I clutched his neck as we came together; each contraction of my muscles forcing another spurt of cum from his cock; each jerk of his shaft inside me making my pussy spasm harder.

Finally, spent, exhausted, sated... at least for now... I collapsed on top of him. "Now you can say thank you," I teased breathlessly.

Mike's arms tightened around me. "Thank you."

I chuckled softly. "You're welcome." Then I kissed his cheek and slid from his arms.

As I scooped my clothes up, I couldn't help assessing the mess on the office floor. At least it didn't look like anything had been broken. Thank God, I hadn't been using my laptop today. Still, I knew it would take days before I had my desk back the way I liked it. Next time, we'd do things differently.

Turning back to Mike, I was surprised to see he was still sprawled in the chair where I'd left him. Only his gaze, heavy lidded and dark, seemed animated, his eyes tracking my every move. I stretched languidly, just to tease him. Until a trickle of wetness down my leg reminded me what such teasing could lead to.

Surely not again? I glanced at the open fly of his pants. Was he harder than he'd been a moment ago? *Better stop staring and get dressed before one of us starts getting ideas.*

"I have to admit I'm surprised," I said, pulling several handfuls of tissue from the box in my desk drawer and handing some to him.

"About what?"

"Us. Our... whaddaya call it... stamina. I mean, we're not kids."

Mike shrugged. "That's what I was telling you earlier. What you get from kids... what good is it? That's not gonna last. Experience, maturity, respect, those are things you can count on."

I nodded, not really listening, as I blotted moisture from my legs in an effort to render myself once again respectable. Mature? That was just another word for old, wasn't it? Did anyone ever *really* think that was better? "Yeah, but, experienced or not, we sure haven't been lasting very long."

Mike's eyes widened in alarm. "What?"

"In case you haven't noticed." I gestured at the clock on the wall. "These little trysts of ours have not exactly been leisurely."

"Claire... I'm sorry." The disappointed look on his face, the crestfallen tone in his voice—it was all so pitiful, I couldn't help but giggle.

"No, silly." Leaning in, I rested my hands on the arms of his chair and kissed him lightly. "That *wasn't* a criticism."

Before I could pull away, Mike caught hold of my wrist, and kissed me again. His open palm, sliding up the back of my bare thigh, made me ache for him all over again; left me moaning with pleasure, with wonder, with *need*.

"Enough!" Wrenching my wrist free of his grip, I took a step back. "See what I mean? I can't hold out either. I feel like I'm—Like I'm eighteen again and just discovered sex."

Actually? That was more like fifteen and a half. But he didn't have to know that now. Or ever, for that matter. In fact, there was a whole, wide range of details I had no plans to share with him. When it came to some parts of my past, I figured the less he knew, the happier we'd both be. I liked Mike a lot. We were friends now, at least I liked to think we were, and I wanted to keep it that way.

And the one sure thing I'd learned about keeping friends was this: Never hand your friend a weapon that can be used against you. Not unless you're looking to test the friendship or end it—fast.

* * * *

Mike

Reaching for Claire, I dragged her back against me. I wrapped my arms around her waist and held her tight. *Eighteen*, huh? Well, it was good to know I wasn't the only one feeling overwhelmed by this situation developing between us. The shaky intake of her breath as I pressed a kiss against the soft flesh of her belly had me closing my eyes and sighing with bliss. *Claire*.

"Let me go now, Mike," she murmured breathlessly. "I have to dress."

I thought about saying no. I thought about slipping my hand between her legs instead. Thought about urging her onto my lap, so I could make her come once again. I wanted to make her prove what she'd just implied, that she was helpless to resist me.

Just knowing I could have that effect on her was intoxicating. Knowing she'd probably let me pleasure her like that or, even better, that she might be wanting me to—*that* was nothing short of astonishing. But she'd asked me to let her go. I had to honor that. So I kissed her lightly, one more time, and opened my arms.

Neither of us spoke much as we dressed. I felt a slight qualm when I saw the tangle of objects on the floor by her desk.

"Sorry about the mess," I told her, as we tackled the chore of restoring order.

"That's okay," Claire murmured, her cheeks suspiciously pink. Though she didn't say it, the words, *it was worth it*, seemed to hang in the air between us.

To be honest, I wasn't all that sorry either. I seldom lose control like that and I was surprised to find I liked it. But, even more importantly, if Claire's reaction was anything to go by, she'd liked it too. That alone was reason to plan for similar *spontaneous* events in the future.

"Well, I'm about done in for the day," Claire sighed, when we were finished. She looked like she was waiting for me to say something.

I can take a hint as well as the next guy, I hope. "Let me take you out to dinner," I suggested.

"Like this?" She glanced down at herself doubtfully. "I'd have to go home and change first."

"Why don't I follow you home then? You can leave your car there and we'll go in mine?" The moment I said it, I wondered if I'd made a mistake. It was only two weeks ago she'd accused me of stalking her. On the other hand, this was as good a way as any to find out what she really thought about that.

Claire shrugged. "Okay, sounds good. Let me get my purse and we'll go."

Yes! It was all I could do to keep from pumping my fist in the air. She hadn't even hesitated. My jubilation was short lived, however. I turned back toward my desk, saw the papers scattered on its surface, and groaned. "Oh, hell."

"What's wrong?" Claire inquired, lifting her purse from its nest in the bottom drawer of her own desk.

I gestured at the papers. "I forgot. I wasn't finished."

"Oh. Right." A smug smile seemed to flirt with the edges of her mouth. "Well, what do you want to do?"

Smiling? What I wanted to do, at this present moment, was think up some way to pay her back for that bit of insolence. I stared fixedly at her mouth, unable to look away. "I guess I could take it home with me." I could bring it in to the office tomorrow and let one of my employees finish it up. Only I didn't want to do that. Working on Claire's account was a pleasure for me, an act of devotion. It was *my* task and I didn't want to share it with anyone. "But why don't I check my schedule tomorrow and see if I can't find some time to come back next week and finish it?"

"All right." Claire flashed a brilliant smile as she slipped the strap of her purse over her shoulder. "Good idea," she said as she headed for the door. "Two weeks was too long to wait anyway."

Now, what the hell does that mean? I wondered. Did she think I'd let her account sit, untouched, for two weeks? Or did she mean two weeks was too long to wait to see me again? *Does she only intend to see me when I come to do her books? The hell with that!*

Before I could ask, however, she'd reached the door and pulled it open.

"Was that unlocked the whole time?" I was surprised into asking.

Claire glanced at me slyly. "You just figure that out?"

I felt the blood warming my cheeks and knew I was once again blushing. "I, uh, yes. Sorry. You should have said something."

Claire patted my arm. "Well, you were occupied."

I frowned. Something about her words seemed vaguely familiar. "What?"

"You know how it is," she murmured, blinking innocently. "I didn't want to interrupt." Then she skipped blithely down the stairs.

I trailed behind her feeling once again bemused.

"Good night, everyone," Claire called cheerfully to her staff as she breezed through the small reception area, receiving a chorus of good-byes in response.

"Night, Claire," Derek murmured. As he glanced up from the clip-board he'd been examining, his expression changed. His initial smile faded into a look that bordered on displeasure.

I felt myself bristling as his gaze lingered on her in what seemed to be entirely too proprietary a manner. *He looks like he knows exactly what we've been doing.* Then his gaze shifted to me and the open hostility I read there removed all doubt. *Damn. He does know.* Not caring to conjecture how that was possible, I returned his look with one of cool disdain and passed him by without a word. *Tough luck, kid. You didn't know what you had, did you? Well, now she's with me.*

Picking up my pace, I managed to overtake Claire before she reached the front door. "Allow me, milady," I murmured as I held it open for her.

"Why, thank you, kind sir." She flashed me another smile, then her eyes narrowed inquisitively. "What's going on with you?"

I looked at her in surprise. "I don't know. Why?"

"It's just... all of a sudden, you have this kind of cat that ate the canary look about you."

Oh. I felt my lips stretch until I knew I must be grinning from ear to ear. "Close. Now, where would you like to go for dinner?"

Chapter Seven

Mike

Claire's house was not what I'd expected. I'd thought her home would reflect her personality, her tastes and passions, her career. I thought it would tell me something about her that I didn't yet know. Maybe many things. Instead, it seemed... impersonal.

"I know," she agreed when I questioned her about it. "It's not really me, is it?"

"It's not really anyone."

Claire shrugged. "Why should it be? I don't own this place, you know. I lease it. Furnished. There's a maid who comes in once a week, a gardener, a pool boy. I didn't hire them, I rarely see them, I don't even sign their paychecks. I just live here."

"I see." I glanced around the living room again. "Kind of like living in a hotel."

"One that's severely lacking in room service and other amenities, but yeah. Pretty much."

"Why?"

"Money for one thing. That's simple enough, right? Until my settlement went through I couldn't afford to buy anything and, once I had the money, I decided I'd be better off investing in my business." She sighed. "Plus, I guess I just got tired of having to re-invent myself every few years. The thought of starting over again... I just couldn't do it."

I suppose I must have looked puzzled because she shrugged and added, "You know. Marriage, divorce, remarriage. At this point, I probably wouldn't recognize my own tastes in furnishings if I were plunked down in the middle of 'em. Really, the only things here that are mine are my clothes, and that's just fine with me."

"What about memorabilia? You must have boxes of stuff from all your movies."

Amusement glimmered in Claire's eyes. "Oh, but you know, Mike, those charity auctions do take their toll." Then she shrugged. "*Boxes*? No. I did used to keep a scrapbook with my clippings and whatnot. And I suppose I might still have *a* box in storage, somewhere. But, you know, things tend to get lost when you move as much as I have. It's an occupational hazard. Besides, I prefer clothes anyway. And shoes, of course."

"Okay, but there had to be something about this house that you liked." I suppose I was still hoping I could get some kind of insight into her mind. "What was it that made you choose it over... well, any of the other places you could have rented? When you first saw the place, what did you think of it?"

"Well, let's see..." Claire swept the room with a thoughtful glance. "I think it was something along the lines of... this'll do."

"This will do?" I repeated, in disbelief. "That was it?"

Claire nodded. "Pretty much. Or maybe, this'll do. For now."

I felt myself frowning. There was something about that statement, something about the way she said it, that bothered me. Maybe because I couldn't imagine ever feeling that way myself. Not about anything, really.

"Well, enough of this standing around," Claire said, her eyes twinkling as she smiled at me. "I'm going to go change now, so why don't you... oh, I dunno... make yourself at home? If that's possible?"

"I will," I said as I returned her smile. "Take your time."

As I waited for her to return, I tried hard to dispel the disappointment I was feeling. There was so much about her I'd yet to learn, so much I wanted to know. Luckily, things improved over dinner.

I took her to Ocean Avenue in Santa Monica. It's the kind of place that's popular rather than trendy with an emphasis on good food and good service. The kind of place where I knew we could sit and talk and get to know each other better.

The first thing I learned was that, contrary to all the preconceptions people tend to have about stars and their egos, this one really didn't like to talk about herself. Not about herself, not about her career, not about her past. Especially not about her past.

"Oh, but that's such *old* news," she protested after humoring me for several minutes. "And not at all interesting. Honestly, Mike, if you really want to know this stuff, I'm sure it's all been written up somewhere. You could just... look it up and read it sometime. Right now, I'd much rather talk about you."

Talk about 'not at all interesting'! "You'd be bored."

She smiled at me from across the table. "I bet I wouldn't either. I suspect you're actually quite fascinating."

Fascinating? I shook my head. "Now, Claire, you're a very talented actress, but not even you can pull off a line like that and expect anyone to believe it."

Her laughter was lyrical, musical and just loud enough to turn several heads. "I really do want to know more about you, Mike. Truly. Please?"

When she looked at me like that, when she used that voice and asked so sweetly, I could deny her nothing. And so we talked about me. And then we talked about other things. About everything. About food and wine. Places we'd traveled to, or lived in, or wanted to see someday before we died. And, finally, after I'd worn her down and slipped past all her defenses, we talked about her.

We lingered a long time over dessert and coffee and, with every word she spoke, I felt myself falling deeper and deeper in love. I didn't think I'd ever seen anything as lovely as she looked that night, with the lamplight gleaming in her hair and her eyes glowing.

When I could no longer put off the inevitable, I took her home. I walked her to her door and there, standing in the soft glow of her porch light, I wrapped my arms around her and let her kiss me. Bracing her hands on my arms, she went up on her toes and I closed my eyes to better revel in the sweet softness of her lips, the gentle hesitancy of her mouth on mine.

She broke off the kiss, at last, with a little sigh. Resting her head on my chest she asked, "You're not coming in, are you?"

The wistful tone in her voice could have been an act. I knew it wasn't. That, all by itself, was almost enough to compensate for the words I had to say. "I can't. I have to get back to Zoe. If I come in now, I won't be able to make myself leave until morning."

She nodded, saying nothing.

After a moment I asked, "Can I call you?"

"You have to, remember? You were going to tell me when you can come back next week and finish up."

"I've been thinking about that," I said. "I know I'm free next Thursday afternoon, so why don't I just make it then? Same time as usual, okay?"

"Sure." She angled her head to the side and glanced up at me. "So, I guess, when you asked if you could call me, you must have meant... socially?"

I nodded. And then waited for what seemed an eternity while she appeared to ponder the matter.

"Yes," she said at last, speaking slowly, clearly, making that single word sound so very, very serious. She waited a beat and then added, "Now, that wasn't too vague, or anything, was it?"

Smiling, I pulled her close for another kiss. "No. Not too vague at all."

I'd wait until Saturday, I decided, right there on the spot. One day, so as not to seem too eager. One day to wait, this time, not fourteen. And then, if I was lucky, we'd have almost the whole weekend, two full days, to share together. Two days of heaven.

* * * *

Claire

"Talk to me, Claire," Derek said Saturday morning. He'd come to my office to discuss changes to the upcoming schedule, which was not unusual. But then he'd stayed to chat, something he hadn't done in quite awhile. "What's new with you?"

I hid my surprise at the question as best I could. "Nothing much. Same old, same old, really. Why do you ask?"

Derek shrugged. "It's just... well, it's been great seeing you get back into things in the last few weeks. Exercising. Working out. You're looking more like your old self these days."

"Exactly which 'old self' would that be?"

For just an instant, Derek looked uncomfortable. "You know. More like before. Like you were when we first—Well, like you were when I first met you."

"You mean before you tortured me into shape with your endless *asanas*?" I teased. I wondered if he was feeling slighted because I'd been avoiding his classes.

"No, I mean happy."

I stared at him. "Derek... I'm happy."

He nodded. "That's what I said. And I'm happy for you. But..."

I waited. "But?"

Derek sighed. "It's just—You and the accountant, Claire? That's a little random, isn't it?"

"I don't know why," I answered, feeling suddenly defensive.

"Well, for starters, he doesn't seem like your usual type."

"Maybe that's because I don't have a usual type. Come on, Derek, you know how much I like variety. Mike and I are friends. I had dinner with him. End of discussion."

"Dinner?" Derek's smile turned sardonic. His eyes bored into mine with that annoying all-seeing, Secrets-of-the-Mystic-East kind of way he likes to affect at times. "Well, good. 'Cause I'm sure you needed it. I'm sure you and your *friend* worked up quite an appetite while he was here."

It was a struggle to keep my mouth from dropping open. Derek knew about that? No. He couldn't. "What's that supposed to mean?"

"Exactly what you think it means," Derek replied dryly. "I've been your friend too, right?"

Oops. "Does everyone know?" It shouldn't bother me if they did. No, it *didn't* bother me. Not really. But still, that was *not* the image I was trying to project right now.

Derek shrugged. "Probably not. No one's saying anything about it. If they were, I would have heard it. But I know you better than most of the others do. Besides," A look of distaste curled his lips. "The guy was looking too smug for me to think anything else."

I nodded. "I noticed that too. Like the cat that ate the canary, right?" *And I still don't know why.*

Derek's eyebrows rose. "Okay, I'm not sure which of you was the canary in that scenario but yeah, kinda like that."

Which of us was the canary? What the... oh. As Derek's *entendre* hit home, Mike's reply the other day suddenly seemed a lot less cryptic. *Close.* Right. He hadn't eaten a canary, but—Wow, color me stupid for having missed that one!

To cover my confusion, I went into character. I'd been playing a vamp for over half a lifetime—both on and off screen. Leaning back seductively in my chair, I let my gaze turn smoky. "Now, Derek," I purred in lecherous tones, "You *know* that's always been my favorite part."

Derek's reaction was just what I hoped it would be. A carnal grin lit up his face just as the phone on my desk began to ring. "That so? And here I always thought your favorite part was when I..."

"Hold that thought," I said, waving him to silence as I picked up the receiver. "Hello?"

"Good morning, beautiful lady." Mike's voice poured through the phone like a river of dark, melted chocolate, coating each and every nerve I had with sweet, sweet longing. "What are you doing?"

I smiled. Oh, if only I'd been alone. I knew just what my response to his question would have been then. My hand would already be reaching between my legs. I'd be closing my eyes and murmuring dark words back to him. Between us we'd spin out a lush, forbidden fantasy...

But I wasn't alone. Was I?

I cleared my throat. "Actually, I'm kind of in a meeting right now." Angling my chair so that I was no longer face to face with Derek, I asked, "What's on your mind?"

"Well, I was just wondering—I mean, if you're not doing anything, I thought—Would you like to go out tonight?"

He couldn't be serious? I felt like someone had just thrown a glass of ice water in my face. Tonight? As in *last minute, no advance notice, aren't you glad I called because you couldn't possibly have had anything else planned for this evening?* That tonight? *I don't think so.*

"Mmm, no, sorry, I'm afraid that timing doesn't work for me. I have a prior engagement."

"Okay, how about tomorrow then?"

I gritted my teeth. "Still not so good." Even with my back to him, I'd swear I could feel Derek's I-told-you-so grin mocking me. Damn him for putting ideas in my head. I mean, what was the big deal? So Mike called at the last minute, isn't that exactly the kind of thing friends did? But, smug, Derek had called him and that's just how it felt to me now too. Mike was acting way too sure of having me. My own fault, of course, but still not acceptable. "My weekend is all booked up."

"Oh." The disappointment in Mike's voice was palpable. "That's too bad."

I found myself nodding agreement. It really was too bad, because I *did* want to see him. "I could maybe make time on Tuesday," I said, relenting a little. There was no point in spiting myself altogether.

"After work?"

"Mm-hm. That sounds about right."

"Great. So, did you want me to come by and pick you up there, or...?"

"Why don't you call me Tuesday morning? We'll discuss details then. I can't really talk right now."

"You really *are* in a meeting, aren't you?" The surprise in Mike's voice made me laugh.

"Of course I am. Didn't I say so?"

"Yes, but I thought..." Mike's sigh was audible even over the phone. I could just imagine him shaking his head. "Okay. I'm sorry. Never mind what I thought. Is everything okay?"

"Certainly. Everything's fine."

"Okay then, I guess... I guess I'll talk to you Tuesday."

"Sounds good," I murmured, spinning my chair back to face the desk. "Bye now."

I returned the phone to its holder and looked up to find Derek observing me quietly.

I raised my eyebrows. "What?"

"Nothing. I'm still waiting for you to tell me what's up with you and the accountant."

"His name's Mike," I snapped, irritated with both of them, and myself as well. "You know that as well as I do. Quit calling him 'the accountant'. You make him sound like some kind of second-rate mob enforcer."

Derek smirked, but said nothing.

"Why the sudden interest in my sex life, Derek? No, don't tell me. Trouble in paradise? Already? Or are you just annoyed that I've found someone to replace you?"

A dull red stained Derek's cheekbones as he stood, signaling our little chat was at an end. At least I'd shut him up, though not for long.

"Cheap shots, Claire," he muttered, obviously trying to rein in his anger. He shook his head sadly. "I was just looking out for you, all right? I didn't want to see you get hurt."

Again. He didn't say that, but he might as well have. I nodded, accepting the sentiment, even if it *was* a little late in coming. Our affair had ended amicably. That didn't mean the breakup had been painless, it just meant I'd never admit to the fact. As a face saving strategy, I thought it worked well for both of us. And I certainly wasn't going to be the one to spoil things by arguing with him about it now.

I smiled, willing to forgive and forget. "I appreciate that, Derek. I do. I just don't understand the reason for your concern."

"Why wouldn't I be concerned, Claire? I'm your friend. And I know you. You're not as tough as you like to pretend."

Oh, please. "How tough do I have to be, Derek? He's an accountant. You know what they're like."

Derek sighed. "Okay. Whatever. You'll do what you want, I guess. Just remember, I'm here if you need me."

"Thank you," I murmured, really meaning it. "For everything."

After Derek left, I thought about what he'd said. Yes, he knew me, but not nearly as well as he thought he did. Our affair had been fun. I'd loved being seen with him, loved the boost it gave my battered ego to know I could still attract someone that young, that desirable. Someone who didn't view me as simply a convenient vehicle to advance his career. We'd been 'friends with benefits'. Maybe that was all he wanted from our relationship or maybe it was all he'd been able to offer. Either way, I told myself it didn't matter because that was all I wanted too—not just from him, but from anyone.

After six failed marriages, I was through with getting serious. It was a good idea, marred by just one fatal flaw: I hadn't really meant it. I hadn't yet learned my lesson. I hadn't yet learned to stay detached. Now, I had.

Chapter Eight

Mike

I had just finished dinner Saturday evening and was clearing up in the kitchen when my phone rang. Afraid it might slip through my wet hands, I tucked it against my shoulder while I finished drying them. I nearly dropped it anyway when the sound of Claire's breathy murmur reached my ears. "Michael. What are you doing?"

"I—uh, *hi*," I replied, stammering as I tried to catch my breath. "I'm, I'm well, I'm washing dishes, actually."

"Oh." Silence. And then, "So, um...are your hands all slippery wet now?"

I felt myself frown. "What?"

"Are your hands *wet*," she repeated slowly, emphasizing the last word. "You know, slick and dripping with... soap?"

"Uh, no, not—I just dried them, why?"

More silence, this one followed by a heavy sigh. "Okay, let's try this again. What are you wearing?"

Did she just—What am I *wearing*? "What are *you* wearing?" I asked cautiously.

"I... am wearing... a gown," she answered slowly, her voice ripe with suggestion. "A loooong, white gown made of very soft, sheer silk."

"Are you?" I asked, blinking in astonishment. Had she really called just to seduce me over the phone?

"I am. And, mmmm, I wish you could feel how soft it is, how... sheer."

Smiling now, I took the bait, "How sheer is it?"

"Oh, so very sheer, Mike, you can't imagine. It's like the softest, sheerest, tissue-thin fabric in the world, and, I think, if it got even the slightest bit wet..."

"What would happen? Would it turn invisible?"

"Oh, yessss. I'm so afraid it would."

"Ahh." Clutching the phone in my hand now, I braced my other fist on the counter and closed my eyes, the better to imagine it. Phantom Claire shimmered into view, a seductive smile on her face. "Claire?"

"Yes, Michael?"

"I've just put my hands back into the sink."

"Have you?"

"Yes," I said, elaborating on the lie. "I accidentally dropped the towel into the water while we were talking and when I reached in to get it my hands got wet, all over again."

A soft sigh escaped her. "Uh-oh."

"Come closer," I whispered. "Let me feel your gown. I want to see how soft it is."

"It's so soft, Mike, but your hands—if you touch me now..."

"Where, Claire? Where should I touch you?"

"My breasts," she answered promptly. "If you put your hands on my breasts..."

"Are you imagining it? How does it feel when I do that? Tell me."

"Sooo good. But, ohhh, I can feel the water soaking right into the front of my gown." She gave a startled gasp. "Oh, no, it's all wet! You can see..."

"Everything, can't I?"

"Yes."

"Can I see your nipples through the wet fabric?"

"They look like they're about to poke right through the material. They're so hard."

"They're dark against the white fabric, aren't they? I bet they look like little pebbles. I can't help but run my fingers across the front of your gown to feel them, standing so stiffly at attention."

"Mmm, your hands are so warm and..."

"No," I corrected quickly. "They're cold."

"What?" I could hear the surprise in her voice. It made me smile. "Why cold?"

"I was interrupted by your call, remember? The water in the sink grew cold while we were talking."

She laughed softly. "Oh, so it's *my* fault you're cold?"

"Yes. It's all your fault. Now my hands are like ice. And as I fondle your breasts, you start to shiver."

"Do I?"

"You beg me to help you. You ask me to please get you out of your wet clothes and warm you up."

"And will you?"

"Of course. I've already started. I've stripped you to the waist and now I'm gently blowing on your nipples to warm them."

"Mmm, that's nice. I love to feel your mouth on me. But why did you stop?"

"I didn't. Now I'm circling your nipples with my tongue, first one, then the other. They're growing even harder now. They look little cherries so ripe and sweet, I can't resist taking one into my mouth."

"No, I mean, why didn't you finish undressing me?"

"Oh." I had to pause for a moment and decide how far I wanted to go with this. How much of my true feelings should I reveal? "I like seeing you this way," I admitted. "With your clothes in disarray and your hair tumbling in your face. It's like you... well, it's like you'd let me have you any way I wanted. Like you're so hot for me, you just can't wait, not even until you're all the way naked."

"Ahh. Slutty. I see."

"No," I snapped, much more sharply than I'd intended. "That's not what I'm saying." She'd touched a nerve with her teasing. What I'd just described was so similar to the first time we'd made love; both of us too hot, too hurried to undress. The fact that she could be that passionate for me still seemed miraculous. To have that mocked...

"I'm sorry," she mumbled contritely, reminding me that the silence had become uncomfortably long.

"It's all right." In an effort to restore the teasing tone we'd lost, I added. "But if you use language like that again, I might have to spank you."

"You what?" She sounded scandalized, amused... curious. "Michael! Stop it. You would *not.*"

I felt myself smiling. At the shock. At the curiosity. At the hint of interest, the hint of challenge in her tone. At all of it, really. "Don't tempt me like that, Claire."

"And why not?"

"Because I just might have to do it."

"You would? You'd actually..."

"Yes. Under the right circumstances, I most definitely would. With pleasure."

"I see. Exactly what circumstances would those be?"

"If it was what you wanted me to do to you."

"What *I* wanted?"

"Of course."

"Hmph. And, for some reason, you think *I* would... would ever—?"

"I don't know. Would you?"

Claire was silent for way too long. I could almost feel her hesitation and I held my breath as I waited to learn how she would answer.

Finally, she cleared her throat. "You know, Michael, I do believe there might be several other ways in which I might... atone... for my bad behavior."

"That's entirely possible. What did you have in mind?"

"Well... I could kiss you, for starters. All over your body."

"All over? Would I be naked?"

"Entirely," she purred, sending chills racing over my skin.

"Okay. Where would you start?"

"Wherever you wanted me to."

"How about my mouth?"

"A classic choice. Is that where you'd like me to start?"

"Kiss me like you did the other night, when I brought you home," I told her, freeing my cock from my shorts and leaning back against the counter.

"Ahh." A soft laugh escaped her. "Liked that, did you?"

"Yes," I admitted, taking myself in hand and beginning to stroke slowly up and down my shaft. "Very much."

"Well, I'm going to kiss you just like that and then I'm going to nibble on your lips, very lightly, just because I can. Because I know you won't do a thing to stop me and because I can't resist. You taste so good, Mike, I just want to eat you all up."

I think I groaned aloud because she laughed again even more softly.

"Do you want to know what I think you'll be doing while I take your mouth like that?" she asked, not waiting for an answer. "I think you'll be clenching your hands at your sides, struggling not to grab hold of my head and kiss me back."

My hand faltered. I was surprised at how well she seemed to know me. "Probably."

"Have I mentioned how much I like that? The way you frame my face with your hands and kiss me like you can't ever get enough?"

"I can't," I told her, then asked. "What will you do next?"

"Next I'll kiss your throat. Then your shoulders. You have such broad shoulders that it will take a very long time."

"Keep going," I muttered, stroking harder.

"I'll trace the pulse at the base of your neck with my tongue and then start on your chest. Your hair tickles my nose and scrapes against my cheek as I move lower."

I swallowed hard. "Sorry about that."

"No, I like it. It makes my skin feel alive."

Good to know, I thought, sending up a silent prayer of gratitude and wonder. How had I gotten so lucky?

Claire's voice was husky, barely above a whisper as she continued, "I'm going to take a long time teasing your nipples because I like to hear you moan, so low and deep. The sound of it makes me wet. It makes me tremble inside. Eventually, I'll let them go—maybe I'll wait until you beg me to keep going. And then I'll slide slowly, slowly, slowly down the length of your stomach until I reach your cock."

I did moan then, low in my throat, just as she'd described. I couldn't help it. Just remembering the way she'd teased me in her office the other day was enough to make me sweat. As Claire went on to describe how she'd give me head, taking me into the heat of her mouth, swallowing me inch by inch, my heart was pounding. Any louder, and she probably would have heard it through the phone. By the time she'd gotten to the point in her narration where she had my dick wedged between her breasts and was rubbing herself, up and down, around me, I had reached my limit. If she were here, if this were real, I'd no doubt be giving her the pearl necklace she seemed to desire. Instead, I pressed the phone against my chest to muffle the groans I could no longer contain as I shot my cum into the empty sink.

I listened to the rest of Claire's recital in silence, waiting for my heart rate to return to normal, stopping her as she was working her way down my legs. "Tell me more about this gown you're wearing."

"The what?"

"Your gown," I repeated. "Enough about me, I want to hear more about you now."

"You mean the gown I'm only *half*-wearing," she corrected after a protracted pause. "Don't you?"

"Mm-hmm. The very same."

"Well, it's long, like I said, but it has a slit going up the side."

"How high?" I asked, adjusting my clothing and once again closing my eyes to imagine it.

"Alllll the way to the top of my thigh."

I smiled. "Good girl. I like that."

"I thought you might," she murmured sweetly. "In fact, it's cut so high that, from the right angles, or if I move a certain way, you can see the curve of my ass without even trying."

Maybe it was the mention of her ass that did it. I'd been

hoping for a way to regain control of the conversation, now I thought I had it.

"And are you wearing anything underneath it?" I asked, mentally crossing my fingers that she'd give me the answer I needed.

"Mm-hm. Just the teensiest lace thong you've ever seen."

Bingo. I clucked my tongue. "Tsk, tsk, tsk. You must have known that wouldn't make me happy."

"What?"

"I want your pussy bare. You should have removed any... impediments... before we started."

Shocked silence met my remark. "Did I mention it was v*ery tiny*?" Claire asked at last, sounding not at all pleased. "And lace, Mike. Incredibly flimsy lace, almost like fishnet, actually. Even more sheer than the gown."

Fishnet, huh? "Doesn't matter," I replied, quietly searching through drawers and cabinets until I'd located the tools I needed to carry out my mission. "I want to be able to see *and* feel all of you, all the time, whenever I want. I love how your pussy is so clean-shaven, it's so amazingly sexy that way."

"Waxed, actually," she corrected dryly. "If you really want to know."

"It's so soft," I murmured, aligning a sheet of paper along the edge of the counter. "So smooth, so perfectly exposed. I like to pretend you keep it that way just for me."

"Well, *of course* I do it for you, Michael," she drawled sweetly. "You *know* there's no one else."

I winced at the arch, seductive tone of her voice. What I knew—or at least strongly suspected—was that she hadn't just started shaving, *or waxing*, her mound in the past two weeks. She was *not* doing it just for me. And that left the rest of her statement in doubt as well. "Well, I'd better be the only one right now. Otherwise one of us had better start wearing a condom."

More silence. "Michael? What is this? What's going on here?"

"Nothing," I said as I reined in my anger. It was out of place, completely uncalled for. We hadn't discussed whether or not she was seeing anyone else. I'd never really thought about it, until now, and I certainly hadn't asked. Stupid? Without a doubt. But it was my mistake, not hers, and now was not the time to correct it. "It's time to get rid of that thong."

"All right," she replied, her tone poisonously sweet. "Shall I remove it?"

"Allow me," I said as I loudly ripped the paper in half.

"Wh—what was *that*?" Claire was startled into asking.

"That was the sound of your panties being ripped from your body."

"Oh." A gurgle of laughter escaped her. "Okay, very good. Nice job on the sound effects."

"I'm glad you liked it. I'd hoped it would please you."

"Oh, it did. It was extremely... umm... masterful. I'm all a-tingle."

Masterful. Good. She'd just given me another piece of what I needed. "Now, it's time for your punishment."

"Excuse me?" she asked, sounding startled again. "Punishment? What are you talking about?"

"Just what we discussed earlier. I'm going to spank you."

"Mike, that's just.. just..." her voice trailed off.

"What? Kinky? Provocative? *Exciting*?"

"Pointless! We're not even in the same *room*. I mean, what are you..."

"It's just a game, Claire," I reminded her, intrigued by the discomfort in her voice. "Are you saying you want to stop playing now?"

She ignored my question to ask a couple of her own. "Besides, I thought you said you'd only do something like that if I wanted you to? Have you changed your mind all of a sudden?"

"No, not at all. I just figure that's why you keep misbehaving. You're *asking* for it."

"I'm what? Oh, really. Am I?"

"I think you must be."

She sighed. "That's rather presumptuous, don't you think? At the very least."

I smiled triumphantly. "Possibly. So why don't you clear things up for me? Tell me."

"Tell you... what?" she asked hesitantly.

I lowered my voice, speaking slowly and clearly. "Tell me you want to be spanked."

Silence greeted me. I waited. Her breath sounded shaky, as though she wanted desperately to say something. But she didn't . She didn't say yes, didn't say no, she simply sighed.

"You do, don't you? The exposure, the stinging heat, the uncertainty—not knowing when or if the next stroke is coming—I bet you're wet just thinking of it."

"Michael..." Claire's voice was soft, uncertain, a plea for... something.

"If I'm wrong, just say so. Tell me no and we'll never discuss it again."

More silence. More waiting.

"Are you imagining it?" I asked at last. "Is that why you're so quiet? Are you thinking about how you'd lower yourself to lie face down across my legs? How I'd wrap an arm around your middle, trapping you there, holding you fast. My hand is splayed across your abdomen and I can feel how fast you're breathing. Are you nervous? Or excited?"

"Probably both," she answered, breaking her long silence with a breathy little laugh.

"With my other hand, I rub slow circles on your bottom to relax you. To calm you."

"To lull me into complacency, I think you mean." She sounded tense and what I was about to say was calculated to increase the tension even more.

"To prepare you for what's yet to come. To help focus your attention right there, right where my hand's going to strike you. Is it working?"

"Ohhh, you bet."

"Are you thinking about it? Now? Can you feel your skin tingle as it warms to my touch?"

"Umph."

I smiled. "Good." Her response, just barely a grunt, showed me how deeply she'd sunk into the fantasy. "Now it's time to get this gown out of the way, so I slide my hand down the back of your thigh, as far down your leg as I can reach. And then, slowly, very slowly I raise your gown inch by inch."

I paused. The only sound to be heard was Claire's labored breathing. I figured either she was mesmerized by the images I was conjuring, or she'd fallen fast asleep.

"Can you feel the silk trailing up your legs now, Claire?"

"Yes."

"It tickles your calves, doesn't it? Then the backs of your knees, the backs of your thighs. Cool air strikes your exposed skin as I drag it higher, up your legs, over your ass, all the way to your waist. And now..."

I paused, letting her wait, letting her think about it. I knew she was hanging onto each and every word. Just as I was hanging onto every sigh.

"Now I have you," I continued, even more softly than before. "I have you right where I want you. When I rub my hand over your bare bottom, your body trembles. Your back arches to meet my touch and that's when I know. You're right where you want to be, as well."

Another shuddery sigh escaped her. "Mike..." The passion throbbing in her voice when she spoke my name was almost my undoing. My dick, which had been stirring back to life for some time, was demanding attention. I had to struggle to keep my focus where it belonged: on the faint sounds coming to me through the phone.

"The scent that rises from your hot flesh makes my heart race, Claire, and I can't resist tracing it back to its source. So I slide my hand lower until I can fondle your pussy. And what do you think I find there?"

"I don't know." Her voice was husky and thick. "Wh— what?"

"You tell me. I want you to reach between your legs, right now, and touch yourself. Tell me what you feel. Tell me if you're really as wet and ready as I think you are."

The heavy silence was broken by a deep sigh. "I, I—Yes."

"Tell me. Tell me how slick and swollen you feel, tell me your pussy is dripping for me, throbbing for me."

"Yes."

"It's imagining what's going to happen next that's making you so hot, isn't it?"

Silence.

"It's thinking about what it would be like if I were really there with you, if this were really happening. Now. Tonight."

More silence.

"You want it. Don't you?"

"Mike, please."

"Answer me, Claire. You want it. Say you do."

Another sigh and then, finally, finally, she answered, "Yes."

Smack! My hand made contact with the phone book I'd placed on the tile counter. Glasses rattled in the cabinets overhead. On the other end of the phone, Claire gasped.

"Are you still touching yourself?" I asked.

She hesitated for a moment and, in the silence, I slammed my hand down once again: *smack*.

"Well? Are you?"

"Yes."

"Good. Don't stop. I want you to keep fingering yourself while I give you what you've been asking for. You can't see me, you can't see my hand, so you won't know when the next blow is coming. But, know this: I'm not going to stop—neither of us is going to stop—until you come."

The night had closed in while we spoke and I hadn't turned on any lights. Now, I stood in the dark and whispered hot words into the phone, punctuated now and again with sudden slaps. Claire's breathing grew progressively more ragged and I closed my eyes and imagined right along with her.

"Your breasts were pressed against my thigh when we started." *Smack.* "And your arms were hanging loose. But you've been pushed forward by my blows..." *Smack.* "Now, your breasts are exposed and your hands are clutched so tightly around my leg that your nails dig into my skin." *Smack.* "I lean down to whisper in your ear, 'Don't move,' but I know you're not going anywhere. Are you?"

She groaned in reply. "No."

Smack.

"I remove my hand from around your waist and use it to brush lightly back and forth across the front of your breasts, across the tips of your hard, hard nipples. You like it when I do that, don't you?"

She groaned again, louder this time. I smiled.

"Now I'm pinching them, lightly at first, but harder each time. One... then the other. One... then the other. You like that too, don't you?"

"God, yes," she panted. "Like that, Michael, please. Don't stop."

Stop? Never. "Ah, Claire, you have such gorgeous breasts. I've waited years to get my hand on them. Years." *Smack.* "I'll never stop, my darling." *Smack.* "Nev..."

"Ahhh!"

Her shattered cry of release took me by surprise. I slumped against the counter, suddenly aware of how hard my heart was pounding, of the sheen of sweat that had gathered on my forehead.

"Well," Claire murmured several long moments later. "That was... um, interesting."

I laughed weakly, not certain how to take that. Not sure whether to feel awkward or relieved. Or disappointed. "It was that," I said, moving into the dining room and sinking into a chair. Adding, just in case she'd forgotten whose idea this was, "Thank you for thinking of it."

"Hmm." She sighed. "You're welcome. I suppose now you're going to tell me you used to work as a sex phone operator?"

I blinked in surprise. "No. Why would do you say that?"

"Just that... you seem to have had a lot of practice."

"Actually, this was my first time."

"Are you serious?"

"Of course. I'd never lie to you, Claire."

"Oh, shit." She laughed. "Sorry, but I've heard *that* before."

I frowned. "Meaning?"

"Meaning 'that's what they all say'."

"This time it's true," I replied flatly.

"Hard to tell the difference, I'm afraid."

I nodded. "I guess it can be. *Though all things foul would wear the brows of grace, yet grace must still look so.*'"

"Shakespeare?" she asked, after a moment's shocked silence.

"Who else?"

"Who, indeed." She laughed again, but less harshly than before. "You're a very interesting man, Mike Sherman."

Interesting. There's that word again. This time, however, I had no trouble knowing how to take it. "If that means you'd like to get to know me better, then thank you."

"You're welcome," she answered warmly. Then her voice turned regretful. "But that will have to wait for another time. I should go now. Good night, Mike, see you Tuesday."

Tuesday. Three long days away. I sighed, clinging to the regret in her tone, hoping it was genuine. "Good night, Claire." *My darling.*

It was only after she hung up the phone that I thought to wonder what had happened to her plans for this evening, her prior engagement. How, if she had no time to see me, had she found the time to call?

Chapter Nine

Claire

I don't know how I made it until Tuesday without losing my mind. No, scratch that, I do know. The several exercise classes I sat in on each day went a long way toward leaving me centered, peaceful, serene and much too tired to think. I even braved one of Derek's legendary Power Yoga classes, although only after pulling him aside ahead of time to ask a favor...

"Go easy on me today, okay? We both know I'm out of shape."

Arms crossed, he studied me without speaking. His expression was thoughtful and a little too grim.

What now, I wondered. Is he going to tell me I'm too out of shape to take his class? Too old? Too lazy? "What?" I demanded impatiently.

"What's wrong?" His voice, so patient, so surprisingly gentle for someone notorious for being a hard ass, only added to my discomfort.

"Nothing's wrong, Derek. It's just your classes are not the easiest in the world. I'm out of practice and I don't particularly feel like being shown up by your regular students. Is a little consideration really too much to ask?"

Dropping his gaze from my face, he shook his head. "If that's what you want, you got it."

True to his word, Derek stuck me in the back of the class where my performance was more likely to go unnoticed. Then he left me strictly alone, other than to toss an occasional, 'that's good, Claire,' in my direction, just to make it seem like he wasn't ignoring me.

Still, even despite Derek's unprecedented gentleness, by Tuesday evening I felt wrung out and exhausted.

"I'm not in the mood to go out tonight," I told Mike when I called him with a change in plans. "Why don't I just order dinner in and we can stay here and relax?"

"Anything you want me to bring?" he asked, after a slight pause.

"Nothing I can think of. Just bring your handsome self. You can leave the whips and chains at home tonight."

This time the pause was longer. Long enough to make me cringe.

"Mike? You know that was a joke, right?"

"Sometimes jokes are a way of saying what we really mean."

I sighed. "Sometimes they're just an attempt at being funny."

"Which is this?"

"Funny," I answered as I rang off and immediately dialed the number of my favorite Pacific Fusion restaurant.

Was he kidding, I wondered as I waited for Mike to arrive. If he wasn't... well, it would be my own fault, wouldn't it? And hardly the first time my big mouth had gotten me in trouble. "Whips and chains," I muttered, disgusted with myself. "Jesus, Claire, *what* were you thinking?"

I suppose I was thinking about the way I'd responded to Mike's little game Saturday night. Having had my fill of controlling ex-spouses, I would have considered myself the last person to find discipline arousing. One bad alpha can spoil more than a bushel—take it from someone who's been there.

It was a relief when I answered the front door a short while later and found him empty handed, except for a bottle of wine and a showy arrangement of tropical flowers—anthurium, heliconia, ginger, bird of paradise, orchids.

"How lovely," I murmured, as he handed them to me.

Mike's eyes lit up as I pinched off a single dendrobium to wear in my hair. "I was hoping you'd like them."

"Oh, I do," I said as I kissed his cheek. "Hawaiian flowers have always been my favorite." He was so eager to please, so easy to be with, I felt myself relax for the first time in three days. I'd been silly to be so apprehensive. What had I been worried about? True, it was a bit uncanny the way he seemed to know my tastes in far too many things. But nothing to be alarmed about. After all, look how many things we had in common—our appreciation for fashion, flowers, similar music, mutual vacation choices, exotic birds. Even our tastes in food were nicely matched. Mike clearly approved of the meal I'd ordered, while I thought his choice of wine was superb.

Our conversation throughout dinner was light, lively, and likely to lead us into bed. Or so I thought, envisioning a long, leisurely night of love-making. But then, as we were finishing dessert, Mike abruptly switched gears.

"We need to talk," he said quietly, after a brief but pensive pause. I tried to stop my eyebrows from crawling right up my forehead, but failed miserably.

"Not an auspicious opening." I leaned back in my chair in what had to be a completely transparent attempt at distancing myself from whatever was coming next. "What's on your mind?"

Mike leaned forward, snagging one of my hands in both of his, as though to keep me from withdrawing. I should have pulled it away, refused to be drawn in, but it felt nice, the stroke of his fingers against mine. "Claire, these past few weeks have been wonderful, probably the greatest couple of weeks of my life. But there are things we should have said, long before now. Issues we should have settled. We didn't. And I apologize for that."

"What kinds of things?" I had to ask. "What are we talking about?"

Mike's lips pursed. "This. Us. Our... our relationship."

"Ah." This time I did disengage. Resting my folded arms on the table, I tucked my hands away, out of sight, out of reach. "Look, Mike, I like you. I like spending time with you like this. I like sleeping with you. But, that's really all I'm looking for. So why don't we just leave it like that?"

"Because," he replied. And now it was he who leaned back. And folded his own arms. And gazed at me sternly. A faint chill slithered along my spine. He looked so unexpectedly intimidating it made my 'mob enforcer' joke seem just slightly less far fetched. "We at least need to establish certain ground rules."

I forced myself to speak calmly. "Such as?"

"Such as whether either of us is going to be sleeping with anyone else while we're together."

I let 'together' slide. There was no *together*, I thought I'd made that clear. Just like there was no 'us'. We were two people who enjoyed each other's company—end of story.

I also let all the ugly implications, the snide allusions—things I'd heard too many times before—go unchallenged. *Either of us* rarely meant *either* of us. It usually just meant *me*. Perhaps it didn't, in this case. But, just in case it did, I let my displeasure show. I glared at him coldly. "Well? And are you?"

To my surprise, a flush colored Mike's cheeks. "Fair enough," he muttered gruffly as he unbent just a little. "I wish I could say for sure that I'd have acted differently if I'd been seeing someone else when we got together. But I can't. I've never been a cheater, Claire, but, given the circumstances, I'm pretty sure I'd have caved just the same." He shook his head. "But, no, as it happens, there's no one else. And there won't be. I can't even imagine wanting to cheat on you."

And then it was my turn. The expectant look on his face left me with no doubt about that. "Well, thank you, Mike. That's nice to know. But... why, exactly, is this conversation necessary?" I asked, balking a little. This was precisely the type of complication I'd wanted to avoid. Anger. Hurt feelings. Raised hopes and dashed expectations. Promises that begged to be broken. Who needed them?

"Well, for health reasons," Mike snapped, sounding annoyed. "If nothing else."

Shit. Trust him to have a point—and a good one, too, damn it. "You're right," I admitted. "And, for what it's worth, I'm actually kind of a 'one-man woman' by preference myself." All things being equal, which they very rarely were. "Contrary to what you might have heard." And not counting some of those early movies, where the role required me to fuck practically the entire cast. "I probably haven't even met half the people the tabloids have linked me with over the years."

Mike frowned. "Claire, I didn't mean to suggest—I just..." He gazed at me appealingly, obviously hoping I'd rescue him from the hole he'd dug for himself. Unfortunately, I wasn't in much of a rescuing mood tonight.

"So there's no one else?" he asked at last.

"No. There's no one else."

"Thank you," he said simply, looking all too happy to take me at my word. "That's all I needed to hear." The expression in his eyes was one of sweet relief, which only made me feel worse. Then he flashed that shy smile I'd grown so fond of seeing. Tonight it made my spirits sink.

Clearly, Mike knew nothing about some parts of my past. And here I'd been afraid he knew too much!

How would the way he looked at me change if he learned the truth? Would he judge me as harshly as others had? Why should I assume anything else? It suddenly occurred to me to wonder if this was what Derek, one of the very few who *did* know and *hadn't* cared, had been trying to warn me about. Shit.

Unable to sit still any longer, I got up and began to clear the table. "Well," I muttered, slamming dishes together viciously as I pondered whether to claim a sudden headache, or just ask him straight out to leave. "I'm so glad we got *that* out of the way."

"I've upset you," Mike said, getting to his feet and standing in my way.

I looked at him pointedly. "Excuse me. I need to get into the kitchen."

Instead of moving, he took the plates from my hands and

put them back on the table.

"Michael," I said warningly, but he ignored that, too and took hold of my shoulders.

"I'm sorry I handled this badly. I think part of the reason I put it off so long was because I knew I'd make a mess of it. I just wanted to clarify where we stood with each other. That's all."

Where we stood? That was easy. "I want a friend, Michael, no more, no less. After six marriages and umpteen relationships I'm through with the drama and the misunderstandings, the betrayal, the *pain*. All I want is a friend." That and regular sex with a man who knew what he was doing and who I could count on for a good time.

"A friend with benefits—isn't that what you mean?" he replied, just as though I'd spoken the last part aloud.

"Exactly."

"Like a... like a fuck buddy."

The scorn in his voice brought the blood rushing to my face. "If you prefer."

"If I—? No," he thundered, looking just as flushed as I felt. "I don't *prefer* that, Claire. I don't prefer *any* of it. I think the whole arrangement stinks."

"I see." We stared at each other. I waited a beat, but he said nothing more. "So are we through?" I asked at last.

Mike's brow creased. "What's that mean?"

"It means are we through? You asked where we stood. I told you. You don't like it. I don't see where we can go from there. So, again: Are. We. Through?"

Mike's eyes widened. His expression went blank. Next thing I knew, I was crushed against his chest. His arms were around me, banding us so tightly together I could hardly breathe. "No. God, no. Claire..." His voice trailed off and he took a deep breath. A shudder ran through him and then he was holding me away, far enough that he could see my face. "Is that what you *want*?"

"I already told you what I want, Michael." I wanted companionship. A warm body to curl up against when the nights turned cold. A warm smile to wake up to in the morning. I wanted someone who wouldn't take *my* past and make it all about *him*. Someone who wouldn't feel insulted by it, disgusted, ashamed. Who wouldn't use it as an excuse to turn vicious or violent or cold. Someone I could laugh with and joke with. Someone I could eat with, travel with, maybe even shop with. But not cry with—I'd already cried enough.

"A friend."

"Yes."

"Someone to spend time with and have sex with and, and... date."

"Yes."

"And that's it."

I nodded. "No more, no less." I'd had it with the other kind. Relationships where we'd started out so close it was as though we were in each other's blood. Only to end with each of us striving to see how much of each other's blood we could draw. Marriages where we amassed all the trappings—houses, jewelry, cars, all that money could buy—and ended up trapped. With nothing *but* money. Or, sometimes, with not even that.

"Okay," Mike sighed. "We'll give it a try."

I looked at him questioningly.

He smiled. "I can't promise I'll like it, but I want you, Claire. And you want a friend. So let's start with that and see where it goes."

"It's not gonna go anywhere, Mike," I warned. "It's going to stay the same."

"Nothing stays the same, Claire. But, for even a few more weeks like these last few, it's worth it."

"Thank you," I murmured, resting my head against his chest, wondering how it would all work out, whether I was stupid even to try.

"So you wanna kiss and make up now?" he asked at last.

I looked at him. Was he purposely reciting the same line I'd used on him last week?

The smile on his face suggested he was. "Well?"

I hesitated. Part of me did and part of me didn't. Part of me felt bone tired and wanted to curl up in a ball and hide. And, part of me... well, part of me didn't want to be alone tonight. I grabbed his face with both hands and planted a big, wet kiss on his lips. Not surprisingly, his arms closed around me and he kissed me back, deepening and lengthening the kiss until I started to swoon.

"I'm tired," I murmured, pulling my mouth away. I wasn't really. I just needed a break. The sizzle in my blood was too hot tonight, when all I wanted was a little warmth. "Just hold me?"

I suppose I have to give him credit for trying. He held me close for several minutes without complaint, although his hands did rove restlessly, up and down my back and through my hair. And he pressed so many ardent kisses against my head, murmured so many soft endearments, that I soon lost count.

"All right," I sighed, giving up at last. I took hold of his hand. "You win. Let's go."

"Where are we going?" he asked.

"The bedroom." I slanted a glance at the bulge in his pants. "I'm putting you out of your misery before I send you home."

Mike frowned. "Claire. No. If you're too tired... we don't have to do this."

I smiled. "Yes, we do. Come on."

We stripped and screwed in record time.

Afterwards, I lay in bed and watched as he dressed. "One of these days, we really should try something a little different," I observed, yawning widely. "Like maybe taking more than five minutes to do this."

Mike turned a reproachful gaze my way. "You wanted it fast," he reminded.

I nodded. "I know." I hadn't really wanted anything, to be honest. But, hard as he was, I could hardly have called myself a friend if I'd sent him away like that. And, I have to admit, I felt tons better now myself. "Mind if I don't get up?" I asked sleepily when he'd finished dressing.

"No, that's fine." He stood looking at me for a moment. "So. Thursday?" he asked at last.

I nodded, my eyes already closing. "Mm. Same bat time, same bat channel."

"Two days," he whispered as he leaned down and kissed my cheek. "I'll see you then."

* * * *

Mike

Two days had never seemed so long. I wish I could tell you why that was, but I can't. Maybe it was because, in the wake of my confrontation with Claire, I was so unsettled I could barely bring myself to concentrate on anything else.

I should have been ecstatic. What had been an Impossible Dream for years and years had become reality. Yet, the fact that she wanted nothing from me but sex and friendship left me deeply dissatisfied. Because I wanted more, much more, from her. I wanted to make her mine in all ways possible. I wanted to win her love entirely.

Instead, I found myself proscribed from even trying. The

restriction rankled—as good an explanation for what happened next as any other, I suppose.

Claire was nowhere in sight when I got to the studio. Rather than waste time wondering where she might be, I buried myself in my work. I made such great progress I had all but finished by the time she appeared looking red faced and breathing hard.

"What have you been doing?" I couldn't help asking, upon noticing her condition.

She downed half a bottle of water before panting. "Exercise."

"More Capoeria?" I not-quite joked.

She shook her head and drank the rest of the water. "Derek."

She'd been doing Derek? "Ah." Great. Even better. "So he's his own form of exercise now?"

Eyes twinkling, she grinned appreciatively. "Well, I'm sure *he'd* like to think so. I sat in on one of his infamous yoga classes."

"Oh." I forced myself back to work, hoping the simplicity of the task would prove soothing. But the questions in my head were not so easily quelled. Finally, I had to ask. "So how come?"

Claire glanced up questioningly from her own work. "How come what?"

"This sudden resurgence of interest. All these exercise classes you're taking..."

"It shows?" Her expression dismayed, she looked down at her body. "I know I was slacking off these past few months, but I didn't think it was noticeable."

I sighed. "Of course it's not noticeable." Not in the way she meant. How did one say, *I notice everything you do,* without sounding a little too obsessed?

When I first met Claire, she'd been a regular in Derek's classes. Every Thursday, from what I observed. And several more times each week, from what I intuited from our conversations.

As far as I could tell, she'd dropped them all when she and Derek parted company. The fact that she'd started up again now, so soon after taking up with me—That couldn't be coincidence, could it?

Aware that she was still gazing at me inquiringly, I shrugged. "I just wondered."

"Well, I don't know," she answered, looking almost puzzled. "I guess it seemed like time." Which was as good as saying nothing at all.

She's perfectly free to do as she pleases, I reminded myself. *And if she wants to spend every spare, waking moment with her former lover, who are you to complain?*

Maybe she *was* making another play for him. So what? No matter how foolish I thought it, no matter how angry it made me, as no more than a friend, I could say nothing.

In fact, unless she were somehow using me to accomplish her goal, unless she'd taken up with me for no other reason than to make *him* jealous—and unless I could prove that was the case—

But, no. I would *not* think like that. It insulted us both and, besides, I was *not* about to be jealous. Although, if it turned out she preferred some steroid-enhanced, muscle-bound, wet-behind-the-ears exercise instructor to me...

"Well, I'm done here," I said, as I closed the books and began to clear my desk.

Claire's eyes widened. "So soon?"

I shoved the papers into my briefcase. "Not that much to do today. I was just finishing up what was left from last week, remember?"

"Oh, I remember, all right," she said, smiling suggestively, lighting me up with just a look.

As I felt my body tighten, I frowned crossly. It really wasn't fair that she should have this effect on me. I remembered last week too. I remembered how incredibly hot she'd been. How badly I'd wanted her then, still did now, probably always would. How she'd left the door unlocked...

I felt the color drain from my face.

"Is something wrong?" Claire asked, not smiling at all now.

How she'd left the door unlocked so that anyone could have walked right in...

"No," I said, trying to disguise the sudden disorientation I was feeling, the sense of not knowing which way was up. I stood and reached for my briefcase. "Nothing at all."

So that anyone could have walked right in...

Her eyes widened. "You're leaving?"

I gazed at her helplessly, feeling lost, feeling torn. "No sense in hanging around, is there? I mean, you're busy and... and..."

Anyone. Like Derek.

"Well, would you like to do something later?"

"Like what?" I snapped. That had to be the world's stupidest question. Dinner? Sex? Dinner and sex? Given the parameters she'd set for us, that was pretty much all the options we had. Which should have been enough. More than enough. Which should have been fantastic. For the life of me, I couldn't have explained why it wasn't. I shook my head. "Maybe another time."

Claire's eyes narrowed. "Something *is* wrong. What?"''

I opened my mouth to deny it again, but what would another lie accomplish? "Why'd you leave the door unlocked last week?" I asked, instead.

"What?" Red flags appeared on her cheeks. "Wh—why? What are you suggesting?"

"Did you want to get 'caught', is that it? Were you hoping someone would walk in and see us?"

Claire's mouth dropped open. She looked shocked, almost stricken. For a moment, I let myself believe I'd been wrong. But no. There was too much awareness, too much guilt in her gaze for her to claim ignorance. I felt my heart sink.

"Why me, Claire? There's something like six billion people on this planet, why'd you pick me to sleep with? Was there anything about me that attracted you other than proximity? Or was that it? Did I just get lucky because I happened to be in the right place at the right time?"

In the time it took her to blink once, the bruised look in her eyes was replaced with one of absolute fury. "Let me get this straight," she snarled, getting slowly to her feet and planting her fists on her desk. "You're upset with me because I slept with you? Is that what I'm hearing?"

"No, that's not what I meant. Stop twisting things around." But she rode right over me.

"Why, Mike? What's the problem? Did I use you? Or manipulate you into bed? Did I take advantage of you in some fashion?"

"Cut it out, Claire."

"What next?" she continued blithely, ignoring the warning in my tone. "Are you gonna claim sexual harassment? Or maybe you'll just sell your story to the tabloids?"

"You know what I'm talking about," I insisted, growing angrier by the second. *If she's smart*, I thought, *she'll stop this now*. She didn't.

Instead, she smiled spitefully. "Actually, I don't. But, if you want some free advice, I'd try the tabloids first, if I were you. They'll publish any old shit. Harassment might be a little too hard for you to prove, especially considering how many times you thanked me."

"All right, that's enough!" It stung, hearing my words thrown back at me like that. I stormed over to where she stood. Unfortunately, I didn't think to drop my briefcase first. As tightly as I had gripped the handle, I'm not sure I *could* have dropped it. Furious, I slammed the case down on the desktop. The sound of it echoed off the walls. Claire didn't so much as flinch.

"Enough, Mike?" Her eyebrows rose. Her voice did the same. "Oh, I don't think so. I'll decide when I've said enough. How dare you come in here, blustering like an old fool, accusing me of... of... of what exactly?"

"I haven't accused you of anything," I roared in reply.

"Oh, no?"

"No! All I want is an explanation. And I think you owe me that much."

"An explanation for what?" she asked, her tone continuing to rise with every word.

"Why are you with me?" I repeated. "What kind of game are you playing here, anyway?"

"Games?" Claire glared at me wide-eyed. In the silence that followed, the sound of someone tapping softly on the office door could be clearly heard. We both ignored it. "You're the one who likes to play games, Mike. And, as for why I picked you, I—I... I don't know!"

"You don't *know*?" My eyes felt like they might bulge out of my head. I could not believe my ears.

The door was edged open. "Excuse me," a man's voice murmured. We ignored that, too.

"What the hell does that mean?" I demanded. "How can you not know?"

"Easily." Claire tossed her head. "The way you're acting right now? I can't imagine *what* I was thinking. Other than I must have been out of my fucking mind!"

"Claire!" the voice rapped out, sharper this time, louder. Derek's voice.

Claire rounded on him angrily. "Well? What is it?"

"I have a class starting in just under five minutes," Derek announced, barely controlled fury evident in his voice and in every line and muscle of his body.

"And?" she snapped impatiently, eyes flashing, when he paused.

"And that wall," Derek growled with a nod toward the glass behind Claire's desk. "Is *not* sound proof." He glanced at us both and then focused his attention on Claire once again. "So you might want to keep it down up here. *Capesce?*"

"Oh, crap." The color drained from Claire's face and she collapsed into her chair. "Sorry. I'm sorry. Shit."

Watching her I felt sick. Not because we'd been overheard, I couldn't care less about that. But I could not believe I'd been yelling at her. I could not believe it had all gone to hell. I could not believe Derek's was the lone voice of reason.

"Is everything all right?" he asked, eyes still trained on Claire's face.

She nodded mutely, then her gaze met mine.

The tragic look in her beautiful eyes tore at my heartstrings I opened my mouth to apologize; to say something—anything I could think of—anything that might help to erase that look. But Derek's next words put an end to that.

"You want him to leave?" His voice was flat, cold; the implication clear. At her word, I was gone. Either I'd leave on my own, or he'd make me go.

"Don't bother," I said, my gaze still locked with Claire's. "I'm going."

"Mike," she murmured softly. "Don't."

But I shook my head. "If you ever do come up with an answer, Claire, maybe you'll give me a call and let me know."

Then I turned and left. I'd reached my car before I realized I'd left my briefcase behind. There was no way I was going back to retrieve it, however. Not until we'd both had a chance to cool down.

* * * *

Claire

After Mike left, Derek quietly closed the door behind him. Then he came and sat down by my desk. "So," he said, in a voice that strove to be conversational. "What was that all about?"

"I don't know," I replied, sighing tiredly. I thought I knew—back in the beginning, when Mike had started ranting about the door, about my wanting to be seen. In his words I heard the echo of all the sordid accusations that had been thrown at me over the years:

"You liked it, didn't you? Putting out for the camera. Your body

exposed, your sex on display. All those men watching you, touching you, drooling over you. I bet you needed that. Isn't that so, Claire? Isn't that what you really want, what you need to get off? Isn't that why you can't make it with me, why I don't do it for you?"

Well, of course it wasn't. And as for liking it? No. In the beginning, it made me sick. Each and every time. But I got used to it. I learned.

It wasn't really me, after all. That girl on the screen, making love to a room full of strangers, she'd just been using my body to tell her story.

"Claire?" Derek's voice penetrated my thoughts.

I glanced up at him. "Hmm?"

"I said, are you all right?"

I nodded. "I think so. Maybe." I'd overreacted. I could see that now. Flicked on the raw, I'd jumped to conclusions. Stupid. I'd been stupid. "It was just a little misunderstanding."

"It sounded like it was a little more than that," Derek answered dryly.

"Not really." I shrugged. "People argue, Derek. They get upset. They say things they don't mean."

"We didn't."

"No," I agreed. "We didn't." Not like that. Then again, what would we have argued about? I glanced at the clock on the wall. "I thought you had a class?"

Derek nodded. "I do. But they can wait."

I stared at him, almost speechless with surprise. "They can what?"

He shrugged. "It's not gonna kill them to warm up for a few extra minutes. If you need to talk, they can wait."

"Thank you," I said, smiling at the gesture. "But you should get down there. I just need to figure a few things out, that's all."

"Well, that's for certain," he said as he got to his feet. He glanced at the briefcase Mike had forgotten. "Want me to take that downstairs, leave it at the front desk?"

"No, that's okay," I said quickly, laying a hand on the worn leather.

Derek shook his head in disapproval. "All right. If you say so."

"Thanks," I repeated, continuing to smile until the door closed behind him.

My hand absently stroked the leather briefcase. Mike's voice and the anguish in his eyes haunted me.

Why me, Claire? Was there anything about me that attracted you?

How did you answer a question like that? Why would he even ask it? I slid the case closer, turning it 'til I could grip the handle. I imagined Mike's hand clenched here, holding it just so... as though I could somehow intuit what he'd been thinking.

A few minutes later, a burst of applause from the studio below drew my attention. I got up and glanced through the glass. Derek was on the floor doing push-ups. One handed. While a bevy of leotard-clad women looked on, cheering and counting. It wasn't hard to imagine what that was all about. He always exacted a penalty for lateness. No doubt his students had decided to do the same to him.

I suppose I should have felt just slightly guilty about that, but I didn't. A couple dozen extra push-ups wouldn't do him any harm. In fact, he was probably enjoying himself.

"Show off," I muttered affectionately, watching until, his penance completed, he jumped to his feet. He wasn't even out of breath.

"All right, let's go." He clapped his hands together briskly. "Places, everyone."

As Derek's class scurried into position, I went back to my desk. Without doubt his biceps, freshly pumped and lightly sheened with sweat, would be compelling his students to make an extra effort today. They'd probably exert twice as much energy as usual in an attempt to impress him.

Just as I would have once.

I thought about that for a moment, remembering how Derek's arms had felt locked around me. How they'd supported me while I balanced above him. How they'd caged me while I lay below him. They'd felt nice. Damned nice, in fact. But, strangely, I felt no sense of loss, no pang of regret.

Nice, yes, but nothing I couldn't live without. Whereas Mike...

He wasn't hot or flashy or young. He wasn't influential or connected. He wasn't wealthy—certainly not by Hollywood standards. He wasn't... oh, so many of the things I'd looked for in a man over the years.

Maybe I'd been looking for too many of the wrong things?

"You old fool," I muttered as I stored his briefcase out of sight beneath my desk. "I wonder how long it'll take you to miss me."

* * * *

In the end, I gave him twenty-four hours. For most of the first twelve, I was sure he'd call; sheepish, penitent, eager to reconcile. Of course, for most of that same time, I was asleep and likely dreaming. By noon I'd resigned myself to the reality.

Obviously, if anyone was going to fix things between us, it would have to be me.

Chapter Ten

Mike

I was surprised to find Claire waiting for me when I got home from work Friday evening. Surprised and more than a little confused by her care-free smile, by the relaxed way she leaned against the side of her little white Lexus convertible, by... Oh, hell, let's face it. I'd been nothing *but* confused for three full weeks now.

The only difference was that now I was angry, too. *You don't know what the woman wants*, I reminded myself. *Could be she's just toying with you.*

Frowning cautiously, I got out of my car and walked over to where she stood waiting for me. She was dressed all in white—to match her car, I supposed—in a snug, white tank top that made it almost impossible not to stare at her chest and slim, white pants that molded to her body and ensured that her breasts were only the first things you noticed.

"Hello, lover," she said cheerfully. "Miss me?"

I had, of course. But there was no way I'd admit it. "Claire. What are you doing here?"

Her lips pursed in a little moue as she slid her hands up my chest and over my shoulders. "Now, what kind of greeting is that?" she pouted, dismissing my query in turn. My hands found their way to her hips—and I'd swear it was of their own volition—even as she locked hers behind my neck. Then she hit me with her best come-hither gaze, her softest murmur, her most inviting smile. "Well?"

Fool that I am, I caved, giving her what I knew she wanted, kissing her for all I was worth. My fingers tightened on her flesh and, at their slightest urging, she willingly canted her hips into mine.

Her lips parted, inviting me in, and I was unable to resist. I deepened the kiss, plunging my tongue into her mouth, thrilling to the sweet play of her nails along my nape. A growl emerged from my throat and I tugged her closer, banding her against me. Another moment and I think I would have taken her right there in the drive.

"Mmm. That's better," she purred, smiling slyly as she disengaged.

"What are you doing here?" I repeated stubbornly, when I could speak again.

Claire sighed. "Is that all you can think to say?" Twisting around, she reached into the car behind her. "Here." She lifted my briefcase from behind her seat and presented it to me. "If you must know, I thought you might want this back."

My hands reached automatically to take it. "Thank you," I muttered, partially in dismay. "You didn't have to do that." In fact, I kind of wished she hadn't as I'd planned on using its retrieval as a pretext for seeing her on Monday.

"Well, of course I didn't *have* to, Michael," she replied, arching an eyebrow at me. "Since when have I ever done that? I do things because I want to, don't you know that by now? Anyway, here." Reaching back into the car, she pulled out two medium-sized, brown paper bags. "Take these, too."

The bags, surprisingly hefty for their size, were warm and smelled faintly of garlic. However, their folded-over, stapled-down tops, which seemed to present no difficulty for Claire, offered precious little for my fingers to clutch. "What is all this?" I grumbled, juggling bags and briefcase as I struggled for a better hold on them.

"Dinner," she replied, already turning back to the car once again. This time the back seat gave up a large Coach tote bag. "I hope you like Italian?"

"Sure, I..." I stopped juggling and stared at her in surprise. "You bought me dinner?" That made two times in a row! The fact was just slightly unsettling. It's not that my masculine pride is such that I insist on paying every time I share a meal with a woman. But most of the time is certainly not too much to expect, is it?

"Well, no, actually, I bought *us* dinner," she replied, oblivious to my discomfort until, after slipping the tote's strap over her shoulder, she turned back around to face me. Her eyebrows rose. "What's with the face, Mike? You're the one who insisted on ground rules. Remember? We agreed we wouldn't see anyone else? So, when you didn't call me, I figured we both were gonna end up eating alone tonight. That doesn't sound like much of a plan for a

Friday night, does it?"

"We said we weren't *sleeping* with anyone else." Even as the words left my mouth I wondered what in the hell I was doing. Only an idiot would choose to split hairs like that. Especially since I preferred her version better anyhow. But, fair was fair, and *she* was the one who'd insisted we could be nothing more than friends. "I hope you know I'd never suggest you curtail your social life like that on my account, Claire. You can eat dinner with whomever you want."

"Why, thank you," she replied, eyes dancing with suppressed laughter. "And, as it happens, that's just what I'm trying to do." She glanced pointedly at my front door. "So? Are you going to invite me in?"

"Of course," I murmured politely, taking a step back and gesturing for her to precede me. "After you." But it seemed my manners were at an exceptionally low ebb. As we made our way toward the house I couldn't help asking, "What's Derek up to tonight?"

Claire slanted me a puzzled glance. "I have no idea. Why?"

I shrugged. "I just wondered why you weren't eating with him."

At that, Claire stopped dead in her tracks. The tote she'd been carrying hit the gravel with a thud. I stopped as well. Turning, I found her glaring at me; nostrils flaring, her hands fisted on her hips, her eyes bright and angry. She was breathtaking, in a fiery, furious sort of way, even if I was almost too annoyed to notice.

"Mike Sherman. Am I hearing this right? Are you telling me you think I drove all the way out here for no other reason than because I couldn't find a single person in all of Los Angeles willing to eat dinner with me?"

"That's not what I said at all." Even though I strove to keep my voice as cool as possible, I could feel my temper spike even higher in response. When had I *ever* suggested any such thing?

Eyes narrowing, Claire eyed me suspiciously for a moment. "Ah. So this is about Derek? Well, make no mistake, Mike, if I'd wanted to eat dinner with Derek tonight, that's exactly what I'd be doing."

This time, I think I failed to mask my emotions. I'm sure she read the skepticism in my gaze. A bitter little smile curled her lips.

"Even if he *is* head over ears in love with that blonde he's seeing, Mike, if I'd asked him to dinner tonight, he'd have made time for me. I can assure you of that. In fact, if I wanted to use him as nothing more than a piece of arm-candy for the evening, Derek would have been *happy* to oblige me."

"Just as long as you realize that's probably the best use you could have for him," I replied dryly.

Claire snorted in response. "For Derek? Hardly. If you really want to know the truth, Mike..."

"I don't," I said, interrupting quickly, before she could launch into a litany of praise for her former stud-muffin. "I think we've already wasted more than enough time on the subject."

We eyed each other for a moment in silence. I waited for her to remind me that it was I who'd brought up the subject in the first place. But, once again she surprised me. "Fine. As it happens, I totally agree with you." She sighed. "I want you to understand something, Mike. I drove out here tonight for one reason and one reason only."

I waited.

"Yesterday's little *scene* notwithstanding, I happen to enjoy your company and I wanted to spend some time with you. That's it. Now, are you going to be able to accept that, or am I going to pick up my bag, get back in my car and go home?"

"Stay," I replied, not certain which part of the question to respond to. "Please."

Claire nodded and bent to pick up the tote she'd dropped.

"I owe you an apology," I murmured, wincing inwardly as I thought about yesterday's scene—and tonight's.

Claire froze. Her gaze snapped to my face. "For...?"

I shrugged. "For all of it. Yesterday. Today. I behaved badly. I'm sorry."

"Oh, don't worry about it," Claire sighed as she slid the bag's strap back on her shoulder again. "I think we both overreacted a little. Hopefully, we can put it behind us now and move on."

"I'd like that," I said, although I was still uncertain as to exactly *where* she saw us moving on *to*, given her previous avowal that she wanted nothing to change. However, since voicing that sentiment now would likely result in her leaving, I said nothing.

"Good," Claire replied, all smiles again. "So, let's go already. Before that food you're carrying gets any colder."

As we fell into step once more, I couldn't help but remember the first time Claire had been here. I think I was more nervous now. I'd been in shock that other night. I had no idea what to expect and was trying hard to keep my hopes down. Tonight, both my hopes and my expectations were soaring high.

I opened the door and let Claire in. Her eyes immediately assessed the room, just as they'd done the first time. I'm not inordinately house-proud, I don't think, but the approval in her gaze and the smile on her lips made my heart swell with pride and satisfaction like nothing else could have done. It was all I could do to keep from murmuring, 'welcome home'.

I'd no sooner put the bags containing our dinner down on the kitchen counter when an impatient squawk from the spare bedroom reminded me that we weren't alone.

"Do you mind if I take care of Zoe before we eat?" I asked. "She's been on her own all day and she really likes company."

"Of course not." Claire smiled eagerly. "Are you going to bring her out here? I've been looking forward to getting reacquainted with her."

When I returned to the kitchen, a few minutes later, Claire had set the table and was already plating our food. I paused for a moment, grateful for the pinch of Zoe's talons against my shoulder. No, I wasn't dreaming. The cozily domestic scene unfolding before my eyes was real. I sighed happily.

Claire glanced up. Her eyes went immediately to my shoulder, her entire face lighting up as she smiled. "There's the baby," she cooed. "Hi, Zoe, remember me?"

The feathers rose on the back of Zoe's neck. She twisted her head around to the side and gazed at Claire curiously.

"I think she does." I don't know why it surprised me. How could anyone forget Claire?

"Do you want a treat, sweet girl?" Claire asked as she picked up a breadstick and headed towards us.

Without warning, Zoe launched herself from my shoulder and instantly plummeted toward the floor. I lunged and caught her before she hit the ground.

Claire stared at me in alarm. "Mike?"

I smiled tightly. "Well, I'd say that confirms it, don't you think? She obviously remembers you."

"But what's wrong with her? Why can't she fly? Is she hurt?"

"No, no," I assured her. "She's fine. It's just that I clipped her wings last night. Sometimes it takes her a few tries before she remembers she's been grounded. Especially since it had been a while since the last time I'd done it."

"Hmph." Claire frowned at me darkly and held her arm up for Zoe to perch on. I handed her off, reluctantly. "Is that the problem, baby?" she murmured, hugging Zoe protectively against her chest. "Is the mean man spoiling all your fun?"

"It's just feathers, Claire," I felt compelled to point out. "They'll grow back, you know. Besides, it's really for her own good."

She shot me a reproachful look. "Yes, and don't they always say that? She's a bird, Mike, they *need* to fly. It's like hobbling a race horse, or that hood thing they put on falcons. Or de-barking a dog. It's just cruel."

Cruel? I stared at her, appalled. "It's nothing of the sort. Claire, you have *no* idea how much trouble she can get into on her own—between flying into windows and attempting to eat things that would make her sick. If I didn't clip her wings I'd have to keep her locked up in her cage all day while I'm at work. That would be cruel. She hates that."

"Uh-huh." Sounding utterly unconvinced, Claire carried Zoe over to the table. "I don't know what you want to drink, Mike," she said as she seated herself. "I didn't pick up any wine, because I assumed you'd have some." Her gaze went to the empty wrought iron wine rack hanging from the ceiling. "But it looks like you're out."

I shook my head and headed for the kitchen. "I'm not out of wine. It's just that I keep it in a special, climate-controlled cabinet most of the time. That rack up there is mostly for show—especially during the warmer months." Despite the trees that surrounded the house, the canyon has a tendency to get hot in the summer; hot, dry and prone to wild fires. "Wine doesn't do well if it's left in the heat too long, you know. And since I buy most of mine directly from the vineyards I tend to be a little particular about how it's stored."

Claire coaxed Zoe to perch on the back of her chair. "I think I may have been underestimating you, Mike." Her voice sounded pensive.

I gazed at her curiously. "How's that?"

She shrugged. "Well, I tend to be a little too impulsive, myself. Sometimes I forget that not every one's like that. But you... you really think things through, don't you? I can tell."

I looked at her in surprise. "Why? Because I like to store my wine properly?"

She shook her head. "Not just that."

"Well, I hope I do," I replied, carrying glasses, wine and

corkscrew over to the table. "It's not a bad trait, is it? Although, there's a lot to be said for spontaneity."

Claire nodded. "I suppose. But jumping to conclusions, rushing to judge—or really just jumping into anything, for that matter—has its risks."

I don't like taking a position when I don't know what's at stake. Since I had no idea what we were talking about, it seemed best to stay as non-committed as I could. "Ah, but what's life without a few risks?" I uncorked the bottle and poured a little wine into Claire's glass. "Here, see what you think of this."

Claire took a sip. "Lovely. You always pick the perfect wine for every meal too, don't you?"

I shrugged. "That's not hard to do when you provide such delicious food. You make things easy for me."

"I do, don't I?" Claire smiled teasingly. "So we make a good team. Is that what you're saying, Mike?"

I poured more wine into her glass and then filled my own before I answered. "I'd like to think so. Sure."

"Hmph." Claire sipped her wine and retreated into a thoughtful silence.

I sat down and gazed at her curiously. "I take it that means you don't agree?"

She shook her head. "I didn't say that."

"But is that what you think?"

Again she surprised me. "No, actually I just hadn't really thought about it before now."

I waited. Then pressed her again. "And now that you have?"

Claire sighed. "Well, nowwww..." She folded her arms on the table and leaned forward, closer to me. "I think you may—possibly—be right."

Hopes soaring even higher than before, I couldn't help but point out, "I usually am."

Clare's eyebrows rose. "You're usually what? Right?"

"Most of the time. Yes." I smiled. "That's one of the benefits of all that thinking you've credited me with doing."

"Oh. I see." A hint of challenge glimmered in her hazel eyes as she smiled at me. "So, as a result of *all that thinking*, you think this is one of those times, huh?"

"Yes," I answered, mirroring her position, folding my arms as well, leaning towards her until only the slightest of efforts on either of our parts would result in a kiss. "I do."

I spoke the words softly, but I think my voice carried

conviction. Claire's reaction, however, was not what I'd hoped or expected. Oh, her eyes did turn molten for all of a moment, her lips parted... but then the moment passed and instead of leaning closer, she withdrew.

"Well, I guess we'll see, won't we?" Her tone was teasing. A slight smile curved her lips. Her face appeared serene. But she couldn't hide the sudden bleakness in her eyes and, as she lifted her glass to her lips, I could see her fingers were trembling.

She's afraid. I stared at her thunderstruck. Though she hid it well, the woman before me was clearly, suddenly nervous... but of what? Of me? Of my being right?

No, that was ridiculous. It had to be more than that.

Commitment?

Well, I guess, with half a dozen disastrous marriages behind her, how could she not be at least a little bit gun-shy? But, if that's all it was, if that's what was motivating her...

Oddly, the realization filled me with hope. It put everything she'd said the other night into a perspective I hadn't ever considered. This business about us staying friends—no more, no less—was nonsense. We could be so much more than that. In her heart of hearts, I'd bet anything she knew it, too. She knew it and if frightened her.

But I could live with that, couldn't I? I could wait until she came around. If she was a one-man woman and I was that one man? I was pretty sure I could wait as long as I had to.

"So, what are we waiting for?" I asked, returning her guarded look with a calm smile—a friendly smile—just like she wanted. "Let's eat."

* * * *

Dinner went well. Zoe stayed perched on the back of the Claire's chair for at least part of the meal, before moving onto her shoulder, snuggling against her in a way I'd thought was reserved for me. I pretended not to notice, just as I pretended not to notice all the snacks Claire gave her. Seeing Zoe again seemed to spark all sorts of memories for Claire. And, for once, she didn't seem to mind talking about them. We discussed some of the movies she'd made, directors she'd worked with, other actors. Our conversation, while not as light as on previous occasions, seemed to cover a lot more ground.

We'd made it all the way to the dessert course when Zoe craned her head around suddenly and nipped at Claire's ear.

"Ow! Bad bird," she gasped, covering her ear.

"I'm sorry," I said rising from my seat to take Zoe away. "I should have warned you."

"No, no, it's okay." Still holding one hand pressed to her ear, Claire put out her other hand to stop me. "Sit down, Mike. Warned me about what?"

"At least let me see if you're okay," I protested.

She shook her head. "Really, I'm fine."

Reluctantly, I returned to my chair. "Zoe loves to chew on earrings. I guess it's the sparkle, or something. It's her only bad habit, really, and I just can't seem to break her of it." I pointed at my own ear, at the stud I'd been wearing ever since the night Claire had admired it. "That's why I practically had to stop wearing this."

"Oh." To my surprise, Claire's face went pink, her eyes danced with laughter. "Well, in that case, I suppose I owe *you* an apology."

"How's that?" I asked.

"Um, because I'm the one who taught her to do it?"

"You taught her—" I felt my eyebrows rise.

"Fraid so," she answered, lips quirking up in a guilty grin. "And, oh, wasn't her trainer just furious with me? Luckily, there was no way they could ever prove I was responsible. But I think everyone knew—or guessed. I mean, it wasn't the first trick I'd taught her."

I was still staring at her, open-mouthed. "Why would you do that?"

Claire sighed. "Oh, you know how it is. Long days stuck in the jungle. Too much time on my hands. I was young. I was bored. I was... provoked." She lifted Zoe from her shoulder and placed her on her lap, stroking her gently as she spoke. "It was while we were filming *Inca Gold*. The location was gorgeous but totally remote. The nearest town was... oh, gee, I don't know how many miles away from the set. I think there was only one cantina in the whole place, one crappy little hotel. Not that 'the whole place' amounted to very much, mind you."

"Go on," I prompted, still not seeing the point.

"Well, there was this one, really annoying PA. You know, a production assistant? She had these earrings. This one *particular* set of gold and diamond, two-toned, tassel earrings. Trashy looking things, really. Completely inappropriate for wearing on a set. Never mind the fact that, *hello! We're in the middle of a damned jungle!* They were obviously not the kind of thing she could have afforded to buy for herself either. Not on a PA's salary. They were a gift from her married lover, as everyone knew, and she wore them—No, damn it, she *flaunted* them. Constantly. She was all the time tossing her head, shaking her hair back behind her ears—making sure everyone saw them, hoping everyone would comment on them. Which, of course, everyone did."

Claire paused and heaved another sigh. "Finally, I'd had enough. I couldn't take it anymore. I had some time—two whole days when we weren't shooting any of my scenes and the director had taken most of the crew off with him someplace, supposedly to shoot some B roll footage. So I decided to use that time to teach Zoe a new trick."

She glanced at me and smiled—mischievous, reminiscent, sad all at once, somehow. "By the time they got back, we were ready. And the first time PA girl started shaking her head, Zoe flew into action. It was really quite astonishing. It took everyone by surprise, I think. She landed on the girl's shoulder, ripped the earring from her ear and was off again like a shot. She flew up to a tree branch with it. Sat up there for the longest time chewing on the thing. She chewed the shit out of it, actually. It was almost like she thought it had been dipped in honey, or something."

"Claire!" I gazed at her appalled. I couldn't believe it. I just couldn't picture her doing anything so vicious.

Claire shrugged. "Long days in the jungle, Mike. *Way* too much time on my hands. Anyway, the silly girl was inconsolable. You can't even imagine. She threw such a fit that... well, you'd have thought it was her ear she'd lost rather than just an earring. I tried to help. 'That's how life is sometimes,' I told her. 'Better get used to it. Easy come, easy go. Besides, there's a market in town—right next to the hotel, I'm sure you've seen it—you can pick up all sorts of cheap trinkets there.' 'They were a gift,' she screamed. As if I didn't know that! 'Well, see?' I said. 'There's a bright side for you. You didn't even have to pay for them, right? So what did you really lose? Next time, why don't you see if he'll get you a pair more like these?' And then I showed her the ones I was wearing, which, as I told her, had been a gift from my husband on our wedding day. They really were much more classy."

I stared at her. "That wasn't very nice of you."

"No, it wasn't, was it?" she answered still smiling, looking not the least repentant. "Oh, well."

"So, what ended up happening?"

Claire looked at me questioningly. "What, to the PA, you mean? Actually, things turned out pretty well for her. Not long after we got home, her lover left his wife. Ripped her off for an absolutely obscene amount of money in the divorce settlement—most of which she'd earned, I might add. Then he married the little bitch, had a couple of kids with her and, a few years later, she caught him doing their nanny in the car port. Or so I hear."

I shook my head. "If you disliked her so much, I'm amazed you bothered to keep tabs on her."

"It's a small town," Claire said, with another small shrug. "You hear things."

"So, did you do any other tricks?" I asked.

Claire glanced at me quickly. "I'm sorry... what?"

"You and Zoe—did you teach her anything else?"

"A coupla things." Claire studied my face for a moment and then plucked a grape from the bowl of fruit on the table. "Here, Zoe," she called softly until she got her attention. Then she placed the grape between her lips.

"Claire, no—" I felt my heart lurch as Zoe attacked the grape—but gently. Delicately. Eating it, bite by bite. And, if I didn't think too much about it, it appeared disturbingly erotic, as though they were kissing. But macaws can crack nuts with their beaks and the fear of Claire's soft lips being pierced or torn held me immobile, almost afraid to breathe lest I startle either of them into moving the wrong way.

"That was really dumb," I scolded when it was over. "I can't believe you did that. Do you know how easily she could have ripped your lip apart with her beak? You might have needed stitches, surgery..."

Claire grinned. "Relax, Mike. We practiced this. A lot."

"You must have."

"Long days, lotta hours."

"But still, what were you thinking? And, if you'd gotten hurt—wouldn't that have delayed shooting?"

She nodded. "Oh, sure. It might have set the whole production back. The producers would have been pissed, our director would have been furious. He had a bunch of other projects lined up too, all waiting for when we got back. He probably would have lost... at least some of them if we'd fallen too far behind. But I figured it would have served him right. After all, it was mostly his fault I had so much spare time to waste."

"Anything else?" I asked, trying to hide my displeasure. Her unprofessional attitude seemed completely out of character for her and I have to admit I was disappointed.

"Well, here's one the guys on the crew especially liked," Claire replied, reaching for another grape. "Although, as I recall, I had to use olives for this one. Not that I recall too much about that, actually."

"I don't believe this," I muttered as she tucked it into her cleavage and then looked at Zoe.

"Gosh, Zoe, I seem to have dropped my grape. Can you find it? Can you give it to me?"

Zoe seemed to take her time, twisting her head from side to side as she eyed Claire up and down—almost as if she were actually searching for something hidden. Then she reached out with her head, deftly plucked the grape from between Claire's breasts and held it aloft.

"Ohhh, thank you!" Claire murmured. Leaning forward, she used her teeth to take the grape from Zoe's beak. She swallowed it down and then turned to me, eyes glinting, a frosty little smile on her face. "What about you, Mike? Want to play hunt the grape with me?"

"Is that what you did with the guys on the crew?"

"What do you think?"

I met the challenge in her gaze and smiled back faintly. "Well, I, guess they would have had a lot of long days to fill too, huh?"

"No." She shook her head, unbending a little so that she looked more like her usual self, only sadder. "Not really. For them I think it was more a matter of too many long nights packed into that one cantina. They were good guys though, most of them. Very good guys. They took care of me." Her smile peeked out again, warmer this time. "So, how about it, Mike? Wanna play? Just you and me?"

I nodded, my eyes cutting briefly to the window. Night was settling in. "Yes. But not here. And, anyway, I think it's time for Zoe to say good-night."

"I suppose you're right," Claire answered, kissing Zoe's head. "Not the kind of thing we want the children watching, is it? Good-night, sweet girl."

Chapter Eleven

Mike

By the time I got back from getting Zoe settled for the night, Claire had disappeared. The bowl of fruit was also missing from the table. I found them both in my bedroom—waiting for me.

The light from the table lamp bathed Claire in a soft, warm glow. I felt my gut clench at the sight of her kneeling primly in the center of my bed; her hands clasped demurely in her lap, her smile a mere glimmer on her lips. She was naked from the waist up and, though her lower body was hidden by the sheets, I had no reason to suspect she was wearing anything at all. I went and sat beside her, trying not to stare, as usual. Failing miserably. Also as usual.

I touched her cheek, feeling grateful for her presence, feeling happy just to be alive. I tucked her hair behind her ear and gently kissed the slight redness that still lingered in the spot where Zoe's beak had scraped it.

"Such a sweet little ear," I murmured as I laved the spot with the tip of my tongue. "It would be a sin to damage it. You should be more careful."

I heard her breath catch. "Mmm," she whispered. "Nice." Then she ruined it by adding, "I'm always careful."

I pulled back and looked at her. Her eyes were luminous in the lamplight. Her lips...

My gaze hardened as I studied them. They were so damn beautiful. Soft and full and... perfect, just like everything else about her. "You are *not* always careful," I told her as I traced the line of her bottom lip with my thumb. Then kissed it, just like I'd kissed her ear. Soft. Gentle. Sweet. "I know I said spontaneity was a good thing but you scared me tonight. Never do that again. You're far too special to risk injuring yourself out of boredom or as part of some silly prank."

"Special, huh?" Her smile mocked me. "Why's that? 'Cause I make movies? 'Cause I'm a 'star'? You know what that's been good for, Mike? Not much."

I shook my head. "You know better than that, don't you? You're not special because you're a star. You're a star because you're special. You have a quality about you that would shine through even if you were a... even if you were a garage mechanic in work boots and greasy overalls."

"If I were what?" She laughed softly. "Oh, I'd be a real special mechanic, all right. What are you thinking? I don't know anything about cars, other than how to drive one!"

I sighed. "Okay, maybe that was a bad example, but you know what I'm saying. Don't you?"

"Actually," she murmured, maneuvering herself around on the bed until she was facing me, still on her knees, the sheet still gathered just below her waist. "Right now I'm more interested in what you're *not* saying."

Huh? Distracted by the slipping of the sheet, by the jiggling of her breasts as she repositioned herself, it seemed I'd missed a connection. "What am I not saying?"

"You're not saying, 'where's the grape?'."

"Oh. Right." My glance went to the bowl on the nightstand. How could I have forgotten? Dinner and sex. The two things we were still pretending were all we had going for us. Stifling a sigh, I reached over and plucked a grape from the bowl, rolling it between my fingers while I considered my next step. "So, how shall we do this?" I mused aloud. Not really a question.

"However you want to," Claire murmured quietly, as she continued to kneel before me, hands clasped loosely in her lap. Waiting. Smiling.

If I'd had any lingering questions left about whether or not she understood how much it turned me on to take control, her smile would have put them to rest. Oh, yeah. She knew.

"Open," I ordered quietly.

Her lips parted. I thrilled to the sight, to the quick flush that warmed her cheeks, to the look in her eyes as they locked with mine. I held the grape between her lips. She waited.

"Close."

She did.

It was hard to tell whose heart was beating faster.

As I clasped her face between my hands, her eyes fell shut. Tilting her head to the side, I lowered my mouth to hers. One bite of grape. Two. Three. That's all it took and then it was just my mouth on hers. Nibbling. Licking. Feasting on her sweet taste, her soft lips.

"Kiss me," I murmured. And she did; her lips questing, searching. Her tongue matching mine, stroke for stroke.

She sighed softly when I pulled away. Her eyes opened slowly, mischief sparking within them. "I have to admit it. You do that much better than Zoe."

I snorted. "Thank you."

'Better than Zoe—or anyone else I've played this game with.' That's what I wanted to hear her say. I picked another grape, stroked it across her cheek, over her lips. Her mouth opened.

I shook my head. "Nope. Not there."

Over her chin and down her throat, I dragged the grape; down to the middle of her chest and then I stopped. As beautiful as her bare breasts were, there was no way they could hold a grape between them—not without some help.

I withdrew my hand. "It seems we have a slight problem."

Claire glanced down, following my gaze. "I see what you mean. Not much cleavage that way, is there?"

"Not really."

"All right," Claire murmured as she crossed her arms at the wrists, re-clasped her hands and pressed. "What about this?"

"Perfect."

Dipping my head, I kissed the soft juncture of her breasts and then lodged the grape between them. I sat back, smiling. "Why, my dear Miss Calhoun, it appears you have a piece of food caught in your décolletage." I peered closer. "Is that a grape?"

"Is it?" Claire's eyes widened in a look of mock alarm that would have been perfect were it not for the hint of a smile on her lips. "Oh, no!" she gasped breathlessly. "Whatever shall I do?"

"Allow me to assist you in removing it," I said gravely, leaning into her.

"No!" she gasped again and shrank away from me.

What? I jerked back, staring at her in confusion. "No?"

Eyelashes fluttering, she bowed her head and coyly murmured, "I mean, I couldn't possibly impose on you like that. It's far too arduous a task."

Actors. I chuckled as I lifted her chin on the edge of my hand and trailed kisses down the length of her neck. "Oh, but I insist."

I licked along the seam of her breasts, flicked my tongue across the tips of her nipples, enjoying the happy little gasps and murmurs. "Arduous tasks are my specialty." Finally I scooped the grape up and sat back. I gazed at Claire commandingly, grape between my teeth, and waited.

But not for long. Hands still clasped between her knees, she leaned forward, obligingly, to take it. I let her take a couple of bites, loving the way her lips brushed softly against my own.

As soon as the grape was gone I recaptured her mouth. The

taste and the heat and the softness of her made my head spin. I grabbed hold of her shoulders and fell back, taking her with me.

"Wait. Not yet," Claire protested as she pulled away and sat up again. "There's more."

"More?" I blinked up at her, trying to get my thoughts on track. Not that I wanted to have to think right now—any more than I wanted to wait. "What more?" What *now*?

"More to the game, silly." She eased herself back until she was leaning on her hands, half-reclining on the bed, still partially swathed in the sheet. She smiled wickedly. "While you were in the other room with Zoe, I hid a grape."

"You hid it? Where? Here in the bedroom?"

"Yup." She nodded. "Definitely *in* the room."

I met her gaze, met the mischief and the fire there and felt my interest rise, felt my cock grow harder in anticipation of what I knew was to come. "And I'm supposed to find it. Is that what you're saying?"

"That's the general idea."

"I see."

I took hold of the sheet, gave a sharp tug, and whipped it away from her. She gasped in delight, heat rose in her cheeks.

My smile widened. "Am I getting warm yet?"

Swiveling her hips provocatively, Claire peeked up at me from between her lashes. "Well, I certainly hope so, Mike. Otherwise I'm gonna think I've lost my touch. But I don't see you looking yet."

"Oh, I'm looking. Believe me, I'm looking."

"For the grape," she replied with false asperity.

"Right." Sitting up again, I lifted one of her feet to my mouth. "The grape. I think I'll start my search here."

She moaned as I bit her big toe softly and then edged my tongue into each of the spaces between her toes.

"Nope, no grape here," I murmured as my mouth moved slowly down the sole of her foot.

Claire's eyes were half closed, her voice heavy with desire. "No, huh? Better check the other one too, while you're at it."

"Good idea." I switched feet, sucked each of her toes in turn. "Not here either."

She sighed happily, wiggling her toes 'til I had to bite down on them to make her stop. "Mm. Mike, you really have the most wonderful mouth."

"Thank you," I said as I kissed them one last time and took hold of her ankles. "I try. But now I believe it's time to widen the search parameters." I ran my hands up the insides of her legs easing them apart. "Widen being the operative word here, of course."

Claire laughed softly. "Of course."

Grinning back at her, I pushed at her knees, spreading her legs even wider. Her sex glistened invitingly; soft, pink folds that almost concealed the curve of the grape. "Well, what have we here?" I leaned closer, reached out and ran a finger around the grape, circling it, stroking and teasing her swelling flesh until her body trembled beneath my touch. Then I glanced back up at her face. "That wasn't so hard to find. Now was it?"

Claire sucked in air and forced a smile. "Game's not over yet, sport. You still have to get it out. And mouth only. No hands."

"There are rules for this sort of thing?" I stared at her in surprise. "Oh, no, I don't think so." And if there were, I was pretty sure *I* should be the one to be setting them. "What do you have against hands, anyway?"

"There have to be rules, Mike. Otherwise, what kind of game would it be? And I don't have anything against hands. It's just... well, Zoe doesn't have any, does she? And if she can do—What? What's wrong?"

"Zoe?" I felt my mouth gape open. "Damn it, Claire. *Tell* me you did *not* try this with that bird?"

"What?" She stared at me, her eyes blank, her face perplexed, and then, "Oh!" Comprehension flooded her face and she collapsed backwards onto the bed, shaking with laughter. "Oh, my God. Mike! Of course I didn't! That would, that would just be... *bent.*"

"To say the least." And while I had nothing whatsoever against being bent or twisted, in general, in this particular case... just thinking about it made me wince.

"That's not even funny. I can't believe you thought of something like that."

"Me?" I stared at her outraged. "No. *You're* the one who thought it!"

"Well, clearly I didn't. Farthest thing from my mind."

"Then why bring it up? You mentioned Zoe and if you hadn't..."

Claire sighed. "Don't be ridiculous. I was just going to point out that Zoe does amazing things using nothing but her mouth.

And that I would have thought someone like you could do... well, almost as much."

"*Almost* as much?"

"Can you climb ropes, Mike? Or open doors, or swing from a perch using just your mouth? Or crack nuts? I don't think so."

I clamped my lips together to keep from pointing out that, at the moment, she was doing a fine job of cracking mine. *And* using just her mouth. But that was sure to spoil the mood. I shook my head.

"And, so, fine. If you think you can't do this..." She smiled at me—kindly—probably the worst thing she could have done under the circumstances, and shrugged. "Or if you just don't want to, then don't worry about it. Forget I mentioned it. Use your hands all you want. Hands are good too."

If that didn't count as a challenge, I don't know what would. I gazed at her sternly. "Claire, any man who can't eat a grape out of a woman's pussy without using his hands is..." Useless? Pathetic? Better off dead? "Well, he's no one a woman like you ought to be wasting your time with, I can tell you that."

"A woman like me?" Heat blazed in her eyes. Heat and speculation. "What exactly is that supposed to mean?"

I met her gaze dead on. "It means a woman like you deserves only the best." And, tonight, that was exactly what she was going to get.

I think something in my expression must have finally gotten through to her because her face, already rosy, turned a warmer shade of pink. "Oh?" Her tongue peeked out to wet her lips. "Okay, Mike, you're on. Show me what you got."

"I intend to." I didn't care how many men she'd played this particular game with, my goal tonight was suddenly crystal clear. I was gonna make her forget every last one of them. Starting right now.

I stretched out on the bed between her legs. Sliding my hands beneath her, I tilted her hips toward my mouth—certain that little bit of assistance wouldn't count against me. I started off with one long swipe of my tongue up the center of her sex, ending with a quick flick across her clit that had her sucking in air.

"Mm. Grape flavored snatch," I teased. "Like a lollipop, only better." I then proceeded to make pass after pass along the length of her slit, making no attempt to dislodge the grape.

"You're not even trying, are you?" Claire's voice sounded

shaky.

I glanced up at her. "Are you complaining?"

"Not a bit."

"No point in rushing things," I told her, striving to look serious. "Besides, I think I need something else to practice on first."

"Practice?" she repeated after me. "Are you kidding me?"

"This'll do," I said as my lips latched onto her clit.

"Oh, God," she moaned as I sucked the little nub. "Oh, that's good. Don't stop."

Finally, when she was thrashing and bucking beneath me, when her pussy was flooded with so much cream it was a wonder the grape hadn't poured out on the tide, I curled my tongue inside her, scooped up the fruit and popped it out.

I lifted my head, grape between my teeth, and met her gaze. Just to make sure she saw it. Then I swallowed it down and licked my lips. "Well? Any other games you'd like to play?"

Claire's eyes looked glazed. "Maybe you ought to try that one again," she suggested, adding a helpful, "There are still plenty of grapes left."

Not the response I was expecting. "What?"

"Yeah, I think so." She nodded, her voice tight, breathless. "We don't want to be too... be too hasty, right? You know it, it *could* just be... beginner's luck."

Beginner's luck? For an instant, I didn't know what to think. *What's she trying to say?* Then my eyes registered the rapid rise and fall of her chest, the greedy, hopeful look in her eyes. I smiled. "If you want more, you just have to say so."

She nodded again, fingers prodding at my shoulders. "Okay, then, yes. More. Now."

"My pleasure." Smiling, I bent once more to my task and then paused. "So how'd that stack up against your crew's performances?"

"What?" Claire blinked at me as if I'd lost my mind. Probably I had. Even I couldn't believe I'd asked that. "You think I did stuff like this with the guys on the *crew*?"

I felt my forehead furrow. Hadn't she said as much? "I was just curious."

"Why would you think something like that?" Claire asked, her voice wooden. "And is it the whole crew I'm supposed to have done, or just a select few?"

"What do you mean, 'why do I think that'? You said they'd

liked your tricks, remember? All those long days and nights? Bored and lonely? The jungle? You said they'd been good to you. And how am I supposed to know how many? You tell me." Or, better yet, don't!

She was silent for a moment, then she sighed, her shoulders sagging, her expression bleak. "Okay, look, Mike, yes, I was bored. A lot. And very unhappy and there may have been a few nights... or more than a few, even... when I was upset and I had too much to drink and things maybe got... a *little* out of hand. But, when I said they were good to me, I meant they weren't the kind to take advantage of something like that. Trust me, they saw a lot more skin on the set than off. At least where *my* skin was concerned. I didn't get naked with any of them."

I must have looked surprised or skeptical, or maybe just confused.

She shook her head, her voice flat. "You don't believe me."

"Of course I believe you." Why would she say that? Belief was not the issue here. Why had she led me to think otherwise— that's what had me confused.

"For what it's worth, I was married when I made that film," she continued bitterly. "And I was still young enough to think that *meant* something. I can't imagine why. It certainly didn't seem to mean much to my husband."

The pain in her voice struck at my heart. In that moment, she looked and sounded very young indeed. Young and forlorn. I pressed a kiss against the soft skin of her inner thigh, wishing I could somehow take away the hurt, longing to protect her. "I'm sorry I brought it up. I didn't realize it was a painful subject. I guess it's gotta be tough on a marriage, what with one of you being gone on location for so long. All the separations, that can't be easy."

She sighed. "That's what I thought too. That's exactly why I fought for the project in the first place—despite my agent's objections. I thought it would be good for us, good for our marriage. We weren't separated, Mike. He was directing the film."

I stared at her in surprise. Her husband was there? Through all those long days and drunken nights, he was there? What the hell? No wonder she'd divorced the loser.

"Anyway, I don't know why we're even talking about this."

"He must have noticed how unhappy you were."

Claire's eyes flashed. "Did I *say* he didn't notice? Of course he did! Everyone noticed." Then she stopped and shook her head, looking even sadder than before. "No. No, you're right. I don't suppose he did notice, come to think of it. Either that or he just didn't care."

"Impossible."

Claire stretched out on the bed and stared at the ceiling. "Not really. He was... busy."

"Doing *what?*"

She waved a hand in the air. "Oh, you know. Director stuff. Lighting, camera angles, thousands of details I know nothing about and probably couldn't even understand if he tried to explain them. Movies don't just happen on their own, you know."

"Claire?"

She sighed. "He was screwing his PA, Mike. Is that what you wanted to hear?"

His PA. "The girl with the earrings?" So that was why—

Claire's mouth twisted. She shrugged. "Easy come, easy go. I warned her about that, but girls in lust rarely ever take the wife's advice. Guess she found that out too."

"Stupid," I growled angrily, wishing there was something I could do; something to make her feel better, something to make it up to her, just *something*.

"Hey!" Claire sat up, scowling. "I hope that's her you're talking about and not me? I mean, at least *I* didn't have *kids* with him. That would have been really stupid. Bad enough to have him as a husband, at least you can walk away from that. But as a father, he's been a total disaster."

I shook my head. "I wasn't talking about either of you. I was talking about him. About me. *You* didn't do anything you should feel stupid about and her— Her I'm not interested in."

She frowned at me, curiously. "So what did *you* do that was so stupid?"

"I misjudged you. Horribly. When you told me about the earring, I should have known you wouldn't have done something like that without there being a reason—a good reason—for it. I thought you were just young and spoiled and acting irresponsibly. I should have known better. I'm sorry."

"Mike." Her gaze softened. Her eyes glistened with what might have been tears. "I *was* young. *And* irresponsible. And probably spoiled as well. That thing with the earring—you were right about what you said. It was a lousy thing to do. It was spiteful. Mean."

"No." I shook my head again, more firmly this time. "You'd

been hurt. You had every right to be upset. They were wrong to treat you so callously. It I'd have been there..." But it was foolish to even think it. What could I have done to protect her, even if I had been there?

"I see." A teasing smile had curved Claire's mouth. "So now you've decided to see me as perfect? Is that it? Well, that makes for a nice change. Thank you."

I met her gaze. "I've always seen you that way. Don't you know that? To me you've never been anything less than perfect. Right from the start."

The smile disappeared from her face. "Mike, I... I..." Her voice trailed away. She stared at me for a moment. A very long moment. And then, "Come here," she murmured brokenly, reaching one trembling hand toward me. "Please."

I surged up the length of her body, thrilling to the sweet caress as her hand found my shoulder and then my back. Sighing softly in regret as I bypassed all the interesting places I'd planned to linger along the way—her navel, the swell of her hip. Pausing only to kiss the tip of one breast, the curve of her neck, before settling above her. Her eyes were hot on me as I bent to kiss her cheek, my hands clenching in the silky waves of her hair.

"Love me, Mike," she whispered and I felt my heart stall.

I raised my head to stare at her. "Claire?"

"Now." She tugged at my shirt. "Right now. I can't wait. Make love to me now."

Disappointment crashed over me. I shook it off, swallowed hard and nodded my consent. I'd been asked to make love to a goddess. Disappointment was the last thing I should be feeling.

I levered myself up on one arm so I could unbutton my shirt, but again Claire stopped me.

"No. Leave it on. Leave it all on. All your clothes."

"What? Why?"

"I want it like you said the other day. Fast. Hard. Like you're too hot to wait. Like you want me so badly you can't take the time to undress."

Fast? I nearly groaned aloud. *Again?* She was giving me my fantasy, or something close to it—as though just making love to her at all wasn't fantasy enough! It was a gift I couldn't refuse but it wasn't at all what I wanted. "Not slow this time?" I teased hopefully.

She shook her head. "Like you need me, want me, have to

have me. Now."

Well, that was easy enough. I unzipped my pants and slid hot and needy into her slick, wet passage. It was easy because it was true. "I do."

Need her. Want her. Love her.

Slipping a hand beneath her, I tilted her hips up to meet my thrusts. Pounding hard and fast, just like she wanted it. Hard and fast, to match the pounding of my heart.

She moaned soft and low as her body contracted around me. As she crested below me, her nails dug hard into my shoulders through my shirt and I ached to feel more. I longed to feel her, skin to skin, and mourned the loss.

I looked into her face, watching it go taut and blissful as her body spasmed and she came undone. *For me, all for me.*

"Claire."

She opened her eyes and, in the instant when her gaze met mine, I knew. *She* was my fantasy—here, now, always. Fast or slow, it didn't matter. Making love to her was all I'd ever need or want.

I bent my head, kissing her fiercely, as I felt my balls tighten, as I felt my muscles seize. *Mine!* I pumped my hot seed into her waiting pussy and pulled her tight against me as I claimed her and came.

Need her. Want her. Love her.

Yes.

"I do. I do. I do."

* * * *

A moment later, I was rolling off of her to lie on my back, sweaty and uncomfortable in my clothes, cum soaking through the front of my pants. She rolled to face me.

"Will you hate me if I go to sleep now?" she asked.

I smiled at the absurdity of the question, while I used a tired hand to brush the hair back from her face. Hate her? Impossible. "Of course I won't."

"I'm so tired, Mike, and it's been such a long week. Now I just want to curl up in your arms and sleep until morning. Right here with you. Is that okay?"

I nodded. "Anything. Whatever you want."

"Thank you." A brief smile glimmered on her lips as she stretched up to kiss me good-night. "You're very sweet." Then she rolled again to spoon with me, her head resting on my outstretched arm, the soft curve of her ass pressing against my open fly and my softening cock.

I slid my other hand up her bare thigh, coasted it over her hip, until she stopped me. Until she grabbed my hand and pulled my arm snug around her. Until she clasped my hand in hers and pressed it to her chest.

Perfect. I sighed as I folded my other arm around her. As I rested my chin on her head, swung my leg over hers, wrapped myself around her and held her tight.

I wanted to stay like this forever. I wanted to lay my body down for her—be her pillow, her blanket, her shelter, her shield. I wanted to protect her against anything or anyone who might hurt her.

She tightened her grasp on my hand—the one that covered her heart—and I smiled. *Just perfect.* I wanted to protect her, every part of her. Now and forever. But that part most of all.

Chapter Twelve

Claire

I woke up early the next morning to the soft scratchiness of a bearded cheek rubbing along my neck. To warm lips pressing kisses against my shoulder and a firm hand that slid around my waist and then down between my legs. To these tender words whispered in my ear: "Are you awake?"

Groaning a little—because I was, but I didn't want to be—I turned my head and looked up into Mike's face. "I am now."

"Good. Turn over." He prodded at me until I'd rolled into his arms, then he cupped my face in his hand and kissed me. His lips—warm, wet, demanding—moved over mine with increasing urgency until I pushed him away.

"Okay," I gasped, trying to catch my breath while my heart fluttered out of control. Heat pulsed in my pussy to the point where I was almost ready to hump his leg to get some relief. "Okay, now I'm *really* awake."

"Good," Mike repeated as his arms tightened around me. "Now, come here."

"Whoa." I held him off again. "Hello to you, too." His chest felt warm and solid under my hands and I couldn't keep from kneading my fingers in the crisp hair that blanketed his pecs. Any more than I could keep my gaze from straying down along his naked torso, past the comfortable bulk of his muscles, to his thick cock—already hard and spoiling for action. "Nice outfit," I murmured as my eyes traveled back up to his face.

He gave a short bark of laughter. "Thanks. Yours too." Then he raised his eyebrows inquisitively. "Are you gonna let me kiss you again, or not?"

"Maybe. Are you usually this frisky in the morning?"

"No. That's your fault. What do you mean *maybe?*"

"*My* fault? Nice try. As I recall, last time I spent the night here you were gentlemanly enough to let me sleep in."

He nodded. "Exactly. And look what that got me: you left."

Mike's words caught me off guard. Yes, I'd left. I'd called a cab and fled. I'd gotten scared. And, this morning, it was happening all over again. "What is it about you anyway?" I grumbled, feeling angry with us both as I remembered how easily he'd gotten me to open up again, to talk so much about myself last night.

Years, damn it. I'd been distancing myself for years. How was it he kept getting to me like this?

"I at least expected breakfast in bed this morning," I said, desperately seeking a distraction. I needed space.

"An excellent idea." Mike pulled back the covers and sat up. "That's just what I'm in the mood for too."

"Good." I shivered at the sudden chill of cool air against my bare skin, then frowned as I watched him slide between my legs. "Wait. What are you doing?"

He glanced up at me; eyebrows raised, a faint, sardonic smile on his face. "Eating breakfast."

His gaze was hot and frank and far too sure of itself. I felt the rush of heat in my cheeks and was appalled. Claire Calhoun was *never* embarrassed by a lover's attentions. And yet, I had to clear my throat before I could speak and still my voice sounded weak. "Mike, you know that's not what I meant."

"Really? It's not?" Still smiling, he spread my legs wider. "It's what I meant though."

"Last time you offered me an omelet," I said, trying again.

"Last time *you* called a cab."

Irritated now, I frowned at him. "You're never gonna forget about that, are you?"

Mike shrugged. Burying his face in my crotch he inhaled deeply. "Mm. Never's a long time, Claire. I'm sure I'll get over it eventually."

His lips tugged gently on my labia and it was all I could do to keep from wriggling beneath his touch. I wanted more. And less. Both at once. "And in the meantime you plan to starve me. Is that it?"

Mike raised his head. "You want food?"

Deprived of his mouth on my flesh, that was suddenly all I wanted, all I could think about. Still, "Food would be nice," I managed to say, faintly.

"Fine." He nodded toward the nightstand. "Have a grape."

"Excuse me?"

"Sure. Eat the whole bunch, if you want. Or, better yet, why don't you pass a couple of them down here to me?"

"Michael!"

Sighing, Mike stroked a hand up over my belly. I shivered at the touch. "Tell me you don't want this and I'll stop," he said quietly.

I bit my lip to keep from whimpering. I tried to speak, but I couldn't make the words come out of my mouth.

Mike's eyes glinted. A smile curved his lips. "Hmm. Didn't think so."

Cupping his hand over my mound, he pressed upward, pulling the flesh taut, exposing my clit. Then he used his tongue to flick the little nub, circling, stroking, over and over until I had no choice but to give in. Crossing my arms over my face, I closed my eyes. I focused on the sensations flooding through me and tried hard to let all the rest of it go.

Just give him what he wants, I told myself. *Stop thinking and do it. Come for him. Let him have you. Get it over with.*

It should have been easy. It shouldn't have been anything out of the ordinary, nothing I hadn't done a thousand times before. The heat went everywhere. My legs fell open wider. His tongue set all my nerves alight.

Then he spoiled it.

"Gosh, you're sweet," he murmured. Once again his hand stroked lightly over my belly, teasing, tormenting. Once again I shuddered. "I love that," Mike breathed, sounding reverent, sounding amazed. "The way you respond... it's so pure, so hot, it's almost like you've never been touched."

I groaned aloud. *Great. Just great. What the fuck am I doing? I'm in bed with a man who says 'gosh'. Who thinks I'm the next best thing to a virgin. Who thinks of me as perfect, for Chrissake. What happens when he finds out I'm not?*

But I already knew the answer to that one, didn't I? It was always such a long, hard fall from the top of a pedestal and it hurt like hell all the way down to the ground.

Mike's fingers trailed circles around my navel and my body arched against his hand. Shivering harder now, I sucked in air. I dug my nails into my palms to keep from crying.

Goddamn Derek. Why'd he have to go and fall in love with that girl? What we had was perfect. We'd both gone into it with our eyes wide open, knowing just what we were getting, just what to expect. And when it ended, even though that wasn't what I would have chosen, at least it had been quick, clean, honest. A single cut, easy to heal.

This affair with Mike could never be like that. Could never end clean or easy. Could never be anything less than a train wreck, or like taking a shotgun blast to the chest.

"You're killing me," I muttered.

I was only barely aware I spoke the words out loud until Mike chuckled in reply, "At least we know you'll die happy."

I opened my eyes and looked at him. His expression was sweet and warm and tender. I think that's when it really hit me how big a mistake I'd made.

I'd looked forward to our appointments every other Thursday. Having Mike around—even though we'd never discussed the matter—had helped to soften the blow when Derek left me. The admiration in his gaze had soothed my wounded pride, my battered ego and, yes, even the bruises to my heart. The ones I'd sworn I didn't feel.

What would I do when this ended; when the laughter that blazed now in his eyes died out, to be replaced with a look of loathing and disgust?

Get out now. Stop thinking. Just fuck him and leave.

I told myself I could figure it out later. I told myself that naked and on fire was no time to be making decisions that could affect the rest of my life.

"Fuck me," I ordered, lifting my head, propping myself up on my elbows.

Mike just looked at me, the smile on his face slowly fading.

"Take me now," I said, changing it from an order to a plea with a whispered, "Please?"

He shook his head. "Not this time."

"Michael..."

"You had it your way last night," he said, still refusing me. "This morning it's my turn."

"Meaning what?" I groaned.

"Meaning... you'll just have to wait and see."

"I don't like to wait."

He grimaced. "Believe me, I've noticed."

"I don't know what this game is you think you're playing, Mike, but this isn't the time for it."

"You're really not a morning person, are you?"

"Michael!"

"Patience," he murmured soothingly, trailing kisses along my inner thighs. "It'll be good this way. You'll see. You'll like it."

Well, that wasn't the problem, was it? I already liked it, just like I liked *him*. Too much. Liking any of it more wasn't going to help.

I gazed at him helplessly while he slipped one finger, then two fingers inside me, gliding deep and then withdrawing.

"Mm, sweet." He stuck his fingers in his mouth and sucked noisily. "Like honey."

"More," I pleaded.

He laughed. "Just what I was thinking." Then he repeated the caress, dipping and sucking and dipping again, inching me closer to climax at glacial speed, until my pussy was on fire and my entire being was alive with need.

"Now." I pumped my hips frantically, straining toward his hand. "Fuck me now."

"So impatient," he chided, pressing another kiss against the inside of my thigh. "See what you missed last time you were here? See why it was a mistake to call that cab?"

Oh, dear God. "Mike," I groaned, not sure if I wanted to laugh or cry. I lay back on the bed once more and covered my eyes again. "I swear, if you don't take me soon I'm gonna call a cab right the hell now and screw the cabbie while you watch!"

I froze. He froze. In the silence that followed my outburst, I could hear the echo of my words, could hear how they must have sounded and I wanted to throw up.

I can't do this. I'd rather end it now than stay and see the disappointment in his eyes.

I could have tried explaining, I suppose. I could have told him that I had a bad habit of saying things I didn't mean, that I'd simply never learned to keep my mouth shut. But, eventually, it would all turn out the same. I could see where we were headed and I would *not* go there. Not with him.

I don't want to beg. I don't need to beg. I don't beg.

I pushed him aside and got out of bed, slipping past him without meeting his gaze.

"Where do you think you're going?" he called after me, sounding amused. "Did I say you could get up?"

I shook my head. "Don't start."

"That better have been a joke about the cabbie," he warned teasingly. "You'd better not be looking for a phone."

I felt my shoulders start to sag and I straightened my spine. "I'm not," I answered coolly. "I'm just looking for my clothes."

He sat up quickly. "Claire? What's going on? What are you doing?"

"What's it look like I'm doing, Michael?" I replied, still not looking at him. "I'm getting dressed."

"I can see that! But why?"

"I've got... things to do today. I'm pressed for time."

He got up from the bed. "You're not leaving?"

I nodded. "Sorry."

"What the hell? Claire... okay, come on, very cute. Now, cut the crap. This is ridiculous. Get your ass back in bed."

"Don't talk to me like that, Mike. I don't take orders from you."

"I don't get this," he mumbled, pulling a pair of jeans from his dresser drawer. "What the hell just happened here? This *can't* be about breakfast. What are you so upset about?"

"You! All right? You're just... just..."

"Me?" He stopped dressing and stared at me. "You're angry at *me*? What'd I do?"

"You're much too controlling, for one thing," I said, struggling with my voice, which had begun to shake. It didn't so much matter if I didn't sound calm, but I *would* sound cool, I *would* sound collected. "I don't think it's gonna work out. I'm not used to being treated this way. I think this was a mistake."

"A mistake." Mike zipped up his jeans and fisted his hands on his hips. "Okay, fine. What's a mistake? What are we talking about? Tell me so I can fix it."

"You can't fix it. It's not that kind of thing."

"Everything's fixable, Claire. Most things, anyway."

"Not this."

"Why not?"

"Because."

He arched an eyebrow . "Because...?"

I sighed distractedly. He looked damn good in those jeans. I don't know why that should have mattered, or why I was even noticing. But, it was the first time I'd seen him wear them and, somehow, seeing him like that, barefoot and bare-chested, wearing nothing but a pair of softly faded jeans, only made things harder somehow. Even to my own ears, my excuses sounded feeble and weak.

"That's it?" Mike prompted, after a moment. "That's all the answer you got for me?"

He looked so... normal, so solid and sane. A little distracted, perhaps, a little vulnerable, but decent, warm, concerned. Patient. He looked like someone I really wouldn't have minded getting to know better. The kind of person you could grow old with.

Someone I could easily have seen myself having breakfast with every morning for the rest of my life. But I couldn't start thinking like that. Not again.

I shook my head. "Because I'm talking about us, Mike. And I think maybe we... maybe we never should have started this."

"What?" At that, anger flared in his eyes. Anger, disbelief, or maybe hurt. It was hard to tell at a glance and I couldn't meet his gaze long enough to be certain.

Moving quickly, I began to toss things into my bag. "Sorry."

"Sorry? Un-fucking-believable. And what do you mean 'we' anyway? Maybe *you* shouldn't have started something you didn't want to see through to the end."

"I don't think so." I slid the bag's strap over my arm and turned toward the bedroom door. "I think maybe you just don't want to admit that this *is* the end."

"Is that what you're saying?" he demanded. "This is it? The end? You're calling it quits?"

"Yes," I said as I crossed the living room, intensely aware of him stalking behind me, praying he'd just let me go. "That's exactly what I'm saying."

"Over what? This is bullshit, Claire. You can't just—just... what the hell? You can't do this!"

Oh, yes, I could. "I'm sorry, Mike." I pulled open his front door and turned to look at him. I forced a small smile. "I'll see you Thursday, okay? Same as always?"

"Same as always? Are you kidding me?"

I shook my head, closed the door behind me and ran down the drive. My hands were shaking so hard I could barely get the car door open, could barely get it started, could barely drive.

I pulled away from the house expecting every second to see the front door burst open, to see Mike come running out of the house. I was relieved when he didn't. Mostly relieved, except for the small, obstinate part of me that felt only disappointment. *Stop me*, it called out to him silently. *Tell me I'm wrong. Make me stay.*

But he didn't. And that, I told myself, was Just As Well. All for the Best. A Huge Relief.

I'd made it as far as the coast before it dawned on me I didn't know where the hell I was going.

Not to work. I'd told already told them not to expect me until Monday. I couldn't show up before then without having to answer a lot of awkward questions that I'd rather avoid.

And not home, either. I hadn't liked it all that much in the first place. Now that I'd seen it through Mike's eyes, I despised it. Besides, he knew where I lived. There was nothing going to stop him from showing up there if he wanted. Nothing to stop him from making another painful scene, from running through the same fruitless argument with me over and over again until I gave up or gave in or did something stupid. Something I'd regret. Something that could only end up hurting us both in the long run.

I just wasn't up for that kind of pain.

Digging my cell phone out of my bag, I dialed the number of my favorite spa and breathed a prayer of thanks when they told me they had a vacancy. I hung up, turned the phone off, and tossed it back in my bag. Then I turned left and headed south.

I'd give myself two days to disappear, to relax, to breathe. Two days to put myself back together.

And if that didn't work? Then at least I'd have two days to think of something else.

* * * *

By Monday morning, I was feeling about a thousand percent better. Traffic was brutal on the drive back into the city and there seemed to be more than the usual quota of helicopters aloft. I was still feeling a little out of sorts, but at least my mind was much, much clearer—which was more than I could say for the air. The sky was hazy and brown along the horizon, a shade you rarely ever see this far west of San Bernardino.

I didn't reach The Body Electric until shortly after noon. I found most of my staff gathered around the small TV at the receptionist's desk. It was only then that I learned about the brush fire raging out of control.

"...*almost a thousand acres already burning,*" the grim-faced newscaster was saying. "...*several houses have been destroyed and dozens more are in danger... authorities say area residents have been evacuated from Topanga Canyon and the neighboring communities of...*"

"Topanga Canyon?" I asked, feeling suddenly light-headed. "When did it start?"

"Yesterday, I think," Damien replied with a shrug. "I'm surprised you didn't hear about it. It's been on the news all day."

But I hadn't been listening to the news. I'd been playing CDs on the drive in this morning, trying desperately to hold onto the serenity I'd spent two days working to find. Trying desperately not to think.

Just as now, I was trying desperately not to panic.

"Excuse me," I murmured as I headed up to my office. My hands were once again shaking as I dialed the number for Mike's office.

His secretary was somber but unhelpful. Mike wasn't in. The phone lines were down in the canyon and he wasn't answering his cell. They had no idea where he was, how he was. No one there had seen or heard anything from him since he'd left work Friday night.

I hung up the phone feeling cold and frightened. Feeling more alone than I could ever remember being.

Suddenly all the things I'd been so afraid of, all my petty, personal, everyday concerns, seemed monumentally unimportant. And my choices lately, the supposedly clear-headed decisions that I'd spent the past two days congratulating myself on making, seemed a twisted joke, a huge mistake, an absolute, total lie.

I'd convinced myself I was okay with losing Mike. If someone had to be hurt, why did it have to be me? Why couldn't someone else take the hit—just once? Better to hurt him now and lose his friendship than to lose my heart once again; or my peace of mind, my hard-won serenity. Or any more of my money. But maybe that was only because I didn't think I had—or even could— ever *really* lose him.

Until now.

Unable to sit still and do nothing, unable to work, I wandered back downstairs. I was still carrying my keys and my purse, I was still wearing my sunglasses atop my head. My stomach roiled, my skin felt cold. Unable to think, unable to settle down, I gravitated back to the TV, hoping for better news. But it seemed the situation had only gotten worse in the past few minutes.

"Hey," Derek greeted me quietly, coming up behind me, radiating concern, comfort and support as he gently massaged my neck. "Are you okay?"

"Not really." I turned my head to look at him. He was beautiful. Tall, fit, gorgeous face, gorgeous body—any woman's dream.

"Anything I can do to help?"

I shook my head. "No. Nothing."

He gave my shoulders a final squeeze. "Okay, well, if you think of anything, you'll let me know. All right?"

I nodded, tried to smile. "Thanks, I will." But we both knew there was nothing that he, or anyone else, could do to help.

Derek and I were friends. What I felt for Mike was

something else entirely. And it had taken something like this; it had taken being faced with the possibility that he might be hurt, might be injured, might be dead to make me see that.

Fear tore up my insides with razor-sharp claws as I stood there, staring at the screen. *No. Not dead. He can't be.*

"I have to go," I said, my voice shaky and dull as I turned away from the desk and headed blindly for the door. I couldn't stay here and wonder. I couldn't stay here and hope. I couldn't stay here and wait to hear... something.

I'd been wrong. I'd been stupid. And I had no idea if I could ever fix things, ever make things right. Maybe I'd never even get the chance to try.

"Hey, where are you going?" A voice called out behind me. "Claire?"

But I didn't answer. What would I have said?

I'm going to hell.

That seemed like a good explanation and a real possibility. Either in this life or the next, I certainly deserved to suffer a stint in hell for my sins, for my lies, for my stupidity. For my cowardice.

I'd tried to save myself. I'd tried to hide from the truth, and look where it had gotten me. Now, my only hope lay in trying to face it.

Chapter Thirteen

Claire

The wind had picked up by the time I was back on the road—or maybe I just hadn't noticed it earlier. The air was hot and dry. The sky was definitely darker. Huge, angry, bruise-colored clouds billowed and swelled to the north of the city, to the west, straight ahead. The sun was a flat, orange disc in the dull, bronze sky.

I didn't really have a clear idea where I as headed, or what I'd find when I got there. But, as close to the canyon as I could safely get *had* to be the best place to search for either Mike or information about him. There had to be someone who knew where the evacuated residents might be gathered.

I got to the point where traffic was stalled and cars were being turned back much sooner than I'd expected. I had to park my car and walk to get closer, cursing my poor choice in footwear. Who knew, when I'd got up this morning, that I'd be hiking through weeds and gravel?

I wasn't the only one either. It seemed like dozens of other people were making the same trek, singly or in small groups. Their faces either grim or urgent, most appeared concerned, some merely curious. Their voices were hushed—or maybe it just seemed that way due to the buffeting wind, the din of helicopters overhead, the crackle of radios and static. No sirens though. Apparently all the fire-trucks available were already on the scene.

Badly parked cars were scattered along both sides of the road here. Despite the heat that poured from their shiny glass and metal surfaces, I felt cold inside, chilled to the bone. Even if Mike was here, how would I ever find him? Between the crowds and the confusion, the noise and the smoke, I could pass within feet of him and never even know it. The air itself was dark, heavy and thick with ash. It was hard to breathe, hard to see through. The tightness in my chest and the watering of my eyes made it harder still.

LA is a strange place at the best of times, but today it seemed absolutely surreal. Being a celebrity in LA can leave you with a sense of entitlement, can make you think you're invulnerable. That you can do no wrong. Like ambassadors to the community, we expect to receive special treatment, special favors, a certain amount of immunity. Most of the time we get it, too.

This, however, was clearly *not* one of those times. At least not as far as the police officers whose job it was to keep people out of the canyon were concerned. When I reached the final barricade—still miles away from the fire, still acres away from where Mike might be trapped—I was stopped. Just like everyone else.

Oh, I tried everything I could think of to get information from them. I tried begging, crying, cajoling, reasoning, demanding, threatening, name dropping, all to no avail.

A sensible person might have let it go at that point, but I couldn't. I had to know. I had to know now. *What next*, I wondered, as I paused for breath. *Do I start shedding clothes, try to bribe them, or what?* Suddenly, a hand was clamped firmly down on my shoulder. I shrieked in surprise as I found myself being spun roughly around, and then started to cough on a lungful of smoke.

"Claire, what the hell are you up to?" Mike barked at me angrily. "Have you lost your mind? Why are you here?"

"Mike." Relief washed over me in great, warm waves and made me dizzy. Or maybe it was his handling of me that had done that, or the lack of breathable air. I didn't care. I didn't even think about being angry with him for his callous treatment. I drank in the sight of him and felt myself start to shake as reaction set in. He looked so good despite the sooty streaks that marked his jeans and polo shirt. And not dead! Not even injured! Only angry—as if I cared anything about *that*.

I started to sway and reached a hand toward him, hoping to steady myself, but he flinched away from my touch. Muscles freezing in response to his rejection, I stared at him, stricken. Okay, maybe I did care after all. The look on his face was arctic.

"I asked you a question, goddamn it," he growled

He'd asked three, actually, but who was counting? And, anyway, I'd started coughing again and couldn't answer.

"Folks, I'm not gonna tell you again," the police officer nearest us warned. "If you don't clear this area…"

"We're going," Mike snapped, taking hold of my arm and hauling me away. "I don't believe you," he muttered, scowling furiously. "Why were you arguing with those cops? Aren't they busy enough already? What the hell are you even doing here?"

I tripped on a rock, stubbed my toe and abruptly lost my temper. Pulling my arm from his grasp, I scowled back at him. "Well, that's a stupid question, Mike. Why do you think I'm here? I was looking for you!"

"Looking for me? Oh, that's just—Shit, that's just perfect." His eyes narrowed. "Wait a minute. You're not gonna tell me you've been out here all along? You weren't here last night, were you?"

I shook my head. "No. What are you talking about? I only heard about the fire when I got to work today. No one knew where you were. I had to come see that you were okay. I was worried."

"Go home, Claire," he said, sounding exhausted. "There's nothing for you to do here."

"Okay." Well, that was fine with me. Now that I'd found him, I had no reason to stay. "Let's go."

"Stop it," he snapped. "No more games. I'm not going anywhere and you know it."

"Then neither am I." I dug in my heels. "If you stay, I stay."

"Not a chance. It's too dangerous. Now get the hell out of here before I really lose my temper."

I shrugged. "Go ahead and lose it. You think I haven't seen a man get mad before? Besides, if it's that dangerous, neither of us should be here."

"I have *a reason* to be here!"

I nodded. "I know. So do I."

He looked at me for a moment then shrugged. "Whatever." Turning away, he headed down the road to where the cars were parked.

"Wait," I protested hurrying to keep up with him. "Where are you going?"

"Back to my car," he called over his shoulder. "There's no telling how long we'll be here and I can't see the sense in just standing around all day, can you?"

I shook my head. "Not with all this smoke and heat."

"Well, don't expect it to be any better in here," he cautioned as he held the passenger door open for me. "You really should leave, you know."

I ignored that. "At least you still have your car," I blurted without really thinking.

He looked at me, surprised. "My car?"

I nodded. "That's something, isn't it? I mean, I know how much you love your house—and it's a beautiful house, Mike, really. But, look, you haven't lost everything and it's just stuff. It can be replaced."

"Not everything can," he said quietly, sounding so bitter it made my heart ache.

"But you can rebuild. If it's even damaged—and it might be fine, you know. But, either way, you're strong. I know you. You won't end up like me, giving up and settling. And you know what? You'll probably make it even better than it was before. It'll be fine. You'll see."

An impossibly sad smile curved Mike's lips. "Aren't you forgetting something?" he asked softly.

I looked at him, blankly. "No. Like what?"

"Zoe. I think I might have a little trouble replacing her."

"Z-Zoe?" I stuttered as the bottom dropped out of my stomach and once again I felt like throwing up. "Are, are you telling me sh—she's...? No. You mean you...no. No!"

Mike nodded, looking wretched.

"Why?" I wailed, tears welling up in my eyes as I thought about it. "How could you? Why would you leave her behind like that, Mike?"

"I didn't leave her behind," he snapped. "Not intentionally. I wasn't home when the fire broke out and by the time I got back here they'd already started evacuating people and they wouldn't let me in." He glared at me coldly. "Obviously, if I'd known ahead of time there was going to be a fire, or if I'd been there when it started, I'd have taken her with me when I left. But I haven't been home since Saturday. I'd have had to be a psychic to know she wouldn't be safe there when I left her. Clearly, I'm not."

"Sorry," I mumbled, lowering myself into the Jaguar's front seat before my legs gave out. "I didn't mean to accuse you. I know you wouldn't do anything like that on purpose. Sometimes I... sometimes I say things without thinking. Dumb things. Things I don't even mean."

"I've noticed," Mike replied dryly, walking around the car and opening the driver's side door. "So, where were you anyway?" he asked as he settled himself in the driver's seat.

Where was I? Confused, I looked at him questioningly. "What do you mean?"

He shrugged. "Just for curiosity's sake. So I can see exactly *how big* an idiot I've been."

"I don't understand," I said, still puzzled. "Where was I when?"

Mike turned to stare out through the windshield. "When you didn't return my calls on Saturday, I figured you were ignoring me.

That made me mad. So I decided to drive into town and have it out with you." His lips twisted. "But I couldn't find you. I went to your house first. You weren't there. Next I stopped by the exercise studio, but they didn't know where you were either, or so they said."

"They didn't," I interjected quickly, not wanting him to think I'd told them to lie.

"Right." He sighed and went on. "So, I didn't know what else to do. I drove around town for a bit but I was too angry to go home. I went back to your house and... ah, crap, I still don't believe it."

He passed his left hand over his face, scrubbing violently. His other hand was fisted on the console between us. I covered it with mine. "And what?" I asked finally.

He shook his head. "And...congratulations. I've finally become the stalker you always thought I was. I spent most of the weekend camped out in front of your house waiting for you to return. It's a wonder none of your neighbors noticed or called the cops." He turned his head and met my gaze. "So? Where were you?"

I opened my mouth to answer, to tell him all that I'd been doing while he was searching for me, waiting for me, risking embarrassment for me, sleeping in his car...

The soothing Acutonics sound therapy, the relaxing Thai massage, the crystal infusions, the oxygen facial, the full-body mojito sugar scrub, the mud bath, the herbal wrap, the manicure, the pedicure, the sauna...

Oh, hell, no. I could *not* tell him about the spa. I shrugged. "It doesn't really matter, does it?"

"I guess not." Glancing down at my hand clasping his, Mike shook his head. "We really fucked this up good, didn't we?"

I didn't ask him what he meant by 'this'. He could have been referring to any of a half dozen things and his assessment would still have been accurate. I nodded. "Yes, we did."

We lapsed into silence. He didn't withdraw his hand though, I counted that as a good sign and left my own where it was as well.

Time passed slowly. *It's just like a wake*, I thought at one point, but again held my tongue. *I'm learning*, I thought sadly, even though it seemed like a clear case of 'too little, too late'. *I'm finally learning to keep my mouth shut.*

Shortly before dark, word filtered down that the fire had been contained. We hurried to join the crowd clustered around the barricades, eager for news and listened while the Fire Marshal announced that, although the danger was past, no one would be allowed back in until morning.

"Why don't we go back to my house now," I suggested as we turned away.

Mike shook his head. "No. You go. I'm staying here."

"Mike, come on, you can't spend the night in your car."

He snorted. "Sure, I can. What's one more night?"

"Really dumb, that's what," I snapped. "And what about food? Have you eaten at all today?"

"I'm not hungry," he replied sounding petulant.

"No? Well, I am." I hadn't eaten since breakfast. Considering the amount of food I'd eaten the two days before that, it was no wonder I was suddenly famished. The break-up/brush fire/spa cuisine diet might not ever catch on, but it was effective as hell. I felt like a wraith.

"Claire, just go," Mike sighed. "I'm not driving all the way back into town tonight. I doubt I can even get my car out until they open the road back up in the morning anyway. And even if I could, I wouldn't go. I want to be here early."

"There's lots of motels out on the highway," I pointed out. "That's not very far, is it? And I'm parked out that way anyway. Let's get a room. We'll still be close enough to get back here early in the morning. Plus you'll be in a lot better shape to deal with... with whatever you have to deal with... if you've had a meal and a shower and slept for a few hours."

He said nothing, but I could tell he was wavering.

"Come on," I pressed. "You know I'm right."

"Fine," he said, giving in at last. "You win." Then he glanced down at my feet. "You walked all the way up here in those? Nice shoes."

It took me a moment to realize he was being sarcastic. I looked down at my feet and wiggled my toes in my strappy, open-toed pumps. They had been nice—once. But they hadn't been designed with this type of terrain in mind and their metallic, cracked-leather finish was all but wrecked now. I shrugged. "What can I tell you? It seems like neither one of us have been very lucky with our plans lately."

* * * *

It took us a while to get back to my car and I have to admit my feet were aching by the time we did. I slid behind the wheel, kicked off my shoes and sighed in relief.

"Omigod," I groaned when I checked my reflection in the vanity mirror. My face was in worse shape even than my shoes! Tracked by sweat and coated in dust and soot, it was almost unrecognizable. "No wonder I couldn't get those cops to listen to me. Look at this—I'm a wreck!"

Mike rolled his eyes. "Could we just get going, please? I'm sure we're not going to be the only people looking for a place to stay tonight."

"All right, all right," I muttered, making a couple more ineffectual swipes at my face with a tissue I'd taken from my purse. "I can't really do anything about this now, anyhow."

We had to try several motels, but eventually we got a room, took quick showers to wash away the heat and the grime and then went down to the adjacent restaurant for a light dinner—salad, burgers and iced tea for both of us, most of which Mike left untouched.

He was still acting distant and uncommunicative and as much as I would have liked to talk about my change of heart, I didn't. He had other things on his mind tonight, I thought, and, frankly, I didn't even know where to start.

On the television over the restaurant's small bar the news showed pictures of the fire. Mike's gaze strayed back to the screen again and again. My heart broke at the despair in his eyes.

"She's going to be okay," I murmured finally.

He looked at me, saying nothing, his disbelief obvious.

"Birds have all sorts of instincts, don't they? Like with earthquakes and things. They probably face this sort of danger all the time in the wild. I'm sure they always know how to get to safety."

He shook his head sadly. "Not always. Not when they're trapped in a house. Besides, she can't fly. I clipped her wings, remember?"

I hadn't remembered, actually, although I nodded just the same, just as though I had. In my mind, however, I'd seen a different picture. I'd seen a smoldering tree branch fall through the bathroom skylight, opening up a hole in the roof. I'd seen Zoe winging her way to safety, a small, bright spot of gold, brilliant and beautiful, against dark clouds of smoke.

In my mind, I still refused to see it any other way. She was free, safe, untouchable, clever. Smart enough to know when to stick and when to make a break for it, to know how to avoid injury, how to protect herself, how to stay alive.

"You have to believe it Mike," I said as I picked at my salad, doing my best to appear confident, unconcerned. "You have to tell yourself, over and over, that she'll be okay. You have to see it with your mind's eye."

He stared at me for a moment, then he shook his head, picked up a fry and began to eat. "Sure," he mumbled between bites. "Okay. Why not? I'm good at imagining stuff."

After we ate, we went back to our room. Mike sat down on one of the beds and stared at the floor between his feet. I went into the bathroom to brush my teeth and change my clothes—having finally remembered during dinner that I still had my overnight bag in the car. When I returned, wearing my very favorite, brandy-colored satin and lace peignoir, he still hadn't moved.

"You look tired," I told him.

He nodded, his face wooden, his eyes still focused on the carpet. "I am. Very tired."

He also looked like he'd stopped believing and was back to fearing the worst. "Maybe you should get into bed, "I suggested.

"I will," he muttered. "In a minute."

I busied myself applying face cream and hand cream, covertly watching him through the mirror. I wondered if we would be using both beds tonight or just the one. I wondered how to ask without embarrassing us both. Or whether I even *should* ask. Maybe I should just assume.

A minute passed. Two minutes. He got as far as taking his shirt off and then stalled again. He looked so sad, it wasn't hard to guess what he must be thinking about. His house. All the bad choices we'd made recently. Zoe.

To be honest, I was having a hard time staying positive myself. Every time I thought about it, I found it hard to breathe. And even though I knew it wasn't *really* my fault, it still felt like it was. My chest felt tight, weighted down with guilt and grief and shame. I was sure Mike must be feeling and thinking the same.

If Zoe was dead, even if Mike didn't blame me for it, I would still be a reminder of everything that had gone wrong, of everything he'd lost. But, most likely he *would* blame me and, either way, I wouldn't be surprised if he never wanted to see me again.

If Zoe was dead... but no, I could not, would not think like that. Until I knew otherwise I would keep believing, I would keep hoping. And I would do whatever I could to keep both our minds focused on something—on anything—other than what we might find tomorrow.

That decided me. Crossing the room to where he sat, I went down on my knees on the cheap carpeting.

"What are you doing?" Mike asked, sounding alarmed, as I lifted one of his feet.

"Taking off your shoes," I replied calmly, evenly, even though I thought that should have been evident. "And your socks. You weren't planning on going to bed with them on, were you?"

He shook his head. "No, but I can undress myself, you know."

"Well, obviously you can't, Mike. You're just sitting there."

"Claire, that's not the point."

"Hush," I said, quieting him with a finger against his lips. "You're tired. Don't fuss so much."

He looked annoyed for a moment but I pretended not to notice. Taking his foot between my hands, I began to massage it. I sighed in relief as I felt him begin to relax. He wasn't the only one with talent in this department. If he didn't already know that, he was about to find out.

"Stop it," he protested when I switched feet. "You don't have to do this."

I looked up at him. His face was bleak, stern. I smiled at him anyway and murmured playfully, "I know I don't *have* to, Mike. I *want* to."

His gaze slid away from my face. He shrugged. I took that for acquiescence and continued. But a couple of minutes later, when I'd finished with his feet, when I'd slid my hands up his legs and was reaching for the waistband of his jeans, he stopped me again.

"No," he said as his hand clamped down on my wrist. "That's enough now."

I looked up at him questioningly. This time his eyes met mine and stuck. Emotions I couldn't identify swirled in their depths. Anger, hurt, pain, longing, lust... or maybe a little of each. I swallowed hard. "Please, Mike, I want to. Let me do this."

I took my free hand, the one he wasn't holding, and reached up to frame his face. "Please?" I repeated quietly. "Please let me." *Let me help you, let me have you, let me love you.* I didn't know how to phrase it, what to ask for, so I didn't even try. I just repeated, "Please, Mike?"

He squeezed his eyes shut for a moment and then finally, reluctantly, he nodded, braced himself on his hands and leaned back.

I undid his jeans and began to tug at them. He lifted his hips briefly to help.

"So... do you go commando often?" I teased when I realized he was wearing nothing under the jeans. *Maybe that's why he didn't want me undressing him*, I thought hopefully. *Maybe he was just feeling shy.*

But he shook his head and his expression hardened, dashing my hopes. "No, hardly ever. But I got distracted Saturday morning. I guess I wasn't thinking straight."

Saturday morning. Right. My spirits sank lower as I thought about it, as his meaning became clear, as I remembered his rush to dress Saturday morning—perhaps in hopes of stopping me before I left.

I should have recognized the jeans when I first saw him today and, perhaps, without the smoke and the soot and the two-days' wear, I would have. He mustn't have changed, or undressed, or even really slept all that much in the two days since I walked out on him. No wonder his cock was so soft now.

It had been a rough couple of days for him and a lot of that was my fault. I could hardly blame him for not wanting me. But I wanted him and I refused to be disheartened. He might not be all that interested right this second, but I could change that—I had to believe that, too.

Once his pants were off, I pried his legs apart and pressed closer, licking slowly along his inner thighs until he groaned softly, helplessly, low in his throat. Glancing up I could barely keep from smiling at the sight of his shaft lengthening and swelling. He groaned again and the sound set all my nerves to vibrating. My pussy throbbed, aching to be touched, to be filled. But tonight wasn't about me. Tonight was for Mike. Even if I never had him again, I'd have him now. And I'd for damn sure give him something to remember me by.

The musky smell of him filled my lungs as I kissed and tickled and teased his sac with my lips and tongue. I breathed in deep. I wanted to remember him, too. I wanted to remember his scent, the way he looked and felt and tasted. I wanted to imprint it on my brain for always, forever.

I took my time as I worked my way up his shaft, licking and nibbling, drawing it out, making it last. Pressing closer and closer until I felt my breasts brush against him, teasing him, teasing us both.

Since he'd released my arm, he hadn't moved once, and I wouldn't ask him to. But, oh, how I longed to feel his hands moving over me now. To feel them hard on my breasts, kneading and squeezing. To feel them reach between my legs and stroke my pussy.

Finally I reached the top of his shaft. I rubbed my lips against his cock's swollen, purple head, flicked my tongue along the ridge, nibbled at his frenulum. The rasp of his breath would have kept me apprised of his rising excitement, even without the drops of pre-cum leaking from his slit. I licked them up, one by one, treasuring the taste, swirling my tongue around his crown, hoping for more and yet more.

A quick glance at his face assured me he was watching, half-closed eyes focused hotly on my face. I opened my mouth wider. His own mouth gaped open in unconscious imitation. Then I wrapped my lips around his cock and slowly, slowly, inch by inch, swallowed the length of him down.

I loved the feel of him stretching and filling my mouth and throat. Loved the salty-sweet taste of him. Loved the ragged intake of his breath and my name on his lips. "Claire."

Down and down my mouth moved over him, until my lips brushed against the hair at the base of his shaft. Another groan escaped him as I slid slowly back up, releasing him inch by inch. Then I canted my head to the side and took him again. And again. Closing my eyes as I settled into a steady rhythm—in and out, up and down, over and over. I'd braced myself with one hand on his thigh. My other hand grasped his sac and softly milked it.

"Claire." Mike's voice was harsh but his hand, as it stroked and tangled in my hair, was gentle, "Oh, Claire."

Yes, I thought happily as I felt the faint trembling in his legs, felt his fingers as they clenched on my scalp. *Yes. You want me. You know you want me.* I sucked harder, letting him feel the edge of my teeth along his shaft. *Let me have you, all of you, now.*

He broke suddenly, filling my mouth with cum. I swallowed and swallowed and swallowed again.

Then his hand slid out of my hair and he collapsed backwards. He lay on the bed, not saying a word. I ignored the faint sense of disappointment I felt when I raised my head and found he'd drawn his arm across his face, covering his eyes. I felt like he was closing me out, shutting the door on his heart.

Would he even object if I got dressed now and left? Would he even notice?

I got up and turned down the bed, prodding and nudging him until he got under the covers. Then I turned off the lights and got into bed beside him.

If he doesn't want me here, he can damn well tell me to leave, I thought feeling angry now. *And maybe I'll listen. Or maybe I won't.*

I curled up against him hesitantly, half expecting to be rebuffed. Instead he reached for me and pulled me to him, holding me tight, kissing me desperately. His hands roved everywhere, hot and urgent, as though he were attempting to commit my body to memory.

Maybe he is, I thought sadly as I pressed closer. *Maybe he knows this is the last time we'll be together like this. Maybe, tomorrow, everything will change, everything will be different. Everything will be lost.*

Maybe. But that's tomorrow. We still have tonight...

Tonight, there would be no games, no resistance and no conversation. I think I missed that the most as I let him take me slowly to the edge and over. But he didn't stop then, either. He continued to touch and stroke and fondle me until I was once again trembling on the brink. Then he rolled me beneath him and slid between my legs. His cock was hard again, thick and solid. "Good. So good. So good," I moaned as I curled into him, biting gently into his shoulder as he thrust into my wet and willing pussy.

We came together in a rush; in a white hot explosion that had my nails digging into his shoulders, his fingers biting into my hips. And then... he was gone. Rolling off of me with a final whispered, "Claire," but without so much as a single kiss, and well before the aftershocks had ended. I think he was asleep before his head even reached the pillow. I lingered on the edge of consciousness only a little longer myself; floating on a soft wave of ecstasy and regret. I missed him already.

Through the crack in the curtains I could see the sky. Night had already begun to fade to gray. Morning would come too soon. I closed my eyes and curled up against Mike once more, clinging to what was left of the night, to the shadows that surrounded us, to my hopes for tomorrow. And, most of all, to him.

Chapter Fourteen

Mike

Despite the exertion of the night before, and the exhaustion of the two days before that, I woke up early. Too early, if the aching in my bones and joints and muscles, or the weariness in my mind, were anything to go by. I suppose the smartest thing I could have done, at that point, was to stay in bed, to rest if I couldn't sleep. But I was too anxious, too impatient for that option.

If I were alone, I'd have gone ahead and checked out. I wanted desperately to be home. Not that I knew if I even had a home anymore.

The next smartest thing would have been to wake Claire up and make love to her again. With any luck, I could have tired myself out enough to fall back asleep for another couple of hours. But considering how badly things had turned out the last time I'd tried something like that... maybe not such a smart choice, after all.

The worst option—short of stealing her car and leaving her stranded here, I suppose—would be to get up, to wait by the window, and watch while the sun rose. To sit alone in the dark and think about everything that had gone wrong, everything that still might go wrong. To dwell on my worries, my fears, my regrets.

So, of course, that's precisely what I did.

I drew up a chair, pulled the curtains aside and sat down. All was gray—sand, sea, sky—glistening darkly, wet with dew, with fog, with salt-spray; beautiful and bleak.

It had been sweet of Claire to try and console me, to try and make me believe that things would turn out okay. But that kind of faith had been damn hard to sustain last night, for even a short while. Now, in the cold, dim, pre-dawn light, it was completely beyond me.

Zoe's fate, and the fate of my house, were a *fait accompli*, at this point. There was nothing I could do about either of them now but wait and see. And the situation with Claire, which should have been dwarfed by the rest, not even a blip on my radar, loomed instead like a vast, unsolvable puzzle, defeating all my attempts to grasp either its secret or its solution.

It had been clear from the way she'd run out on me Saturday morning that I'd screwed up somehow. What still wasn't clear was what it was I'd done wrong. How had I upset her?

Whatever it was, I knew I'd only made things worse by chasing after her. I had taken a bad, but potentially fixable situation, made it worse by acting precipitously, and then turned the whole thing into a full-on disaster, yesterday, by admitting my mistakes.

It seemed hopeless. I knew Claire cared for me. But would she ever care *enough*? Would she ever give us a chance to settle our differences? Could we ever reach a resolution that would satisfy us both?

I knew what wouldn't work: going back to the way things had been. We'd fucked that up too good. We were both finally in agreement on that count.

Last night I'd been worn down, exhausted, weak. I'd let her make love to me out of pity—I was sure it was that, more than anything else, that had motivated her. But, fool though I was for her, I did have some pride and I would *not* let it happen again. Unless, or until, she convinced me she'd had a change of heart, that she wanted me as more than a friend, there'd be no repeat performance. No more sex, no more dating, no more anything.

"What time is it?" Claire asked in a soft, sleepy voice.

"It's still early," I said, turning to look at her. A thin strip of daylight had slipped into the room through the gap I'd put in the curtains. It fell right across the pillow where her head had lain. I guess I should have felt guilty at having disturbed her sleep, but I was full-up with guilt already. "I'm anxious to get going though. Do you mind if we leave?"

She said nothing for a moment, then nodded. "Give me a minute," she said as she threw back the covers.

I tried not to watch as she headed for the bathroom, tried not to pay too much attention to the way the silky fabric of her gown clung to her figure. I failed. I guess some things never change.

"Do we have time for coffee?" she asked, stopping to indicate the coffee maker set up on the vanity outside the bathroom.

I shrugged. "If you'd like." Then I shook my head as she picked up the carafe. "No, leave it. I'll make it while you dress."

But as she disappeared into the bathroom, I turned back to the window, wondering if I wasn't making yet another mistake. I had no idea what we'd find in the canyon today—anything from a miracle to total devastation was possible. If it was the former, my joy would be that much sweeter with her there to share it. But though I'd need her presence even more in case of the latter, I wanted to shield her from it too. I guess I wanted to shield us both, since I knew nothing would break me faster than the horror in Claire's eyes if... if...

"Are we keeping the room?"

"What?" I turned, rubbing my eyes to clear my vision, chagrined to realize Claire was already dressed and I'd made no move toward the coffee maker.

At any other time, I would have appreciated her performance. She didn't cast so much as a single glance in its direction, she just smiled serenely, not a care in the world. "Well, I'm sure it'll be days, at least, before the power's restored in the canyon. And this place is convenient, if nothing else."

"Let's just go," I answered, ignoring all the questions, spoken and unspoken. I had no answer to any of them this morning.

* * * *

The day was treacherous in its normalcy, deceptively bright and beautiful until we neared the canyon where haze and the smell of burning hung in the still air. I felt my chest start to tighten.

"Wait," I said as we passed my car, parked by the side of the road.

Claire slowed. "Did you want to stop and pick up your car?" she asked.

"Yes," I told her then, "No," then, "I'm not sure."

She pulled over and stopped while I thought about it. Even if I still had a house, she'd been right about the utilities. It might be days, weeks, even months before they were fully restored. It would be at least a few days until I could stay here. "No," I sighed at last. "I'll come back for it." Claire nodded and pulled back on the road.

We had to stop and show ID before proceeding into the canyon. Only residents were being allowed in, to prevent looting. I took the fact that someone thought there might be anything left to loot as a good sign and tried to cheer up. It was hard to maintain any kind of optimism as we passed through once lush terrain that was now as barren as the moon. So much that had been familiar had been destroyed. But not everything was burned and, now and again, we passed houses—sometimes one, sometimes a cluster of two or three or four—that had survived seemingly unscathed.

"Look, there's another one," Claire said, pointing out another small grouping. I nodded and tried not to think about the odds.

Just before we reached the point where my property should

be visible, I tensed in my seat. Claire took one hand from the wheel to briefly squeeze mine. A moment later... there it was. It took my eyes a second or so to adjust to the sight, it took my brain a little longer than that to process the scene before me.

"Oh." Claire's soft gasp sounded dismayed. "Oh, Mike..."

Well, what was she expecting? I wondered, staring, taking it all in, trying to grasp what I was seeing and put it in perspective, somehow. It was... not as bad as it could have been, I guess. I let out a deep sigh of something. Relief? Resignation? Regret? I was too numb to decide.

The hundreds, or perhaps thousands, of gallons of water that had been dumped on the property had not landed gently. Not that I was complaining, you understand, but it's called water bombing for a reason, and, this morning, that reason was abundantly clear. The landscaping was an almost total loss, several trees had come down, along with part of the stone wall that had bordered my garden.

Part of the roof had collapsed, including the chimney, but considering the scorched vegetation all around, it appeared the helicopters had arrived just in time, had prevented the structure itself from going up in flames.

"I'm going to park here," Claire said as she pulled up on the shoulder. She nodded toward the drive. "I'm not sure I trust my tires on that."

"I sure wouldn't," I sighed. The drive leading up to my house was not exactly drive-able, at present.

I got out of the car and stood for a moment, surveying the mess. Claire came to stand beside me. "Well? Are we going in?" she asked.

I nodded, then happened to glance down at her feet. She was wearing a pair of sneakers today—bright white, spotlessly clean. "You're gonna ruin those too, you know."

Claire slanted me an exasperated look. "Well, gee, I'm sorry. Next time you have a fire, I'll be sure to pack more appropriately."

Next time? Did that mean she planned on being here? "Next time I have a fire..." I growled, then I stopped myself. "There's not gonna be a next time." I sincerely hoped not, anyway.

Claire winced and nodded. "I know. Sorry. My mouth again."

"C'mon," I said, starting toward the house, feeling wretched. She'd had no breakfast—no coffee, even, thanks to me—and not a lot of sleep. And here I was snapping at her. I was definitely not winning any points today. Not that it mattered, I supposed.

The front door was blocked by debris—tree limbs, shingles, bricks from the chimney. We weren't getting in that way. I had taken my keys out—acting on instinct, I guess. Now I returned them to my pocket, feeling stupid.

We picked our way around to the back. Things were in a little better shape here. The glass doors were intact, coated with greasy soot and locked from the inside. We could neither see nor get into the house through them. As we continued to circle the house I was aware of my growing anger and increasingly helpless frustration as it morphed into a howling fury that was bound to come out sooner or later.

The bathroom's greenhouse ceiling was gone, although the retractable glass walls that surrounded the tub still stood. When I found myself staring at them, measuring their height and giving serious thought to the idea of boosting Claire over the top of them, I knew I'd lost it.

So that... what? I asked myself angrily. *So that she can tumble down into a room filled with broken glass? There's a plan.*

Clearly, my mind was gone. "Stand back," I ordered as I bent to pick up a boulder that had once been part of the garden wall.

"Why? What're you..." Claire asked, her voice changing to a shrill cry of, "Mike, no! What the hell?" as I charged at the house and hurled the rock through the glass wall. "Omigod, are you crazy?"

I was breathing hard from exertion but feeling much better overall. "No, I just didn't feel like waiting for the locksmith to get here," I joked as I reached inside, undid the latch and slid the wall open a couple of feet.

"Oh, that's great," Claire sighed, unhappily. "Very funny. Like there's not enough damage already? You have to cause more? Besides, you could have hurt yourself."

I glanced at the wall. It had been one of my favorite features when the house was first built. But, with the ceiling gone... "It was going to have to come down anyway. Now, later, what's the difference?"

Without waiting for an answer, I turned and slipped inside the house, feeling insanely grateful for the fact the ceiling had caved in since it made seeing where I was putting my feet that much easier.

I took a couple of steps into what used to be my bathroom and looked around, trying to assess the damage until a sound behind me made me turn my head.

"Claire, don't," I cautioned, annoyed to find her trying to follow me inside. "It's too dangerous this way. Why don't you go back around to the back door and wait for me? I'll let you in there."

"Why don't you shut up and give me a hand?" she snapped, clearly at the end of her patience, as well. "And stop telling me how dangerous everything is. *I'm* not the one throwing rocks. 'People in glass houses', Mike. After all this time, I'd have thought you'd know better."

"Funny." I reached out a hand to steady her as she climbed over the wreckage that had fallen into the tub. "I can see now why you never really made it big in comedy."

Claire's mouth fell open, she stared at me, eyes wide and hurt.

"Sorry." *That's not me talking,* I wanted to tell her, *it's some crazy person whose house has burned down, whose bird might be dead, who's lost his mind to the woman he loves and no longer knows what the hell he's saying.* Instead I mumbled, "Guess you're not the only one who says things without thinking, huh?"

"I guess not," she said, climbing out of the tub and glancing around.

Using the side of my foot, I swept the worst of the debris away from the door that led out to my bedroom.

"Let me at least go first," I said, still wanting to shield her from as much as possible.

She looked at me crossly. "Fine, it's your house, be as manly as you want. But I'm gonna be right behind you."

I nodded, feeling a pang of remorse. We were behaving this morning like some bitter, estranged couple whose only child was sick or missing. Linked by our common emotions of love and fear, our attempts to get along with each other were sabotaged by sniping attacks that tore our thin veneer of civility to shreds. How had things come to this?

The bedroom was dark, the walls smoke-stained and water-streaked, the carpet sodden. I didn't imagine I'd ever completely eradicate the burnt-out smell.

"Why is it so wet?" Claire asked.

"All that water had to go somewhere," I replied. Adding, "From the helicopters," when she gazed at me blankly.

"Oh, right," she sighed. "I forgot about them."

I pulled open the bedroom door and water splashed over our feet. The rest of the house—the mostly uncarpeted sections, anyway—appeared to be under a couple of inches of water, most of which appeared to have come down the chimney. I half expected to see Zoe's charred remains floating on the tide. But no, probably not charred, I thought as I looked around. It seemed we'd at least be spared that.

"Do you see her anywhere?" Claire asked quietly.

I shook my head. "No." I didn't hear her, either, which was a lot more ominous. If she were alive, I'd have expected Zoe to be complaining. Loudly.

The living room was a disaster—it appeared this was where most of the damage had occurred. "Guess it's time to redecorate," I half-joked, but I don't know if she heard me.

"Where is she?" she whispered, looking around, biting her lip.

"I don't know." Considering how much of the ceiling had come down, I wasn't sure we really wanted to know, either. But there was still one more room to check. I thought about asking Claire to wait here while I went into the second bedroom, but I doubted she'd listen. What did it matter anyway? "C'mon," I muttered as I headed across the living room. "Just watch where you step."

The door leading into the bedroom was open. Had I left it that way? I couldn't be sure, but the door was in a more-or-less direct line with the fireplace. I suppose the force of the water could have pushed it open. The room seemed to have sustained little damage, just the usual smoke darkened walls. A very good thing. But there was still no sign of Zoe anywhere.

Her big, wrought iron cage was empty, but that wasn't a surprise, I hadn't left her in there and she'd be unlikely to go in on her own. For the better part of twenty four hours, I'd been consoling myself with the idea that at least she hadn't been trapped in her cage, unable to flee as the fire crept closer. Now, having seen the rest of the house, I had to ask myself if she wouldn't have been safer in there.

Her perch was also deserted, a layer of black ash floated on top of her water and soot coated what was left of her food.

Claire looked around the room calling, "Zoe? Zoe, where are you, sweetie? You can come out now," very softly. Only silence met her plea.

I sighed, feeling defeated. "You stay here and keep calling her, maybe she's asleep or hiding or something. I want to check the living room again." It was a lie and a bad one, at that. Zoe rarely slept during the day. But, if she'd been crushed under falling rubble from the ceiling, and if I could keep Claire from seeing her like that, then I guess that was the best I could hope for.

I don't think I was out of the room for more than a couple of minutes when I heard Claire call me. "Mike, come here. I found her!"

"Shit," I muttered as I raced back towards the bedroom. Was that panic in her voice, or excitement? And what were the odds she'd find her the minute my back was turned?

"You were right," Claire said, getting to her feet with a black and bedraggled Zoe cradled in her arms. "She was hiding under the bed. But I think she got herself wedged in there somehow, or maybe she's just frightened? She wouldn't come out on her own, I had to reach in and pull her out. Do you think she's okay?"

"I don't know." Crossing the room, I held out my hands. "Let me see her."

Was it that my hands were trembling, I wondered a moment later, when I had her in my arms? Or was Zoe shivering? And from what—fear, cold, pain? Blindly I sat down on the bed and stared at her. Was it too soon for relief?

"I'll go get something to wipe her off with," Claire said as she hurried from the room.

Good idea, I thought, stroking Zoe's grimy feathers. At least she didn't appear to be burned—that was something. She was alive, conscious, neither burned nor bleeding—all good things. "I'm sorry I left you alone for so long," I whispered. "I didn't mean to."

Zoe blinked up at me; not moving really, not speaking, just staring. Let me just point out that birds don't have the most expressive features, so I think I can be excused for not knowing what—if anything—was going on in her head. Was she in shock? Half-asleep? Dying? What do you do in situations like that? What *can* you do, other than to make a mental note to call her vet as soon as you can locate a working phone?

"Here, let me have her for a minute," Claire murmured, back again with a couple of dish towels and a handful of grapes she must have taken from the refrigerator. She sat down and reached for Zoe, I handed her off reluctantly and then watched as Claire ministered to her. She wiped Zoe's feathers, paying special attention to her face—her beak in particular. "There's my pretty girl," she crooned softly as Zoe's bright plumage was slowly restored. "There she is. That's gotta feel better now, doesn't it?"

Then she coaxed her to eat the grapes, tearing the fruit apart with her nails, using her juice sweetened fingertips to tempt Zoe with tiny tastes.

Watching her with Zoe, watching the way Zoe responded to her—perking up a little as Claire hand-fed her another grape, looking more like her usual self—I found myself growing inexplicably angry all over again.

I felt like I was the one being teased, tempted, toyed-with. Claire kept showing me these tantalizing glimpses of herself, of this sweet, soft side that she never revealed to the public. A side of her I might never get to see again. And I wanted to. I wanted to see it again and again. Always.

Oh, God, how I wanted that, wanted her, wanted *this*.

Watching her with Zoe... it was almost like we really *were* a family. Almost like she really *did* belong here. Almost like she'd never ended things between us.

But she had. And I had to remember that.

I guess I must have sighed in frustration because Claire glanced up at me and smiled. "I think she's feeling better now," she said, indicating Zoe. "I think she wants her daddy."

"Thank you," I murmured as I reached for her, too startled by Claire's choice of words to say anything else.

Her daddy? Why did she say that? Was she teasing me, mocking my cozy little family fantasy, or does she feel it too—this connection between us, this link?

I didn't know and not knowing only made me madder still. And then, just when I didn't think things could get any more strained or impossible between us, when I was already close to breaking under the hopelessness of the situation...

"We need to talk," Claire said.

I don't think I'd ever realized before how ominous those four words could sound.

I guess I could try and blame what happened next on lack of sleep, on exhaustion, or reaction, or who knows what. But I think it was just inevitable. I think we'd been building up to this moment, to this confrontation, from the very beginning.

"Talk about what?" I asked, as I resettled Zoe on my lap and fed her another grape. She was standing up now, croaking softly under her breath, as she attacked the fruit.

Claire didn't answer right away. In fact, she was silent for so long I began to wonder whether she was ever going to speak again. When she did, I wondered why she'd even bothered, because the words she said made no sense.

"What if I told you something about myself that completely upset everything you think you know about me, what would you do?"

I stared at her blankly. "I have no idea. What are we talking about?"

"I'm not who you think I am."

I felt my eyebrows edge up toward my hairline. "Okay, so who are you then? Or, maybe a better question is, who do you think I think you are?"

"This isn't funny," she snapped, eyes flashing.

"And I'm not laughing," I replied, probably a little too coldly. "Am I?"

Claire's lips pursed but she said nothing.

"Is this the lack of caffeine talking, Claire? Or are you being intentionally cryptic?"

"You have this... this *vision* of me, Mike, and it's a fantasy. It's not realistic. It's not *me*."

I felt my breathing stall. "What do you mean?" She couldn't know about my imaginary Claire, my phantom, my... "Fantasy? What fantasy?"

"Like the other night, when you were talking about how perfect I was? I'm not perfect. I've made mistakes. I'm only human."

"I don't believe I've ever tried to suggest you weren't human," I pointed out, just before the other shoe dropped. "And what do you mean, the other night? Does this have anything to do with what happened Saturday morning, with why you left?"

She nodded. "It has everything to do with it. Or, at least, maybe not everything, but it has a lot to do with it."

"You broke things off with me because I said I thought you were perfect? What am I missing here? Most people..." Most people wouldn't mind being adored. "That's not generally considered a horribly objectionable thing to say."

Claire looked away, her cheeks flaming. "You said a lot of things, Mike. Perfect was just the first one that came to mind."

"What things did I say?" Try as I might, I couldn't think of any of them. None that were offensive, anyway. Not since..."This isn't about Derek, is it?"

"What?" Claire scowled. "No, of course it's not. Would you forget about Derek?"

"I'd love to."

"There are things you don't know about me. Things I really haven't wanted you to know. That I still don't want you to know." Sighing, she dropped her gaze again, mumbling, "But, the thing is, if you don't know, then what you think you know is a lie, and when you do find out, or *if* you find out—Oh, it's hopeless."

"So what if I don't know everything about you?" Having lost track of her logic, I clung to the last thing she'd said that made sense. "There are a lot of things you don't know about me either. Give us a chance. We're just starting out."

She looked at me sadly. "It's not that simple, Mike. This isn't the first time I've had this conversation with someone. I've been here and done this before. And it's just... it's too big a chance to take. There's so much I could lose. I don't know..." She fell silent. I fed Zoe another grape while I waited for her to continue. "I don't think I can do this. Not right now. I thought I could but... I'm sorry."

"I still don't even know what you're talking about," I reminded her.

Claire nodded. "I know. That's the whole problem."

She looked unhappy and I wanted to help. But we were sitting in the burned out wreckage of my home, I still didn't know for certain that Zoe was going to be okay, and this talking in circles was getting us nowhere. My patience was worn thin. "So tell me."

"I can't. Not now. Maybe... maybe some other time."

"Damn it, Claire! What the hell's going on?"

"Nothing. Forget it. Just forget I said anything. It was a mistake."

"Another mistake? Terrific. Does that mean I can forget about what you said Saturday too?"

"Mike..."

"Because you said *that* was a mistake as well."

She shook her head.

"I don't get it Claire—any of it. Why are you doing this?"

"Because!" Getting up, she began to pace around on the damp carpet. "Do you think this is easy for me? What if I tell you the worst thing I know about myself and you decide it's something you can't handle? What if it changes the way you feel about me, the way you look at me—what happens then?"

"I don't know. Try me and see."

"I can't."

"Why not?" I set Zoe down on the bed where she could help herself to the rest of the grapes. She complained a little about that, but I ignored her. I stood, intending to go to Claire, to take her in my arms and tell her that the only thing I couldn't handle was the idea of losing her. That nothing could change the way I felt. But before I'd taken more than a step in her direction, she shrank away from me. She crossed her arms defensively and, with that one move, derailed all my good intentions. I glared at her. "What the hell'd you do, Claire? Kill a man in Reno? Whatever it is, it can't be as bad as you think it is."

She glared back at me for a moment before her face changed. She looked away, biting her lip, almost smiling. "Well, when you put it that way..."

"I have a lot to lose too, you know."

She shook her head, looking sad again. "Not really. What do you have to lose besides your fantasy idea of who I am?"

Plenty, I wanted to tell her. Should have told her. Didn't. "Don't knock fantasies, Claire. You're a fantasy for a lot of guys besides me, you know, and I doubt any of them would mind trading that in for a little reality."

"Oh, you'd be surprised." Her lips twisted bitterly. "Like I said, Mike, I've been through this before. More times than you might imagine. Men always say they want reality, they rarely ever mean it. And even then..."

"Try me," I suggested again, stepping closer, taking hold of her arms, trying hard to ignore the anger I felt at being lumped in the category of *Men Who Say Things They Don't Mean*. Trying even harder ignore the helpless, pleading look in her eyes, as well as the insidious voice in my head that clamored, *shut up and kiss her.*

"Who are these other men, anyway? It doesn't sound like it could be that much of a secret if you've had this conversation so many times."

She sighed. "No one. They're no one. That's not what's important. And I never said it was a secret."

"Well, if it's not a secret, then what's the big deal? Tell me and get it over with."

"Oh, Mike." Reaching up, she framed my face with her hand and smiled wistfully. "What am I going to do about you?"

"Tell me what's bothering you? I know you don't think I can fix it, but why not let me try?"

She studied my face for a long time until my nerves, already stretched taut by exhaustion and stress, were on the verge of snapping. Finally she nodded. "All right, you win. I guess it's only a matter of time before you find out anyway. I just hope..." Taking a deep breath she said, "There were these movies I made, back when I was first getting started in acting, that were... well, they weren't the kind of film you'd really want on your resume. They weren't... good. In fact, they weren't ever intended to be good. There was never any 'redeeming social value' to them, if you know what I mean?"

She paused. I nodded. "Okay," I said with what I hoped was a sympathetic and encouraging expression. "Go on."

"See, the thing is, I didn't always use the best judgment in picking projects. And when I was young and naïve, people told me I had to do certain things to advance my career and I believed them. I know it was stupid, Mike, but you hear so much about 'paying your dues' in this industry and I thought this was part of it. And that's really why I did them. A lot of people haven't believed me when I've said that. They thought I must have done it for the money. I didn't. Although, it *was* nice, for a change, not having to choose between paying the rent and eating. And I didn't get off on doing them either... well, I mean, I *did*, but that wasn't why."

Again she paused, looking pained, uncertain, worried. Again I nodded. "Okay."

"There ended up being quite a few of them, actually, and they were pretty edgy for the time—what I believe they call 'gonzo' nowadays."

I nodded again, trying to curb my impatience. I supposed there was a reason she was giving me all this background information, but I still had no idea where she was going with it. "Okay," I prompted once again, hoping to speed things up.

She frowned. "Okay? Is that all you're going to say? Aren't you the least bit shocked?"

"By what? You haven't told me anything I didn't already know, have you? You're an actress. You've made a lot of movies. Some of them were better than others. I'm still waiting for you to get to the point."

"That *is* the point," she answered coldly. "I made adult movies. You know—porn?"

I nodded. "Yes, I know." Then it hit me. "Wait. That's it?" I stared at her in disbelief. "*That's* your big issue? The thing I couldn't handle, the thing that's supposed to change the way I feel about you?" The back-draft of emotion left me speechless for half a second, then everything inside me detonated. "Are you fucking crazy? Do you know the kind of hell you put me through these last few days? You broke up with me. I thought I was never going to see you again. I thought I'd done something horrible. Not to mention all that 'I just want you for a friend' bullshit—Do you know how lousy that made me feel? And it was all because of *this*?"

She'd wrenched herself away from me when I started yelling. Now, she stared at me warily, not saying a word, looking poised to run. But I no longer cared.

Catching my breath again, I continued my rant. "God damn it, Claire! I've been losing sleep for weeks, trying to figure out what the hell I was doing wrong. Wondering why you kept coming on to me, then running away again. And this place..." I swept my arms out, encompassing the room, the house, the canyon. "Look at it! Don't you think if I'd been here, if I hadn't been going crazy looking for you, I could have maybe saved some of it? I could at least have taken Zoe to safety. I wouldn't have spent two days imagining the worst, seeing her go up in flames every time I closed my eyes!"

At that, Claire's eyes blazed. "So that's my fault now, too? I know I said I made mistakes, Mike, but I don't think you can blame the entire fucking wildfire on me! And don't you dare yell at me like that." She stamped her foot in fury. "A few days? A few weeks? Try spending years in hell, then come talk to me about your problems. At least three of my marriages fell apart over this 'issue', Mike, so yeah, I do happen to think it's a big deal. Oh, and, just for the record? I lost houses too, you know. Several times over. I spent a fortune over the years—lawyers, divorce settlements, squelching tabloid stories, paying off photographers, all kinds of crap—fucking blackmail, most of it. And all because of my past. So you have no right to judge me, Mike. None."

"I'm *not* judging you, damn it! That's my whole point. Don't you know me at all? I'd *never* do something like that. I can't believe you'd think so poorly of me."

She shook her head. "Please. Do you know how many friends I've had stab me in the back over the years? You're a sweet man, Mike, but I'm afraid the jury's still out on you. You're not the first person to say it doesn't matter. People always think it won't change the way they feel. But, most of the time, it really does."

She met my eyes, looking tragic, haunted, hurt. Looking resigned. "Now that you know, you'll probably want to see them—out of morbid curiosity, if nothing else. Maybe you'll tell yourself you're doing it just to *prove* that you're fine with it, that it doesn't matter, that it doesn't change everything. I'm sure you'll be able to dig up a few stray copies. After you've seen them, then you come talk to me about your feelings, Mike. Tell me then how they haven't changed. How I still seem so perfect, so pure, so... or you know what? Better yet, don't tell me. Because I've been there before and I don't think I can bear to go through it again. I really don't."

We stared at each other in silence. My brain felt charred, burned out, useless. I could no longer tell if I wanted to hold her close and reassure her—or curse at her for her lack of faith. Just like I couldn't guess how she'd react to what I was about to do. Would she feel redeemed? Relieved? Would she recognize that she'd been mistaken? Or would she simply view it as yet another reason to reject me? She wasn't the only one with secrets.

I crossed to the cabinet where I kept my movies and other memorabilia. I unlatched the door, pulled a few cassettes and a couple of DVDs from the shelves, more or less at random, then returned to where she was standing.

"Here," I said as I thrust them into her hands. "Now, you wanna tell me again how something I've known about since before we even met is gonna change the way I feel about you?"

She blinked rapidly, heat flooded her cheeks. "You—you've seen these?"

I nodded and jerked my thumb in the direction of the cabinet. "I've seen everything. Go check it out if you don't believe me. And you're right, by the way, some of them *aren't* very good. But *you* were always wonderful."

She closed her eyes. "Why didn't you tell me this sooner?" she asked faintly.

"Sooner? I did tell you! I told you weeks ago."

Her eyes opened again. She frowned at me. "When? I don't remember you saying anything about..."

"At the gallery opening. You said you'd made some films out here. I told you then that I'd seen them."

"That's ridiculous." Still looking perplexed she asked, "How could you know where they were made?"

I shrugged. "I recognized some of the locations."

"You... what?"

"I've lived out here awhile, you know."

Speculation crept into her gaze. "I don't even know how that's possible. You must have looked at them an *awful* lot to be able to pick out locations."

Which was just what I wanted to talk about. Not. Grabbing the movies from her hands, I stuffed them back into the cabinet. "You know what? I can't deal with this right now. I've got... *issues* of my own." I indicated the room around us even though I knew the real issues had nothing to do with the fire, and everything to do with her. With her reaction to my own confession. "Why don't you go home now, Claire? Or go to work—I'm sure I've kept you away long enough already. And I really think I need to be alone for a while."

The startled look on her face ever since I opened the cabinet, the fear in her eyes, the suspicion in her voice—*you must have looked at them a lot*—had put me in the mood to break a few more windows. Alone would be a good thing. As I re-closed the cabinet I noticed that my hands had started to shake. Alone would be a *very* good thing.

"You're sending me away?" The tremor in Claire's voice nearly put me over the edge.

"Hell, no," I told her as I picked Zoe up and headed for the kitchen, where I kept my address and phone book. "Why in hell would I have to do that?"

Vet. Insurance agent. Bank. Office—maybe focusing my attention on the list of calls I had to make could help calm me?

"Mike?"

"Your car's here, isn't it? And you've shown yourself more than capable of leaving. So just go."

"But what about you?" Claire asked, splashing after me. "Are you ready to leave too? Do you want a ride back to your car?"

I shook my head. "No, thanks. I can walk."

"Walk?" The softness faded from her voice. She stopped walking and glared at me. "What are you talking about? Why the hell would you want to walk?"

"Why not? It's exercise, isn't it?"

"It's stupid, is what it is!!"

"Thank you. Nice to know your high opinion of me extends to my intelligence now, too." I pulled a chair away from the table. I had to put Zoe down quickly before I dropped her. As it was, my movements were so hasty she had to flap her wings to re-gain her balance. She squawked hoarsely in protest.

"Careful!" Claire warned. "She—"

I turned to scowl at her and she shut up. Abruptly. Too abruptly. I knew it was only a matter of seconds before I lost it entirely—maybe less. She had to go. "So fine. You know what? Maybe I won't walk. Maybe I'll call a cab instead. Is there a particular reason you'd want to hang around and wait while I do that?"

Claire gasped. Any other time the hurt in her eyes would have cut me to the core. Right now, I felt only a moderate increase in the regret that had already nearly crippled me. I sighed wearily. "You know, you asked me once if I'd regret it if I turned down your offer to sleep with you. I didn't have an answer then, but I do now. I think my biggest regret is that I *didn't* turn you down that night. Maybe, if I'd handled things better from the start, if we'd gone about this a little differently, maybe things wouldn't be in such a mess right now." Maybe. Not that we'd ever know for sure.

Without another word, Claire crossed to the back door. She pushed it open and then paused. Tears had filled her eyes when she turned to face me once more. "I just want you to know... I think I could have loved you."

I forced myself to sit down. Not as easy as you might think, since what I really wanted to do was pick the chair up and hurl it across the room. She *thought* she could have loved me? She couldn't even be positive about a *maybe*? Perfect. I shook my head. "Yeah, I think I could have loved you too." Then I closed my eyes, so I wouldn't have to see her leave.

Maybe I should have gone after her. Maybe I should have apologized or tried to explain. Part of me wanted to, but I didn't. I didn't have the strength for another confrontation right now and I figured we'd already inflicted enough damage on each other for one day.

Chapter Fifteen

Claire

I didn't go into work at all on Tuesday. I went to the beach instead. I ate breakfast on the pier, took a long walk in the sand, stared at the waves and the gulls and thought about the course my life had taken in the past few years.

I'd been putting on a hell of a performance, if I did say so myself. To the outside observer, I sure looked like someone who had her act together. And, in one sense, I guess I did. I was proud of the business I'd started. Proud of the new direction I'd taken. But my successes were mostly on the surface. Underneath, I was still a mess.

I could have loved you...

But I hadn't wanted that, had I? After my last marriage ended, I'd crept away to lick my wounds like a whipped pup. Lonely, afraid I'd always be alone, but not willing to risk the pain another heartbreak would cause, I'd never even noticed how wounded, how guarded, how distant I'd let myself become. When I'd picked Mike up that night at the gallery, it was at least partly because I thought he'd be safe. I'd thought an affair with him would be simple, uncomplicated, undemanding. I never thought I'd fall in love. And I certainly never imagined I'd want to. It had taken me a little too long to realize I'd been wrong on both counts.

If nothing else, this morning had been a wake-up call, a cosmic billboard with light-up letters three stories high that spelled out the message, *is this really how you want to end up?* Did I really want to continue being so fearful? Keeping everyone around me at arm's length, afraid to get close, afraid to be touched, to be seen, to be loved?

I could have loved you...

How badly had I screwed this up? That was the real question, and one to which I didn't know the answer. I'd taken a hit this morning—no question. We'd both said things that we couldn't take back. But had the blow been fatal? It was my own fault if it was.

I'd been letting my fears get the best of me these past few weeks. I could have had something good with Mike; instead, I'd pushed and pushed and pushed him away until he'd finally pushed back. How could I blame him for that? This morning, he'd pushed me right out the door and maybe out of his life as well.

At least I'd learned something from the experience. I suppose that's what counts, right? When I got back to town, the first thing I did was to go and see a realtor. By Wednesday afternoon, I'd made an offer on a sweet little bungalow just off Mulholland, small but quaint, with a garden full of flowers and a view of The Valley. I was through running. I was done hiding. It felt good to take control of my life again, to commit to something, to make a stand. It was time. Some might have said it was way past time but I guess there are some lessons that just take a really long while to learn.

I spent most of Thursday holed up in my office shopping for furniture online. I was even considering adopting a pet. A Maltese perhaps, or a Bichon Frise. Not that I'd ever thought of myself as being all that much of a dog person but warm brown eyes and unconditional love were at the top of my wish list, at present, and a dog seemed the surest way to get them.

Anyone who saw me would have thought I was coping, and I was. Sort of. But I was hurting too. I missed Mike. It had only been two days, but it felt so much longer. Probably because I had no real idea when I'd see him again.

I could have loved you...

Unfortunately, I'd only been half-right when I'd told Mike that. There was really no 'could have' about it. Not on my end. Maybe not on his end either? I could only hope that was the case. And, like Scarlett O'Hara had done after Rhett walked out on her, I promised myself that I'd think of a way to get him back... if not tomorrow then sometime in the not-too-distant future.

How hard could it be? The man had apparently spent years collecting copies of every movie I'd ever made. And while that scared the shit out of me on one level, on another level, wasn't the hope of inspiring that kind of adulation what drove people to perform in the first place?

I was at my computer Thursday afternoon, looking at pictures of a charming French provincial canopy bed that I thought would go well with the darling *Louis Seize* chaise I'd already picked out, when the door to my office swung open. I glanced up, breath catching in surprise. "Mike." I felt my heart immediately pick up speed as he breezed in with a small smile and a nod in my direction.

"Hello, Claire."

"Wh—what are you doing here?" My voice, dull with surprise, sounded horribly ungracious, even to my own ears.

There was the slightest check in his stride. "What do you mean? It's Thursday, isn't it?"

I nodded. "I know. It's just... I wasn't expecting to see you today." I'd expected him to send someone else—with an excuse, perhaps, about how he'd had to take time off to deal with his house. Or maybe I'd get a phone call from his secretary, asking me to messenger my records to the office.

"You weren't?" Setting his briefcase down carefully on top of his desk, Mike turned and faced me. "How come? Same as always. Isn't that what you said you wanted?"

Same as always. Right. My words to him on Saturday. Was he using them now to mock me? Unable to meet his eyes, I studied the surface of my desk. "I know, but..."

"Are you saying you've changed your mind?"

"Yes," I breathed, grateful to him for making it easy. "Yes, actually, I have."

"I see." There was a heavy pause and then, "Would you like me to leave?"

"Would I—? What?" My gaze flew to his face. He looked grim. "No! What are you talking about?" Knees shaking, I got to my feet. Why, I don't know. What did I think I was going to do? Throw myself in front of the door? Refuse to let him go? "Of course I don't want you to leave, Mike. Why would you say that?"

And then it was his gaze sliding away from my face. I watched the muscles in his jaw bunch.

"Mike?"

He shrugged. "I just thought maybe you were a little uncomfortable."

"Uncomfortable?" I frowned. "With... you? Why would I..."

"With my film collection, Claire."

"Oh." As his warm, brown eyes met mine once more, I felt my cheeks flood with heat.

"And, before you ask again, yes. I've watched some of them quite a few times."

"I figured you must have," I said, smiling tightly, inviting him to smile along with me. He didn't of course. I don't know why I thought he would. "I was surprised, Mike, that's all. It wasn't what I was expecting."

He nodded. "Well, that certainly seems to be the theme for

the week, doesn't it? You weren't expecting that, you weren't expecting me today..."

"I wasn't expecting *you* at all."

"So what was it you changed your mind about?" he asked, adding, when I frowned in confusion. "Less than two minutes ago. I asked you if you'd changed your mind and you..."

"Oh." I shook my head. It's so hard, sometimes, to find the right words to say. Life really ought to come with a script. "Everything? What I thought I wanted. From you. From this." I shrugged. "You were right. Being 'friends with benefits' really doesn't work for us, does it?"

He was silent for so long I felt my conviction falter. Maybe he'd changed his mind too. Maybe that's all he wanted now. Or maybe he didn't even want that anymore. Finally, "So what are you saying, Claire? Do you want more from me now, or less?"

I felt a shaky smile stretch my lips. "More?"

Mike's expression didn't change. He gazed at me searchingly, saying nothing.

"Please?" I added in a voice as shaky as my smile.

Mike shook his head. "I can never tell if you're acting or if you really mean it."

"I know." It wasn't the first time I'd heard that one either, was it? *'Were you just faking it, Claire? Was any of it real—or just part of your act?'* And it hurt—just like it always did. But not as much as it hurt to admit the truth. Nothing was as painful or frightening as telling him what I'd never told anyone else: "Sometimes I'm not always sure about that myself."

A little of the tension left Mike's frame. "I guess I can understand that. I guess it's not so different than trying to figure out the way I feel about you. Admiring fan, perverted stalker—maybe there's not as much of a difference between the two as I'd like to believe. Maybe you can't really draw a line between them?"

I nodded, even though I was pretty sure you *could*; actually, pretty sure you *had to* draw a line between the two. But I'd already done that, in this case, hadn't I? I smiled. "Maybe, sometimes, the line just gets a little blurry?" For him, maybe. Not for me. But the fact that he was worried about it at all told me I didn't have to be. That told me everything I needed to know. "I really would like another chance to try again, Mike. I think... I think we could be good together."

For another moment we both just stared at each other. Then he nodded. "Yeah. Me, too."

An instant later, I was in his arms. I braced my hands on his chest to hold him away, needing to look into his face first, into his eyes; needing to see if they still held that look, the one I'd feared I'd never see there again. They did.

"Mike..." Sliding my arms around his neck, I melted against him, sighing in blissful relief as his mouth claimed mine.

"How much more, Claire?" he asked between kisses. "How much more than friends do you want us to be?"

"A lot more," I replied, hoping he wouldn't ask me to be more specific—it was still too soon for that. "I'm sorry I've made things so difficult, Mike. It's just that I've been so afraid, so certain that I'd lose you once you knew."

He shook his head. "You should have trusted me."

I sighed. "How could I? I've been hurt so many times I barely trust myself anymore. And Tuesday... you were so cold, so distant. I didn't know what to think."

"Well, I was angry," he protested. "I was hurt, I was upset about my house. You weren't really seeing me at my best, you know."

"Not your best?" I felt my eyes widen. "Is that all you can think to say about it? You made me think you'd never want to see me again. I thought I'd blown it with you."

"Then you need to listen better. I told you my feelings hadn't changed. Besides, you weren't winning many points for tact either, you know." He looked at me for a moment and then he shrugged. "So, fine. Now you know the worst thing about me. I can be a real jerk when I'm angry. And I know the worst thing about you, too—right?"

I shook my head. "Yeah, well, you know something, Mike? Right now, my worst isn't looking all that bad."

He chuckled softly. "I never thought so. As it happens, seeing you at your 'worst' has given me a lot of enjoyment over the years."

Heat flared in my cheeks and, for a moment, I was speechless. "Excuse me?"

"Well, what did you think? That I was watching those movies just for the locations? I wasn't."

"No, really? I'm shocked." The wicked gleam in his eyes sent the blood flooding to several other places now, besides my cheeks. "You're not going to expect me to re-enact all your favorite scenes for you, are you?"

"Some of them maybe," he replied hopefully. "But I think I'll have to draw the line at threesomes."

"Michael!" I stared at him in surprise. "I'm sorry— *threesomes?*"

"Hey, you're the one who mentioned the cab driver."

"I don't even believe you're bringing that up again! And after the way you threw it in my face the other day?"

He sighed. "Did I not mention I was angry? And, anyway, I don't think it's fair to use Tuesday as our standard of reference for behavior."

"You're right." I nodded. And then I reached up and ran my hands along his beard, just because I could. "So how is this all going to work out anyway?"

"Beats the hell out of me," he murmured in reply.

I stared at him. "That's not the kind of reassurance I was hoping for."

He shrugged. "You want reassurance? Try this. Nothing's going to change the way I feel about you, Claire, so you can stop thinking you're gonna get rid of me so easily. I'm willing to try it any way you want until we get it right and if either of us decides to walk away, I can pretty much guarantee it won't be me. Especially not over something as completely trivial as some movie you might have made or the fact that you've been married nine times or..."

"Six!" I corrected. "It was *six* times—not *nine*. Who gets married nine times, Mike? That's just..."

"Whatever." He shrugged impatiently. "It's just a number."

"You're an accountant," I reminded him. "You're supposed to be good with numbers."

"Yeah, but what I'm really good at is keeping things in perspective."

I looked at him. He rolled his eyes.

"Most of the time, okay? When I'm not angry or hurt, when my house hasn't just burned down. And, besides, you're a fine one to talk."

I nodded agreement. "I know, I know."

"You're what's important to me, Claire. Just you. And as for all the rest—how many movies you've been in, how many times you've been married, how old you are—none of that matters. It's just numbers; the only thing they're good for is counting."

He pulled me close again then, and I let him. Sighing contentedly, I rested my head against his chest feeling very grateful, very happy. Maybe I didn't need to get a dog after all. "But, what's all this about my age, Mike? You don't know how old I am."

A soft laugh rumbled out of his chest. "Wrong. I don't care how old you are. There's a difference, you know. Besides, to me, you'll always be ageless. Ageless and beautiful, just the way a star is supposed to be."

I sighed a little as I thought about that. "I was never a very big star, you know."

His arms felt good wrapped around me, solid, comforting, secure; and his voice was deep and gentle and warm. "Oh, no?"

I shook my head him and nestled closer. "Not really."

I knew that had been important to me once, but, for the life of me, I couldn't remember why that was. And I really couldn't make myself care. Especially not when Mike hugged me tighter and whispered softly, "You were to me. You still are. To me, you'll always be the brightest star that ever shone."

About the Author

P.G. Forte wrote her first serialized story when she was still in her teens. Documenting her very exciting and (sadly) completely fictitious exploits, the sexy adventure tales were very popular at her oh-so-proper, all girls, Catholic High School, where they helped to liven up otherwise dull classes…even if her teachers didn't always think so.

These days she inhabits a world that's only slightly less strange than the ones she creates. Filled with serendipity, coincidence, love at first sight and dreams come true… it also bears an *uncanny* resemblance, at times, to Berkeley, California.

www.ingramcontent.com/pod-product-compliance
Lightning Source LLC
Chambersburg PA
CBHW071206250626
47159CB00001B/216